Classic Yiddish Stories

Judaic Traditions in Literature, Music, and Art
Ken Frieden *and* Harold Bloom, *Series Editors*

Other books in Judaic Traditions in Literature, Music, and Art

Badenheim 1939
  Aharon Appelfeld; Betsy Rosenberg, trans.; Ken Frieden, ed.

Contemporary Jewish American Writers and the Multicultural Dilemma: The Return of the Exiled
  Andrew Furman

The Dybbuk and the Yiddish Imagination: A Haunted Reader
  Joachim Neugroschel, trans. & ed.

God, Man, and Devil: Yiddish Plays in Translation
  Nahma Sandrow, trans. & ed.

The Image of the Shtetl and Other Studies of Modern Jewish Literary Imagination
  Dan Miron

The Jewish Book of Fables: The Selected Works of Eliezer Shtaynbarg
  Eliezer Shtaynbarg; Curt Leviant, trans. & ed.

Jewish Instrumental Folk Music: The Collections and Writings of Moshe Beregovski
  Mark Slobin, Robert Rothstein, and Michael Alpert, trans. and eds.

Nathan and His Wives
  Miron Izakson; Betsy Rosenberg, trans.; Ken Frieden, ed.

Nineteen to the Dozen: Monologues and Bits and Bobs of Other Things
  Sholem Aleichem; Ted Gorelick, trans.; Ken Frieden, ed.

Polish Jewish Literature in the Interwar Years
  Eugenia Prokop-Janiec; Abe Shenitzer, trans.

The Stories of David Bergelson: Yiddish Short Fiction from Russia
  Golda Werman, trans. and ed.

A Traveler Disguised: The Rise of Modern Yiddish Fiction in the Nineteenth Century
  Dan Miron

The Wishing-Ring
  S. Y. Abramovitsh; Michael Wex, trans.

Classic Yiddish Stories *of*

S. Y. ABRAMOVITSH,

SHOLEM ALEICHEM,

AND I. L. PERETZ

Edited by Ken Frieden

Translated by Ken Frieden,
Ted Gorelick, and Michael Wex

SYRACUSE UNIVERSITY PRESS

First Paperback Edition 2011
11   12   13   14   15   5   4   3   2   1

Translation of Abramovitsh's novellas and Peretz's stories © 2004 by Ken Frieden
Translation of Sholem Aleichem's monologues © 1998 by Ted Gorelick
Translation of Sholem Aleichem's *Tevye* stories © 2004 by Michael Wex

∞The paper used in this publication meets the minimum requirements of American National Standard for
Information Sciences—Permanence of Paper for Printed Library Materials, ANSI Z39.48–1992.

For a listing of books published and distributed by Syracuse University Press, visit our Web site at
SyracuseUniversityPress.syr.edu.

ISBN (paper): 978-0-8156-3291-7
ISBN (cloth): 978-0-8156-0760-1

Library of Congress Cataloging-in-Publication Data
The Library of Congress has cataloged the hardcover edition as follows:
Classic Yiddish stories of S.Y. Abramovitsh, Sholem Aleichem, and I.L.
Peretz / edited by Ken Frieden; translated by Ken Frieden, Ted
Gorelick, and Michael Wex.— 1st ed.
     p. cm.— (Judaic traditions in literature, music, and art)
   Includes bibliographical references.
   ISBN 0–8156–0760–1
   1. Short stories, Yiddish—Translations into English. 2. Jews—Social life and customs—Fiction. 3. Mendele
Mokher Sefarim, 1835–1917—Translations into English. 4. Sholem Aleichem, 1859–1916—Translations into
English. 5. Peretz, Isaac Leib, 1851 or 2–1915—Translations into English. I. Mendele Mokher Sefarim,
1835–1917. Short stories. English. Selections. II. Sholem Aleichem, 1859–1916. Short stories. English.
Selections. III. Peretz, Isaac Leib, 1851 or 2–1915. Short stories. English. Selections. IV. Frieden, Ken, 1955– V.
Gorelick, Ted. VI. Wex, Michael, 1954– VII. Series.
PJ5191.E8 C53 2004
839'.13010803—dc22   2003026524

Manufactured in the United States of America

I dedicate this book to my wife Tamar,

to my children Tal and Maya,

to the entire younger set entering the twenty-first century,

and to their continuation of Eastern European culture

in American Jewish life.

K. F.

Ken Frieden holds the B. G. Rudolph Chair in Judaic Studies and is a full professor in the departments of English, Literature, and Religion at Syracuse University. His book *Classic Yiddish Fiction: Abramovitsh, Sholem Aleichem, and Peretz* is a study of the works anthologized in this volume. Frieden's other books include his editions of Sholem Aleichem's monologues and of S. Y. Abramovitsh's *Tales of Mendele the Book Peddler* (with Dan Miron).

Ted Gorelick was born in Israel and educated in the United States. He specialized in the translation of Eastern European literature and won critical acclaim for his English renditions of S. Y. Abramovitsh's *Fishke the Lame* (contained in *Tales of Mendele the Book Peddler*) and Sholem Aleichem's *Nineteen to the Dozen: Monologues and Bits and Bobs of Other Things*.

Michael Wex has published two best-selling books about Yiddish: *Born to Kvetch* and *Just Say Nu*. He is also a novelist, whose most recent work is *The Frumkiss Family Business*.

Contents

Biographical Essays

ILLUSTRATIONS

Introduction

The translation of a complex literary work often sounds simplified or diminished, like the piano reduction of a symphony. While its themes and variations remain, the voices and timbres differ. Our goal in this book has been to translate classic Yiddish stories in ways that express — in addition to their special melodies and harmonies — the diversity of voices and colors, overtones and undertones.

Classic Yiddish writing contains three essential movements associated with three names: S. Y. Abramovitsh, the "grandfather" of modern Yiddish literature; Sholem Aleichem, the "grandson" who raised it to new comic heights; and, in a different sphere, I. L. Peretz, the "father" of a new literary generation who founded Yiddish modernism. The reader of this volume will experience the vast range of classic Yiddish writing through the new translations collected here.

While preparing my study *Classic Yiddish Fiction* in the 1990s, I realized that not all of the seminal works I discussed were available in English; many of the existing translations are out of print or outmoded. I have edited this anthology to make available essential texts that have been neglected or misunderstood.

This book brings together the best short fiction by the three classic authors, whose Yiddish literary careers spanned half a century, from 1864 to 1917. To orient the reader with pertinent information about their lives, moreover, I include three previously untranslated biographical essays by a contemporary of each author.

Sholem Yankev Abramovitsh (1836–1917) played a central role in the development of modern Yiddish fiction. He was the first writer to produce Yiddish novels on a par with nineteenth-century fiction in other European languages. Included here are two of his powerful novellas from the 1860s. Abramovitsh's fiction, typified by *The Little Man* and *Fishke the Lame*, is multifaceted: it satirizes the rich, questions traditional customs such as arranged marriages, represents life among underprivileged members of Eastern European Jewish society, and shows the author's sympathies with the poor. *The Little Man* introduces the fictional character of Mendele the Book Peddler, who eventually became so popular that many readers confused him with the author. At times Abramovitsh himself deliberately blurred that line, although he reestablished the dichotomy in the opening section of his autobiographical novel.

Sholem Aleichem (1859–1916) followed the direction set by Abramovitsh, whom he dubbed the "grandfather" of modern Yiddish literature. Sholem Aleichem continued his mentor's satiric bent, but at the same time he moved toward a popular humoristic style. In the monologues by Tevye and other characters, humor softens and disguises the implicit social criticism. Yiddish readers appreciate Tevye's ability to "laugh through tears" as he tells Sholem Aleichem about his misfortunes. In the face of adversity, Tevye and the other monologists seem to draw strength from the very act of retelling their experiences.

Isaac Leybush Peretz (1852–1915) greatly influenced twentieth-century Yiddish fiction by introducing a compressed style and avant-garde techniques. Some of his most remarkable fiction consists of neo-hasidic stories, which draw from hasidic traditions in the service of modern literature. While some of Peretz's earliest works in this genre satirize the hasidim, his best stories such as "Between Two Mountains" present a balanced picture.

Taken together, the stories in this volume provide an unsentimental look back at Jewish life in Eastern Europe. We may feel nostalgia for nineteenth-century shtetl life, but these authors don't let us forget its shortcomings. One of the classic Yiddish authors' primary goals was to reform Jewish communities through social criticism.

In 1857 Abramovitsh began writing in Hebrew, like many other Enlightenment authors; he switched to Yiddish in the early 1860s. Abramovitsh discussed this switch in an autobiographical essay from 1889: "Then I said to myself, here I am observing the ways of our people and seeking to give them stories from a Jewish source in the Holy Tongue, yet most of them do not even know this language and speak Yiddish. What good does a writer do with all his toil and ideas if he is not useful to his people?" In 1862 the Hebrew newspaper *Ha-melitz* launched *Kol mevasser* (A Voice of Tidings), a Yiddish supplement that gave Abramovitsh a forum in which to publish his first Yiddish fiction. *The Little Man*, S. Y. Abramovitsh's first Yiddish novel, appeared serially in the journal *Kol mevasser* in 1864–65.

The turn to Yiddish had wide-ranging significance. Leaders of the Jewish Enlightenment *(haskalah)* preferred Hebrew—the language of the Bible, prayer, and scholarship—to Yiddish, but only a small elite read secular Hebrew literature. Moreover, because it had not been used as a language of casual conversation in two thousand years, Hebrew lacked the everyday vocabulary needed for effective fiction. By switching to Yiddish, Abramovitsh both broadened his readership and enhanced his ability to represent everyday life in Eastern Europe.

The Little Man conveys a didactic message and, at the same time, possesses remarkable literary power. The fictional narrator, Mendele the Book Peddler *(Mendele Moykher Sforim)*, first introduces himself, after which he provides the frame around a confessional memoir by Isaac Abraham. As Isaac Abraham describes his benighted quest for "the little man," he vividly describes shtetl life. In particular, he shows the difficulties that beset a young Jewish man—who starts out as the exploited apprentice to a craftsman—as he tries to find an occupation. Abramovitsh enlists the reader's sympathy for Isaac Abraham, despite his increasingly blatant flaws.

Abramovitsh's masterpiece *Fishke the Lame* is translated here from the original 1869 edition; previous English translations have been based on the expanded novel dating from 1888. The shorter 1869 version contains much of the same plot but less descriptive detail.

One of the most unusual aspects of *Fishke the Lame* is its portrayal of the poorest members in Jewish society: Jewish beggars who traveled from town to town, seeking alms. Critics have generally agreed that Abramovitsh drew from his own experience of traveling with Avreml the Lame in about 1853 (as Lev Binshtok also suggests in his essay about his friend Abramovitsh, contained in the biographical section of this book).

From a literary perspective, *Fishke the Lame* is a tour de force in its sequence of narrators—most centrally, Mendele the Book Peddler, Alter, and Fishke. Their distinctive voices correspond to three different socio-economic levels of Jewish life in Eastern Europe. Mendele stands above the others as a traditional, yeshiva-educated man of Eastern Europe; Alter is an average guy, trying to make ends meet as a tradesman; and Fishke hobbles along at the bottom of the social hierarchy.

Sholem Aleichem (born Sholem Rabinovitsh) was even more successful in representing the voices of Yiddish speakers. This volume focuses on his monologues, the most famous of which are ascribed to Tevye the Dairyman. Tevye encapsulates the demise of the old patriarchal order by telling stories about the growing independence of his daughters. As misfortunes befall him, he relies on his sense of humor, irony, and unshakeable faith in God's benevolence.

Most of the previous translations of the *Tevye* stories did not adequately convey their humor. Yet Sholem Aleichem is rightly known as one of the greatest comic authors in Yiddish. Hence I asked a talented humorist, Michael Wex, to retranslate two of the Tevye stories. His new versions of "Hodel" and "Chava" will provide readers with a fresh look at the original *Tevye* stories that inspired *Fiddler on the Roof* and many other adaptations.

Sholem Aleichem's monologists come from a range of social classes. This anthology includes two monologues by higher-class characters, who appear to be at odds with the implied author and may be called "unreliable narrators." The monological narrators in the stories "Advice" and "Joseph" often undermine themselves as they speak. Whereas our sympathies lie solidly with Tevye in spite of his outmoded ideas, we are likely to be critical of the wealthy monologists.

Under the title *Nineteen to the Dozen: Monologues and Bits and Bobs of Other Things*, Syracuse University Press published a complete English edition of Sholem Aleichem's collected monologues. The four monologues included here are reprinted from that volume, translated by Ted Gorelick of Haifa, who conceived distinctive voices for each of Sholem Aleichem's characters. I have opted to reprint several stories narrated by some of the more eloquent speakers. The final monologue conveys a thick Yiddish accent in English—reflecting the original Yiddish which, ascribed to a ruthless businessman, is intertwined with English words.

I. L. Peretz read widely in Polish and incorporated current literary forms into his fiction. At a time when internal monologue technique was just being invented, for example, he employed it effectively in two stories published in 1890.

Like Abramovitsh and Sholem Aleichem, Peretz began his literary career in Hebrew. But when Sholem Aleichem invited submissions to the anthologies of Yiddish literature he edited in 1888–89, Peretz sent his ballad "Monish" and several short stories. During the 1890s Peretz continued to write in both Yiddish and Hebrew, and he later played a dominant role in the literary life of Warsaw.

Peretz moved from a satiric style in early stories such as "The Shtrayml" to a complex re-creation of hasidic storytelling. Although Peretz was neither an orthodox Jew nor a follower of any hasidic leader, he was able to use this tradition as the basis for some of his most memorable works. The subtle balance of conflicting views reaches its fullest expression in "Between Two Mountains."

Having translated the selections from Abramovitsh and Peretz in this volume gives me an opportunity to reflect briefly on the development of their Yiddish fiction from *The Little Man* (1864) to "Between Two Mountains" (1900). Abramovitsh's early goals were clearly didactic: influenced by the Jewish Enlightenment *(haskalah)*, he attempted to reform Jewish society in Eastern Europe by showing and caricaturing its flaws. In the 1860s, his Yiddish novellas exposed the corruption, exploitation, and superstition that contributed to the misery of Jews living in tsarist Russia.

Abramovitsh was encouraged by the major changes that took place during the Reform Era under Tsar Alexander II, who ruled from 1855 to 1881; Alexander II became known as "the Liberator Tsar" after freeing the serfs in 1861. The reforms of the 1860s also accorded new rights to the Jews of Russia, who subsequently became eligible to study in Russian-language schools and in the universities. Previously, Jewish boys seeking education moved from a private Hebrew elementary school *(heder)* to a yeshiva. If they wished to receive higher learning, they then faced a narrow choice between the rabbinical schools in Vilna (Vilnius) or Zhitomir. Hence many Eastern European Jewish intellectuals in the nineteenth century, after receiving a rigorous training in Bible, Talmud, and Hebrew commentaries, were essentially autodidacts in the realm of Western literature. (Sholem Aleichem benefited from the social reforms under Alexander II, for he was able to study in a Russian high school—called a *gymnasium* on the German model. As a result, Sholem Aleichem received a strong education in Russian literature, which deeply influenced his later Yiddish writing.)

The Reform Era ended abruptly with the assassination of Tsar Alexander II in 1881. Pogroms followed, spurring the mass emigration of Eastern European Jews to America, and new ideologies arose in place of the Jewish Enlightenment views that had made inroads during the 1860s and 1870s. By the late nineteenth century, the assimilationist goals of the Enlightenment no longer seemed realistic. Other cultural movements sought to preserve Jewish identity either in a Jewish homeland or in the Diaspora. The Hovevei Zion were proto-Zionists, linked to others who worked for the revival of modern Hebrew as a Jewish cultural language. In contrast to the cultural Zionism of Ahad Ha-am, one interesting ideology that originated in Abramovitsh's Odessa circle was the historian Simon Dubnov's "Diaspora nationalism." Secular literature in Yiddish and Hebrew served Dubnov's goals by strengthening Jewish culture without relying on a territorial base.

I. L. Peretz's stories encapsulate the shift that occurred at the end of the nineteenth century. Early in his career, Peretz satirized shortcomings in Jewish life, as in his "Bontshe the Silent" and "The Shtrayml." By 1900, however, Peretz was working to enrich Jewish culture through an artistic return to hasidic storytelling. His work was embraced by a generation of Yiddish writers, especially in Poland, who sensed that it could help them create a new identity for secular Jews. Peretz's neo-hasidic stories revisit an aspect of Jewish religion — not in order to choose that form of life, but to draw from it in the service of secular art and culture.

This volume moves from Abramovitsh's Enlightenment beginnings, through Sholem Aleichem's humoristic monologues, to Peretz's neo-hasidic tales. The ideology of social reform with an assimilationist bent was gradually supplanted by an artistic agenda of cultural rebirth.

Unlike most other collections of short fiction, this book includes biographical stories about the authors themselves. Now that cultural studies and New Historicism have displaced New Criticism, biography is once again being recognized as an important object of study. One should not limit literary works by reducing them to or equating them with biographical details. Nevertheless, there is much to learn from reading biographical sources together with literary works. For this reason I have included three first-hand memoirs about the classic Yiddish writers. Each is distinctive and each provides an important intertextual context for understanding these giants of Yiddish literature.

Lev Binshtok's essay on S. Y. Abramovitsh, in spite of its quaint, flowery style, is valuable for its description of travel experiences that evidently played a role in the author's creation of his early novellas. Y. D. Berkovitsh, as Sholem Aleichem's son-in-law and Hebrew translator, had unique perceptions of him. Although his account is clearly the most hagiographic of the three included here, the adulatory tone does not diminish its importance. Roza Peretz-Laks's memories of her father's cousin Peretz are, in contrast, surprisingly critical. This is significant because Peretz has too often been represented only as a larger-than-life cultural hero. Peretz-Laks's sketch conveys vivid impressions of Peretz during his final years, as a central figure among Warsaw Yiddish writers. The section on his relations with his son Lucian may appear excessive, but it makes an interesting contrast to Berkovitsh's stories about Sholem Aleichem and his children.

To help orient general readers, the stories in this book are followed by a thorough glossary of names and terms. As necessary, explanatory footnotes are also included; in the case of Tevye's stories, I have indicated the sources of his quotations. Where Tevye quotes Hebrew phrases, we transliterate them according to the Ashkenazic pronunciation.

It is a pleasure to thank Michael Wex for contributing his innovative translations of Sholem Aleichem's *Tevye* stories, which he prepared specially for this anthology. Brooks Haxton made many helpful suggestions on my translations. I am also grateful to Sheva Zucker, who checked my renderings of S. Y. Abramovitsh's difficult prose. Rachel May helped me edit Jack Blanshei's translation of the biographical essay by Lev Binshtok. Peter Webber and the staff of Syracuse University Press provided valuable support in the preparation of this volume. I thank Pamela Paul, in the Judaic Studies Program at Syracuse University, for her secretarial assistance. As always, the staff at the YIVO Institute for Jewish Research—now located at the Center for Jewish History in Manhattan—assisted me greatly with bibliographical matters. Thanks go to *Pakn Treger* magazine for granting permission to reprint the opening chapters of *Fishke the Lame*, which were first published in that journal. I conclude these acknowledgments by sadly noting that, while this volume was being completed, Ted Gorelick passed away—depriving us of one of the world's finest Yiddish translators. Publication of this volume has been generously supported by the College of Arts and Sciences and the B. G. Rudolph Endowment in Judaic Studies at Syracuse University.

Ken Frieden

A Note on the Translations

The translators of this volume have attempted to balance literal accuracy with literary readability. When all is said and done, classic Yiddish stories are well served only by English versions that are good literature. In a few places, instead of relying on explanatory footnotes or the glossary at the end of this book, our translations add information in the body of the text. Where Mendele refers in passing to *Kol mevasser* in Abramovitsh's *The Little Man*, for example, the translation refers to "the Yiddish newspaper *Kol mevasser.*" Only Sholem Aleichem's two Tevye stories have been accompanied by extensive footnotes, which are designed to inform readers of the sources of Tevye's quotations. This textual apparatus draws from prior work by Michael Stern and Hillel Halkin, as well as from research carried out by students at Tel Aviv University.

In most cases, we have translated the original text of each story. This is the first time that the short first edition of *Fishke the Lame* has been translated into English; the translations of Peretz's stories are also based on their earliest Yiddish printings. Relying on later versions sometimes obscures the development of the author's work. While translating Abramovitsh, I benefited from Shalom Luria's Hebrew translations of the early Yiddish texts.

Two of I. L. Peretz's stories that are represented here, however, "Kabbalists" and "Teachings of the Hasidim," were first written in Hebrew. These Hebrew texts were landmarks in the Peretz's creation of his neo-hasidic genre. Because this is a collection of translated Yiddish stories, we have based the English translation on Peretz's subsequent Yiddish versions.

For the most part, these translations preserve the writers' original paragraph breaks and other distinctive features. But Sholem Aleichem often represents dialogue within a long, unbroken paragraph, and in the Tevye stories we have sometimes broken dialogue into separate paragraphs. Finally, where Peretz's texts seem to overuse ellipses and exclamation marks, by today's standards, some of them have been omitted.

In the biographical section, we have added in brackets the dates of many lesser-known writers mentioned by Berkovitsh and Peretz-Laks. The glossary also provides information about some authors whose names appear in this book.

S. Y. Abramovitsh

The Little Man; or, Portrait of a Life

As for me, I was born in Tsviatshits and my name is Mendele the Book Peddler. Most of the year I'm on the road, traveling from one place to another, so people know me everywhere. I ride all over Poland with a full stock of books printed in Zhitomir, and apart from that I carry prayer shawls, fringed undergarments, tassels, shofars, tefillin, amulets, mezuzas, wolf tooth charms, and sometimes you can even get brass and copper goods from me. Truth is, since the Yiddish newspaper *Kol mevasser* started coming out a couple years back, I've also taken to carrying a few issues. But actually that's not what I'm driving at—I'm getting off the point. I want to tell you about something else entirely.

Last year, just before Hanukah in 1863, I rode into Glupsk, where I reckoned on selling some candlesticks and wax candles. Well, actually that's not what I'm driving at either. On Tuesday after morning prayers I came to Glupsk and, as I often do, I went straight to the House of Study. But I'm getting off the point again. When I arrived at the House of Study, I saw groups of people standing around arguing, shmoozing, laughing, and looking worried. The people didn't stand still—three circles would join and then split up again into three. How does the saying go, eh? My heart isn't made of stone, and I'm also flesh and bone.

Well, you can imagine that I was curious to know what was going on. In this world you've got to know everything, hear everything, because you never know when it will come in handy. But I'm getting off the point. I had scarcely unhitched my horse when the groups of people moseyed over toward me. One person greeted me, another took a look into my wagon, and others started poking and groping around at my goods, as we Jews are wont to do. The street urchins and schoolboys even managed to pluck hairs from my horse's tail. But I'm getting off the point. In the meantime, I heard the following conversation:

"*Oy, vey! Oy, vey!* Blessed be the true Judge. He was just a young man, I think about forty. *Oy, vey!* How could this happen? And to such a good man!"

3

"Why are you getting all worked up, Reb Avromtshe? As if you care! What's it to you? Who was he, after all is said and done?"

"Nothing matters to you, Yosl. Reb Avromtshe is right—how could this happen to such a man? Have mercy! As sure as I'm a Jew, have mercy!"

"Lookit the new minister of mercy, Leybtshe Temes! Now he's agreeing with Reb Avromtshe. What was it that you said a little while ago, Leybtshe?"

"Who, me? Yosl, what did I say? I mean it, Yosl, what did I say?"

"You and nobody else, Leybtshe. You, with your kosher mouth, said: 'Big deal! It's just Isaac Abraham Takif.' Whether he'll forgive me for saying so or not, he was a coarse fellow, heartless and a bit of a fool."

"What? Who? Yosl, you mean me? Good day, I'm in a hurry."

"Good day, Leybtshe, and a good year at that, too. Come on, Reb Avromtshe, into the House of Study, let's take a drop of brandy. Today the shammes has very good brandy."

"You know, Yosl, a little brandy never hurt anyone, eh? You sure outsmarted that liar Leybtshe. Gave it to him good, Yosl. What nonsense he was talking! The man, may he rest in peace, was an ignoramus, a meddler, and a bloodsucker. And he left behind a pile of money."

"That's why, Reb Avromtshe, I like you so much. Because you always insist on telling the truth."

I heard all this and more, but now I'm getting off the point again. It was time to unpack my wares. I shifted my horse around in the harness so she faced the wagon, to cheer her up with a bit of straw; as for me, I went to work. As soon as I had pulled out a candlestick, a prayer shawl, and a package of tassels, the assistant to the rabbinical court ran up panting like a goose and said:

"Oy, gevalt, Reb Mendele! Sholem aleykhem, Reb Mendele! The Rebbe kindly requests that you come to him as fast as you can."

I told the rabbi's assistant that I'd come right away. Left by myself, I began to wonder what it could mean that the rabbi had called for me in such a hurry; I knew that he used oil wicks instead of candles for Hanukah, because he'd bought his menorah from me the year before. So why did the assistant come running all out of breath? Whatever it was he wanted, I had to go. I thought it over and brought along a few candlesticks, some amulets, and a women's prayer book that was hot off the press, which might be of use to the rebbetzin. But I'm getting off the point.

As I entered the rabbi's house, he ran to meet me and cried out:

"Oy, Reb Mendele! Oy, sholem aleykhem, Reb Mendele! God must have sent you, dear, kind Reb Mendele! This must be a miracle, Reb Mendele, really and truly a miracle from Heaven!" But I'm getting off the point again.

Another bookseller would surely have thought that they were anxious to see my wares, but I'm no babe in the cradle. And I wasn't hatched yesterday, like a chick that has no idea what's going on. You should know that, as a rule, the world consists of deception. When a person needs to buy something essential, he pretends that it has no value to him at all. That way he can buy it for a song. When he urgently needs a prayer book, he haggles over a pamphlet of penitential prayers, lamentations, or a package of tassels. Then he picks up the prayer book as if on a whim, glances at it and puts it down, furrows his brow and smiles, saying: "For a small sum I might have bought this, too." Believe me, all the world is a marketplace. Everyone wants the other guy to lose so he can gain. Everyone is looking for bargains. But I'm getting off the point. I guessed from the rabbi's face that he didn't want to buy anything; otherwise, he wouldn't have let on that he was waiting for me. It's true that the rabbi is a fine and honest man — I should only have his good name — although still, in this world, one has to deceive people. Even the angels had to follow the way of the world and put one over on Abraham, when the Torah says that they ate, although they only pretended to eat.[1] But that's really not at all what I'm driving at. The rabbi led me into his house. There sat the rabbinical judges and all the wealthy men in town, looking lost in thought. Rich people always seem a little bit lost and worried, I don't know why. If you've got money, what's there to worry about? Seems to me that you don't need any fancy ideas to spend money. But I'm getting off the point.

The rabbi addressed his assistants and the wealthy men with these words:

"Gentlemen! I've brought you here regarding a serious matter. And by a miracle, Reb Mendele also arrived in our community today. For this reason I asked that you wait a moment, while I troubled Reb Mendele to join us. Forgive me! Now that everyone is here, gentlemen, I'll tell you something strange and remarkable."

For the life of me, I couldn't understand what it all meant. I even started to ponder what the deeper meaning could be. But then I thought it over and told myself not to be so impatient — soon enough I'd know everything.

---

1. In Genesis 18:8 Abraham feeds three men who visit him. Rabbinic tradition interprets these visitors as divine messengers, angels who could have only pretended to eat.

The rabbi, he should live and be well, took a thick sheaf of paper out of his pocket and said:

"Gentlemen, Isaac Abraham's widow sent me this letter earlier today. Before he passed away, he asked that it be given to me. You see, gentlemen, my name is written at the top of the letter. I won't go on any longer than necessary—I'll just read it to you. Sit, Reb Mendele," he said to me. "Sit down and put your candlesticks over there on the floor."

I sat down. The rabbi unfolded the sheaf of paper, shrugged his shoulders, and started to read these very words:

Rebbe, this letter contains a description of my entire life and my will. I beg, Rebbe, that you follow my request and carry out everything I ask of you. Forgive me that I have burdened you with such a long letter; at the end you will see that it is very useful.

I was born to poor parents in the small shtetl named Bezliude. I don't remember my father because he died while I was still a suckling child. My memories of what happened go back only to when I was five. From what I remember, in my youth no one thought I had any brains, and whenever I said or did anything, people used to burst out laughing. No one spoiled me—I wasn't kissed, caressed, or hugged like other children. When I cried, no one comforted me with candies or toys, but instead they silenced me with slaps and blows. I never heard anyone use the word "pity" or "mercy." No one ever said, "What a pity that he has to go barefoot," for example, or "What a pity, he's cold and his face is all swollen," or "Poor thing, what a pity that he hasn't had anything to eat." No one said, "Have mercy on the child, he's exhausted and shivering to the bone." I only heard people say: "Look at that pretty face, what a puffed-up mug! His feet are red as beets! Look at the glutton, he's up to his old tricks again, shivering and making his teeth chatter." Nobody wants a poor man's child, who just sticks out like a sore thumb. Even his parents have no pity on him unless he's sick because hardship and distress harden a person's heart.

I had a habit of looking into everyone's eyes and mouth when they spoke. Sometimes I stared into my mother's eyes, and she always used to hit me for this. But once when I was looking deep into her eyes, and I saw that she didn't stop me, I couldn't resist asking:

"Tell me, Mama, what sort of little man is that in your eyes?"

My mother smiled and answered, "That little man is the soul. That little man isn't in everyone's eyes, and not in the eyes of animals. It's just in Jewish eyes."

My mother's answer awakened in me a lot of new and fresh thoughts. From then on my imagination was preoccupied with the little man. I saw the little man in my sleep and dreamed I was playing with him. I held the little man and imagined that I myself was a little man. In short, I thought of nothing but the little man, and I so wanted to be one. It was no small matter—the little man is the soul! I started to think about how to catch the little man. Once I had a clever idea. When mother leaned over to take a pot out of the oven, I ran up from behind her and struck her head with my fist so that the little man would fall out of her eyes. You can guess how many pinches and slaps I earned for that, and then I went without food all day because my poor mother had broken the pot of corn mush with her forehead.

Another time I got into even deeper trouble. I was curious to know whether animals also have souls, so I walked up to a cow on the street. While I was getting ready to stare it in the eyes, the beast tore into me with its horns and gave me a serious injury. The scar on my left cheek is still there. All these blows didn't drive thoughts of the little man out of my head; on the contrary, they roused my curiosity.

I studied at the Talmud-Torah. It seems to me that I was no coarse lout—I'd learned the Bible with Rashi's commentaries for seven or eight years. Apparently it's possible to have a little learning and to be a great fool anyway. My mother called me a shlimmazl, and she was quite right about that. Among the children in the Talmud-Torah, I was the greatest shlimmazl of them all, and I received more slaps than anyone else. At the end my teacher had it in for me and beat me so hard that I had to stop going to school. This is what happened. The teacher told me all about the biblical verse near the beginning of Genesis, "And Lemekh said to his wives, Adah and Zillah. . ."[2] He must have been quoting Rashi or a midrash when he explained that Lemekh was blind and that his son Tubal-cain led him around. When he saw his great-grandfather Cain from afar, he thought it was a wild animal. Actually, just to explain it better, my teacher said that Tubal-cain thought Cain was a fox. So he told his father Lemekh to shoot an arrow at the fox, and he killed him. When Lemekh realized that he had killed his grandfa-

---

2. Genesis 4:23. The midrash alluded to here is contained in *Tanhuma* and in Rashi's commentary on the passage in Genesis 4:23.

ther Cain, he slapped one hand against the other—and he struck his son Tubal-cain dead. Because of this, his wives became aloof from him. He begged forgiveness from them and said, "Adah and Zillah, hearken to my voice. . ."

And then the fateful day arrived. Suddenly an inspector from Saint Petersburg showed up at the Talmud-Torah. He was beardless and dressed in a short jacket, just like a German. Along with him, to examine the children, came all of the school officials. It was just my rotten luck that he asked me to translate a short passage from the Bible—none other than the good verse, "And Lemekh said to his wives, Adah and Zillah. . ." I had never talked with such an important person before, and certainly not with a clean-shaven German Jew. I was trembling like a fish out of water, my ears were buzzing, my hair stood on end, and I felt as if I had been blinded by the sun. I didn't think I'd be able to tell a long story about Lemekh, like the one in the midrash. But I had to say something. I got confused and started:

"*Vayomer*—And he said, a fox. And Lemekh was blind. He said to his wives—Tubal-cain led him around—Adah and Zillah, and he killed him."

The German Jew almost jumped out of his skin, he was so angry. He called over my teacher and said to him, "Is it possible? Can this indeed be how you instruct your pupils? Is it possible?"

The teacher scratched his head, picked his nose, and stammered, "My lord, sir, the child became frightened. He's a good lad, you can believe me!"

Then the German Jew said to me, "Have no fear, child, nothing will happen to you. Translate these words for me. *Vayomer*—tell me, what does *vayomer* mean?"

I opened my eyes wide, like a clay golem, and said, "*Vayomer*—a fox." Because when my teacher taught me the verse, we hurried past the phrase *Vayomer Lemekh l'nashav*, "And Lemekh said to his wives." The main thing was to tell the long story.

My poor teacher looked like he wanted to die. It was a black day for him, and later he poured out his bitter heart on me. He always used to bother me; after this he beat me like there was no tomorrow, until I stopped going to the Talmud-Torah.

My mother apprenticed me to a tailor so that I would learn the trade from him. But I, shlimmazl that I was, didn't lick honey at his shop either. For an entire year they wouldn't even give me the honor of letting me hold a needle in my hand. My job was to empty the slop buckets, carry wood, sweep the house, go to the marketplace for kosher thread, or take a bit of work back to a customer, together with the tailor. I ate nothing but blows and anguish. The lady of the house was a mean, malicious person who wore the pants and led everyone at home by the nose. Just as she needed brandy every day, she needed someone to pinch and flail, tear into and torment, curse and scold. When she ran her little hands over my cheeks, she dug down to the bones. In those days I thought an apprentice had to be treated like this. Otherwise he wouldn't be able to become a tailor, in exactly the same way that you can't become a scholar without being beaten by your teacher. Because of this I used to receive all of the blows lovingly, and I didn't even cry out loud.

Once, during the busy season before Passover, the tailor said to me: "Isaac Abraham, hop over to the store, pick up a penny's worth of kosher thread, and sew together the front and back parts of this dress. Hurry it up, you little bastard!" I remember how happy I was to have the honor of sitting at the table and holding a needle; it was as if I'd been given the honor of holding up one of the poles under a wedding canopy. I marched over and sat down beside the table, happy and content. The tailor sang a bit of the Kol Nidrei prayer, shifted to "King Above," hummed a march, and then he told a little joke. Finally he sang a tune for seating the bride before the ceremony, and he made up a few rhymes like a wedding bard. "Hurry it up, Isaac Abraham," he said, his voice rising, "and trim that wick! Faster, you bastard! Sew faster, you puffed-up mug!"

And stitch by stitch, I stuck the needle into the skirt and into my finger, into the dress and into my finger. But who notices a pinprick when the heart is gay? Suddenly a cloud came over me—the house began to smell of something burning. They looked everywhere until, finally, they noticed that the skirt I was sewing was smoldering. When I trimmed the wick, a piece of it had fallen off. Up went a hue and cry, then curses, which were followed by slaps and blows that rained down on me like broomsticks. I got what was coming to me and then some. The tailor attempted to turn the skirt into a blouse with sleeves, but it didn't work. Poor man, he even took out the remnants of fabric that were lying around and tortured himself for a long time trying to make something, but it didn't work. No matter how hard he tried, stretching the cloth this way and that, it didn't help. The skirt would have to remain a skirt.

"Listen up, Isaac Abraham," the tailor said, "get lost, you bastard. I have no energy left to beat you. Anyway, when the lady of the house returns from the market, she'll probably get at you with some warm-up punches. But that's nothing to what you'll have coming if I can't pull this off."

The tailor puzzled over the skirt for a bit and said to himself, I'll make that hole into a pocket. . . . Why not? Yes indeed. Then he shouted at me, "Get lost, you bastard!"

I crawled out from under the table like a wounded kitten. That was on a Wednesday. On Friday the tailor ordered me to bring the dress along to the tax collector's wife. She took one look, had a fit, and burst out like thunder:

"A pocket way back there!³ What's that supposed to be, my dear tailor?" She cried out as if the sky had fallen, "How come there's a pocket in back? Never in my life, swine, will I accept such a dress!"

"Ai," the tailor answered her with a sweet little laugh. "Ai, please don't shout, Breindl, I've sewn you the dress according to the latest fashion. These days all of the landowners' wives wear pockets in back, and nowadays only a madman makes pockets in front. So wear it in good health, and give my apprentice here a tip—he worked hard on that pocket."

He was the best tailor in the shtetl, and people said that he even used patterns from fashion magazines. And the tax collector was the richest man in Bezliude. So when people saw that his wife, the tax collector's wife, was going around with a pocket in back, all of the modish women in Bezliude followed her example. That didn't help me any, though, because the tailor beat me until I had to run for my life.

After that I was apprenticed to one worker after another for a week at a time. My luck didn't improve, I remained a shlimmazl. More than one boss gave me the honor of letting me carry the slop buckets. One of them even said, "Carry them, Isaac Abraham, carry them. I should see the day when we carry wine to your wedding ceremony in a sieve. Carry them, Izzy; when I was your age I also carried a ton of slops." I had another boss, a cobbler, who used to send me to pluck boar's hair from the backs of pigs that were rolling in the gutter.

Once a cantor traveled through our shtetl, and on Sabbath he led services accompanied by his boys' choir. He even had a little pipsqueak singer who

---

3. The tax collector's wife literally complains about "a pocket way down below" (a *keshene same untn*). According to Shalom Luria (1984), however, "below" *(untn)* is a euphemism for "in back" *(hintn)*. This idea gains support from the tailor's later claim that "nowadays only a madman makes pockets in front" *(fun fornt)*.

was my age. I was so jealous of the way he stood and sang tra-la-la in front of everyone, that I would have given the shirt off my back to become a singer like him. I watched that boy with awe during the prayers, while I was hanging around with all of the other kids in a side room of the synagogue. Nothing in the world, I thought, could be better than a choirboy—except maybe a little man. When the boy opened his mouth, well, I just began staring in as if I wanted to drop everything and jump down his throat. As if only that could cure what ailed me.

After I came home I tried to imitate the singer. During our Sabbath singing I let loose with such a tra-la-la that my mother was delighted. It wasn't the Sabbath songs that had me going, but the idea of imitating the choirboy. When she saw that I didn't want to stop and wouldn't give her any rest after lunch, she gave me a good thrashing and threw me out of the house. And where does a boy run to on Sabbath afternoon? To the House of Study. I thought it was just me, but lo and behold! The entire gang was there, same as me, copying the singers. All of them were standing around, busily practicing. One squeaked, one roared, one hummed like a bass, one mimicked the cantor, one meowed, one piped, one chirped, and even the tax collector's boy was in the midst of the flock, poor kid, torturing himself to sound like the choirboy. It turned out that all of them, like me, had been thrown out of their homes. So we gathered in the balcony, in the women's section of the shul, and we let out such resounding shrieks that the synagogue attendant splashed water on us and drove us out.

But I really had a fine voice, and I started begging my mother to apprentice me to the cantor. I pestered her and made myself into such a nuisance for so long that she took me to the cantor. She was a poor widow and, in the end, she wanted to get rid of such a bargain as me. When the cantor asked me to yammer a few notes and then said he'd take me on as a choirboy, I thought I was on top of the world. I'm incapable of describing just how I felt inside.

I traveled around with the cantor and saw the world for more than six months. For me, the shlimmazl, things turned out worse than they did for any other choirboy. That time I really sold myself short and got myself into trouble. It went like this: while the cantor was leading services, the choirboys were supposed to watch the congregation to see whether they liked his davening or not. After we got home, the cantor would call out someone's name and ask him how the services had gone. As chance would have it, he almost always called on me. Maybe it was more than chance because right after services the other choirboys used to run away and make themselves scarce. When he turned to me and said, "Avromke!" I answered him: "Cantor, they laughed at you. I swear, they laughed really hard." Then he'd grab me by the ear and twist and pull, twist and pull—until, I tell you, the tailor's blows looked like child's play.

One time he beat me so badly that I could hardly talk and lay sick in bed for a month. This is the story. In some town, he once davened for the special Sabbath with the Torah reading "Shekalim."[4] He worked hard to prepare for that service, because he hoped to become a steady cantor for that shtetl. Saturday evening people gathered around him, a large crowd. The cantor sent for wine and rum and invited everyone to celebrate the Melave-Malke; his intention was to win over the congregation. He wanted to send me out for something, and he called to me, "Avromke!" Ha, ha! Then I opened my little beak and chirped these words: "Cantor, they laughed at you." The poor man made a face, turned red as a turkey's comb, and everyone, the whole crowd, shot daggers at me with their eyes. I thought the cantor didn't believe me, so I started to swear: "As true as I'm a Jew, Cantor! They laughed at you, these very people. Not to mention that man right there beside you, who's drinking and whispering secrets now, he even laughed while we were saying the *Kedusha*." The cantor pretended to laugh and told the crowd that I was an idiot and a fool, but that he had to keep me because of my fine voice. You can guess what I had coming to me after that. In short, I was sick in bed for a month.

I went on traveling around, almost all summer, with the cantor. Just in time for Sabbath "Nahamu," we arrived in Tsviatshits. The cantor was counting on a steady position as cantor of Tsviatshits, and while we were there he pulled out all the stops. They told him that he would lead services during the High Holidays, and afterward they would close the deal. In the meantime, I got to know the tough kids of Tsviatshits and they treated me with some respect. When they managed to steal the shofar from the synagogue attendant's drawer, for instance, they honored me with the first blow. My life even started to improve, but nothing helps if luck isn't on your side.

Listen to how things ended with my cantor. You can imagine how hard he worked on Rosh Hashanah; he really let loose and just about climbed the walls. The bass singer went hoarse because in almost every verse he sang the

---

4. Exodus 30:11–16, a passage relating to a half-shekel tax, read in traditional synagogues on the last Sabbath before the winter month of Adar.

accompaniment. The poor tenor also lost his voice because using falsetto he had to outsing the bass, and all we could hear was a warble and a squeak. Each singer was screaming at the top of his lungs, and every few moments I had to give a little cry, *Tatenyu!* Father in Heaven!

But in the congregation there was one rich young man who had modern leanings. He was a kind, fat man, and he liked to clown around with children. Well, he really hated the cantor. When the cantor started to go all out during the "Ata zokher" part in the Eighteen Benedictions and, good man, threw off beautiful ornamented phrases, the rich joker silently came over to me and asked: "Can you pucker up your lips like a cherry?" And then and there he puckered up such a big cherry that I broke out laughing. But at exactly that moment, the cantor reached the end of a blessing and was expecting me to answer with a *"Tatenyu!* Father in Heaven!" When the congregation saw that the cantor had stopped, they started to knock impatiently on their prayer stands. The cantor angrily turned around to look at me, his face reddening and boiling over like a carrot stew. The bass hummed a note, signaling to me that I should answer with a *Tatenyu!* But just as I was getting ready to squeak out my part, the rich man puckered up another cherry and I let out a squeaky laugh. The cantor took fright, broke loose, galloped off, and jumped over some of the Eighteen Benedictions, making a few mistakes along the way. The congregants knocked and rapped on their stands, the women became frightened and cried out, *Fire!* Then the men also got scared and started to run out of the synagogue. In short, the services were spoiled. On the day after Rosh Hashanah the cantor threw me out, and he himself quit the town in disgrace. I was left behind, shlimmazl that I am, stranded in Tviatshits.

During the holiday I ate meals at the house of a certain man. He was neither poor nor rich, neither a hasid nor from the modern world, and neither gloomy nor happy—just some ordinary Jewish guy. After I'd been left alone there like a lost sheep, I thought things over, went to that man, and told him my troubles. He heard me out in silence, smoothing his whiskers. Then, looking pensive, he waved his hand indicating that I should stay in his home, and called for someone to feed me. That night at about eleven o'clock, when everyone in town was already sleeping—and it was so dark outside that you thought you'd gone blind—he took me to a godforsaken corner of the shtetl, and down a dark alley. There it was still as a graveyard, except for the rustling of trees that shook in the wind and the sound of a mild autumn rain that drizzled on dry, fallen leaves. When the wind let up for a moment, I could hear the whirring of a mill in the distance, and when the wind picked up again, it mingled with the crowing of a cock and barking of a dog. Apparently Jews didn't live on that alley—if they had, there would have been no trees lining the path or leaves on the ground.

My new friend walked on and on with me without speaking a word. Finally we entered a small, squat house. In a tiny front chamber a candle flickered, and there he took off his coat. He went into the next room but told me to wait in the front. Because I was standing right beside the closed door, I heard the following conversation in German:

"Good evening, Herr Gutmann!"

"Welcome, Herr Jacobsohn! What a surprise! You haven't visited in three weeks. What's the meaning of this, Herr Jacobsohn?"

"Dear Herr Gutmann, how could I visit? You know that these are the Days of Awe, and the local Jews are more fanatical than ever. You know my position and how dependent I am on them. And if they saw me going to visit you. . ."

"You're absolutely right, Herr Jacobsohn, you're right. You are dependent on them and have a family to support."

"Have you already finished your work, Herr Gutmann?"

"Oh, yes. The book has gone remarkably well. It's too bad that in this entire city only a few people read Hebrew."

"What's worse, Herr Gutmann, is that you receive no payment for your work. You often want for food, and on top of everything you suffer undeserved scorn."

"Believe me, Herr Jacobsohn, a writer really needs no other payment than being understood. Scorn and want merely inspire him to do his work. Undeserved disrespect is just as pleasant as deserved respect. To suffer for the sake of truth is not real suffering. I would call it suffering if I had to flatter, be a hypocrite, deny myself, and sell my conscience, my mind, and my heart. Do you think that being a flatterer is an easy job? It's just as hard as being a thief. The flatterer and hypocrite, like the thief, must always worry and be on guard. Do you think that all of my persecutors, the hasidim, are happy and pious? Oh, no! A certain group of them persecutes me just out of envy, out of jealousy."

"Really, Herr Gutmann, with such fine qualities and thoughts, you truly are enviable. People must indeed be jealous of you. But do you know why I've come to you tonight? Several times you've said that you need an errand boy to send around town, and now I've found one and brought him along. He seems like an honest lad, though a bit of a fool."

"Many thanks, my dear friend. Where is he?"

I understood bits and pieces of their conversation. That is, I didn't catch the meaning, although I understood almost all of the words. They were a mixture of Yiddish and German, and I was able to understand the German words—because when I traveled around with the cantor I heard all sorts of people talk. In conversation, the cantor himself liked to throw in an occasional German word, as it suited him. He often used to boast that he sang from sheet music and could lead services *chorisch*.

Suddenly the door opened and they called me into the room. My new friend was sitting there without his hat, and the German Jew took my hand and said kindly:

"Well, my dear young man, you want to stay with me? Here you won't have any hard work, you'll just have to run an errand now and then."

My eyes bulged and I gave such a foolish look that the German Jew smiled. But I liked him a lot; his face showed such goodness, and he spoke so kindly to me—unlike the tailor, the cantor, and even my mother. I was drawn to him. I put my hand to my lambskin cap, which I always wore, winter or summer, even if I was going barefoot. I lifted it a bit off my head, then I put it back down at an angle. I pulled it down toward my face, then pushed it up, and with the other hand I pulled at my side curls and scratched my neck. I didn't know what to do with myself and with my cap. Finally I took courage and quickly snatched it off my head. I felt as if a cool breeze was blowing over my bare head, as if my head had been shaved. I kept reaching up to touch the hair on my head.

"You're a good fellow," the German Jew said. "What's your name?"

I stood there dazed, just like the time with the German Jew in the Talmud-Torah. I peered at him with a couple of calf's eyes.

"What's your name?" the German Jew asked me again.

"I don't know."

"Can it be that you don't know your own name?"

"My mother," I answered, "used to call me Itzhak Avromtshe. My teacher in the Talmud-Torah called me Itshe Avremele. The tailor called me Itsik Avreml the bastard. And another craftsman, when he wanted to get me to carry the slop buckets, would call me Itshiniu Avrominiu. The cantor called me Avromke. So how should I know my name?"

"Your name is Itsik Avrom," the German Jew said with a smile. "It's a very fine name, taken from the Patriarchs. And that's what I'll call you—that is, Isaac Abraham, or Abraham. Do you want to stay with me, Abraham?"

"So long as you don't beat me. Already there's not a whole bone in my body."

Tears welled up in the German Jew's eyes. He put his hand on my shoulder and said, "Poor thing! It seems that he has suffered a lot. So young, and already he doesn't have a whole bone in his body! Yes, yes," he said to my new friend, "he really is coarse, even dumb, but still a good, honest fellow." My new friend remained silent and just smoothed his whiskers.

"No," the German Jew said to me. "I give you my word that I won't touch you. You're a human being, no less than I am, apart from which you've had enough misfortunes. So will you stay with me?"

"Yes, but you just shouldn't ask me to sing the high notes. My throat is already sore."

In short, I moved in with the German Jew. He had a wife and two children. He was very poor, but his house was always clean, everything was in its place, and the corners sparkled. His daughter owned only one dress, but it was always pretty and clean, as if it had just been sewn. The missus, his wife, took care of every nook and cranny and was always cheerful. The German Jew sat in his room writing, day and night; books lay all around him, on the table and under the table. I didn't need to polish his boots much because he so seldom went out. On the other hand, his robe and slippers were tattered and torn. My main job was to run errands. Now and again he'd send me to someone with a book. It seemed like easy work. But in fact it was worse than with the tailor and the cantor. I would carry a bill to someone, and I'd see how he turned up his nose, angrily telling me to come back the next day. The next day he put me off again, and the following day I wouldn't find him at home. If I came back to him with a bill, he would shout at me: Whatever does this boy want from me? I can't get rid of him. Another person told his servants not to let me in, and a third would read over the bill, hesitate, and then walk away without saying a word. A fourth person would say: Tell your boss that I'm not home, you understand?

In general, they avoided me, and if they saw me coming they simply locked their doors or sicced a dog or a servant on me. When someone had mercy on me and accepted a book, he'd hide it right away under a bed or under a bench. For payment they gave me a torn ruble you couldn't read. That's how I spent more than a year with the German Jew. My friend, Herr Jacobsohn, would often visit late at night. And when I wasn't tired I would eavesdrop on their conversation from the next room. Once I heard Jacobsohn tell a story about a Doctor Steinharz and was surprised. Herr Gutmann said that all of the other doctors were quite virtuous and honorable men (at the time I didn't understand these two words), but why was he surprised about Doctor Steinharz?

"He is really a little man. That's why he's rich and everyone's favorite — their very soul."

I shook like a leaf when I heard that. Even Guttman says that a little man is the soul, and rich! My imagination got the better of me again, as I thought about trying to become a little man. It was no joking matter, a little man — and rich! Another night I heard Jacobsohn tell about Isser Varger, how rich and fortunate he was, practically running the whole town.

"What else is new?" said Gutmann. "Isser Varger is a little man and serves the landowner as his very soul."

There it was again, the little man! I was back to my old ideas. All night I tossed and turned and thought it over. Isser Varger is a little man, a soul, and a rich, fortunate man. So it appears that if you are a little man, you are rich and fortunate. It seems that people can become little men at will, and when they do, they become rich and fortunate. I thought I must have always been right when I wanted to be a little man. Yes, that's all well and good, but how does one become a little man? How do I get in on the action?

Even if I could roll up into a ball and shrink to a tenth my size, I still wouldn't be a little man. It seemed that there was some great trick to being a little man, otherwise everyone could be little men — souls, fortunate, and rich people. I thought all that over in bed, and when I fell asleep, I dreamed I met a little man on the street, dressed up like a prince in gold and silver, just like a doll. I so envied him that I pulled myself together, wrapped my arms around my knees, and held my breath until I stopped feeling and thinking, seeing and hearing. And suddenly I became a little man! As tiny as a flea. It was exhilarating. As soon as I became a little man, I began to feel better — next I became a soul, drove in a carriage, and I led the whole town by the nose. Everyone showed me respect and pointed at me, saying: There goes the soul in his carriage, take a look at how he talks and laughs! If you've got a dowry set aside, keep it safe with him! If you have some legal matter, go have a talk with the soul! But suddenly I started to stretch, daylight started to shine through my eyelids, and there I was again, Good morning! Just me, the rascal Itsik Avreml.

It really was me, stretched out on my bed, imagining I was lying in the lap of luxury. I pinched myself and, yes, it really was me. How did I get here all of a sudden? Oh, was I angry with myself for waking up and being myself again! Well, I thought, no matter, I'll figure out how to become a little man. I had to become a little man. Then I mulled it over. Before I dreamed that I was a little man, rich and fortunate, I first stopped feeling, thinking, seeing, and hearing. There must be something to that. One couldn't become a little man except if one first stopped feeling and thinking; one just shouldn't feel and think. But how does one do this? How do you stop feeling and thinking? That was the whole trick! I had the idea that I would ask Herr Gutmann. Then I thought again and realized that if he knew the secret, he himself would have become a little man! He would have been rich and, poor man, he would have spared himself the shame of sending around books and bills. I thought it all over and decided that I should leave Herr Gutmann and offer myself as a servant to Doctor Steinharz. There I would learn the secret of how to become a little man. I promised an agent a big commission if he could pull some strings and make me into a servant for the doctor, and the very next day I left Herr Gutmann and the agent took me to my new job. The doctor himself was not home, his wife gave me work to do, and all day I worked like a donkey. I accepted everything quietly in hopes of seeing the little doctor. At nightfall the door opened and in came a tall, coarse man with a belly as round as the cantor—he was as big and tall as Gog and Magog. When I caught sight of him my eyes bulged and I stared at him foolishly. The boor cried out in Russian:

"What are you looking at, blockhead?"

I started to tremble and shake like a leaf, and I said, "Oy, oy, oy, my name is Itsik Avreml. I'm Abraham. I'm an orphan. I'm a servant here."

"Well, we can see that you're a great fool," the coarse man said. "From now on, watch for me, and when I come in you should quickly take off my coat and my boots, you hear?"

I was so scared of him that I got down on the ground and wrapped myself around his legs to take off his boots. The lummox went into the room, I brought in the samovar, and I served him and the lady of the house all evening. At night, in bed, I thought about who the coarse fellow could be. He could sit for an entire evening alone with the doctor's wife. And where was the doctor himself? For the next two days I served the lummox, and whenever he went out or came in I stretched out on the ground to put on or take off his boots. As I did this he would hold his sides and look at the ceiling, not even caring if he stepped on my fingers. And I still couldn't figure out who the lummox, the lout, could be. Once when the man had already gone to bed, I went down to the kitchen and asked the cook, with a pathetic expression: "I beg of you, who is the man that comes every evening and sleeps in the bedroom?" The cook looked at me, astonished: "What are you saying, what? What do you mean, someone sleeps in the bedroom? What are you talking about?"

"I swear it," I started to say. "I should only see the Messiah as clearly as I've seen him with my very own eyes. We should only live and be well."

"Well, and what about the master of the house?" asked the cook, with a cheerful face, and her eyes blazed like an oven baking challah.

"The master of the house," I answered, "doesn't seem to be sleeping at home. He must have gone away somewhere."

"Well," the cook said, "now I'm curious to go up and see for myself. I'll make some kind of excuse."

A few minutes later the cook came back down all red in the face and opened her big mouth to curse me: "What's the meaning of this? You're so young and already you've learned to make up gossip about something that never happened! Blockhead, hoodlum, I ought to tear you into shreds! How do you dare, you worthless loafer? You brazen rascal, Abraham! A pox on you, and may an evil spirit take you away, so help me! After all that, the master of the house is sitting in bed and talking with his wife!"

"What do you mean?" I said. "What do you mean? God be with you. Not that overgrown lout. . ."

"A curse on your grandpa, you impudent boy!" the cook started to shout and brandished the poker she was holding. "You mean to call the master of the house a lout, you smart aleck? I'll crack your head open!"

I hurried out of the kitchen and went back upstairs. Everything was quiet. When I lay down to sleep in the front room, I mulled it over. What was I seeing and hearing? The doctor was a big, fat fellow, so why did Gutmann say he was a little man? Had Gutmann told a lie? It couldn't be, Herr Gutmann never deceived me, and what Gutmann said always turned out to be true. Something was wrong.

A few days later, when I was standing behind the door to the doctor's office, I happened to hear this conversation between him and his barber-surgeon:

"Doctor, I procured quite a lot for you this week, and you haven't given me anything."

"What are you saying, Getzl? And what about yesterday?"

"What about yesterday, doctor?"

"He has a short memory! What's the meaning of this? You've forgotten, Getzl, that just yesterday, for your sake, I was a little man. I had thirty leeches applied to the sick man—only in order that you would make a profit. Just between us, he needed leeches about as much as you or me. All he had was an upset stomach. Truly, Getzl, just for your sake yesterday I was a little man."

"Yesterday you were a little man, as you say, and for your sake I was also a little man. Between us, today's patient didn't need a doctor. All he had was a cold. But I advised him to call you, and you gave him a prescription so that he'll be sick for at least two weeks. In the meantime you can visit him twice a day."

"Well, what do you want, Getzl?"

"Doctor, I still have quite a few leeches left!"

"Calm down, Getzl! Tomorrow I'll order leeches for all my patients. Just calm down, Getzl!"

So that's the story?! I thought it over as I lay in bed. Ha, ha! From what I've seen and heard, a little man isn't just a little man. One can, pardon my saying so, be a big and a little man at the same time.

My guess was that being a little man meant drawing other people's blood and cheating them out of their money. Now I started to understand what it meant to rub elbows with respectable people! I began to know the secret, but what did that help if I wasn't a doctor and couldn't apply leeches? I had to look for another means to become a little man—something similar, but in a different way. There was nothing more to be done in that line.

Then it came to me. I had to wheedle my way into service with Isser Varger! I was sure that was all it would take. Isser Varger was a little man—a rich, fortunate person.

That's what I thought, and I worked it all out in bed. The next day I promised the agent another commission, and in a few days he sneaked me into Isser Varger's house.

Isser Varger was one of the richest men in Tsviatshits. He worked everyone up into a fever, and everyone trembled before him when he spoke. It was no small matter, Isser Varger! He himself didn't do business or get his hands dirty; but just the same, things were always cooking at his house. One person came in and another person left—everyone showed up at Reb Isser's door. You might think that he was a great scholar, from a long line of rabbis, but not at all! He wasn't even the least bit of a scholar and barely knew how to pray; he came from a family of tailors. I found out about all of this later. The truth was, as I learned, that the secret of his success was being a little man—and with that he made a sea of money, more than anyone else with his Torah or his trade. He was in tight with the richest man of Tsviatshits—and was his very soul. It was always *this* Isser, *that* Isser, everything was just Isser. Isser was his soul, his legs, his hands. True, I never did get to know the rich man, and maybe he was a great man, a fine person, wise and learned; but Isser was some soul, a real little man. From Reb Isser, my rebbe, I learned a vast number of things. He opened my eyes and showed me the way to become a little man. I was a fool, a numbskull, but it turned out later that I wasn't an idiot by nature. That came more from being beaten and abandoned as a child. I was raised on beatings, and whoever wanted to went to work on me with slaps and blows. From beating your breast you don't get blessed. And from being beaten again and again, you get beaten down. It was no joking matter that, whenever I saw a hand, I expected it to hit me. I was dazed, confused, and stunned. What's more, I was born in a little shtetl, and a small-town Jew stays a small-town Jew. People from the shtetl are different—neither great nor small, neither wise nor foolish, neither good nor bad, neither fish nor fowl, just folk.

I won't waste any more of your time, but you shouldn't be surprised that a simpleton like me occasionally had a levelheaded thought and even came up with some bright ideas. I was a simpleton, for sure, but not by nature—just by being dazed and hazed and beaten. No screw was loose, but I was still unformed. That's how I was. This is why I was still able to learn some things, and I could soak in Reb Isser's teachings. I won't go on at length about Reb Isser, because he passed away and moved on to the true world a long time ago, and why should I reopen the book of his sins? I'd rather not talk about them. It's enough for you to know that I was his student, and from my tricks you'll understand what kind of man he was. I'll just explain to you Isser's system and his worldview, to which I adhered.

Isser had a close friend to whom he would tell everything. Especially when he was a bit tipsy, he would let down his guard and spill out everything that was bothering him. Once they came back cheerful and dead drunk, and they went into his room together. I was already quite good at standing behind doors and listening to conversations.

"Listen, my friend, I worked out a shrewd deal today. That is, I didn't really work, as fools might think. I worked just as little as you. I only pretended to work, you understand."

"But did you take in any money, Isser?"

"Hah! Did I ever!"

"How did it happen?"

"It's an old story; you know it well. Yankl might as well have walked to Siberia, though it wasn't really his fault. He'd been asking me to help him out for a long time. You know that I always answer: We'll see, we'll see. I say that with a shrug and let him think that I've seen what's going on—although I've seen as much as I can see my own ears. Then I take a hefty fee. If his plan fails, I still don't lose my standing, my influence. He thinks he lost just because I didn't *want* to look into the matter, and that if I'd *wanted* to get involved, I would have surely carried it off. He can come and make demands, even want to strangle me or just plain call me names. It's no skin off my back, and I haven't spoiled my reputation. He'll get over it and return asking for another favor, and as always I answer: We'll see, we'll see. You understand.

"Well, that's what I said to Yankl: We'll see, we'll see. I saw full well that my seeing could help him about as much as last year's snow. Let's not be fooled about the limits of my power. But Yankl thought I saw and would ask the rich man to look into it. I didn't even have to open my mouth or get my hands dirty. After the documents came out, I knew that when it came to a decision Yankl would lose his lawsuit. So early this morning I went running to him out of breath and said: Yankl, I've been wearing myself out to win your case. Give me some bottles of wine—I still have to go see the secretary. You should have seen how happily Yankl and his wife embraced. They said to me: We have only you to thank, Reb Isser. If not for you, we could have really suffered, and we'll tell everyone what you did for us. They sent me home and I took along a small fortune.

"Believe me, my friend, you won't get anywhere in this world with the truth, and work won't earn you anything. No matter how hard you sweat, you'll still go hungry ten times a day. In this world, only a little man gets results. Wisdom is worthless, because the main thing is to be cunning. You must be able to flatter, lie, and be hypocritical whenever it's called for. What else? You've got to have money, for without money you're nothing. What's a beggar? Do you want to know why rich people hate a beggar? They talk to him once and pretend to have pity on him, but in truth they can't stand him. To them he seems superfluous, and they feel a pinching in their chest when they see him. I have no words to describe it to you fully. But everything depends on money, my friend. If you have money, you own this world and the next. To get money you must be a little man. And to be a little man means flat-tering, being a hypocrite, and doing whatever it takes to succeed."

"Well, and Isser, what about the rich man who depends on you as if you were his soul? He has money and yet he's a fine person."

"I won't speak of him, my friend. You understand? So long as he's under lease to me I won't speak of him."

"What do you mean, Isser, he's under lease to you?"

"Oh, my friend, you're still just a straitlaced gent, so let me explain it to you. You should know that in this world everyone must seek only his own good. Do you understand? A rich man has great power, and everything falls into his lap. People humble themselves before the rich man, though they get nothing for it, just because a rich man deserves respect. And I, Isser, say that one should judge a rich man by his money, you understand? Just by his money; the man himself comes second. A rich man who doesn't serve your ends should have no importance to you. Pay as much attention to him as they do to the Purim Megillah in Czernovitz. A clever, shrewd man should, in this world, do everything for his own benefit. Do you understand? I'll repeat it once more: every person must seek his own good. A rich man has great power, and the clever man must take advantage of everything—so you need to know how to make use of the rich man, and not just for his money. You should stand next to the rich man like a comedian at the entrance to a comedy, or like a circus gypsy beside his bear. If you've bought a ticket, enter the comedy and watch the pretty play. If you give me some money, I'll make the bear dance. You understand? The rich man is under lease to me, so if you want to see him, pay me for a ticket. I'm his manager, his soul, his landlord! That's enough. Now do you understand, my dear friend?"

At first, of course, Isser's system was too advanced for me, and many of his expressions were unfamiliar. But right away I understood: "To get money you must be a little man. And to be a little man means flattering, being a hyp-ocrite, and doing whatever it takes to succeed." I had found the secret. But I didn't fully understand what it meant to flatter and be a hypocrite. I should note that, at the time, I didn't know the difference between what one may or may not do. The sins I knew about were things like peeking during the Priestly Benediction, not slaughtering a scape hen at Yom Kippur, not going to Tashlikh during Rosh Hashanah, not believing in a wonder-worker, not be-lieving that Elijah the Prophet goes from house to house on Passover drink-ing glasses of wine, not believing that the dead pray at night in the Great

Synagogue, or not believing that sinners wander in limbo. That would have meant not believing that there are hordes of people among us who trade, do business, travel, buy and sell, while in fact they are living dead. One fringe of their prayer shawl is defective and they are not called to the Torah. And not believing in the transmigration of souls—that would have meant not believing that the sacred soul of a person is transformed into a black cat, a pig, a calf, a hen, a stallion, or a canary. Or not believing that the dead come for judgment to the Bezliude rabbi, led like soldiers by the Angel of Judgment. Not believing that a shtrayml is sacred, and that even in Egypt the Jews wore fur hats and because of this they were redeemed. In short, these were the kinds of sins I knew—not flattering, being a hypocrite, or being a little man. Why not become a little man, rich and happy? No one dares to beat up a little man, and I knew how much a beating hurts. When a tailor or his wife hits you hard, you see stars; and when a cantor twists your ear, you can forget you were ever born. It's also unpleasant to stretch out on the floor putting on or taking off the master of the house's boots while he puts his hands on his hips and looks at the ceiling. So of course I wanted to be a little man, to suffer less, and to be happy and rich. I'd started to eavesdrop on all Isser's conversations with his good friend, and I began to understand his words. He was easier to understand than my teacher at school.

I served Isser for many years, during which time I polished my skills and learned all the things a little man needs to know. I listened carefully and was a diligent student. Then I started to look at myself and ask: When shall I build my own abode?[5] That is, when will I start to do something that will raise me up in the world? I was getting on in years and was already a young man. It was true that I knew Isser's Torah well, but the main thing is to learn the craft, not the commentary. I thought about it for a long time before I came to this conclusion. Indeed, I told myself, what a fool I was! Isser himself says that everyone must seek his own good, and one should have a rich man under lease, taking a profit. Well, Isser himself was a rich man, so I decided I would have him under lease and become his soul. It was as if I had roast goose in my mouth and still thought I needed to beg for food. I won't drag it out, but just tell you that I started to play the hypocrite and flatter Isser, finding a thousand ways to ingratiate myself with him until I caught him and became his soul. Isser was also a human being, and he liked to be flattered and pampered, al-

5. A Hebrew phrase based on Genesis 30:30.

though he knew how false flattery was. When he told someone, for example: You're wise, good, pious, generous, and highborn, it meant just the opposite: You're are a fool, a villain, a rogue, a miser, and lowborn. But that's just how it is, that everyone in the world likes to be deceived.

Still, it was easier said than done. It took a long time before I was able to become important to Isser. You may wonder: how does a servant become important? Ai, don't hold it against me, but if you need to ask this, you must not know the world. Almost all servants are important, and almost all important people are servants. When people saw my importance, because I had become Isser's soul, they started to treat me with kid gloves. Aha! Someone wanted to see Isser—and who didn't?—so he asked me to intercede for him. There was no need to talk of gifts or bribes. The person thought he'd gotten somewhere with me, that I would put in a good word with Isser, and he was happy. I knew that Isser could help him about as much as bloodletting helps a corpse, but I let him think it helped, and then hand over some money. That's how I gathered a few thousand rubles. I might have gone on that way and collected millions. But I was still a shlimmazl and, in the midst of everything, it happened that the rich man who was under lease to Isser died. Suddenly Isser was nobody's soul and had no influence. And when that happened, obviously, I was also nobody's soul and lost my influence. People stopped going to Isser because he was no longer a lease-holder; he no longer had a dancing bear. And when Isser lost his importance, you understand, I also lost mine. True, I was still important to Isser, but when he could no longer employ me, I needed him like a hole in the head. Then I listened to him about as much as they listen to the Purim Megillah in Czernovitz. I learned that from Isser himself—it was his own philosophy. I had a few thousand rubles, so I could afford to make light of him. My next thought was how to get another position where I could play a leading role, and I had the idea of moving to Glupsk. A certain rich man had a reputation there; I decided to take him under lease.

On the way to Glupsk I went to see the leader of the city. If you want to take a rich man under lease, you have to set things straight with the local rebbe. He's the first stop. That's how Reb Isser acted in his heyday. I gave the rebbe a hefty sum and he gave me his blessing so that I should succeed. With his blessing I rode into Glupsk. At that time I was maybe twenty-three, twenty-five, twenty-seven—I didn't keep track of the years and didn't know when I was born. What good would it have done me to know? In Glupsk I let on that I was a widower, because a young unmarried man gets no respect. I wore a prayer shawl decorated with a thick silver collar that shimmered and sparkled. In those days, as Reb Isser Varger used to say, a beautiful collar was the best recommendation among Jews. I had money, too, which made it easy to meet all of the fine creatures of Glupsk. I told them I was thinking of opening a business, but really I was thinking of my lease, because I didn't know how to do anything else. God lent a hand and I came to know the rich man. He was very coarse and liked to be involved in all of the foolish goings-on around town, which suited me fine. That's just what I needed. I won't drag it out; my business went on smooth as butter, and it wasn't very difficult for me to become his soul. In short, in the course of two years I was lucky and came to hold him under lease. The whole city, rich and poor, needed his favors and bowed down to him, so you can imagine how it went with me, his soul. I said earlier that it isn't my nature to speak ill of others, and to this day I hold with Isser, who used to say: I won't talk about my rich benefactor. I don't need to confess his sins—he's still alive and will have time to confess for himself. Here I'm talking about myself.

I repent for my sin of deceiving others.[6] When townspeople saw my importance, they all thought I was immensely rich and powerful. Whoever had a business venture in mind went straight to Isaac Abraham Takif—that's what they called me, as you already know, Rebbe. I would accept piles of gold and say, We'll see, we'll see, just as Isser had answered. A person thought I would help, but in truth I would forget all about him after I took the money. I just made a fool of him.

And for the sin of hardening my heart—I repent. I stole from the poor, from widows, and from orphans. When a poor man cried rivers of tears, I turned a deaf ear. What good are your tears to me? I thought. Render unto me the capital, and desist from weeping and wailing. That is, hand over the dough, Jew dog, and drown yourself in your tears.

And for the sin of hurrying to do evil—I repent. Doing evil is far easier than doing good. Even a cat can spill the milk. Most of the time, to do good requires wisdom, money, and so on, but to do evil is easy as pie. It doesn't demand any great wisdom and doesn't cost a thing. To keep my reputation as a

---

6. Starting with this phrase, Isaac Abraham's repeated use of the formula "I repent for my sin" (or "for the sin . . . I repent," *'al heit she-hetati*) echoes the Yom Kippur ritual of atonement.

takif, I often did evil deliberately, so that people would fear me and not take me lightly.

And for the sin of slander and holding a lease—I repent. I had to speak a lot of slander and secretly carry out a lot of schemes in order to make my benefactor into a leading light, adorn him with a shtrayml, and become his soul, the takif, the lease-holder.

And I repent for my sin of insolence and of being a little man. When I had to entrap an honest man who stood in my way, or to deceive an intelligent, honest man who had guessed my fraud, then I showed my full power and impudence, my insolence, just like a little man.

In short, I was a little man, and because of this things went well for me. I married a rich wife and lived in wealth and honor. I earned a great deal of money from my lease and I have accumulated wealth during the twenty years or so that I've been living in Glupsk.

Earlier I said that I wasn't born a fool, I was no idiot; I was just beaten down. By nature I wasn't an evil person, either, but I was led astray. When I did something low down, afterward my heart pounded faster and a gloomy mood would overtake me. I myself didn't know where to hide my head. I recall that Isser said that a little man shouldn't envy men like Gutmann, who write books. God forbid: one should hate and persecute them, because they are more dangerous than fire. They crawl down your throat with their wise words. He used to say it's a miracle that donkeys don't have horns; well, it's a miracle that men like that don't have money and are usually paupers. Otherwise, we'd never hear the end of them and we'd never get rid of them, like lice. Obviously, Isser's sayings were the Holy Torah to me, and though it disturbed me to make an enemy of Gutmann, who had found a way to enter my soul, I only listened to Isser. If not, I couldn't become a little man, a lease-holder, and I'd have to go on suffering blows and misfortunes by the pound. Of course, I tortured men like Gutmann. But when I was already rich and didn't need to fear suffering and misery, then my heart used to throb; I would imagine the good, calm Gutmann. Oh, what a good man he was! How he liked me and didn't treat me like a servant! Even though he was poor, he was always cheerful and happy.

Once his wife cried long and hard when it was close to Passover and there wasn't a trace of the holiday at home. He sent me out with books for an entire day, and no one wanted to touch them. When I took people invoices, they turned up their noses; and so, in short, the dear lady cried. Oh, Gutmann said, why are you sinning with tears? We're better off than all of the rich — we're honest people, and we suffer for the truth. It's much better and finer to suffer for the truth than to be happy from deceit. Don't worry. God has helped in the past and He'll go on helping us. What do I need with two jackets and a fur coat, when I can only wear one? And who needs a fur coat, anyway, with summer coming? The moths may chew it up. Abraham, take my fur collar and my coat, pawn or sell them, and we'll have matzoh for Passover.

The scene replayed itself again and again before my eyes. I saw that Gutmann was happy without money, which showed that happiness wasn't made of money, but of something else. He would even say, "We're better off than all of the rich, since we're honest people," which meant that only honest people are happy and rich. I always remembered what he said to my friend Jacobsohn: "Being a flatterer and a hypocrite is worst of all. The flatterer and hypocrite, like a thief, must always worry and be on guard." I began to see how true this was: Gutmann, with his intelligence, understood that things are as bad for a flatterer and a hypocrite as they are for a thief. Both must always be afraid of being caught, and they must always guard against people finding out their tricks. It is unpleasant to live secretively all the time. And I really did feel, in my heart, that a false person is always in a bad way. Life lacks all flavor, it weighs on him like a stone on his heart; his blood boils, his head bothers him and burns like a flame. Yes, I felt that real suffering was having to flatter and be a hypocrite. I was rich, but still not happy!

I would have harsh, bitter dreams. I'd imagine I was holding a knife and slaughtering with it; I'd hear moans, groans, and death rattles, and my coat would be soaked in blood. In one dream I saw Gutmann sitting with his family, happy and cheerful. When I went in, he looked at me and shook his head with regret.

"Oh, Abraham," he said sadly. "You used to be a much better man, although you were a bit of a fool. It's a pity. Feh, you've been led astray and ruined. You've become a little man!"

This year these dark thoughts so tormented me that I took sick. I felt that I wouldn't last long, and I hurried to write my life story — how it happened that I went astray. Perhaps by writing I can atone for my sins, and also set down my last will.

My fortune is worth about a hundred and fifty thousand rubles. I wish to give fifty thousand rubles for my two small children. That's enough for them;

their father didn't even have fifty kopecks at their age, and until they marry they can earn interest. My wife shall receive fifteen thousand rubles.

For God's sake I ask of you, Rebbe, that you send for Herr Gutmann in Tsviatshits as soon as possible. The two of you should make use of my money, as I will direct here. You, Rebbe, are a saint and an honest man, which I can see from the fact that you're very poor. If you had wanted, you could have been rich like any other rabbinical judge. Gutmann is also a saint and a good man, though he wears no head covering and trims his beard; he has your precious character. I ask, Rebbe, that you treat him kindly, as he will treat you, for he likes everyone and is a lover of the Jewish people. Herr Gutmann will be very useful to you in the matters I will request of you.

With the remaining eighty-five thousand rubles, as an endowment in perpetuity, I ask that you first improve the local Talmud-Torah. In what way? You yourself will know, and Herr Gutmann also knows about such things. The main thing is that the teachers shouldn't beat the poor children. And one shouldn't give them all kinds of twisted interpretations of biblical verses. Believe me, that just confuses them.

Second, one should make a vocational school for craftsmen, so that apprentices won't have to suffer abuse from tailors and their wives, and they won't have to carry slop pails. God have mercy! Many orphans who become apprentices, poor things, spoil their health and are left crippled, with bruises all over their bodies. Why doesn't anyone think about such unfortunate children?

Third, when a traveling cantor comes to Glupsk, you should give him expense money to continue on his way. A cantor is no comedian who drags himself all over the world. If you're a cantor, stay home and take care of your synagogue; but if you're a musician, travel around and sing in theaters.

Other than that, you should spend the money as you and Herr Gutmann wish. I know that because both of you are fine people, great humanitarians, you'll know what to do without answering to anyone. I bequeath my entire house with all of its household objects to you and Herr Gutmann; the property earns about five thousand rubles a year. You should live in the house and both of you should provide guidance for my children.

You should read this letter to all of the wealthy local men. It will atone for my sins and teach them a lesson. Afterward you should print it. Let the whole world know that wealth doesn't bring happiness; a person is happy only with a good heart and good deeds. It's better to suffer torments, so long as one is honest, than to live in luxury and be a little man. Please give this letter to Reb Mendele the Book Peddler, because he knows all about printing books. And apart from that, he travels all around Poland and will be able to distribute it. Pay him well for his troubles—he's very poor.

When the rabbi finished reading the letter, I took a look at the people gathered around. The rich men were angry and bit their lips with resentment, but they kept quiet. One of the rabbinical judges was enraged and he tore at his whiskers. But the other judges remained calm and said:

"A Jew stays a Jew. Even sinners fulfill as many commandments as there are seeds in a pomegranate. Look at what a Jewish heart he had—he sinned unintentionally, and now he has repented. We'll study a chapter in the Mishna every day and say Kaddish for him, for a year, free of charge."

"Now, Reb Mendele," the rabbi said to me, "I ask you, first, who is this Herr Gutmann of yours in Tsviatshits? Is he really an honest man? Do you know him?"

"Rebbe," I answered, "Gutmann trims his beard, but still he's an honest man."

"Well," the rabbi said, "so long as he is an honest man, his trimmed beard doesn't bother me. As we say: better a Jew without a beard than a beard without a Jew. Second, since you're from Tsviatshits, I ask that you please travel there today—you'll be well paid for it. You should deliver my letter to Herr Gutmann and ask him to come quickly, for God's sake, so that we may fulfill the wishes of the deceased. And third, dear Reb Mendele, you should print and sell this letter at a low price all over Poland, so that many people will buy it. Of course, I will pay you well."

I went over to pick up my candlesticks from the floor, and suddenly we heard a voice outside calling, "Charity saves from death," as beggars do at funerals. All of us—the rabbi, long may he live, the judges, the rich men, and I—went outside to accompany Isaac Abraham to the cemetery. The rabbi asked the Talmud-Torah boys to walk ahead and say: "Righteousness will go before him and give direction to his steps."

I hurried to hitch up my horse. While I was sitting at the rabbi's house, the street urchins had pulled out almost all of the hairs in his tail, so that only about forty remained. But I'm getting off the point. I hurried on my way to Tsviatshits, where I hadn't been for almost two years.

When I arrived home, they told me that Gutmann had left Tsviatshits long ago, and no one knew where he was. I hastened to print the letter, and I hereby let it be known that as soon as Herr Gutmann reads it, he should travel to Glupsk. The rabbi there is looking for him, so that together they can improve the Talmud-Torah and do many other good things.

Translated by Ken Frieden

Fishke the Lame

A Story of Poor Jewish Folks

1

Last year, in the summer of 1868, after I stocked up some fresh goods and packed my wagon with all sorts of books, I headed out on my travels to those distant places where, thank God, Reb Mendele and his wares are still valued. You've got to know those Jews. They like it when the pages of a book are all colors and sizes, the letters are a little blurred, and every page is printed in different type: Rashi script, pica, elite, bold, pearl, italic, you name it. Don't worry about mistakes because a Jew has a head on his shoulders and can figure things out. One printer from Obmanov, may he rest in peace, discovered the secret of what Jews like, and his books—even the most insignificant—sold like hotcakes. But I'm getting off the point.

It was afternoon on the seventeenth of Tammuz, in the heat of the summer, when I turned off the main road a few miles short of Glupsk. The sky was clear and blue without a trace of clouds; the sun scorched and burned the land. There was no air to breathe and no breeze. From the wheat in the fields to the trees on the hill, nature stood still. You remember the dreadful dry heat last summer, when not a leaf stirred. Jews moved heaven and earth—everywhere they said Psalms, wailed, fasted—but for the longest time God didn't want to grant even a single drop of rain. The grass in the pastures turned brown. The miserable cows lay exhausted with their necks outstretched, ears twitching, chewing the cud. Others rooted around in the ground with their horns, scraped their hooves, and bellowed at the heat. Nearby stood horses leaning their heads across each other, making a bit of shade, and chasing away flies with their tails. It broke my heart to see them, and yet God didn't want to give a drop of rain, even for the sake of the innocent beasts. Everywhere it was calm and you could hear each rustle or peep, but not a single bird was out—only mosquitoes swarmed, like evil spirits. Now and then they would dance by, take a bite, and buzz and hiss in your ears. As if they'd come to whisper a secret and then march on. But I'm getting off the point.

In the intense heat I sat stretched out on my wagon, stripped down—if you'll excuse my saying so—to my undershirt and fringed garment. A stitched plush cap was pushed back on my head and woolen stockings from Breslau were rolled down to my heels. I wear them even in the summer, to atone for my sins, and I sweated heavily. Actually, if the sun hadn't been full in my face I might have enjoyed this because I like to sweat and can lie for hours on the upper benches of the bathhouse at the hottest time of year. My father, may he rest in peace, was a hot, burning, fiery Jew who got me used to the heat since childhood. He so liked to steam up and sweat that he was famous for it. Sweating is, after all, a Jewish business, and who in this world sweats more than a Jew? But I'm getting off the point. My wretched horse also worked up quite a sweat. I should tell you that he hasn't changed a bit except that now he limps around with a swollen back foot wrapped in rags.[1] One of his eyes oozes pus and there's a nasty cut where the bridle rubs against his neck. What difference does it make if a Jew's horse isn't pretty, so long as it can walk? I took pity on him and tied long strips of paper to his chewed up tail—let me tell you, this is a great trick to drive away flies and mosquitoes. But I'm getting off the point again. Behind me followed a second wagon made of old, torn straw mats. It bounced along on four uneven, squeaky wheels, pulled by an old nag that was tall, thin, with a bruised and scratched back, and big ears. Its knotted mane was tangled with hay and straw that stuck out of the fraying bridle. Leaning his head on his hands, high up on the wagon lay a heavyset Jew with a fat belly, red as a beet, sunburned, dripping sweat from his hairy chest, and it broke my heart to look at him. It was Wine 'n' Candles Alter, my good friend, a book peddler from Tuneyadevke. We had met up along the way a few minutes earlier.

At about one o'clock we came to the woods at the foot of Green Mountain outside Glupsk. Green Mountain is known almost the world over from an old song about it. Everywhere children sing this song; nurses and nannies sing it

1. "My wretched horse . . . hasn't changed a bit": an allusion to descriptions of Mendele's horse in Abramovitsh's previous two Yiddish works, *The Little Man (Dos kleyne mentshele)* and *The Wishing-Ring (Dos vintshfingerl)*.

to suckling babies. My mother, may her soul rest in Paradise, when she wanted to distract me so that I wouldn't cry, used to sing these words:

> High up on Green Mountain,
> Tall grass brushing their hips,
> Stand two stylish Prussians
> Brandishing whips. . . .

I always liked the song, and it amused me more than any other lullaby. From a distance, Green Mountain seemed so beautiful that I imagined it was made of something other than earth. Green Mountain brought to mind the hills of Lebanon and the Holy Land. Not to mention those Prussians who seemed, begging their pardon, like oxen, wild beasts, mythical creatures grazing on the tall grass of Green Mountain. But I'm getting off the point.

We unhitched our horses, which were ready to drop, and let them drag themselves off to graze on Green Mountain. Then we propped ourselves up under a tree.

2

Reb Alter could scarcely breathe because of the heat, and he was covered in a cold sweat. He cackled like a hen and so moaned and groaned that hearing him pierced me to the heart.

"Hot enough for you, Reb Alter?" I said, trying to make conversation.

"Bah!" he answered and moved deeper into the shade.

"I reckon the fast has got you feeling really lousy," I said.[2]

"Bah!" said Reb Alter again.

But I couldn't leave it at that. I was getting bored and wanted to talk a bit, so I tried again.

"From what you've said, Reb Alter, I gather you're coming back from Yarmolinetz. Do any good business at the town fair?"

"Bah!" said Reb Alter once more and twisted his lips.

"Bah, what?" I asked, getting annoyed. "Why can't you just answer my question?"

2. "I reckon the fast has got you feeling really lousy": Referring to the complete fast observed by traditional Jews on the seventeenth of Tammuz, in commemoration of Nebuchadnezzar's capture of Jerusalem in 586 B.C.E.

"Don't ask, don't ask," Reb Alter finally said with a sigh. "I got what was coming to me at the fair. It serves me right, and I should give up the business."

I kept bothering Alter, long and hard, until he told me all about his mishap at the fair.

"When I arrived at the fair," he began and groaned again, "I tied up my wagon as usual and laid out my wares on the main square. I had great hopes for the Yarmolinetz fair, you should know, because I'm in a bad way. The printer wants me to pay up or he won't send another book. My eldest daughter is getting on in years and needs to be married off. My wife bore us another son not long back, and so, praise God, I'm raising a brood of kids without a penny in my pocket."

"Excuse me for interrupting, Reb Alter," I said, "but why, at your age, did you go and marry a young wife who'd bear you so many children?"

"God help you," Reb Alter answered. "I needed someone to keep house. Why else does a Jew get married?"

"Then why," I said, "did you divorce your first wife? She was a good housekeeper, wasn't she?"

"Bah!" said Reb Alter with a grimace.

Among us Jews, "bah" is a very useful word. It seems no other people or language has such a word that answers every question. "Bah" comes in handy at any time and will always serve. Even Reb Yosl, who gives advice to all the people of Glupsk, waits until a person has talked himself blue in the face, puts on a serious look, and says, "Bah!" Though Reb Yosl hasn't been listening to a single word, it comes out like a pearl of wisdom and everyone is satisfied. Or when some hapless man chances upon Reb Nisl, the town arbitrator, and says, "How can it be that I put myself at your mercy, gave you a fortune, and yet you sold me cheap like a sheep for slaughter? Come on, speak up!" Then our Reb Nisl calmly answers with a simple "Bah!" And he stays in the right. People take this as a valid explanation and the very next day another loser entrusts his fate to Reb Nisl. Or when a Jew puts a ruble in front of Reb Abba, our rabbinical judge, for a legal decision, and asks if it is enough, Reb Abba makes a face and says, "Bah!" The Jew catches his drift and, with a heavy heart, adds a few coins. When someone asks Reb Azriel, just to be polite, whether he'd like another glass of wine or piece of fish, he answers with a coy "Bah!" And then you have to give him the last drop. "Bah" has so many meanings that a Jew can always use it to wriggle out of a tough spot. Language experts of our day tell us that the word "bah" is as old as Balam's ass: when it opened its mouth to speak, it said "Bah, bah!" But I'm getting off the point again.

I, too, had to honor Reb Alter's "Bah!" before asking him to continue his story.

3

"Standing beside my wagon," Reb Alter began, "I watched the town fair. The crowd was thick as molasses, and Jews were busy making a good profit. Among the other merchants I saw Berl Teletse, once a mere teacher's assistant, then a servant, and now the owner of a big shop, favored by fortune and wealth. Over there I saw a man running and working himself into a sweat, wearing a cap on his head and raking in money. Then some other people ran by, out of breath—agents, matchmakers, ragtag tailors, hucksters, henwives, all of them with flaming red faces and apparently all on the verge of success.

"Deep down I envied everyone who was making out so well, mining gold—while I, like a shlimmazl, stood idly beside my broken-down wagon with my arms folded. Some of my wares, charms and four-cornered fringed garments, were hanging over the sides of the cart. Inside were a few packages of books—Passover Haggadas, prayer books for Shavuot—that were out of season and no one wanted to touch. I was also selling a bit of old brassware, some shofars, yarmulkas spun from yarn for children, and some rags. Silently I cursed myself, the wagon, the printer, my broken-down nag—all of us would be better off dead. I saved the best curses for the printer. If not for him, I wouldn't have known from any wagon, nag, or the rest of my troubles.

"Suddenly, driven by envy and desire, it occurred to me to try my luck at a new trade—making a match between the children of two wealthy merchants, who had brought their goods to the fair. You must know them; one is Reb Elyakim Sharograder, and the other is Reb Getzl Gredinger. I neglected my book trade and spent the next day and night going back and forth between the families like an utter madman, running from one father to the other. I worked at it, nose to the ground, determined to make a match then and there. What more suitable place could there be? God helped out by bringing together the in-laws, who luckily agreed to the dowry and other expenses. Overjoyed, I thought I had the world in my pocket, not to mention the matchmaker's fee. I even started to think how much I would give my poor daughter as a dowry, and I haggled over some fabric for a featherbed.

"But listen to what can happen if luck is against you. When they started to write the marriage contract and needed the names of the bride and groom, it turned out—I can hardly bear to tell you—that it was all a pipe dream. Listen to what can go wrong: both of the families had boys! You can imagine the reward I got from both sides, *vey iz mir*, and how I felt as I left the fair without a penny in my pocket."

I couldn't help it—I burst out laughing and said:

"How's it possible, Reb Alter, that you got mixed up in such an idiotic scheme? I don't want to insult you any more than I would my own mother, but how could you make a match before you were sure that one family had a girl and the other had a boy?"

"Of course, don't I know it?!" answered Reb Alter with feeling. "I haven't totally lost my marbles. I knew very well that Reb Elyakim had an unmarried daughter, and once I even saw her with my own eyes. But nothing in the world can help if luck is against you. It was just my luck that Reb Elyakim's girl decided to get married in a hurry last year. I hadn't heard anything of it. So when I planned a match between Reb Elyakim and Reb Getzl, I was thinking of Elyakim's girl and Getzl's boy. No need to spell it out—it seemed so simple there was nothing more to say. Two boys don't get hitched up, obviously it would be a boy and a girl, the way of the world. I think I acted as befits the trade, and I swear no one could have done it better. I went straight to the heart of the matter: dowry, wedding gifts, and other expenses. Don't forget that at a fair there's no time to mince words, you keep it brief and to the point. Reb Elyakim himself must have assumed that, if there was going to be a match, it had to be with his son. How could it be any other way? He knew that Reb Getzl would be his in-law, but how could that be? Neither of them had a girl to marry off. Now you see what goes on in the world and how I got into such a mess. Take it from me, nothing you do will succeed unless you have luck. The devil put me up to it, and I got what was coming to me."

Poor Reb Alter lay there quietly, licking his wounds and beset by cares. His story brought to mind many things about arranged marriages among Jews. I decided to talk with Reb Alter and draw him out of his gloom.

"Yes, Reb Alter, yes," I said, "anything can happen in this world. I want to tell you a fine tale about what goes on among Jews."

Reb Alter wiped the sweat from his face with his sleeve. Then he stretched himself out under the tree, smoking his small pipe. I coughed a few times, drove away some mosquitoes, and started to tell the following story.

4

"In the brick bathhouse of Glupsk, there lived for many years a fellow named Fishke the Lame. One might say that Fishke had perfected every possible flaw. That is to say, there wasn't a single flaw or failing that Fishke didn't possess. He had a big, flat head with long, flaxen sidelocks, a wide mug, fat lips, and crooked, yellow teeth. Cross-eyed, one arm twisted back, limping heavily on one leg, Fishke was no delight to behold. He was such a freakish creature that the town didn't even want him as a cholera groom. When people panicked during epidemics and conscriptions, the Glupsk community hastily matched up cripples, scoundrels, and beggars with unmarried girls, raising the wedding canopy amid the tombstones at the cemetery. They did this in the hope that it would put an end to the disease. Instead of Fishke, the community first selected the famous cripple Yontl, who pushed himself along on his buttocks holding two low wooden platforms in his hands. They paired him off with the illustrious, poor old widow with no lower lip and huge teeth that hung down like shovels. The second time, the community chose the town bum named Lekish. At the graveyard, this Lekish placed the veil on a bride who, if you'll excuse my saying so, was better off with her face and bald pate covered. In town there was a rumor that she was either sexless or androgynous. They say that the guests were very festive at their wedding and drank a sea of brandy among the tombstones. Jews should be fruitful and multiply, everyone agreed, and poor cripples should also be able to enjoy life. But I'm getting off the point.

"The short and long of it was that they all skipped over Fishke, even the old auntie who'd lost her nose.[3] She was the one who—when the klezmer musician used to squeak out a tune on his fiddle and sing along—used to go and hop around like crazy in the middle of the street. She took up a collection so that two corpses could dance; that is, she gave new life to cripples and poor girls so that, God forbid, they wouldn't become old maids. But even the merciful old auntie kept forgetting Fishke and let him go around for a long time without a wife. It was too bad, let me tell you, for if Fishke had been in good health, Glupsk might already have been blessed with some of his children.

---

3. "The old auntie who'd lost her nose": possibly a matchmaker (shadkhen); or perhaps a local prostitute or madame in a brothel, because before the discovery of antibiotics, syphilis was known to deface its victims.

"Most of the time Fishke went around barefoot, without a coat, wearing a patched shirt over his long, grease-stained four-cornered garment and coarse, wrinkled underwear. His work consisted of going through the streets calling people to the bathhouse in his stammering voice. In the summer, when vegetables came into season, the streets would ring out with his sweet cries: 'Jews, over here! Fresh garlic for sale!' I knew Fishke well, because I went straight to the bathhouse whenever I arrived in Glupsk. First things first, and on such occasions I always stopped in at the brick bathhouse to fumigate my clothes, rinse the lice off my socks, and stretch out my aching bones on the top bench. Whatever anyone else may say, to me that's the greatest bliss; what could be better than to sweat? As I already said, even now it would be a pleasure to sweat, except for the sun beating down on my face.

"Move over a bit, if you don't mind, Reb Alter!" I said. "Seems to me you've worked up quite a sweat. Move on over, if you don't mind, just a bit farther."

Reb Alter cleaned out his pipe, filled it up again with tobacco, and went on smoking. I moved closer to him, into the shade, and returned to my story.

"When I was in Glupsk last year, I saw Fishke from a distance and was so surprised I almost jumped out of my skin. He was limping along as usual but looking like a dandy in a fine new coat, new shoes and socks, a wide-brimmed hat, a newly sewn shirt of starched calico that sparkled on his chest, and large red flowers decorating his four-cornered garment. What did it mean? I wondered. Did the town finally make him into a cholera groom? Or maybe old auntie no-nose took pity on him, combed the streets, and drummed up some beauty for him. But I was off to the bathhouse for a good cupping on my neck and shoulders, as is the custom among Jews, and to scrub my old bones with twigs. I'd fallen on my back and suffered from aches and pains, God help me, so I decided I would pass a few hours at the bath. I figured that I'd learn everything I wanted to know about Fishke there. Aside from which I would pick up other gossip concerning public affairs—such as, what's gone wrong with the Emperor? Have the Prussians brought him down a notch?[4] And how might the Pope, poor fellow, be doing? Has Rabbi Avigdor Emanuel been bothering him? What did the old folks, who still remembered the time when Napoleon reached our corner of the world, have to say? In order to save their sons during those first days of the conscription, as the French army approached, peo-

4. Mendele is referring to events associated with the Crimean War (1853–56).

ple married off five-year-old boys and girls. What would people say now? Maybe that we could rediscover the mysterious Red Jews or Ten Lost Tribes. According to the bathhouse gossip, the Pasha was already a lost cause, thrown out of Istanbul with everything he owned. I was most curious to hear what was happening in America, because ever since the Civil War started, in our parts the price of wool has risen so that for a prayer shawl and fringes you have to spend everything you've got.

"I mixed all this together purposely in order that you'd understand what goes on in the brick bathhouse of Glupsk. There everything that's doing and brewing in the world gets mooted about, secrets are revealed, business is transacted, and the tumult is greater than at a town fair. If you come on Friday you'll see a marvelous thing: in a corner sit barber-surgeons surrounded by people. One of them gives shaves and haircuts while another marks shoulders with a razor, places cups, and Jewish blood spurts all over the floor, mixing in with papers and newly cut hair. On the walls, on the ceiling, and beside the oven hang more clothes than in the grandest store: socks, shirts, fringed garments, underwear, caftans, overcoats, and sometimes even plush hats. From the top bench you hear frightful shouting while some folks lie there groaning, ready to pass out. Others, armed with twig brooms, cry, *Gevalt!* Have mercy, Jews, steam it up! The bath grows cold, everyone starts to shout, but no one bothers to pour water on the stone. Finally some hoodlum fires it up until it's so hot you choke. High up over a vat sit the rich and well-connected men talking brass tacks: about the lease from the Polish lord, about the kosher meat tax, about the draft, about the elections, and about the new chief of police. A wealthy man shuffles over to them and makes conversation about the Jewish school, the new government edicts, scandals about town, and starts some rumors. Suddenly one smart aleck—who's been sharpening his teeth on the local councilman—grins and invites the best-connected man in town to sit with him on the top bench, so that he can steam him up a bit. The wealthy man gets the same idea and, swallowing his pride, invites someone else to get in on the action. Everyone crawls up to the top bench and the deal is done. Thanks to them, things really start to heat up in the bath—from young to old and small to grand, people grab the twig brooms amid the hubbub, tumult, and shouting. Then I crawl into a corner as high up as I can get and steam up my bones to the limit, until all at once a glow spreads through my limbs. I'll have to take you with me to the bath some day; you should feel the heat and see it with your own eyes. But back to the matter at hand. Listen, Reb Alter, to what the bathhouse attendant told me about Fishke, in these very words.

5

" 'One Thursday evening,' he told me, 'when all of the attendants and I finished firing up the stoves, we stretched out on the benches to catch our breath. Apart from us, stretched out, were a few poor Jews who always hang around and stink up the place. Sorry if I'm being crass. We were all lying there calmly, smoking and chatting cheerfully. You should know that we pass the time much better and more amicably than people do in the town club. There the jealousies and rivalries are so fierce that it's a wonder no one gets his nose torn off. While we were resting, all at once we heard a coach drive right up to the bathhouse. And sure enough, soon three healthy, broad-shouldered fellows came in, each one bigger than the next. They asked whether Fishke the Lame lived there. At first I was terrified, but when I thought it over I realized I didn't have to worry about Fishke. Even if the three louts were kidnappers, what did it matter? With all of his charms, thank God, he wasn't in danger of being drafted into the tsar's army. Since I was curious to know why they needed Fishke, I answered, yep, Fishke hangs around here. He's not here now, but if you tell me what you want with him, maybe I can find him for you.

" 'The three fellows thought it over, after which one of them told me:

" '—Have it your way. To tell the truth, there's nothing to be ashamed of—it's just a common Jewish story. You probably know the blind old orphan who's been begging and praying for the dead in front the synagogue next to the graveyard. One of our local scribblers even wrote a song about her, and everyone sings it. This year she became a widow and soon after she had herself matched up with some porter, promising to clothe him, feed him, and even give him a little money. Today was supposed to be the wedding day. They prepared a fine feast with brandy, baked rolls, fish and roast chicken, as Jews are wont to do, and all of that costs money. But listen to what can happen! When everything was ready and the bride had been decked out and veiled, they went to bring the groom to stand under the wedding canopy. But the crown jewel wasn't at home. They waited an hour and he didn't show, so they waited another hour. He'd vanished into thin air. It turned out that the brat got cold feet when his granny—a cook who'd served the lord of the manor for a long time—started to cry, fuss, and scream that the match would shame her. After all, she'd been in service to His Lordship for so many years! She could make a kugel pudding from the best recipe and there was no match for her cooking in town. No small matter, His Lordship's cook! In the meat market, her opinion was the last word. Why should her grandson disgrace her and spoil their good name in her old age? Now, nothing anyone said helped, he'd decided he didn't want the match. —You can call me whatever you want, he said, do what you like, or send me packing to the rabbi's court. So the rest of us were stuck out in the cold like moldy cheese in the larder. No one was as sorry about the groom as we were about the feast. How could this happen? We killed ourselves running around all day long, and we hadn't eaten a bite. What a crime to waste such fish and roast chicken! We thought and thought, pondered the matter some more, and Fishke came to mind. Good Lord, Fishke could get all of us out of this mess—he should be the groom, what does it matter to him? Anyway, we've come now to take him to the wedding canopy in place of the porter, so the bride will remain a bride and the feast won't get spoiled.

" 'As the three hale and hearty fellows were explaining it all to me, in comes Fishke. We snapped him up like a real bargain and kept our story brief: Get going, boy, take your sick legs and limp over to the wedding canopy. Things were arranged in a hurry, before Fishke had a chance to turn around. The town had a good meal—everyone ate and drank like there was no tomorrow, and we congratulated the new couple.'

"That's what the bathhouse attendant said to me. So now," I told Reb Alter, "Fishke walks around in the overcoat that was meant for the porter, and he's a new man. His job is to take his wife, the blind old orphan, out to her spot beside the graveyard in the morning, and to lead her back home before dark. Fishke no longer has to worry about where his next meal is coming from. His wife is a paragon of virtue with a steady job, the couple is in love, and neither can have any complaints, God forbid, about the other.

"That, Reb Alter, is my story. So you see," I said, "what can happen in this world. In our parts they hitch up the lame and the blind, just for the sake of a meal, so that all the busybodies can eat and drink their fill! And what happens with poor, simple folk happens just the same with the rich community leaders: more than once they've made completely impossible matches for the sake of a different sort of feast. . . . But I'm getting off the point. Don't worry, Reb Alter, if you didn't succeed in pairing off a boy with a lad, with God's help you'll have better luck with another match. Just don't let it get you down and don't lose sleep over it! On the contrary, I see you think you've made a fine start in your new business, acting like a top-notch matchmaker, even if you did try to hitch up a couple of boys. As soon as you sniff out a girl, your trade will start to flow like butter. Whether she's crippled, blind, mute, or lame, you'll tell her: Get going, girl, go under the wedding canopy and may luck be with you! Go on! My wife's given birth to another boy, my eldest daughter needs a dowry, the printer wants to get paid, my nag needs to eat, so go ahead, girl! By the way, Reb Alter, won't you move over a piece? You're sweating like a horse. So move on over just a little farther and sweat all you want."

6

We lay there for a few hours until our horses had grazed long enough. By about six o'clock, I was again sitting with my friend Reb Alter, talking business.

A fresh breeze had begun to blow and clouds began to appear in the sky. To us they were as dear as precious guests. The trees rocked slowly; one leaned its head over to another, and after having kept still for so long, they enjoyed a conversation in their tongue. The breeze roused the sleeping wheat and all the stalks woke up in a flurry, like young children, and kissed warmly. One after another, the birds of the field started to chirp and sing. In a small copse not far off, a nightingale rang out on his flute, bursting into sweet scales and playing delightfully. Every creature with a voice joined in with the world-famous cantor—frogs from the river trilled and even flies and bees weren't left out. A beetle sneaked in on the action, humming as he flew past. It was a concert worth buying tickets for. The whole world became livelier and took on a happy mien. It was a joy and a delight to hear and see everything, and to smell the sweet odors coming from all sides. I pulled up my stockings and, if you'll excuse my saying so, hitched up my pants with a strap before I cheerfully began my afternoon prayers. Beside me, Reb Alter soon let loose in his coarse voice, and we gave praise and thanks to God's name. All of the plants in the fields, and all of the creatures in the forest, sang His praise. But I'm getting off the point again.

When I turned back to the main road, behind the wagon I suddenly heard a voice: "Jews, have mercy on a cripple and take me into town with you. I'm all alone in the world, with nothing but what you see on my back." I looked over and, believe it or not, I saw Fishke the Lame hobbling along—barefoot, scantily clad, worn out, and covered in sweat. His feet were swollen and bloodied up from mosquito bites.

"How did you get here, Fishke?" I called out, astonished to see him. "Where are you coming from? Climb up and tell us what you're doing here all of a sudden."

Fishke crawled up onto the wagon with difficulty, and after he caught his breath he sighed and said, "I curse the day she was born!"

"What's the story?" I asked. "Who're you cursing out?" Turning, I said, "Look, Reb Alter, this is the very person who married the blind orphan girl."

"A curse on her and on him, too!" Fishke cried out angrily. "They played a dirty trick on me!"

"What's the story?" Reb Alter and I asked again. "Tell us, Fishke, tell us. We'll just say our afternoon prayers while you tell what happened."

Fishke started to narrate in his lisping, stammering way.

"You seem to know I married the blind orphan girl, and after the wedding we lived well, like a Jewish couple should. I think I kept my part of the bargain right enough. Every morning I took her, as is fitting, out to her spot by the old cemetery. She'd sit there on a bit of straw and beg alms with a melody from Lamentations that touched everyone who passed. Plenty of shopkeepers only dream of earning like her—they can sit whole days in the store, crying their wares and shouting themselves hoarse, haggling with customers and not bringing in a cent. And still there's rent to pay plus interest on the money they borrowed for stock. Whereas my wife had no expenses and brought in a pretty penny—enough to live on. But people's never satisfied, and when they have potatoes they want meat.

" 'Y'know what,' my wife started to say, 'people like you an' me, such a couple as the both of us, never run afoul in the world. In this trade, our flaws is pure advantages. So listen to your wife who's a bit older an' a little wiser'n you: take me out in the world with folks of the better sort, and you'll see, we'll haul in a fortune. In this place there ain't much more to be done. I sit for hours 'til someone has pity and gives a groschen. People been talking about Lekish, the cholera groom what went out into the world with his wife Perl— how he struck it rich. After the wedding they lit out an' their luck's steady ever since! Motl the pauper met up with 'em making the rounds of houses in Kishinev—he says their sacks was stuffed with scraps of meat, loaves of bread, smoked lamb, sausage, sheep's tail, and Perl's face shone so bright you'd go blind just lookin' at her. People coming back from Odessa say they seen Yontl, our other cholera groom, draggin' hisself around the shops on his buttocks—God sends him everything he needs. An' God won't forsake us neither. While it's still summer let's get moving, because each day we're here is a waste of time.'

"So we headed out. What should I say? We had it good. Whenever we come to a town or a city, we hit the jackpot. Everybody stared at us and not a single person turned us down. Wherever we went, the poorhouse stood open, and for a few pennies the synagogue attendant got the both of us invited to supper at a decent house. My ol' lady taught me the rules of beggary—I was out of touch with the real world and didn't know the ropes when it come to making the rounds of the houses. She was an expert in such things and taught me all I know: how to peer into a house, how to pretend to cough, moan an' groan, how to beg for mercy with a pathetic look, how to beg for alms, how to hang on like a leech, how to haggle or wish people well, and how to swear at 'em with curses that make the blood run cold. I learned all of this in no time.

"We was foot paupers—that is, draggin' ourselves around on foot. Like soldiers, poor folk is divided into infantry and cavalry—them that walks and them that gets around in wagons. Apart from these is also city poor folk, born somewheres in a city, what don't have nothin' to do with people born in the country. And then there's wagon poor folk, born on the road in caravans, whose ancestors always been on the move. These paupers is all like gypsies: day and night they wander from one end of the world to the other—born, bred, wed, and soon enough dead along the way. They's free men and beholden to no one: never pay no taxes, don't carry no papers, don't say no prayers, and don't mind leaving Judaism behind. Nothin' sticks to 'em. They's another type of creature altogether, neither fish nor fowl. My wife and I was infantry paupers, so you can imagine how, with me an' my bad legs, we used to crawl along real slow, like crabs. Little by little, because of this my wife started to scold, curse me, and make nasty remarks. She done give me nicknames, blamed me for my bum legs, said I'd turned her into a fool from top to bottom. To hear her tell it, she'd made a man of me and taken me out in the world to be with proper folks, but I wasn't true to her, I played dirty tricks on her. I used to keep quiet and swallow all she said, I swear!

"Until we come to the city of Balta we'd already gone and dragged ourselves along for a couple months. There we missed the great fair, which is famous round the world—an' she was sick over it, like as if she'd lost a fortune.

When we left Balta, on the road we met up with a large band of country paupers, cavalry. The entire group was riding in three wagons. Among 'em was
old and young, all kinda women, girls, and boys. For some reason they liked
us and welcomed us onto one of the wagons, so after that we traveled around
with the troupe. What should I tell you? A new world popped open to me at
first, and I was very happy. I'd see an' hear amazing things I can't hardly describe. I learned how they'd slander people and mock the whole world, like
when everyone told about stunts they pulled—how they filched loaves of
bread or swiped a hen from a nitwit. They'd curse out rich folk for all they was
worth, just like that, for no reason. I can tell you for a fact, they all hate the
rich a heap more than the rich hate them. I used to hear boys chatting with
girls, jokin' around and pairing up; one whole wagon hitched itself up with
another. But it ain't decent to talk about that. I saw how they was able to disguise themselves, when they come to a city. One person pretended to be
hunchbacked and another lame, one pretended he was blind, another mute,
and another crippled. As soon as they left town the crooked were made
straight, the lame man was healed, the blind could see, the mute could talk,
and the cripple could walk. Just me and my wife was stuck with our flaws.
Later I got the notion that they'd taken to us because of this, we was plain useful to 'em. More than once they blurted out that defects like ours, for paupers,
ain't nothin' but gifts from God, 'cause they bring in good wages. My wife's
blindness was several notches higher'n my limping. On top of that, when she
opened her mouth, which flapped open like it was on hinges, people stopped
in their tracks and their hair stood on end. One healthy redhead on our
wagon kissed up to her like he was in love, made jokes, and talked with her 'til
dawn. Whenever he hustled up a scrap of white bread, a slice of meat, a cake,
or cooked peas, he'd hand it over to her. I didn't give it a second thought.
What did I care about him feeding her, clowning around, admiring her,
and—for all it mattered to me—turning her into a Turk?[5] But they finally
took to mocking me, taunting me, making my life bitter as the gall from a rotten liver, 'til I was the butt of all jokes. Every minute someone played a trick
on me, every second I had another nickname. I was always to blame and
everybody did whatever he wanted with me. If I started to get upset, they just
rubbed salt in my wounds. 'Listen how our fine man moans an' groans, soon

5. "Turning her into a Turk" (*gib ihr fun maynetvegn afile di shmad*): literally, "so far as I'm
concerned, even destroying her Jewishness (converting her to another religion)."

he's gonna bust out crying.' They beat me to death, and when my face was wet with tears, they used to say: 'Fishke, what you so happy 'bout? You grinning like a idiot! Look, everybody, lookit him laugh!' Then someone'd say, 'Give 'm a kick in the shins, or a smack on the back, that's a cure for laughing. If that don't work, we'll slap down the hair on his head or twist his ear and whisper a secret. That should get him started, sure 'nough as bitter herbs at a Passover Seder. After all, we got to take care of our own kind!'

"Sometimes they would throw me off the wagon and—while I limped along struggling to keep up, the best I could—clap their hands, laughing: 'Bravo, Fishke! That's it—dance, Fishke, dance! Hey, everybody, just look at the way Fishke lifts his feet, dancin' along so fine an' dandy. He could dance at any wedding, knock on wood!' Once the redhead who was messin' around with my wife—the devil take him—said: 'Fishke's no cripple! The bastard is putting us on, just pretending to be lame. We ought to straighten him out—jab him hard in the leg and you'll see him kick!' That's how they tortured me. I'd think back on the good years when I sat like a prince in the bathhouse, living like God in Paris. What else did I need? The devil gave me the idea to get married. I wanted to find buried treasure and ended up buried with no treasure."

"Fishke!" I cried out as I finished saying my prayers, "Put off your tears until another day, maybe until Tisha b'Av. You're getting off the point, Fishke. I want to hear more of your story."

"Yep," said Reb Alter, "finish the story—it's a good one."

7

"A plague on 'em!" Fishke cursed before he continued his story. "Whenever we arrived in a city, the gang broke up and went door to door, spreading out every which way. We fell on a town like a swarm of locusts. They called it 'going to work,' and to their way of thinking everyone should come running with alms. They used to say, 'Why do the rich have it so easy, sitting home while everyone works for 'em and spoils 'em? Ain't all they got been earned by the poor man's blood, sweat, and tears? They're so fine and keep so busy saving their souls, but they want to make everyone else work. The fat rich man is respected like nobility, but one of us got to hide his health and be ashamed, like a crook—if not, everyone yells: Why don't such a healthy man go to work? Believe me, we ought to mix things up and let the rich try going to work for a while! We're just as good as they are.' When they stole something, they called it finding a bargain, or playing a prank on some guy. They had nothin' to do with city paupers and avoided 'em like filth. And all of them'd say that the houses in town were as full of beggars as of bedbugs. They complained that people stuff 'em to the gills at each wedding or bris, while we tore our clothes, toiled, an' worked ourselves into the grave.

"At first I made the rounds of the houses with my ol' lady, and it was darned easy. I even learned to haggle with people. The trick was—never be satisfied with what people gave, never thank anyone, always scowl and pout, grumble and even curse at people. We fared no worse 'n anyone else, but the redhead—he should rot in hell—started to shame me, put me down in front of my wife, and make me look a fool. 'I don't get it,' he used to say to my wife. 'How you crawl round with that turtle? I'm a different sort, with me you could really walk the walk . . . and things'd really heat up. Together we could rake it in!' Apart from that, he lied about me, saying I was hooking up with a girl from another wagon and flirting with her. It's true that I often talked with a hunchbacked girl. She pitied me, and many a time she cried about our misfortunes. She was all alone on the wagon, and God knows she'd suffered enough in her short life."

"Say, Fishke," Reb Alter and I interrupted, "what sort of girl is she? Tell us more about her."

"It's a very long story," Fishke answered, "but I'll keep it short. The girl was just a young child when her mother brought her to Glupsk. Her mother was a cook in a well-to-do house. She'd never seen her father, and she wouldn't even have known she had a father if her mother hadn't cursed him fifty times a day. At the same time, her mother complained bitterly to her daughter, saying that—since no one can stand a cook with a child—it was her fault she couldn't hold a job. More than once the lady of the house ran into the kitchen when the dinner didn't turn out well, scolding in a loud voice: Why did God punish me with such a cook, who skims the shmaltz off the soup for her pretty little daughter? In fact, the poor daughter ate nothin' but sorrows and blows. Early in the morning her mother used to push her aside into a corner on top of the large enamel oven, just like rotten goods. There she lay hunched up in one tiny spot and no one wanted to hear a sound from her. When she'd sniff the smells of roast goose and fried livers, her mouth would water and she'd suffer from hunger silently, 'til someone remembered to throw her a piece of dry bread with an old bone, or a scrap that had been left over on someone's plate. Sometimes they completely forgot about her, and if she made a peep, then a poker, a spatula, or a ladle would shoot up over the oven and strike her head, her hands, her feet—wherever the blow might fall. Because she was always sitting bent over and hunched up, in one place, she became a hunchback. She stayed for a few years in the corner beside that oven. But all things in this world come to an end.

"When she got older, she looked down from the oven and saw a young man who come visiting her mother in the kitchen. Her mother would hang on his arm, stuff his pockets with delicacies, and even give him money. He used to come late at night and stay over in the kitchen. As expected, her mother finally married that young man and left the rich woman's house. One lucky evening she took her daughter, half naked, and led her to a dark alley. 'Sit down and wait, Jews will have pity on you. Farewell!' she said, and disappeared.

"For a few hours the cast-off child sat on the street and didn't dare move, just like before, on top of the oven. A cold, autumn rain was falling and chilled her bones. She sat huddled up in a shift, trembling and shivering from cold, her teeth chattering. When someone asked who she was, she answered: I'm my mother's! She told me to sit here, and if I move she'll hit me with a poker, a spatula, or a ladle. She stayed there long into the night, 'til some Jewish woman tempted her with promises and took her home—to a small house that stood in the sand on stilts.

"The girl licked no honey at that woman's house. She was a market woman who sat in the square selling potatoes, sweet cakes, and special pears and apples. At dawn the woman went off to the market and left the hunchbacked girl to sit and rock her baby all day long. When she got back in the evening, she'd send out her little nanny to beg for crusts of bread. The poor girl used to go out in nothin' but a coarse shift to beg for crumbs that she would eat—or even share with her auntie, the market woman! That's how she lived and supported herself for about a year.

"One summer after dark while she was going door to door, she wandered far off to the edge of town and couldn't find her way back. The sun had set long before and a black cloud crept into the sky. She strayed like a lost sheep past the city gate, still dressed in only her shift. Three wagons loaded with people was just leaving town, and someone called out from a wagon: Lookit that girl! Right away one of 'em—the very same redhead, the devil take him—jumped down and asked who she was. 'I'm my momma's,' she answered in a tearful voice. 'I want to go home to my auntie.' The redhead bastard told her, 'Hush, girl, don't cry! I'll take you back to your momma.' Then he grabbed her, threw her into the wagon, and drove on.

"Ever since, she's been wandering around with that gang of poor folk, and she's endured more troubles from them than one could begin to tell. Don't nobody in hell suffer like her, poor thing. My blood boils over when I think of her—I'd give my life just to free her from them. She's the best, dearest soul in the world!"

8

"Listen, Reb Alter," I said with a smile, "it seems to me that Fishke has gone and fallen in love with the hunchbacked girl. Something isn't kosher here."

"Why should I deny it?" Fishke answered. "I was drawn to her and began to love her out of pity. If not for her, I'd have lost all interest in life and died of my troubles, but since I've gotten to know her, a load has lifted from my heart. My life is better now. More than once we talked and cried together after everyone else had gone to sleep, pouring out our hearts to each other. We don't fool around none, God forbid, but the redhead bastard—he should rot in hell—noticed everything and brought reports to my wife along with fifty thousand lies. She was furious and, to make me jealous, she flirted even more with that bastard. They became fast friends and would make the rounds of the houses together like a lord and his lady. By then it didn't bother me, but if I ever tried to say anything, the lout would give me a slap and cry out to my blind wife, 'Lookit, your Fishke is hitting me! *Oy vey*, he's murdering me!' 'Butcher him!' she'd shout back angrily. 'He ain't seen nothin' yet! Give it to the scoundrel and shove him closer to me so I can pay my respects!' Then both of 'em jabbed their fingernails into me, pinched, plucked, and tore at me 'til I was black and blue all over. While he was beating me up, that bastard—he should rot in hell—would stick his tongue out at me and say to my wife, like he was a saint: You hit him yourself, you do the honors. I forgive him—let God punish him. But then he'd punch me in the chest or in the pit of the stomach with his fist, so hard I felt like I was gonna die.

"There was an old fellow, a sly devil, who used to go begging for pennies with me. He'd make such a pitiful face that everyone had to give him something, and then he would point to me, the miserable cripple, with a deep sigh. He'd take the alms and, if I cried out for my share, he hit me and said in a gruff voice, 'What, you want to ride for nothin' in my wagon? I should take you begging for nothin', you smart aleck? Just try to say another word about it, and I'll tell your wife. She turned you over to me, so I'll settle accounts with her. Shut up, you pipsqueak!' Long before I'd realized that, for them, I was just like a circus animal in a gypsy troupe. But sometimes it irked and pained me so that I lost my head and shouted: Do what you want with me, from now on I'll go begging by myself. I swore I'd take care of myself and I've kept my word.

"One time we arrived at a town in the Kherson district and the gang went out to work. The bastard went with my wife and I went alone. I planned to cover the whole town and collect a fortune, so that I could show my wife I knew how to do business and prove to her that I was no shlimmazl. She shouldn't think only her redhead was a real mentsh.[6] Luck was on my side that day, and I hit upon a house where they was having a bris. After the circumcision, they gave me a healthy swig of brandy, a whole kiddush cup, a large slice of cake, a little rose-shaped roll, and on top of that a few pennies. I restrained myself and didn't taste even a crumb, instead hiding everything under my shirt to bring to my wife. Well, you should've seen me then. I walked home thinking with a grin how my wife'd look up to me—she'd have to admit that I ain't no dime-a-dozen sort and she'd send the redhead bastard packing. True enough, I broke off a nice big piece of cake for my hunchbacked girl, who was dear to my heart. I thought to myself: when everyone has gone to sleep I'll give this to her, poor thing, so she can also enjoy it. She was a ruined, homeless girl with a broken spirit who never had a sweet moment in all her life. I was thinking she should know Fishke's a faithful friend who takes care of her and watches over her like the apple of his eye—he'd rather not eat so he can give her the last, best piece. I even imagined, as if I was seeing it with my own eyes, how I'd sit with her on a grassy spot outside the Great Synagogue. The sky would be covered with stars, all around it would be still, she'd sit crumpled and hunched up, tears would run down her cheeks, and she'd sing the familiar song in a tearful voice:

> My daddy, he slaughtered me,
> And my momma ate me alive.

6. Literally, *mentsh* means "person"—in this context, a successful person who can cope with the world; the Yiddish word *mentsh* can also mean "a good, decent person."

"She always used to sing that song. Tonight I'd comfort her, have a heart-to-heart talk, and give her the piece of cake. She'd cheer up a bit, look me in the eyes and laugh. 'Fishke, you're a good man,' she'd say to me. 'You're very dear to me, the only person I have in the world. You're my father, my mother, my brother. Look, Fishke, be true to me and never forget me. Swear to me by the synagogue, where the wandering souls that pray are witnesses—and among them perhaps the father I never knew. Swear you'll never forget me. . . . ' In short, along the way I was overjoyed and thought I was happy. But listen to the end of the story and hear what can happen.

"When I come back to the poorhouse that evening, our whole troupe was gone. A couple hours earlier they'd driven away, along with my wife and the bastard who'd been flirting with her all that time. My heart froze, and I almost burst with anger and pain. My head was spinning, my eyes went dim. Why should I deny it? I was mostly sorry for my hunchbacked girl—what would she do, poor unfortunate thing? Who could she talk to and pour out her bitter heart? *Oy*, Jews, how it hurts!

"To make a long story short," Fishke started again after taking a deep sigh, "I dragged myself and my troubles out to the Odessa highway. I thought if they was on that road, I'd probably hear about it, but it was no use. They'd slipped away like water, and by then I was sick of life from all that walking. I was dying to rest my bones in one place, like I used to do. In Odessa I met up with Yontl, pulling himself along on his buttocks. We was overjoyed to see one another. He told me how things stood with him, that he was eating like a prince and that in some shops people even treated him like a bigwig when they gave him alms. I spilt out my heart telling 'bout all the things that happened to me, and I begged him, if he had some standing in Odessa, to find me a place in a bathhouse where I could support myself like I did in Glupsk. He just laughed and answered, 'For now, Fishke, I won't say nothin' about that idea. First, if you don't mind, go and take a look at the local bathhouses with your own eyes. Then we'll talk it over.'

"I took his advice and went straight to a bathhouse, which was really strange. Have you ever heard of such a thing? There it was brightly lit, clean as a house and furnished with fine benches, believe it or not! They don't steam up and they have separate rooms. That ain't no bath, I assure you, it's a joke! No, I thought, it's not for me, I can't work in such a place. It ain't no place—with the people, or the pleasures—like our bathhouse in Glupsk. Back home it's something else entirely, where people while away the time—

naked men lie around on the benches in groups shmoozing, telling stories, talking about every little thing that's going on in town, no matter what it is. What a delight! . . . I went to other baths, but ain't none like ours—they don't even smell like our brick bathhouse in Glupsk. Now, their ritual baths are a joke. In our *mikve* you can darn near cut the water, 'cause it has a special odor, a different color, and it's somehow thicker'n other water. Right away you know it has a Jewish flavor, but there the *mikve* water is clear, plain old water, you could even drink it. . . . 'So, Fishke, what's up?' Yontl asked me later with a smile. 'You seen the local baths?' I said, 'Not a chance, this ain't for me. My place is in Glupsk, and I'm heading home.' How does the saying go? Strap me up by the ankles and send me home bound and tied, so long as I'm among my own kind. So now I'm going back for some peace of mind.

"A curse on my blind wife! I'm only worried about the poor hunchbacked girl."

9

Fishke ended his story and let out a heavy sigh.

"Don't worry, Fishke," I consoled him. "God can bring you and your girl back together. Just tell us, what's her name? On my travels it's very possible that I'll meet up with the gang."

"Beyle is her name," Fishke answered. "She's called Beyle."

Reb Alter suddenly gave a sigh and fell back, his face white as chalk.

"What's wrong, Reb Alter?" I asked him.

"Bah!" he answered as he slowly sat up again on the wagon.

"Tell me, Fishke, do you happen to know her mother's name and where she came from?"

"Yes," Fishke replied. "My poor hunchbacked girl remembered, like in a dream, that people called her mother Elke, and she was divorced from her husband in Tuneyadevke."

"Divorced in Tuneyadevke!" I cried out, astonished. "Who can her husband have been, that brute who sent away his own child? Hey, Reb Alter, maybe you know someone like that in your shtetl. What's his name?"

Reb Alter was frozen in place like a corpse, and his eyes were rolling in his head. My blood ran cold.

"He is called . . ." Fishke tried to remember his name. "Her husband's name is, I think . . . wait a second . . ."

"Alter's his name," Reb Alter cried out and collapsed onto the wagon.

"Yes, yes!" Fishke said. "That's it, Alter—Wine 'n' Candles Alter is his name."

I had already guessed the whole story and stood there like someone who'd just been doused with boiling water.

It was pitch dark outside. The stars twinkled and shone between the clouds, and on the horizon—as if growing from the earth—the moon began to rise, frightfully large and red as fire. My friend Reb Alter moaned and beat his fist on his chest.

"I've sinned, it's true," he said. "I deserted her and made her life miserable. She's right, poor thing. She's right when she says that her daddy slaughtered her, her father blackened her days and years. *Vey is mir!*"

Out of pity I began to console Reb Alter and showed him with kind words how he could still correct his mistake. He soon sat up, raised his eyes to the sky, and said with emotion:

"I swear by the Eternal One that I will not return home to my wife and children, and I won't marry off my girl, until I find my other unhappy child. . . . You two are witnesses," he said, pointing at Fishke and me.

Fishke fell upon Reb Alter's chest, hugging and kissing him. "Oh!" he begged him in a tearful voice, "have pity and save her. *Gevalt!* Rescue her!"

Reb Alter quickly climbed up onto his wagon, bade us farewell, turned his horse around, and went off in the other direction. Late that night Fishke and I rode into Glupsk.

Translated by Ken Frieden

Sholem Aleichem

שלום-עליכם.

By permission of the YIVO Institute for Jewish Research.

Hodel

You're surprised at Tevye, Sholem Aleichem, it's so long since you've seen him? He's gone way down hill, you say? Out of the blue he's gone gray? Ach, if you knew the troubles, the pain that your Tevye's lugging around with him! Like it says in the prayers, *odom yesoydoy mi'ofer ve-soyfoy le'ofer*[1] —man is formed from dust and ends up as dust; he's weaker than a fly and stronger than iron. . . . And that's Tevye to a T. Wherever there's an evil, a hardship, a calamity, it has to find its way to me, whether it wants to or not. And why me? Because I'm a born sap who takes everyone at his word? *Kabdeyhu ve-khashdeyhu*[2] —our sages have told us a thousand times, and Tevye can never remember it. Respect him and suspect him: in plain Yiddish, *cave canem*, don't trust the s.o.b. as far as you can throw him. . . .

What am I supposed to do about it, if that's my real nature? You know that I'm always looking on the bright side, and with Him Who Lives Forever I don't get into arguments. However He works things out, it's fine by me. Be my guest and try it the other way, go ahead and kick against the pricks—you think it's going to help you? *Ha-neshome lokh*, we say when we pray for forgiveness, the soul is Yours and so is the body—so what does a *person* know, what does he amount to? Not that I don't argue, mind you; it's just that I always do it with her, my better half, I mean.

"Golda," I tell her, "you're committing a sin. We've got a midrash . . ."

"What do I need with a midrash?" she says. "We've got a daughter to marry off. And after that daughter come two more daughters, touch wood. And after those two, another three."

1. From the High Holiday prayers; compare Genesis 3:19. Translated by Tevye in his next ten words.

2. Based on Derekh Eretz Rabbah 5:3, "Always view all people as robbers, yet respect them." In the subsequent passage, the idiom *cave canum* (Latin, "beware of the dog") is meant to convey, by embedding Latin in this English translation, Tevye's unusual use of a Russian phrase (*nye vir sobaki*, "don't trust a dog") in his Yiddish monologue.

"Eh," I say, "Forget about it, Golda. Our sages have got it covered. There's a midrash about this, too . . ."

But she won't let me get a word in. "Daughters," she tells me, "grown-up daughters are enough of a midrash all by themselves . . ."

Try and reason with a woman!

To get to the point, though, it should be clear from this that I've got a full line of merchandise, touch wood, top-quality goods without a flaw in the lot, one more beautiful than the next. Far be it from me to praise my own children, but I hear what everybody says, and what they're all saying is: "Gorgeous!" And the most gorgeous of all is Hodel. She's number two after Tsaytl, the one who went nuts for the tailor, remember? Is she pretty, this Hodel? What more can I say than what it says in the Purim Megillah, "because she was fair to look upon"[3]—a piece of shining gold. And as if that isn't bad enough, she has to go and have brains, too, has to read and write Yiddish and Russian, and pack away books like dumplings.

Of course you'll want to know how Tevye's daughter comes to books when her father deals in butter and cheese? Look, that's just what I want to ask those fine young men who have outlasted their pants but want to study in a university. As we say at the Passover Seder: "We are all wise"—they all want to learn; "we are all intelligent"—they all want to be students. But ask them, "What's with the studying? Goats should know from the neighbor's garden like you guys know from universities!" When everything's said and done, they won't be allowed anywhere *near* a university. What are they gonna be told? As the angel tells Abraham the Patriarch: "Stretch not forth thy hand"[4]—know your place, and scat!

But still, you should see how they pull it off. And who? Working-class kids, children of tailors and cobblers, so help me God in heaven. They go off to Yehupetz or Odessa and bounce from garret to garret, dining on sound and fury and noshing cholera and fever blisters for dessert. They don't lay eyes on a piece of meat for months at a time: six of them buy shares in a roll and herring and it's "rejoice in thy festival"[5]—dog, have your day.

Well, it happened that one of these shlimmazls blundered his way into

3. Tevye associates his daughter's beauty with that of Vashti and Esther. See the Book of Esther 1:11, and compare 2:7.
4. Genesis 22:12.
5. Compare Deuteronomy 16:14.

these parts, not far from where we are now. I knew his father—he was a cigarette maker and, not to speak ill of the dead, a king-size pauper. But that's beside the point. I mean, if sewing shoes was good enough for a Mishnaic sage
like Rabbi Yokhanan the sandal-maker, then a father who rolled cigarettes
was good enough for this boy. The only thing that bothers me is why a pauper
should want to study, want to go to a university. Granted, he wasn't kicked by
a horse when he was a kid. He's got a head on his shoulders, a real good head,
the shlimmazl. His name is Pertchik; we translated it into Yiddish and it came
out Fefferel, Little Pepper. And a pepper is what he looks like, you should
see—a little black squirrel, a freak. But full, overflowing with knowledge. And
a mouth? A flaming fire, sulphur and pitch. . . .

Well, it came to pass one day that I was driving home from Boiberik after
unloading all my wares, a whole transport of cheese, butter, cream, and what-
not. I'm sitting and meditating, as I'm prone to, on the cosmos: on this, on
that, on the fat cats in Yehupetz who have everything so good, and on Tevye
the shlimmazl and his horse, who suffer the days away, and other suchlike
things. It's summer. A scorching sun, biting flies. The outdoors is delightful,
roomy and free—just lift yourself up and fly, stretch yourself out and swim!

Meanwhile, I take a look. There's a boy, a young man with a bundle
under his arm, hot-footing it across the sand, sweating and gasping for breath.

"Let Joel, son of Pole, come forth," I say.[6] "Hop on, I'll take you a bit of the
way. The wagon's empty anyhow. What is it that's written? If you run into
your neighbor's ass, thou shalt surely help unburden.[7] And if you can't ditch a
donkey, how much the more so when it comes to a man?"

He laughs, the shlimmazl, and climbs onto the wagon before I have a
chance to repeat myself.

"Where might a young man be running from?" I ask him.

"From Yehupetz."

"And what does a young man like you have to do in Yehupetz?"

"A young man like me is taking exams."

"And what," I ask, "is a young man like you learning to be?"

6. Ya'amoyd ha-khosn reb Yokl ben Plekl: literally, "Let the groom Mr. Yankl, son of Plekl,
come forth!" This alludes to a formula by which a person is called to the Torah in the synagogue, but uses the diminutive "Yokl" (from Yakov, Yankl) that has a secondary sense meaning
"simpleton."

7. Compare Exodus 23:5.

"A young man like me still doesn't know himself what he's learning to be."

"If so," I say, "then why is a young man like you troubling his head for nothing?"

"Don't worry, Reb Tevye," he says. "A young man like me already knows what he's got to do."

"Well, and since you seem to know me already, why not tell me who you might be?"

"Who I am? I'm a person."

"I can see that you're not a horse," I say. "I mean, *whose* are you?"

"Whose should I be? I'm God's."

"God's, I know," I say. "It's written, *kol ha-khaye ve-kol ha-beheyme,*[8] every beast and all the cattle. I mean, where do you come from? Are you one of us or are you maybe from Lithuania?"

"I come from Adam," he says, "and I come from here. You know me."

"So then who's your father? Let me hear already."

"My father's name was Pertchik."

"Damn you," I say. "Did you have to torture me for so long? So that means you're the son of Pertchik the cigarette maker?"

"I'm the son of Pertchik the cigarette maker."

"And you're studying in the classrooms?"

"I'm studying in the classrooms."

"All right," I say. "A is for apple, B is for bird, and see what the cat dragged in. . . . So tell me, Mr. Classy, what is it that you might live from?"

"From what I eat," he says.

"Aha, very good. And what do you eat?"

"Anything you give me."

"I get it," I say. "You're not choosy. If there's something to eat, you eat; and if there's nothing to eat, you bite your lip and go to sleep on an empty stomach. But what of it? You think it's all worthwhile, so long as you can study in the classrooms. You want to be like the rich folks in Yehupetz. As the saying goes, 'They are all beloved, they are all without flaw.' "[9]

I give him a verse and a midrash in good Tevye style, but do you think he sits there in silence, this Pertchik?

8. Echoes several passages in Genesis, e.g., Genesis 1:25–26, 2:19–20, 6:20, but closest to Genesis 7:14.

9. From a description of heavenly angels in the morning prayers.

"They'll never see the day, those fat cats, when I let myself be compared to them!" he says. "The hell with every one of them!"

"You're getting pretty worked up about the rich folks," I say. "Don't tell me they made off with your father's inheritance."

"You should know," he says, "that it's entirely possible that you and I and all of us have a big share in *their* inheritance."

"You know something?" I say. "You should let your enemies do your talking for you. All I can see is that you're a boy with plenty of gumption and a self-starting tongue. If you've got time, you can come over to my place for a little chat tonight—and while we're at it, we'll have a bite of supper."

He didn't give me a chance to say it again. He turned up right when the borsht was waiting on the table and the blintzes were frying on the stove.

"You've got all the benefits of marriage here," I told him. "You can wash and make a blessing or just go ahead and eat. I'm not God's district attorney, and I won't be taking any lumps for you in the world to come." So he and I talk things over, and I can feel myself being drawn to this fellow. I don't know why, but I am. You understand, I like a man that you can really talk to: here a verse, there a midrash, once in a while a little speculation on things of the spirit—this, that, up, down, sideways. That's the kind of guy Tevye is.

Well, from then on, the kid started coming by nearly every day. Once he finished giving his lessons, he'd come to my place for some rest and relaxation. You can imagine how it was going for him and his lessons when I tell you that the richest man in town was used to paying a couple rubles a month, for which the teacher also had to help read telegrams, write addresses, and even run the odd errand. Why not? The Bible doesn't mince words: "With all thy heart and with all thy soul"[10]—if you eat bread, you have to know what it costs. Lucky for him that he did his real eating by me, and gave my daughters a few lessons in return, as it says: "An eye for an eye"[11]—a slap for a slap.

And that's how he became a regular member of our household. The kids would bring him a glass of milk, the old lady made sure that he had a shirt to wear and socks without holes. And it was then that we crowned him with the name Fefferel, by turning the name Pertchik into Yiddish. You could say that we loved him like one of our own because he was really such a heck of a guy,

10. Deuteronomy 6:5; this is included in the second verse of the *Shm'a Yisrael*—the central prayer, "Hear, O Israel. . ."

11. Exodus 21:24.

just plain folks—"what's mine is yours, what's yours is mine," mine, yours—a free-for-all.[12]

The only thing I didn't like was his disappearing act. All of a sudden he'd get up and leave, and no Fefferel—*ve-ha-yeled eynenu*,[13] the lad is gone.

"Where have you been, O songbird of mine?" He's silent as a stone. . . . I don't know about you, but I hate a man with secrets. What I like is what it says in the Bible: *va-yedaber*, he spoke, and *va-yoymer*, he talked. But one good thing about Fefferel and talking: once he got started it was full steam ahead— he kept on going and wouldn't stop. A mouth on him—don't get me started! He spoke against God and His anointed, and about bursting their bonds.[14] Mostly about bursting their bonds. He was full of wild, oddball plans, crazy, head-over-heels schemes with everything somehow back-asswards. Like, in his cockeyed scheme, someone with money is worthless, and a pauper's a cream-filled dessert. And a craftsman? Top of the heap, worth more than caviar, because according to Fefferel, the labor of your hands is the most important thing.

"Sure," I say, "but it doesn't compare to money."

He gets all worked up and tries to convince me that money is the bane of our world, that it's the root of all untruth, the reason there's no justice here on earth. He brings me ten thousand illustrated proofs that hold water like the wall holds peas.

"So in your crazy system," I say, "it's also unfair that my cow gives milk and my horse pulls a wagon?" I hit him with imponderables like this and hang him up, as they say, "beyond all words of songs and praises";[15] hang him up at every step, as only Tevye can. But my Fefferel can do it, too; can he ever! If only he couldn't the way that he can! If he's got something on his mind, he's sure to let you know.

One evening we were sitting outside, delving into these matters—it's called philosophy. Suddenly Fefferel says to me: "You know what, Reb Tevye? You've got some very clever daughters there."

"Really?" I say. "Thanks for the news. They've got who to take after."

---

12. Alluding to a passage about four types of people in *Ethics of the Fathers*, Pirkei Avot 5:13.

13. From Genesis 37:30.

14. Alluding to Psalm 2:2–3.

15. From Sabbath morning prayers; cp. Berakhot 3b.

"One of them," he goes on, "the older one, she's very sharp, a mentsh in every sense of the word."

"I don't need you to tell me," I say. "The apple doesn't fall far from the tree." That's what I told him, my heart almost bursting with pleasure. I'm asking you, what kind of father doesn't love to hear his children praised? Go be a prophet and know that this praise would lead to such a mess, God protect us. Listen to this.

"There was evening and there was morning"[16]—it happened between daytime and nightfall in Boiberik. I'm making the rounds of the country houses in my wagon when someone stops me. I take a look: it's Ephraim the Shadchen, the marriage broker. One thing you should know about Ephraim the Shadchen is that he's a matchmaker like all matchmakers—he keeps himself busy by making matches.

So when he sees me in Boiberik—Ephraim, that is—he stops me. "Begging your pardon, Reb Tevye, there's something I need to tell you."

"As long as it's something good," I say and rein in my horse.

"Reb Tevye," he says, "You have a daughter!"

"I have seven, they should live and be well."

"I know that you have seven. I have seven, too."

"And together we've got an even fourteen."

"Enough with the jokes," he says. "Here's the story, Reb Tevye. As you are undoubtedly aware, I am a shadchen, and I have a groom for you. Straight from groomsville, cream of the crop."

"And what's your idea of a groom from groomsville, cream of the crop? Because if it's a tailor or a cobbler or a Hebrew school teacher, he can stay where he is and 'relief and deliverance will arise'[17]—I'll find my own match, in the words of the midrash, somewhere else."

"Eh, Reb Tevye, you're already starting with your midrash? To talk to you, people have to go into training. You're going to snow the world under with midrash. Better you should listen to the match that Ephraim the Shadchen is so eager to offer you; just keep still and listen."

That's what he says, Ephraim, and then starts to read me a list. What can I tell you? Really fine and dandy. First off, he was very nicely situated: a boy with a real pedigree, no Tom, Dick, or Harry. And that, you should know, is

---

16. Genesis 1:5 and in the subsequent verses.
17. Book of Esther 4:14.

what's most important to me. Because I'm no nobody, either. I've got all kinds in my family, like it says: *akudim nikudim u-vrudim*, striped, spotted, and mottled.[18] I've got plain people, craftsmen, homeowners. . . . And on top of all this, the boy's an accomplished musician with a thorough grounding in Talmud. And that's likewise no small matter to me, because I hate an ignoramus like I hate pork. A know-nothing is a thousand times worse than a bum; you can go around bareheaded and even walk on your hands — so long as you know what Rashi's got to say, you're one of my people. Tevye's *that* kind of a guy. . . . And he's also, Ephraim tells me, rich, stuffed with money, and he goes around in a carriage pulled by two horses, steeds so fiery that you can see the sparks fly.

Nu, all right, I think. This isn't such a drawback either. Better a rich man than a pauper, as it says: *yo'e 'aniuso le-yisroel*,[19] poverty is becoming to Israel — God Himself hates a pauper, and the proof is that if God loved the pauper, the pauper wouldn't be a pauper.

"Nu, let's hear some more," I say.

"What's more," says Ephraim, "is he wants to make a match with you. He's dying, he's out of his head — not for you, of course, but for your daughter. He wants a pretty one, he does."

"Oh, yeah?" I ask. "He's dying? Then let him die for her sins! Who is he, this gem of yours? An old bachelor? A widower? A demon? Divorced?"

"He's a bachelor — getting on in years, but still a bachelor."

"And what might be the name of his holiness?"

He wouldn't tell me, not even if I burned him at the stake.

"Convey her to Boiberik," he said, "and then I'll tell you."

"What do you mean *convey* her?" I said. "You *convey* a horse or a cow that you want to sell at a fair . . ."

What's there to tell you? A shadchen can seduce a wall. We agreed that I'd *convey* her to Boiberik on Saturday night, and all kinds of nice, sweet thoughts came into my mind. I could already picture my little Hodel in a carriage with two fiery steeds. I could picture the world envying me, not so much for the carriage and steeds as for the benefactions that I'd confer through my wealthy daughter, my interest-free loans to the down on their luck — twenty-five rubles here, fifty there, a hundred somewhere else. As the saying has it, other people are human, too.

18. Genesis 31:10.
19. Talmudic saying from Hagiga 9b, translated by Tevye.

I'm driving home that evening while thinking these thoughts, whipping my horse and chatting in horse talk. "Giddyup, horsie," I say. "Just step a little livelier and you'll get your share of oats, because *im eyn kemakh*—if there's no flour, *eyn toyre*—there's no Torah.[20] As it's written: if you don't grease the wheels, you won't go anywhere."

I'm talking to my horse like this when I see a familiar-looking couple, a man and a woman, come out of the woods, one right next to the other, talking away with gusto. Who could this be all of a sudden? I wonder, and I take a squint through the sun's fiery rays. I could swear that it's Fefferel. And who's he out walking with so late, the shlimmazl? I block the sun with my hand and take a closer look. Who's the woman? Oy, could it be Hodel? It's her, all right; by my life, it's her!

So that's it? *This* is why they were so hot to study grammar and read books. Oy, Tevye, I thought, you're an idiot. I stopped the horse and called out to them.

"Good evening to you," I say. "Any news of the war? What brings you here all of a sudden? What are you looking for, anyway, your vanishing youth?"

My welcome froze the young couple between heaven and earth, as they say; neither here nor there, their behinds out of joint and their faces all red. They stood speechless for a couple of minutes, with their eyes cast down. Then they started to look at me, I looked at them, and they looked at each other.

"Nu?" I say. "You're looking me over like you haven't seen me for a long time. As far as I know, I'm still the same Tevye, haven't changed by so much as a hair." That's what I say, half-angry and half-joking. Then my daughter spoke up, Hodel I mean, blushing even more than before.

"Daddy, wish us *mazl tov.*"

"*Mazl tov,*" I say. "May you live with *mazl*. What's going on? Did you find a treasure in the forest? Or were you just delivered from some great danger?"

"The *mazl tov*," he says, "is because we're engaged."

"What do you mean you're engaged?"

"Engaged," he says. "You don't know what it means? It means that I'm going to marry her, and she's going to marry me."

Fefferel says this and looks me right in the eye. I look right back at him and say, "So when's the engagement party? And how come I wasn't invited? I like to think that I'm a relative, too." You understand, I'm laughing but the worms

20. Quoted from Pirkei Avot 3:21.

are eating me up, gnawing away at my body. But I won't let it show. Tevye's no woman, and Tevye likes to hear things through to the end.

"I don't get it," I say. "A match without a matchmaker? No engagement contract?"

"What do we need with matchmakers?" asks Fefferel. "We've been engaged a long time already."

"You have? Wonder of wonders! Why didn't you mention it before?"

"Why should we shout about it?" he says. "We wouldn't have told you today, either, except that since we're going to be parting from each other soon, we've decided to get married as quickly as possible."

This got me angry. What is it you say? *Bo'u mayim 'ad nofesh,*[21] the waters are come in unto my soul—wounded clear to the bone. Engaged I can put up with. How is it written there? *Ohavti,*[22] I have loved—he wants her, she wants him. But married? What kind of talk is that, get married? It doesn't make any sense.

The groom seemed to have understood that the story wasn't entirely clear to me.

"You understand, Reb Tevye," he says to me, "it's like this: I'm about to leave here."

"When are you going?"

"Very soon."

"Where, might I ask?"

"That I can't tell you," he says. "It's . . . it's a secret."

You hear? It's a secret! How do you like that? A little black freak of a Fefferel turns up disguised as a fiancé, then he wants to get married, he's about to go away, and he won't say where! It's enough to make you sick.

"All right," I tell him. "A secret's a secret—everything with you is a secret. But explain one thing to me, brother: You're a man with a fine feeling for justice, a mentsh from head to toe. So how is it that all of a sudden, right out of the blue, you take a daughter away from Tevye just so you can desert her? Is that what you call justice? Decency? I should count my blessings that you didn't rob me or burn down my house."

"Daddy!" It was Hodel who spoke. "You have no idea how happy we are, he and I, to have told you our secret. It's a load off our hearts. Come here and give us a kiss."

21. Psalm 69:1.
22. Exodus 21:5.

And before you know it, they both embraced me, she on one side, he on the other, and started kissing and hugging. They kissed me, I kissed them, they let the momentum carry them off and stood there kissing each other. Some scene, I tell you, a regular stage show.

"Maybe you've kissed each other enough for now?" I say. "It's time to talk a little turkey."

"What turkey?" they ask.

"The dowry," I say. "Clothing, wedding expenses, this, that, the other."

"We don't need anything," they say. "No this, no that, no other."

"So what *do* you need, then?"

"All we need is a rabbi and a wedding canopy."

You ever hear such a thing? I won't drag it out—my arguing did me as much good as last year's snow. A wedding was held, if you can call that a wedding. What do *you* think? Not up to Tevye's standards, that's for sure. Some wedding, a quiet wedding, *vey iz mir.*

On top of all that, there's my wife. A scab on a blister, like they say. She was driving me crazy, I should just tell her why all the hurry, all the rush. Nu, go tell a woman there's no time. I had to turn out a lie, a great, mighty and awesome lie, just to keep the peace. Something to do with an inheritance, a rich auntie in Yehupetz, a cock and a bull—anything to get her to leave me alone. That very day, a few hours after the lovely nuptials, I hitched up my horse and wagon, and the three of us—me, her, and him, my son-in-law, my poison-in-law, I mean—the three of us got in and good-bye, Charlie—straight to the train in Boiberik.

While we were driving I took a look at the young couple out of the corner of my eye and thought: What a great God we have, and how strange and wondrous is His guidance of our world! And how many different kinds of people and wild creatures He's put here. Like a newly-minted young couple—he's going away, the devil knows where, she's staying here, and nobody's shedding a single tear, not even for the sake of form. But what of it? Tevye's no woman. Tevye can wait. He keeps his mouth closed and his eyes open, to see what's going to happen. . . .

A couple of youngsters, good little Kasrilevke paupers in worn-out boots, came out to the train to bid my songbird farewell. One of them was dressed like a *sheygets*, you'll excuse me, with his shirt hanging over the top of his pants. He was speaking to my boy in a whisper. "Watch out, Tevye," I thought. "If you haven't fallen in with a gang of horse thieves, cutpurses, lock pickers, or counterfeiters."

I couldn't restrain myself on the way home, and I told Hodel everything I'd been thinking. She burst out laughing and tried to convince me that these were all fine people—honest, deeply honest people who lived only for the welfare of others. They never thought about themselves—not a bit.

"Take him with the shirt," she says. "He comes from a good family. He abandoned his wealthy parents in Yehupetz and won't take a single kopeck from them."

"Really? Wonder of wonders!" I say. "Truly, a very fine boy, upon my word. And if God would only help him out with a squeeze box—or a dog to trotting along behind him—to go with the long hair and the shirt hanging out, he'd be the very picture of perfection."

I meant it for him, but I took it out on her, dumped my bitter heart all over her. And her? Nothing. "Esther let not on" [23]—she played dumb.

"Fefferel," I say to her.

"Workers, the commonweal, castles in the air," she answers me.

"What good is your commonweal and your working if it only happens in secret? There's a saying: Where there's a secret, there's a thief. You'd best tell me straight where Fefferel went and why."

"Anything," she says, "but not that. You're better off not asking. Believe me, you'll know everything in time. God willing, you'll hear lots of good news—and maybe very soon."

"Amen," I say. "Let it go from your mouth to God's ear. But our enemies should know as much good health as I know what's going on here and what this game is supposed to mean."

"That's the real misfortune," she says. "You won't understand it."

"What, it's so deep? It strikes me that God's helped me understand greater matters than this."

"This isn't a matter of reason alone," she says. "It has to be felt, felt in the heart." Her cheeks flamed, her eyes burned as she spoke. My daughters— don't get me started. When they get excited about something, it's with their heart, their body, their life, with all their body and soul.

A week passed, then two and three and four and five and six and seven— "no voice and no money," [24] no letter, no news.

23. Book of Esther 2:20.

24. The quoted Hebrew phrase, *"eyn kol ve-eyn kesef,"* alludes to but alters *"eyn kol ve-eyn 'oneh ve-eyn keshev,"* from 1 Kings 18:29. The biblical phrase means that "there was no voice, no one who responded, and no one who heeded."

"Fefferel," I say, "has vanished." I take a look at my poor Hodel. Not a drop of blood in her face, endlessly looking for work around the house, anything to help her forget her troubles. You'd think that at least she'd mention him, but nothing, as if there'd never been a Fefferel.

One day, though, I come home and see Hodel all puffy-eyed and teary. I start asking questions and find out that a long-haired shlimmazl was there earlier, whispering with Hodel. "Aha!" I think. "It's the same guy who abandoned his wealthy parents and pulled his shirttails out of his pants." I call Hodel out into the yard and don't beat around the bush.

"Tell me, you've heard from him?"

"Yes."

"And where is he, your predestined mate?"

"Far away."

"Doing what?"

"Doing time."

"Doing time?"

"Doing time."

"Where's he doing it? And for what?"

She didn't speak, looked me right in the face and didn't speak.

"Just tell me, then," I say. "To the best of my understanding, he isn't in there for theft. I don't get it—if he isn't a thief or a con artist, then what's he doing time for, what good deeds?"

She didn't speak—"Esther let not on."[25] You're not telling? I thought. Then who needs it? He's your shlimmazl, not mine, and good riddance to him! But there was a pain in my heart. I'm her father, after all. Like it says in the prayers, *ke-rakheym ov 'al bonim*[26]—once a father, always a father. . . .

Now, it came to the night of Hoshana Raba. It's my custom to relax on holidays, and to let my horse relax as well, like it says in the Torah: *Ato*, you, which means you; *ve-shoyrkho*, and your ox, by which they mean your wife; *ve-khamoyrkho*, and your donkey, by which they mean your horse. . . .[27] Besides, there was scarcely anything left to do by this time in Boiberik; at the first blast of the shofar, the vacationers scatter like mice in a famine and Boiberik

25. As above, Book of Esther 2:20.

26. First part of a simile in Psalm 103:13, "As a father has compassion for his children, so God has compassion for those who fear Him."

27. Cp. Deuteronomy 5:14: "The seventh day is a Sabbath of the Lord your God; you shall do no work—you, your son or your daughter, your slave or maidservant, your ox or your ass. . ."

turns into a ghost town. That's when I like to stay home and sit outside—it's the best time of year for me. Every day is a gift. Instead of knocking you over like a blast-furnace, the sun comes softly, caressing, invigorating. The woods are still green, the scent of resin wafts from the pine trees; the forest looks festive, as if God had made it His sukkah. Right here, I think, this is where God celebrates Sukkot—not in the city with its hustle and bustle, with people scurrying back and forth, running themselves ragged chasing a piece of bread, where all you ever hear is money, money, money. . . .

And let's not forget about the nights, either. On Hoshana Raba, for instance, it's paradise. The sky is blue, the stars sparkle, twinkle, change, wink like a human eye. And once in a while a star flies by like an arrow, leaving a trail of green behind it: a star has fallen, and someone's luck has gone with it. There are as many different kinds of luck—Jewish kinds of luck—as there are stars in the sky. "May it not be my luck that's turned bad," I think, and Hodel comes into my mind. She'd been cheerier the past few days, more lively, her whole demeanor had changed. Apparently someone brought her a letter from him, from her shlimmazl. I was dying to know what he wrote her but didn't want to ask. If she's keeping quiet, so am I. Mum's the word. Tevye's no woman. Tevye can wait. . . .

And as I'm thinking about Hodel, who should come out but Hodel herself, and sit down beside me. She takes a look around, then speaks to me quietly.

"You listening, Daddy? I have something to tell you. I'm saying good-bye today . . . forever."

I could hardly hear her, she was so quiet. She was looking at me with a strange kind of look, one that I'll never forget. It made me think, "She wants to drown herself." Why did I think that? Because something had happened that never should happen. A girl who lived not far from us fell for a Christian peasant, and on account of the Christian peasant—you can guess what she did with a few drops of water. Her mother sickened and died, her father squandered what he had and became a pauper. Meanwhile, the Christian peasant thought things over and married someone else. She went to the river, the girl I mean, threw herself into the water, and drowned.

"What do you mean, you're saying good-bye to me forever?" I lowered my eyes so she wouldn't see that I was dying.

"It means," she says, "that I'm going away, first thing tomorrow. We'll never see each other again, never."

These words made my heart a little lighter. Thank God for this at least, I thought. What does it say? "This, too, is for the best"?[28] Things could always be worse, and better has no limit.

"And where might you be going?" I ask. "If I might have the honor to know."

"I'm going to him."

"To him?" I say. "Where is he now?"

"At the moment, he's still in jail, but they'll soon be sending him away."

"So that means that you're going off to say good-bye?" I was pretending not to get it.

"No, I'm going to follow him there right away."

"There?" I ask. "What the heck is there? What's the name of the place?"

"We still don't know exactly what it's called," she says. "But it's very far, you take your life in your hands just to get there." She seemed to be boasting, as proud as if whatever he'd done was worthy of the Legion of Honor.

What do you say to this sort of thing? For something like this, a father hauls off and bawls a kid out, gives him a couple of slaps, or else starts to curse until the air turns blue. But Tevye's no woman. As far as I'm concerned, anger is the same as idol worship. So I quote her a verse from the Bible, as usual.

"I see, my daughter, that you are fulfilling what is written in our holy Torah: 'Therefore a man leaves.'[29] On account of a Fefferel, you're leaving your mother and father and going off to some God-forsaken wilderness somewhere, probably on the frozen sea where Alexander the Great once went sailing and got lost on a remote little island full of savages—or so I once read in a story book. . . ."

I said this to her half-joking and half-angry, and my heart was crying all the while. But Tevye's no woman. Tevye holds himself back. And Hodel had nothing to be ashamed of, either: she answered all my questions, one after the other, quietly, unhurriedly, deliberately. Oh, Tevye's daughters can talk, all right.

Even though my head was bowed and my eyes were closed, I still thought I could see her, Hodel, I mean. Her face was as pale and wan as the moon. Her voice was shaky, a little muffled. Should I fall on her neck, swooning, begging her not to go? I knew it'd be a waste of time. Damn my daughters! Once they fall for someone, it's with body and soul, with heart and body and life.

28. Sanhedrin 108 or Ta'anit 21a.
29. Genesis 2:24.

We sat outside like this for quite some time, the better part of the night, more silent than talking. And when we did talk, it was hardly talking, just disjointed words. She spoke and I spoke. I asked her only one thing: who ever heard of a girl getting married to a boy just so she could follow him to hell and gone?

"If I'm with *him*," she answers, "it doesn't matter—even to hell and gone."

Of course, I explained all the reasons why this is foolish, and she explained all the reasons why I would never understand it. I gave her a fable about a hen, a brood-hen that hatched some ducklings. The ducklings were no sooner up on their feet than they set out on the water, leaving the hen to cluck and brood.

"What do you say to that, my dear?"

"What am I supposed to say?" she asks. "It's really a pity about the hen, but just because a hen does the hatching, does that mean that ducklings shouldn't swim?"

You understand? Tevye's daughter doesn't just talk to hear herself.

Meanwhile, time was passing. Dawn was already breaking, the old lady was grumbling in the house. She'd already sent word more than once that it was time to call it a night. When that didn't help, she stuck her head out the window and gave me her usual blessing. "Tevye! Where are your brains?"

"Quiet, Golda," I reply. "As it's written, *lamo rogshu*[30]—what's all the hubbub? Have you forgotten that today's Hoshana Raba? Hoshana Raba is when God does the final audit of our accounts. On Hoshana Raba you're supposed to stay up all night. Do as I tell you, Golda. Fire up the samovar, please, and make some tea. In the meantime I'll go hitch up the wagon—we're going to take Hodel to the train." And as usual, I turned out a spanking new lie: Hodel's going first to Yehupetz and then even farther on account of the same old business—I mean the inheritance—and it's entirely possible that she'll be staying there all winter, maybe even into the summer and on to the next winter. And so, I told her, we've got to fit her out with provisions: linens, a shirt, a couple of pillows with cases, this, that, the whole garden medley.

Thus did I decree, and I also made it known that there was to be no crying—it was Hoshana Raba.

"No crying allowed on Hoshana Raba," I said. "It's an incontrovertible statute."

Of course, they paid as much attention to me and my statute as to a cat in

30. Psalm 2:1, "Why are the nations in an uproar?"

heat and cried anyway. And when it came time to say good-bye, the crying turned to wailing. Everyone was crying—her mother, the children, Hodel herself, and, most of all, my eldest daughter Tsaytl (she and her predestined tailor, Motl Kamzoyl, always come to me for the holidays). The two sisters threw themselves onto each other's necks—we could hardly tear them apart.

But I bore myself with steely resolution; it sounds good, steely resolution—my insides were bubbling like a samovar. But to let it show? Feh! Tevye's no woman, you know.

We rode all the way to Boiberik in silence, and when we were nearly at the train I asked her one last time to tell me whatever it was that Fefferel had done.

"There has to be a reason for everything," I say.

She flew into a passion and swore by everything holy that he was as pure as solid gold. "He's a person who doesn't care about himself," she says. "Everything he does is only for the good of others, for the good of the world, and especially for the laborers, the craftsmen." Go be a sage and figure out what that means!

"He's worrying about the world?" I ask. "Then why doesn't the world worry about him, if he's such a nice young man? Give him my regards, your Alexander the Great, and tell him that I'm counting on his sense of justice. He's a man of the highest probity," I say, "so he probably won't lead my daughter astray. He'll make sure that she writes her old father a letter once in a while."

And as I was speaking, she fell onto my neck and started to cry.

"Let's say good-bye," she says. "Good-bye, Daddy. God knows when we'll see each other."

Enough! I couldn't hold back anymore. I started to think about Hodel when she was still a tot, a kid . . . how I held her in my hands . . . my hands. . . . Don't hold it against me, that I . . . like a woman. You should only know—are you listening?—you should only know what kind of a Hodel this is. You should see her letters. . . . A Hodel from God. . . . She's right here with me, deep, deep inside. . . . I don't know how to get it across to you. . . .

You know what, Mister Sholem Aleichem? Let's talk about something happier: What's doing with the cholera in Odessa?

Translated by Michael Wex

Chava

"Give thanks unto the Lord, for He is good"[1]—however God guides the world, it's for the best. I mean, it needs to be for the best, because just try to be a big brain and do better! Take me—I wanted to be clever. I read the verse frontward, read the verse backward, and when I saw that it didn't do any good, I gave up and said to myself: Tevye, you're a dope! You're not going to change the world. *Tsar gidel bonim*,[2] the trials and tribulations of child rearing, were given to us by the Lord, and you know what *that* means: your children give you the trials and you have to grin and bear the tribulations. Do I have anything against my eldest daughter, Tsaytl, for example? She went crazy over Motl Kamzoyl the tailor. True, he really is a simple soul, with no feel for finery—for the fine print, I mean—but what can you do? The whole world can't be intellectuals, as the saying goes. Anyway, he's a decent sort who slaves till his sweat runs with blood. You should see; they've already got a houseful of little china dolls, no evil eye, and the two of them suffer in gilt-edged distinction. Talk to *her*, though, and she'll tell you that everything's hunky-dory, couldn't be better. Just one minor problem, there's nothing to eat. . . .

'*Ad kan hakofe alef*,[3] that was float number one in the parade of travails.

Nu, my second daughter, Hodel—about her you already know, I don't have to tell you that I've lost her forever. God knows if I'll ever lay eyes on her again before we're both in the World to Come, after her hundred and twentieth birthday. . . . Even after all this time, I still fall to pieces when I talk about her—about Hodel, I mean. She was the one who finished me off! "Forget it," you say? How can you forget a living person? And especially a child like

1. *Hodu lashem ki-tov*: as found in the *Hallel* prayer, from Psalm 118:1; also in Psalms 106:1, 107:1, and 136:1. This phrase is most familiar from the grace after meals.

2. Literally, "the sorrow of raising children," a rabbinic expression found in tractates of the Babylonian Talmud such as Iruvin 100b and Sanhedrin 19b.

3. "Up the this point, the first procession"; that is, of the Torah scrolls on the holiday of Simkhat Torah *(simkhes toyre)*.

Hodel. You ought to see the letters she writes me—you'd melt. She says that they're doing very well out there. He does the time and she does the work. She takes in laundry and reads books and sees him every week and has a hope, she says, that things will turn around down here. The sun will come up and everything will be bright and they'll bring him and a lot of others back. And then, she says, they'll really get down to business and turn the world upside down, with its feet in the air and its head on the ground.

Nu, how do you like that? Good, eh? So what does the Master of the Universe go and do? Being what you call a compassionate and gracious Lord,[4] He says to me, "Just you wait, Tevye, I'm going to do something to make you forget all your troubles." And He did. I wouldn't let anyone else know about it because the shame is even worse than the pain, but you I can tell. Do I have any secrets from you? What does it say in the Bible? "Shall I hide it from Abraham?"[5] Whatever I've got, I tell you—what else am I supposed to do? The one thing I ask is that you keep it between the two of us, because I'll say it again: the pain is bad, but the shame, the shame is even worse.

Anyway, what does it say in the Mishna? "The Holy One, Blessed Be He, wished to impart merit"[6]—God wanted to do Tevye a favor, so He went and blessed him with seven daughters, females yet, all of them smart, beautiful, clever, radiant, bright, healthy—cedars, I tell you! Oy, it would have been better for them and healthier for me if they'd only been ugly *zhlobs*. What happens to a good colt if it never leaves the stable? And what becomes of beautiful daughters when they're so stuck in the sticks that they never lay eyes on a human being, unless you count Anton Poppereleh, the chief of the village goyim; Khvedke Galagan, the village clerk, a lengthy hunk of goy with high boots and a forelock; and the priest, may his name be blotted out. I can't bear the sound of his name, but not because I'm a Jew and he's a priest. Hell, we've known each other for a dog's age. Not that we go to each other's parties or stop by with greetings of the season, but when we happen to bump into each other, it's "Hello, how are you? What's doing?" I don't like to go any farther with him because as soon as anything comes up, he starts with the your God—our God business. I won't sit still for it and I cut him off with a clever

4. *El rakhum vekhanun*, a phrase found in traditional prayers, based on Exodus 34:6, Nehemia 9:31, Jonah 4:2, Psalms 86:15 and 103:8.
5. Genesis 18:17.
6. Pirkei Avot 6:11 and Makot 3:15 (23b).

remark and tell him that in our Bible there's a verse. . . . Then, of course, he interrupts me and tells me that he knows the Bible as well as I do, maybe better, and starts to spew *khumesh* from memory, but like a goy, of course: *Bereshìth barà alokìm*[7] — every time, the same thing every time. So, of course, I interrupt *him* and tell him that by us there's a midrash. "A midrash, he says, "is already what you call Tal-*mud*," and he hates Tal-*mud* because Tal-*mud*, he says, is nothing but lies. So I, of course, get good and mad and start to give him a piece of my mind. You think he cares? Not at all. Just looks at me and laughs, laughs and parts his beard. I'm telling you, there's nothing worse than when you curse someone out, make his name into mud, and he just sits there without a word. Vultures are pecking your liver, and he sits there and smiles. I didn't understand at the time, but now I know what that smile meant. . . .

Anyway, I'm driving home one day around dusk and run into Khvedke the village clerk standing outside with Chava, my third daughter, the next after Hodel, that is. Soon as he sees me, the kid turns around, doffs his hat and takes off.

So I say to my Chava: "What was Khvedke doing here?"

"Nothing."

"What's nothing?"

"We were talking."

"And how do you come to Khvedke?"

"We're old acquaintances already," she says.

"*Mazl tov* on your acquaintance!" I say. "Some friend there, that Khvedke."

"And *you* maybe know him? *You* know who he is?"

"Who he is," I tell her, "I don't know. I haven't seen his pedigree, but I most assuredly understand that he must spring from illustrious forebears — his father was undoubtedly either a shepherd or a janitor or just a plain drunk."

And she, Chava I mean, says to me, "I don't know what his father was and I don't want to know — to me, all people are equal. What I *do* know, though, is that he himself is an uncommon sort of person."

"In what way? What kind of species of person is he? Let me hear."

"If I were to tell you, you wouldn't understand. Khvedke," she says, "is the second Gorky."

7. The opening words of Genesis: "In the beginning, God created . . ."

"The second Gorky?" I ask. "And who, might I ask, was the first Gorky?"

"Gorky is just about the most important person in the world right now."

"And where does he live, this Mishnaic sage of yours? What does he do for a living and what did he do to get so famous?"

"Gorky," she tells me, "is an author, a famous writer, a maker of books. He's a rare person, genuine and unique, who also comes from a humble background. Instead of going to school, he taught himself. Here's a picture of him." And she took a small portrait from her pocket and showed it to me.

"That's him, that's your *tsadek* Reb Gorky?" I ask. "I could swear that I've seen him somewhere, either lugging sacks at the depot or *shlepping* logs in the forest."

"And according to you there's something wrong with a man who labors with his own two hands? Don't *you* work? Don't the rest of us?"

"Yes," I say. "Yes, you're right. The Bible says so explicitly: *yigiye kapekho ki soykhel*[8] —you shall eat the fruit of the labor of your hands. You don't work, you don't eat. . . . But I still don't understand what Khvedke was doing here. I'd like it a lot better if you were acquainted with him from a distance. Don't forget *me-ayin boso u-le'on ato holeykh*,[9] whence thou comest and whither thou goest: who you are and who he is."

"God," she says, "made everybody equal."

"Yeah, yeah. God created Adam in His own image, but you can't forget that not everyone is meant to be together, as it's written: *ish ke-matnas yodo*, each according to the gift of his hand . . ."[10]

"A prodigy of nature!" she says, "with a biblical quotation for every occasion. Maybe you've got one about how people went and divided themselves into Jews and gentiles, masters and slaves, aristocrats and beggars?"

"Tsk-tsk-tsk, daughter of mine. It looks to me like you've wandered off into the next millennium," and I give her to understand that that's the way the world has worked since the six days of creation. "But why," she asks me, "should the world work that way?"

"Because that's how God made it," I tell her.

"So why did God make it that way?"

8. Psalm 128:2.

9. Pirkei Avot 3:1, where this phrase has a more metaphysical meaning that relates to birth and death.

10. Deuteronomy 16:17.

"Ach, if we start asking *questions*—why this and how come that—there's no end, no finish, it's a story with no last page."

"But God gave us reason and understanding so that we should be *able* to ask questions."

"We have a custom that if a hen starts to crow like a rooster, we take her to the *shoykhet*, the slaughterer, right away. As it says in the morning prayers, Who hast given the rooster understanding . . ."

"Maybe it's enough out there with the chin music?" my Golda says from inside the house. "The borscht's been on the table for an hour already, and he's outside singing spirituals."

"There you have it," I say. "The last rose of summer! It wasn't for nothing that our sages said, *shive dvorim be-golem*, there are seven signs of a blockhead—and a woman has nine measures of talk.[11] We're out here talking essentials, and up she pops with her borscht and cream."

"My borscht and cream might be just as essential as any essentials of yours."

"*Mazl tov!*" I say. "A philosopher is born—so fresh from the oven that she's only half-baked. It isn't enough that his daughters are all enlightenheaded, now Tevye's wife wants to fly to heaven through the chimney, too."

"And since we're talking about heaven," she says, "why don't you go straight to hell!"

Some howdy-do on an empty stomach, eh? But let's say good-bye to our princess and turn our attention to the prince, I mean the priest, may his name and his memory be blotted out. I was on my way home one evening, just about to drive into the village with my empty jugs, when I ran into him in his iron-trimmed wagon, driving the horses in all his glory while the wind beat at his neatly parted beard. "I need you like a hole in the head," I thought. "This is a meeting I could have done without."

"Good evening," he says. "You didn't recognize me, or what?"

"If I didn't, it means you'll soon be rich," I say, doffing my hat and trying to drive on.

"Stop for a bit, Tevel. What's your hurry? I've got a couple of things to tell you."

"All right, so long as it's good news," I say. "If not, it can wait for another time."

"What do you mean, another time?"

11. From Pirkei Avot 5:10 and Kiddushin 49b.

"By me, 'another time' means when the Messiah comes."

"The Messiah," he says, "has *already* come."

"So you've told me more than once," I say. "Tell me something new, little father."

"That's just what I had in mind," he says. "I want to have a talk about you, about your daughter, I mean."

My heart went thump—how did he come to my daughter?

"My daughters," I tell him, "aren't the kind of girls who need someone to speak on their behalf. They can stand on their own two feet."

"But this is a matter that she cannot speak about by herself. Someone else has to do it, because we're dealing with essentials here; indeed, we're dealing with her future."

"Whose business is my child's future?" I ask. "Inasmuch as we're talking about her well-being, it strikes me that I'm her father until such time as I slough off this mortal coil. No?"

"True," he says, "You are a father to your child. But you're also blind when it comes to her. Your child is making her way into another world, and you either don't understand her or don't want to understand her."

"Whether it's that I don't understand her or don't want to understand her—that's another matter, and we can talk about *that*. But what's it to you, little father?"

"It's plenty to me, because she's under my authority now."

"What do you mean she's under your authority?"

"I mean that she's under my supervision," he says, parting his beautiful flowing beard and looking me straight in the eye.

I must have jumped right out of my seat.

"Who? My daughter is under your supervision? By what right?" I could feel myself falling into a rage.

The priest's smile was utterly cold-blooded. "Let's not get worked up, Tevel. We'll take things one step at a time. You know that I am, God forbid, no enemy of yours, even if you *are* a Jew. You know that I'm fond of Jews and that my heart aches for them because of their obstinacy, their stubborn refusal to understand that it's their own good that we have at heart . . ."

"Don't talk to me about our own good right now, little father. Every word I hear you speak is a drop of deadly poison, a pistol shot to my heart. If you're as good a friend as you say you are, the only contribution to our well-being I'd like to ask of you is that you leave my daughter alone."

"You're a foolish man," he says. "God forbid that any harm should come to your daughter. She's on the threshold of happiness, engaged to a young man—I should have her luck."

"Amen!" I say, chuckling on the outside as a hell began to burn in my heart. "And who, for example, might this young man be, if I might be so privileged as to know?"

"You must know him," he says. "He's a very honest, respectable individual, very well-educated, even if completely self-taught, and he's crazy about your daughter. He wants to marry her and can't, because he isn't Jewish. . ."

"Khvedke!" I thought, and a strange fever struck me in the head and I burst into a cold sweat and barely managed not to fall off my wagon. But that priest will never live long enough for me to let him see it! I grabbed the reins, gave my horse a little nudge from behind with the whip, and good-bye Charlie, scatted off home without so much as a by-your-leave.

And when I got there, ay-ay-ay—everything was upside down! The kids were lying around weeping, their faces buried in their pillows, and my Golda was more in the next world than in this one. I looked for Chava: Where's Chava? Chava's gone. I didn't want to ask where she was. I didn't bother to ask—I was already getting enough of a taste of the torments of the grave. Rage was burning inside me, but I didn't know at whom: I could have hauled off and slapped *myself* in the face.

So I start to yell at the kids and take my bitterness out on my wife. I can't stay still, so I go out to the stable to give the horse some food and find it with its forefeet splayed, one on either side of the barrier. I grab a stick and start to give the horse what for. I flay its skin. I break its bones. "Burn, shlimmazl! You should live so long that you'll get even one single oat from me. *Tsores*, if it's *tsores* that you want, *tsores* I can give you—afflictions and terrors, plagues and Egyptians."

But before too long it occurs to me that I'm mistreating an innocent animal. What's the horse got to do with it? So I spread a little chopped straw on the ground and make a promise that, God willing, I'll show it some *hey*—the fifth letter of the Hebrew alphabet—when I open up my prayer book on Saturday. Then I go back into the house, bury myself under the covers, and lie there and let everything bleed. And as I think and reflect and interpret what it all might mean, my head damn near explodes. " 'What is my trespass? What is my sin?'[12] How have I, Tevye, sinned so much more than anyone else that I

12. Genesis 31:36, from a passage in which Jacob speaks to Laban about himself and Laban's daughters.

am punished more than the rest of the Jews? Oh, Master of the Universe, 'What are we and what our lives?'[13] What makes me so special that you have me always on your mind, keep me constantly in view and never let loose evils, calamities, and afflictions on anyone else?"

And as I'm lying on this bed of hot coals, I hear my poor wife groaning as if her heart were being torn out.

"You sleeping, Golda?" I say.

"No," she says. "What is it now?"

"Nothing," I say. "We're up a creek, all right. Have you got any idea what to do?"

"You're asking my advice," Golda says, "when I'm as far up the creek as you are? A kid wakes up healthy and strong in the morning, gets dressed, hugs and kisses me, then starts to weep and doesn't say why. I thought, God forbid, she's lost her mind. 'What's wrong?' I ask her. She doesn't answer, just slips out to tend to the cows and vanishes. I wait an hour, two hours, three hours — Where's Chava? Chava's gone. 'Nu,' I say to the children, 'why don't you hop on over to the priest's for a minute?' "

"How did you know," I say, "that she was at the priest's?"

"How did I know?" she asks. "God help me — don't I have eyes? Aren't I her mother?"

"If you have eyes," I say, "and if you're her mother, then why didn't you say something to me?"

"To *you*? When are *you* at home? And when did you ever listen when I talked? Anybody tells you anything, you come back with a verse from the Bible. You bang everyone over the head with your verses, and that's supposed to pass for conversation."

That's what she was *saying*, my Golda, but I could hear her weeping in the dark. She's got a bit of a point, I thought, because what does a woman understand about biblical verses? And my heart ached for her.

I couldn't bear her weeping and moaning, so I say, "You see, Golda, you're mad because I've got a quotation for everything, but I've got to respond to you with a quotation. *Ke-rakheym ov 'al bonim*,[14] it says, a father loves his child. Why doesn't it say, *ke-rakheym eym 'al bonim*, that a mother loves her child?

---

13. From the morning prayer service.

14. As in "Hodel," here Tevye quotes the first part of the simile from Psalm 103:13, "As a father has compassion for his children, so God has compassion for those who fear Him." *Ke-rakheym eym 'al bonim* means, "As a mother has compassion for her children."

Because a mother is not a father. A father," I say, "can speak to his child differently. You'll see tomorrow, God willing. Tomorrow I'll go see her."

"If only you're able to see her—and him, too," she says. "He isn't such a bad person, even if he is a priest. He'll have mercy on another person. Ask him, fall at his feet, and maybe he'll have mercy."

"Who?" I say. "The priest, may his name be blotted out? I should bow down to the priest? You crazy or just out of your mind? *Al tiftakh peh le-sotn*,[15] bite your tongue—my enemies should live so long!"

"Oh, you see. You're starting again . . ."

"What else did you think? That I'd let a woman tell me what to do? That I'd let a woman do my thinking for me?"

We talked away the night like this. No sooner had the first cock crowed than I got up, davened, took my whip, and went straight to the priest's front yard. . . . What's that you say? Henpecked is as henpecked does? Well, where else was I supposed to go? To hell?

Anyway, once I got to the yard, his dogs came to meet me with a hearty good morning. They were trying to re-style my capote so that they could taste the calves of my Jewish legs and see if they were any good for their canine fangs. Good thing I'd brought my whip with me—I used it to explain to them the verse, "Let no dog whet his tongue,"[16] *nekhay sobaka darom nye breshe*. In other words, I gave them something to bark about.

Their screams and my shouts brought the priest and his wife outside in a hurry, and once they'd dispersed the merry crew they invited me inside, received me as an honored guest, and offered to put the samovar on for me. I told him that there was no need for tea, that I needed to speak to him in private. The priest got my drift and motioned the priestess to please shut the door from outside, and I got straight to the point, without any preliminaries. First, let him tell me if he believes in God. Then he should tell me if he understands what it means to separate a father from the child he loves. Further, he should tell me what, according to his system, was to be called a good deed and what a sin. And one other thing that I wanted him to make clear to me:

15. Popular saying that means, "Don't make an opening for Satan."

16. *Lo yehratz-kelev l'shoyno*, from Exodus 11:7. *Nekhay sobaka darom nye breshe* (Russian) means, "Let the dog not bark in vain." In other contexts, this phrase could also mean: "Let people not rumor (or tell lies) in vain." *Breshe* (from *brekhat'*) means both "to bark" and (in colloquial usage) "to tell lies."

what was his opinion of a man who worms his way into another man's house with the intention of turning it upside down, of overturning the chairs, the tables, the beds?

Of course, he sat there like he'd been clubbed on the head. "Tevel, you're a bright guy," he says. "But when you up and put so many questions at once, how can you expect me to answer them all in one fell swoop? Take it easy—I'll answer in the order that you asked them."

"No, my dear little father," I say, "you won't ever answer them. And do you know why not? Because I know all your thoughts in advance. Answer me this instead: Do I have any hope of seeing my daughter back again, or not?"

That woke him up. "What do you mean, back again? God forbid any harm should come to your daughter. On the contrary."

"I know, I know. You're going to make her happy. That's not what I'm talking about. I want to know where my daughter is and whether or not I can see her."

"I'll grant any request," he tells me, "except that one."

"That's the way to talk, short and to the point. Good-bye, and may God repay you many times over."

When I got home, I found my Golda curled up in bed like a ball of black thread. She had no more tears left to cry.

"Get up," I call to her. "Take off your shoes, my wife, and let us sit *shive* as God has commanded. 'The Lord giveth and the Lord taketh away.'[17] We aren't the first and we won't be the last. Let's just go on as if we'd never had a Chava. Or let it be as if she were Hodel, who went off to the back of beyond—God knows if we'll see her again. God," I say, "is a compassionate and gracious Lord—He knows what He's doing."

My tears were choking me like a bone in my throat, but Tevye's no woman—Tevye can control himself. As you can imagine, that's only a manner of speaking, because firstly there's the shame. And secondly, how can you control yourself when you lose a child without her even dying? Such a jewel, so dear to my heart and her mother's too, almost more than all the rest. Why, I don't know. Maybe because she'd been such a sickly child, enduring all the troubles in the world. We used to sit brooding over her for nights on end. Wept, literally wept her back from the grave, the way you resuscitate a chick

17. Job 1:21. Hebrew phrase that is traditionally pronounced when a Jewish person learns that someone has died.

that's been stepped on. Because if God wants, He can bring the dead back to life. As we say in the Psalms, "I shall not die, but live" [18] — if your time hasn't come, you don't die. . . . Or maybe it's because she's a good kid, a devoted child who loved both of us like life itself. Oy, that's the real question: how could she do such a thing to us? Number one, that's the kind of luck we have. I don't know about you, but I believe in Providence — God's supervision of the world. Number two, it's an evil spirit, a sleight of hand, some sort of spell, you hear? You may laugh at me if I tell you that I'm not such a complete fool as to believe in imps, demons, poltergeists, and the rest of that nonsense. But I *do* believe in spells, as you see. Because what else could it be but a spell? Hear me out and you'll say the same thing yourself. . . .

Anyway, it isn't for nothing that the holy books say, "Against your will do you live" [19] — a person doesn't take his own life. There is no blow in the world that doesn't get better, no trouble that isn't forgotten. I don't mean it's really forgotten, but what are you going to do? "Man is likened to an animal" [20] — he has to work, toil, suffer, and slave for the sake of a little piece of bread. So we all went back to work, my wife and children to the jugs, me to my horse and wagon, and *oylem ke-minhago* [21] — life goes on. I decreed that Chava was not to be mentioned and not to be recalled: there was no Chava. Blotted out — end of story. I got a few dairy goods together, fresh merchandise, and went off to my customers in Boiberik.

And when I got there — rejoicing and exaltation. How are you, Reb Tevye? Where have you been keeping yourself?

"How should I be?" I say. "It's 'renew our days as of old' [22] — the same bad luck as before. One of my calves stumbled and fell."

"Why is it," they ask, "that everything happens to you?" And one at a time, they interrogate me: What kind of calf was it? How much had it cost? How many did I still have left? And they were laughing, they were happy, as rich people usually are when they're feeling good after a meal, making merry at the expense of some luckless pauper, and it's nice and hot and green outside, and the urge to nap is strong. . . . But Tevye's the kind of guy who knows how

18. Psalm 118:17.
19. Literally, "Of necessity must you live" (Pirkei Avot 4:22).
20. Psalm 49:21.
21. Literally, "The world according to its customs." Avodah zarah 54b.
22. Lamentations 5:21, quoted in synagogue prayers.

to joke around with people—no goddamned way will anybody know what I'm thinking in my heart. Once I'd finished with all my customers I started back home through the forest with my empty jugs, letting the reins slide so that my horse could amble along and sneak a pinch of grass while I sank into my thoughts and meditations, reflecting on just about anything you could name: life and death, this world and the next, what is a world, anyway, and why people live in it—anything, in other words, to distract me, I mean to keep me from thinking about her, about Chava. And as if to spite me, who of all people should crawl into my head, but Chava. She comes toward me as tall and beautiful and radiant as a cedar, or even as a tiny little thing, sickly, a babe in arms with one foot in the grave, her head resting on my shoulders. "What is it you want, Chavele? A piece of bread? A little milk?" And for a while I forget what she's done, and my heart yearns for her, my soul pines, longs for her. But then I remember and my blood starts to pump and my heart starts to flame at her and at him, at everybody in the world, and at myself for not being able to forget her for one single minute. Why can't I erase her, tear her out of my heart? Isn't that what she deserves? What's the point of being the living embodiment of the word "Jew," if all I get is to suffer every day of my life, plough the ground with my nose, bring up children so they can pick themselves up one day and tear themselves away, fall away like pinecones from a tree and disappear with the wind and the smoke? . . . Here, I thought, for example, here is a tree in the forest, an oak. Somebody comes by with an axe, takes off a branch, another branch, a third branch. What's the poor tree without its branches? Better a person should come, cut it down completely, and be done with it. Who needs a naked oak sticking out in the forest?

And while I was pursuing this train of thought, I felt my horse draw to a sudden halt. Stop! What's this? I lift up my eyes and take a look—it's Chava. The same Chava as before, not a hair unaccounted for—she hadn't even changed her clothes. My first thought was to jump down from the wagon and hug her and kiss her. But another thought pushed me back—"What are you, Tevye? A woman?" And I pulled the horse—"Giddyup, shlimmazl!"—and turned to the right. I take a look, she also veers right, waving her hand as if to say, "Stop a while. I've got something to tell you." Then something broke inside me, something plucked at my heart. I let my hands and feet take over; any second I was going to jump down from the wagon. But I controlled myself; I gave the horse a tug and we both went left. She went left, too, with a wild look on her face, as pale as death. What's to be done? I thought. "Should

I stop or keep going?" And before I could look around, wham! she's holding the horse by the bridle and saying, "Daddy! May I die if you move from this spot. I beg you, first hear me out, for the love of God!"

"Eh," I thought to myself, "you want to take me by force? Oh no, soul of mine. If that's what you're up to, it just shows that you don't know your father." And whack! I whipped my horse for everything it's worth. And the horse obeyed, it jumped, but turned its head back and wiggled its ears. "Giddyup," I say. "*Al tistakel be-kankan*, don't look at the vessel,[23] my sage, keep your eyes on the road." But don't think that I wasn't dying to turn my own head around and take a look, just one look, at the place where she had stopped. But no, Tevye's no woman. Tevye knows how we're supposed to deal with the devil.

Anyway, I won't drag out the story any longer—it's a waste of your time. If I was ever destined for the torments of the grave, I've surely passed through them by now. If you want to know the taste of hell and purgatory and all the other horrible torments described in our holy books, just ask me and I'll tell you. The whole rest of the way, she seemed to be running behind my wagon, screaming, "Hear me out, for the love of God!" A fleeting thought occurred to me: "Tevye, don't be so stubborn. What's it to you if you stop for a while and hear what she wants. Maybe she's got something to tell you that you need to know. She might have changed her mind and want to come back—anything can happen. Maybe he's buried her alive and she wants your help to escape from hell."

Maybe this, maybe that, and a lot more maybes besides went flying through my head. And she appeared before me as a child and I thought of the verse *ke-rakheym ov 'al bonim*[24]—a father's own children are never bad. And I'm tormenting myself, I'm saying that I am *osur le-rakheym*, that it's forbidden to pity me, I don't deserve to walk the earth. What? What are you so worked up about, you stubborn lunatic? Why are you making a hubbub? Come on, you sadist, turn your wagon around and make up with her—she's your child, nobody else's! And strange thoughts and reflections started crowding into my head: What's this thing called a Jew, and what's a non-Jew? And for what reason did God make Jews and non-Jews? If you simply accept that He did, then why should one be so cut off from the other, and why should

---

23. Pirkei Avot 4:20.

24. Psalm 103:13, "As a father has compassion for his children." The verse continues, "so God has compassion for those who fear Him."

they be unable to look at each other—as if one came from God and the other didn't? It bothers me that I'm not as well versed as other people in the sacred tomes and other books, where I could find some kind of proper answer.

To distract myself, I start to daven the afternoon prayers, out loud and with a melody, just as God commanded: *Ashrey*, happy are those who dwell in Your house, always singing Your praises, selah! But what good is the davening and the reciting when there's a different song playing in my heart: Cha-va, Cha-va, Cha-va! And the louder I sing *Ashrey*, the louder Cha-va sings within me; and the more I want to forget, the more—the more clearly—I can see her. And I seem to hear her voice calling to me, "Hear me out, for the love of God."

I cover my ears so as not to hear her. I close my eyes, so as not to see her. I recite the *shminesre* and don't hear what I'm saying. I beat my breast in the confession and don't know why. My life is a mess, and I myself am a mess. I don't tell anyone about my encounter, I speak to no one about her. I don't ask after her anymore, even though I know, I know full well where she is and where he is and what they're doing, but no one will hear a squeal out of me. May my enemies not live long enough to hear me complain to anyone. That's the kind of guy I am.

I'd give a lot to know if all men are like this, or if I'm the only nutcase around. For instance, as it were, for example, it sometimes happens that— you won't laugh? I'm afraid you're going to laugh at me—sometimes I put on my *shabbes* capote and go down to the train station, all ready to plunk myself into a carriage and go to them. I know where they are. I go up to the clerk and ask him to give me a ticket.

"Where to?"

"Yehupetz."

"In my book there's no such place," he says.

"That isn't *my* fault," I say . . . so I turn around and go home, take off my capote and go back to work, to my horse and wagon and dairy products. What does it say in the Psalms? "A man goes to work and Adam doth labor" [25]—the tailor to his scissors, the cobbler to his bench. You're laughing, aren't you? What did I tell you? I even know what you're thinking. You're thinking, "This Tevye is nothing but an idiot." That's why I reckon: "Thus far on the Saturday

---

25. Tevye modifies this verse from Psalm 104:23, "A man goes out to his work and to his labor."

preceding Passover"—it's enough for today, I mean. . . . Be healthy and strong, drop me a line. But for God's sake, don't forget what I asked you— keep it on the q.t., don't put it into a book. And if you *should* happen to write it down, make it about somebody else and not about me. Forget about me, like it says in the Bible, *va-yishkakheyhu*,[26] he forgot him—no more Tevye the Dairyman!

Translated by Michael Wex

26. Genesis 40:23.

Holiday Dainties

Monologue of a Vilna Housewife

They say, your modern breed nowadays, that is, and I wish the whole cheeky lot in a bad place, that people will be happy if a mishmash is made, like mine's thine, thine's mine? . . . [1] Well, I say the day such a thing comes to pass, we'll be all at sixes and sevens. It'll mean mischief. Like with bells on if you take my meaning. Just listen to what happened to me a year ago this First of Tabernacles last. Well, as you may know, I live down what's called Gitke Toyba's Alley? Yes, so I got my lodgings inside Goody Nehama's bit of a courtyard there? Only that courtyard is about as much Goody Nehama's as the alley is Gitke Toyba's, or say you and me was kissing cousins. Well, the courtyard is what's called your "X-squeeze-doory" courtyard, that's to say, with God's bounty five brothers and two sisters share it original. So the brothers died and the sisters died and they left children, which these was quite a few, so you couldn't divide it nor sell it nor pull it down nor even burn it, which God forfend because the whole street would go then and probably half the town. So they are as much stuck with it as I am with my troubles: no roof, no stairs, no stove—it's a henhouse, for pity's sake, which you are supposed to keep a four-poster in and pay all of two and a half ruble the month for, not counting change. And why's that? Heat's included, they say. Well, you only hope your worst enemy keeps breathing as much as anybody ever get round to heating up the place, except Sabbath and holidays; it's body heat keeps the place warm enough, they say. . . . Well, it's warm, I reckon. Too warm! Specially you consider what a blessed sight of lodgers clutter up the one place. There's your glazier, Shmerl, so that ain't but one; and your butcher, Pini Meir, so that ain't but two; and your boys' tutor, Naphtali, what's from that dinky place called Shmargon in these parts, so that ain't but three; and, course, there's

---

1. Like Tevye, this speaker alludes to Pirkei Avot 5:13—where the person who says that "what's mine is yours and what's yours is mine" is called an ignoramus (*am ha-aretz*).

Moishke, the widow man, so that ain't but four. But that one's as much a widow man as you're the governor. He only gets called the widow man because, preserve us, that's what he was once. Only praise God he's a widow man no more. Because the good Lord bless him since with an ill-tempered shrew for a wife, he best keep to himself for God's sake. . . .

Oh, and I forgot the scrivener, Reb Yoshe, and his daughter-in-law. Though you notice I said daughter-in-law and not the son? Well, it's because the son went away to war, so he give up his place to that fortunate pair everybody calls "the Bunimoviches." And know why? It's that he's lame and she's blind, so they both got Mammon's millions. Work the streets, don't you know. Anyhow, word is they got nice capital laid by, handsome nest egg by all accounts. Well, what you expect with both earning the way they do! Though that proofreading gent Reb Leybe don't really count, I suppose, for he's never home, anyhow, except it's weekends Sabbath. Very busy man, Reb Leybe. Got more sidelines than you can shake a stick at. I mean, not counting his employment at the printer's, he's your dealer in pious books, your Tenth Man for worship, your errands-boy dispatcher, your psalm-sayer, your heder boys' six-of-the-bester, your shofar blower, and God forbid somebody's in a dying way, he'll get you up a quorum for deathwatch prayers, too, and, well, other work along such lines mainly. Never fear, though, his old lady don't sit about idle neither. Dips candles and sells horsebeans, for all I know. Only notwithstanding, the man must have devils for friends because he's still a pauper, anyhow. So what's the count now? Say a baker's dozen? Well that's your worshipers' quorum of ten easy plus a bonus even. So you'd think everything was fine and dandy, wouldn't you. And so it would be, too, if everybody was to worship at the same shul. Only this one does his praying away over Wilejka way, and that one does his away over Chandrikowa way. Well, now, if our glazier prays over at the Glaziers' Shul, and our butcher's glad enough to pray in Butchers' Row, and our tutor prays at the Lubavitchers' concern—well, that's only to be expected. Every buzzard after his kind, as we say. Only you, Mr. Widow Man, what in the nation possess you to be doing *your* praying plumb over at the Old Shul? Just to hear the one and only Sirota cantoring there? And don't give me that guff about being such a cockalorum "cornersewer" of pious songs neither, Mr. Smarty Pants, because I know better! For when it comes to Sabbath hymnings at home? Damn the man! Got the voice of a slaughtered rooster and preens himself on it! Why, the old fool so busts my eardrums with his cock-a-doodle-doo grace after meals Saturdays, it sets my ears aching into Sunday morrow. Only you tell me what bounty the man ever received at the hands of that shrew to be praising the Lord so almightily about it. Except it's the dirt she make him eat and the fat ear she give him. But talking to her you must give the woman her due. For she's right, you know: "A husband's like the Jewish exile," she says, "a trial which becomes a habit." Well, you have to hand it to her. The woman's got a head on her shoulders. . . .

Because it seems to me if I do have a bone to pick, it's more with the One Who I Am Unworthy of Mentioning by Name. After all, my husband's one of them, uh, whatcher-call-'ems—yeah, "pious sheep." Not worth much as mutton maybe, but he sure got an uncommon knack for woolgathering. I mean, the man's never done a useful lick of work that I know of. Though mooching around shul, "a-larning and a-praying," as they say, is more in his line. It's called doing the Lord's work. Well, it's a very noble line of work, only where's it leave me? Tucked up with a spade baking bagels, I guess. Though God knows. It may earn me a chair in heaven yet. So I carry on like the faithful ass of the adage so the table may be set royal for his nibs on Sabbaths and holidays. Why Sabbaths and holidays? Because weekdays he must make do with "Deborah-Esther's charitable board." That's to say, he must put his trust in Providence. Only I don't waste any bother over it personal, nor much care to, I reckon. All I know is, come Sabbath and holidays, there's challah loafs with fish, plus what meat I manage to scrape up, with the whole blessed spread with all the trimmings laid out and ready at table for him. And Feast Days? There's got to be holiday dainties for dessert, Feast Days. It's the rule. Passover is prune stew; Tabernacles is carrot stew.

So you like to hear a story? Tabernacles last, carrots suddenly come very dear. Dickens knows why. Seems they wasn't brought in, some such thing. Anyhow, they was dear. A kopeck a carrot maybe. So you think that might be an excuse? Only my husband cherish his holiday dainties more than anything. He will give up his fish and meat both, the whole blessed spread with all the trimmings, if you only let him have his holiday dainty. Course, all that is only in a manner of speaking, as the dainties come last anyhow, so he can afford to be generous with what he already ate. . . Well, I brung home a basketful of carrots that day and got the fixings ready and set the pot to simmer on the stove. Only talk about taste! M'mm! It's not for nothing your quality will make an everyday meal of such things on weekdays; quality isn't fools, you know. Your quality enjoys everything on a weekday which our lot is partial to only on weekends Sabbath. . . . Well, the stew being done, I put it away in my corner of the stove—because don't you know everybody got his own corner in the stove in our place—after which I covered it over in ash and slipped out to my sister's to see how she was getting on. My sister Beiltse, preserve us, she's paralyzed in both legs, which she hasn't had the use of these ten years now. Though she manage to get by on the labor of her own hands, notwithstanding. Plucks poultry is what she does. That's to say, summer she plucks poultry, winter she knits toddlers' stockings and woolly hats. Well, now she lives over by Jews' Street, in Leybe Leyzer's courtyard; which it's also one of your "X-squeeze-doory" courtyards, which there must be about a couple of hundred families at least occupying it besides. Only you tell me how it's my fault I stopped by my sister's for half an hour once in a holiday? And don't think I didn't take a challah loaf and some fish along so the woman might know the taste of a real holiday feast, for once. And only perish the thought I should ever bring her a stranger's cooking and not my own which I cook myself personal. Nor have I to answer to my husband for it, so who else got anything to say to me about it, anyhow?

Though, being as how we don't hardly ever see each other the whole week, except it's Sabbath and holidays maybe, we got to chattering away and lost track of the time, kind of. Well, next thing, somebody come to fetch me home straight away because he already come back from shul—that is, my husband come back—and, gracious me, I hoped the man wasn't too upset because he must have been good and hungry by then and missing his dinner. Well, I tell you it was a terrible state what I dashed home in and found the sixth couple was already at table in the Tabernacles' hut; because all of us we got only this one bit of a hut put up in the courtyard which we can't all be at table feasting at once in, so we take it in turns like. Thank God, though, he didn't say anything to me, that is, my husband didn't. Well, he's not one of your "saying" sorts anyhow, is my husband. The man's more by way of being your quiet kind of a gent, if you take my meaning. Only I could tell he was out of sorts. See, I can always tell by his look: if he is looking into a book, it means he is out of sorts. That's to say, he's always looking into a book, only there's looking and there's looking: the other kind is one kind of looking, and this is another kind of looking, which it's different. Besides which, being he's a mite blind in his one eye, he never have what I care to call the look of holiday cheer about him, anyhow. Course, I set in to making my excuses straight away: this, that, my sister, we don't see each other all week—Nothing! Man wouldn't give an inch. Never look up from his pious writ even once. Hand him the dipper as per usual, aforemeals handwashings, put the fish on the table next. Tastes a treat. Come the dish of boiled doughcrumbs, also the bit of meat—fine and dandy all around. But now the time come round for dessert, I spoke up. I mean the gent's still a man of pious larnin', so it's only right he come in for being treated civil on occasion. "Know what, dear?" I says to him, "got a dainty waiting which make your mouth water sure thing," I says, "fit for a king," I says, "and know what else?" I says, "It's even carrot stew!". . . Well, now, hearing talk of dainties and carrot stew, he perk up marvelous. Actually put his book by. Me, I make for the stove. I give a look— Why, bless me if that pot wasn't clean as a whistle! Not a lick of dainty inside! No dainty! Dainty, dainty, where's my dainty? So I run about amongst the lodgers, here, there, yonder, asking round, "Anybody seen my dainty?" Dainty? Dainty? What dainty, where dainty, never heard of such a thing, they says! My luck, a neighbor got to feeling sorry for me along the way and said she knew where my dainty was. It's a goner, she says. A dainty no more. Passed on, and Godrest! Been ate up, oh, hours ago. Only she didn't care to say who done the deed, she says. Because she wanted no trouble with "sighted" folks. So that's when I knew it was the blind party which done it. Though when I look over my husband's way, you think the rogue wasn't poring over his book again? Not much he wasn't! And back to playing the clam again as always, what's more. . . .

Well, you may be sure I made a beeline for that fortunate pair everybody calls "the Bunimoviches": "Goodnessgracioussakes, woman," I says, "what the dickens you want of my dainty?" Says she, "What dainty?" Says I, "My carrot stew holiday dainty!" Says she, "Bless you, what you talking about anyhow? I had me a frutkick.". . . Well, didn't that get my dander up, just. Nerve of the woman! And me knowing all along, you see, she hadn't a carrot in the house to save her neck, so she goes and says she had a fruitcake. Why, that only mean she had a better holiday dainty than mine! Says I, "So you had a fruitcake?" Says she, "Frutkick!" Says I again, "Fruitcake?" Says she again, "Frutkick!". . . Only that really was the last straw. I mean, if she'd at least tried denying it, say it wasn't her which done away with my dainty, then I may have thought: Well, now, maybe so, maybe it wasn't her which done it, but somebody else. But letting on like she had a fruitcake? Well, that take the cake! . . .

I mean, what's there to say more? A nasty business, very nasty. . . . And whose fault is it anyhow, if you take folks and stuff 'em together higgledy-piggledy like they was hens in a henhouse saving the difference, and just you try to do anything that way! But you only talk to *them*, to your cheeky modern breed, the same lot what's rarin' to bring them newfangled changes into our Old Shulyard only so there be a proper mine's thine, thine's mine, share-and-share alike, lovey-dovey mishmash there—and they got the gall to say that clever folks opine it's all to the good!. . . . Well, I say we'll be all at sixes and sevens then, it'll mean mischief, like with bells on, only you be sure and have yourself a happy holiday anyhow, hear?

Advice

"Oh, by the way, my dear, there's a young man been coming round every morning, noon, and night for three level days now and finding you always out. Just frantic to see you, he says!" That was the greeting waiting for me upon arrival once from one of my trips away.

"Writer, with a 'creation,' no doubt!" was the thought that immediately came to mind, and I sat down at my desk and set to work—when, hark! sure enough, there was the doorbell, door opened, somebody shuffling about out there, dropping his galoshes, coughing, blowing his nose—yes, all unmistakable signs of a writer in the offing. Oh, I do wish the fellow would quit dawdling and show his face! By and by, though, he came in. And, making me a pretty reverence, that's to say, retreated a couple of paces, bowing from the waist, and, rubbing palm in palm, introduced himself, giving out a contrived fanciful name of a sort that, once it is uttered, gets promptly mislaid and slips irretrievably out of mind!

"Yes, well, do sit down. How can I be of service to you, sir?"

"I come to you on an urgent errand, sir. That's to say, urgent as regards myself, most urgent, really, you might even say, vital, and only you, sir, so I reckon, will understand it. I mean, seeing as you write such an awful lot, sir, I should reckon you must know everything, sir, must surely be knowledgeable in all things. So I reckon, anyway. That's to say, not reckon, sir, but I'm absolutely certain of it."

I sat contemplating the person of my visitor. Your very type of a provincial Jewish gentleman of letters. Your author. Your pale sort of a young person, with great saucerlike black eyes, always begging compassion, pleading with you: "Oh, please, please, kind sir, take pity on a poor lost soul." I do not like eyes of that sort. Eyes of that sort scare me: they never live, are never merry, are always a sight too much in an introspective reverie. I hate eyes of that sort.

"Oh, very well, show us what you've got," I said to him, and I leaned back in the chair, waiting for him to pull out a fat roll of manuscript from his breast pocket: doubtless one of your tedious stretched-out three-decker novels that go on forever, or a play in four acts with a cast of characters all called Murtherson, Goodfellow, Piousheart, Bittersprig, and other such names that are a dead giveaway about the sort of folk you are being asked to have any truck with. . . . Or perhaps it is a cycle of New Songs of Zion:

> Yonder towards the Mount he hies him,
> Yonder where the eagle flies in,
> Yonder where the olive thrives in,
> Yonder where the Prophets bend an humble knee
> Before Divine Eternity. . . .

I dare say I'm familiar enough with such verses and rhymes that repeat on you like a bad meal, make your eyes swim and your ears buzz, and leave behind an awful emptiness in the heart and a strange barrenness in the soul.

But do you know—this time I was dead wrong. The young man had *not* reached for his breast pocket nor did he pull a roll of papers out from anywhere else nor even suggest an inclination to read me out a novel or a play or New Songs of Zion. What he did do was set his shirt collar right and give me a couple of propitiatory coughs before addressing me so:

"Well, you see, sir, I've come here to see you, that's to say, I only came to talk to you about my troubles, sir, heart to heart, and obtain your advice. Because you write such an awful lot, sir, I reckon you must know everything and are the only one that can advise me, I mean, properly, so whatever you may tell me, I'll be sure to do it, you have my solemn word as to that. Only your pardon, sir, truly, do I presume on your time, sir?"

"Oh, it's quite all right. Do go on, do go on," I soothed, feeling now genuinely relieved of an intolerable burden. And my young visitor edged his chair nearer to the desk and proceeded to pour out his troubled heart to me, in an easy manner at first, and ever more passionately then as he progressed.

"Well, you see, the fact is, sir, myself, I'm from what you call a small town. That's to say, not all that small a town, but more in the way of a big town, really, more of a city, you might say; only living here as you do, sir, I reckon by your lights you would incline to call it only a small town. I have a notion, too, that you must know the place pretty well, only, I am not naming names because it wouldn't take only that much for you to be writing about it, and that wouldn't suit me for all sorts of reasons. . . . What line I'm in?. . . H'm. . . . Well, I'm in . . . well, the fact is, I don't do much of anything, really, still board with my in-laws, you see, that's to say, not so much board with them as we live together with them, lap of luxury, you might say, because, what with her being an only daughter, that's to say, her being their one and only off-spring, sir, and them having no other children besides, but only the one daughter, they can afford to keep us for the next ten years, pretty much, be-cause you see they are quite prosperous, you might say rich, even, and down our ways—well, they can pass for being very rich there, more of monstrous rich, even, because nobody can touch them for being rich down our ways. Only I have a notion, too, that you must certainly have heard of my father-in-law. So I reckon, anyway. Only I am not naming names as it wouldn't be proper. Fact is, though, he is your sort of gent that is partial to making an almighty splash everywhere, so people might know him. Like the time there was the big fire which burnt down half Bobruisk two years back, that's to say, back in 'ought-two? Well, he gave away a bundle that time, and then, last year, when they had themselves the big pogrom over in Kishinev ways, he went and put his name down for the biggest donation of just about anybody. At home he won't give even a mite of charity, for it's only abroad that he likes making a big splash where folks are sure to hear it. I mean, after all, the man is nobody's fool. He knows everybody in town kowtows to him as is, anyway—so why waste any bother on their account? Which is why he reckons he can get away with cocking a fig at the whole town and give nothing away besides. He is not your giving sort is my father-in-law. He cannot give. Says so himself, even. I cannot give, he says. Anybody comes to him for charitable donations, he goes dead stiff and says: 'What, again? Come for handouts again? Well, here's the keys, gentlemen, and there's the cabinet, help yourself, take all you want!'. . . Only you really don't suppose he takes the keys out then? Because, with respect, sir, you'd be wrong! Keeps the keys to that cabinet hid away somewhere in a desk drawer anyway and got the key to the drawer tucked well away somewhere else besides. That's the sort of person my father-in-law is. Well, it's only as you'd expect. For the name you earn is the name you get. Be-cause between you and me, sir, pretty near everybody in town calls him the Old Hog. . . . But generally only behind his back, though, because it is sick-ening the way people will suck up to him to his face. Though he reckons it is all only honest coin, anyhow, and pats his belly preening himself on it and liv-ing on velvet the while. Did I say, on velvet? On velvet, and how! Because there's living and there's living, and a world of difference between. I mean, judge for yourself: the man never lifts so much as his little pinky, lives like a lord, eats like a horse, sleeps like a top—what more could anybody want? Done snoozing, he'll order the buggy hitched and brought round so he can take an idle afternoon's turn or two over the mud with it. Come evening then, his clutch of cronies from town will forgather, repeating outrageous old slanders and retailing new scandals which nobody believes anyway, telling black lies about everything and everybody in town, and generally having themselves a high old time all round clowning at everybody else's expense. And then the big samovar gets wheeled in, and the time's come for His Nibs to sit down to another game of dominoes with Shmuel Abba. That's Shmuel Abba the town kosher slaughterer, who is a young chap that notwithstanding he has managed yet to hold on to his original side curls and face whiskers, has fallen pretty well in with the new ways and wears spiffy white shirt collars and walks about with a high shine on his shoes and is never one to shy away from the ladies and has got a way with a song, as well, and takes out subscriptions to Russian newspapers and plays a crackerjack game of chess and is the world's absolute whiz at dominoes. And when them two sit down to a game of dominoes, they will be at it all night into next morning with the rest looking on and yawning fit to yank your jaw off its hinges! Well, you'd think any damn fool would know enough to get up then and make for his room and sit down to a book or read the paper there. But no! And why? Ain't fitting. I mean, you can't just get up in the middle like that and be walking out on a guest, now can you. Because a thing like that only gets his back up. My father-in-law's back, that is. That's to say, he won't say anything; only he'll puff himself up and glare daggers, and then you can be talking yourself blue in the face and you won't get a word out of him. Nor from his wife, either—because she only follows his lead anyway. And that loving pair being now of one mind anent yours truly, then it's *her* turn to be glaring daggers—well, after all, her being their only daughter, mummy and daddy's one and only offspring, sir, and them being the light of her life, as is she of theirs, to say nothing of being the apple of their eye, forever petted and fretted over, so if she is ever feeling off color or goes the least bit queer—then it's always, oh, my God, go and fetch the doctor, and heaven help us all! So it's no wonder a creature such as herself reckons the whole world must be made only for her own pleasure and nobody else's. And her being short on wit don't help matters any. That's to say, talking to her, in only the ordinary way, you would think she was no fool, no fool at all, clever you might even say, sharp, even, and I mean really sharp, got a man's head on her shoulders, that woman! Trouble is, she is spoilt, spoilt rotten, a wild goat that won't browse where she is tied. All day long and half the night it's hee-hee this and ha-ha that, and next thing, she's thrown herself down on the bed and is bawling like an infant. 'What's wrong, dearest? What's ailing you? Why are you crying, darling? What do you want?' Not a word! . . . But never mind. Because if that was all there was to it, it would be only half a misery. For if a wife is set to crying, she'll cry until she has cried herself out. But then, you see, you haven't reckoned with the fly in the ointment—the mother-in-law, that is. Because the minute that woman gets wind of the business, she'll come swooping down with her Turkey shawl thrown over her shoulders and her handwringings and that godawful deep-voiced yammering singsong she'll be putting on when she's on about something—got the voice of a man, that woman has—and be saying: 'What is it, child? Is it that wretch again, that awful brute, that wicked, wicked man? Oh, woe is me! What cares he that I've only the one good eye left in my head? What's eating him now— stomach giving him trouble again, got the nosebleeds maybe?' . . . blah, blah, yap, yap, on and on, like meal pouring out of a sack! And it seems to me it won't ever stop, won't ever end, sawing away at my heart, gnawing at my soul, and I get the sudden urge then to snatch that Turkey shawl off of the woman's shoulders, crumple it up in my fists, jump up and down on it, shred the thing into a thousand bits and pieces. Only now I really think of it, I'm sure I can't say why I should have anything against the woman's Turkey shawl, anyway, in particular. I mean, it's only your ordinary variety of Turkey shawl, which it's brought over from Brody, mainly. Know the kind I mean? Those big checkered, polka-dotted old things which come all painted up gaudy in black and red and yellow and green and white checks and polka dots and have got these very, very long fringes all about. . ."

"You'll forgive my asking, young man," I said, interrupting him at full flood, "but it seems to me you wanted my advice about something?"

"Your pardon, sir, truly," he said, resuming after catching his breath. "Do I presume on your time, sir? But rest assured it was all necessary to the matter in hand, sir, for it was done so you may be the better acquainted with the family, sir, with the sort of people they are, because it is only when you have some acquaintance with the family, with those people, sir, that you can understand my situation exactly. . . . So the minute she goes the least bit queer, that's to say, when my wife goes queer, preserve us, then the mother raises a clamor, and my father-in-law orders the buggy out and sends to fetch the doctor, that's to say, sends for the new doctor—because that's really how we call him back home, the new doctor—though, naming no names, I might sooner have wished the devil had fetched him away instead! . . . So there, sir, is where my business with you really begins, that's to say, the matter I have been meaning to tell you about and obtain from you such advice and good counsel on the subject as you may have to offer."

My young visitor paused now to mop the perspiration from his face and edged himself a bit nearer, picking up something on the way to hold in his hands, for there are people who cannot talk without holding something in their hands because they are otherwise incapable of telling you a story. I keep a collection of handsome *objets* and pretty little curios set out on display on my writing table, among them a little bicycle, which is also by way of being a cigar cutter. It is a very great favorite with visitors, so anybody coming in to see me must inevitably seize upon it and begin toying with it. My young visitor, proving no exception, also picked up the little bicycle with which he was evidently much taken. At first he contented himself with contemplating it while he talked, then he took hold of it, then tried spinning its wheels, till at last the little bicycle never left his hands, and, thus, he took up his narrative again.

"Yes, now about the new doctor. You know, it is hard to say which there is a greater abundance of in our town, dogs or doctors, for we have plenty to spare of both and then some. Because there are your Christian doctors and there are your Jewish doctors and then there are your doctors in only a small way of business and, lest we forget, there are your Zionist doctors, as well, that's to say, doctors whose first order of business is Zionism. But the doctor I'm telling you about in particular is still only a very young doctor yet, hometown boy, don't you know, son of a tailor, that's to say, that his father used to be only a tailor—only he really isn't a tailor anymore because how would it look him being only a tailor with a doctor for a son? Or so *he* thinks. Only what I say is, how would it look with the son being a doctor and having only a tailor for a father, and not just any old tailor, but what's called your 'tailor amongst tailors'? That's to say, taken all in all this is only your pint-sized, loud-mouthed, runty sort of a Jewish gent that likes walking about in a cheap padded-cotton caftan and has got a cast in one eye and a finger out of joint and with a clapper in his head for a mouthpiece that is set to clapping nonstop for, oh, just four-and-twenty hours, day and night, jabbering on about 'Coo, you oughtta sheed wot practish my doctor got yeshtiddy! Lordy, wot practish my doctor got! Ain't no flies on *my* doctor!' And if that wasn't trouble enough, the doctor happens also to be a male midwife, that's to say, the town obstetrician, so if there is ever a domestic secret anywhere, it won't keep long but is instantly noised about all over town by that walleyed tailor with the crooked finger, and woe betide either wife or maid who should fall into that doctor's hands, for she must surely fall into the tailor's mouth as well. . . . Because, you know, it once happened that a girl in town. . ."

"You'll forgive my asking, young man," I said, interrupting at full flood again, "but it seems to me you wanted my advice about something?"

"Your pardon, sir, truly, do I presume on your time, sir? I only started out by telling you about the doctor because it's him that has brought about my ruin! If it wasn't only for that man, I'd be wanting for nothing in this life. Because, look, what do I want for otherwise of the good life? I mean, here I've got me a sweet little wife, what's called a 'real looker,' sir, a great beauty you might even say, nor have we got any children, so what with her being an only daughter, that's to say, their one and only offspring, sir, why then in the fullness of time, of which I wish them nothing short of a hundred and twenty years, which is only their due, sir, she stands to get all of it, that's to say I stand to get all of it, to say nothing of social position, sir, because thank God that in matters of precedence, sir, the son-in-law of a town squire, that's to say, of the richest and most powerful Jewish gentleman in the neighborhood, never wants for any of it—touch wood—neither when it comes to first recitals of the Prophets at shul upon the Sabbath or holidays nor receiving first collations at circumcisions, and come Feast of Tabernacles, with the citron fruit and willow branch, I am always first behind His Worship: that's to say, naturally, the cantor always comes first, then the rabbi, then my father-in-law, and then myself with all the rest tagging along behind. And even at the bathhouse (saving the difference!), when I have taken my clothes off and come in naked (saving your presence!), the bathhouse keeper will make a great show of running before me then, bellowing, 'Gangway, gen'men, all make way for His Washup's Son and La-a-a-wr!' But I swear to you that it does embarrass me, sir, because I hate it! Though hate is maybe a bit strong. Because everybody likes being flattered, and I don't know as anybody ever turned down a privilege. Only trouble is, it has just gone too far, sir. I mean why all the fuss, anyway? Just because of being His Worship's son-in-law? So let them be sucking up to him and welcome to it, let them be slobbering all over him, only begging your pardon because, truly, sir, they are all savages, plain ignorant savages, but I am made to sit with them anyway on account of not being allowed to keep company with just anybody because how can any son-in-law of His Worship be allowed to keep company with just anybody? And it's no use talking to him, you know. Why, the man is downright common, sir, dead common, absolute ignoramus, you might even say, for which craving his pardon for saying so—only what he don't know won't hurt him anyway, so why bother? As for herself, she's a wild goat, sir, a one-and-only daughter, as I already told, always laughing one minute and crying the next, one minute it's hee-hee and ha-ha and the next she's thrown herself on the bed and the new doctor must be fetched—who I wish the devil might fetch away instead! Because believe me, sir, it makes me that miserable only to be thinking of him. Why, sometimes I want to snatch up a knife and butcher him on the spot or run down to the river and drown myself because that's how miserable that doctor has made me!"

My young visitor lapsed into thought and grew sad.

"So are you saying, sir, you entertain some suspicion in her regard?" I now said, stopping short of speaking more plainly.

"Gracious heavens, no!" he exclaimed, jumping up with a sudden start, and he edged even nearer to me then. "Suspicions regarding her? Why, sir, she is an honest woman! Come of pious Jewish stock, sir! . . . No, it's only him I meant, that blasted dandy doctor. Nor even him so much as that walleyed daisy of a tailoring daddy of his in the padded cotton caftan, blast him! Goes about four-and-twenty hours, day and night, noising it about all over town. Think there's a word of truth to his twaddle? Why, no! It is all rubbish, sir, pure rubbish! Creature's got a tongue, so he lets it rattle on regardless! Now, I shouldn't ordinarily pay his croaking any more mind than a bullfrog's in high summer. Trouble is, sir, folks have ears, and ears are partial to listening, so if you listen good you are apt to hear things you would rather not hear. Specially in our town, sir, which I tell you is a town which everybody knows, when it comes to folks having long tongues and being mad for scandal, has every other town in the world beat, hands down. Ask anybody, sir, and they'll tell you! Because when a man's reputation falls into people's mouths down our ways, sir, he may as well say good-bye to it forever. Oh, around me they trod ginger enough; only behind my back I had heard such things, sir, it made me take a good look about me, keep a weather eye open, pick up a word here, a word there, and, well, what can I say? Just wasn't anything in it, sir, not a blessed thing—except I noticed one thing, though. Whenever he came round, she'd be a very different person, sir; face had a different look about it, different sort of look in her eye. That's to say, she was the same person, really, same face, same eyes; only the look was different. Know what I mean? A different look, different sparkle, somehow. Think I didn't ask her, 'Why is it, dearest, whenever *he* comes round, you are a different person somehow?' Well, now, you try and guess what she answered me then. Laughed out loud is what, giving out with such a monstrous ha-ha-ha, I thought I was being put into the ground and tucked up in it whilst still among the living! And promptly she was done laughing, she threw herself down on the bed with such a great wail it brought the mother-in-law running in with that Turkey shawl on, trying to buck her up, and then she, of course, started in with that awful yammering of hers, which only caused my father-in-law to have the buggy brought round to send for the doctor, and who do you reckon was sent to fetch him, sir, if it wasn't my own self, and the minute the doctor came in, she took an instant turn for the better, and the color came right back into her cheeks, and her eyes began to sparkle again like a pair of brilliants in the sun. . . . And imagine the fine position I was put in by it; why, having to step into that house was like a journey beyond the grave. Because surely even a descent into hell might have been more agreeable! And having to look the fellow in the face yet! I mean, you ought to see it, sir. Handsome mug he's got, too, I must say. Kind of a beet-red coloring to it, though maybe more of a blue, really, and talk about your pimples, sir, why, he has got the things all over, so even his pimples have got pimples! Chap likes smiling a sight too many as well, and what a smile it is, too — like a corpse laid out before planting! Thing's a fixture, whether it's wanted or no! I mean, it just never leaves his face. Always smiling, sir, affable with everybody to a fault, no matter who. Never mind with myself! Why, the fellow is so constantly sweet and gentle with me, I may as well bottle him to cure my boils with. And there is no end or limit to it, either! Like, just recent, when I wasn't feeling what you'd call in the pink, exactly? Come down with that newfangled whatsit, influenza thing? Well, you should have seen how that man laid himself out for me then. Why, it wasn't human, hardly. Remarkable thing, though! The more he goes out of his way to be nice to me, the more — though God spare me notwithstanding — the more I hate him for it, just can't bear the sight of him, sir, especially not when he sits amongst us and they are all exchanging knowing looks with her! . . . Seems to me if I took him by the scruff and tossed him out, it would do me a power of good! Because it's his way of looking at her I cannot tolerate, sir, his way of grinning at her I cannot stand. So I am resolved once and for all now — let there be an end! How much humiliation is a man to take? Why, it's reached a point where the whole town has made my business its own! So there is no other course to follow—but divorce! Seems to me it is the only recourse I have left. Ah, but! . . . But is it practical, sir? Rich father-in-law? One and only daughter? Another hundred years she stands to get all of it, that's to say, I stand to get all of it? That'll be the day though, won't it! Only what did I do before, anyhow? What do lots of young gents in my shoes do? No other recourse, though, is there! So, what you reckon, sir? No other recourse but divorce?"

Here my young visitor stopped to draw breath again and mopped his face, waiting to hear what I should say.

"Why, I hardly know, sir. But I am inclined to agree you've no recourse but to divorce. Most particularly as the love between you appears not to be so very strong, nor I understand are there any children, so with the town talking, well, what need have you to persist in an unfortunate business you're best out of anyway?"

The whole while I talked my young visitor kept spinning the wheels of the little bicycle and watching me mournfully with his saucerlike deep black eyes, and when I finished he edged nearer to me still and heaving a sigh he replied:

"You say, love. . . . Well, I can hardly say I hate her, sir. I mean, why should I hate her? Because I do really love her—no, I mean, love her really, sir! . . . And what you said about the town talking? Well, let 'em talk, is what I say! Because what really burns me up, sir, is *him*; that's what really burns me up! I mean, why must she always be making such a monstrous fuss over his coming anyway? Because, well, now, you tell me, sir, why don't she go all red and joyful when she sees me? I mean, in what way am I worse than him, sir? Just because he is a doctor and I am not? Because maybe if they was to teach me the same as him, I should be a doctor, too, maybe even a better doctor than him! And believe me, sir, as regards pious book-learning, I am his match on any day of the week, and when it comes to knowing the Sacred Tongue, that's to say, Hebrew, sir, well, I just reckon what that man knows wouldn't make small money for my change purse! So, on second thoughts, sir, I have reconsidered: because, I mean, what fault did I see in her that was so terrible that I must divorce her anyway? You say, the new doctor! Well, as to that, what would I do if it wasn't the doctor but who knows what plaguey no-account instead? And where does it say that a wife must be unacquainted with a doctor anyway? So that's one away. And two, there is the practical side wants considering. I mean, what's in it for me if I was to divorce her. Because you may not know it, but I am an orphan, sir; that's to say, I'm on my own, not having a single close relation or good friend in all the world. So just you try and go back to being only a poor boy again and remarry and start all over again, that's to say, begin everything from scratch again! And who's to say I'd do better this time, anyhow? Because I could as well end up in a worse hell than even now, couldn't I? I mean, better the devil you know because at least I know what troubles I've got. Besides which, I am what you call Crown Prince anyway, sort of, being I'm His Worship's son-in-law, and another hundred years she stands to get all of it, that's to say, I stand to get all of it. . . . Don't you reckon? I mean, why be taking chances anyway, why just speculate? Otherwise it's all only a gamble, just a lottery really. So what you reckon, sir? Ain't it all a lottery? Just a gamble, really?"

"Yes, quite," I said, "I am inclined to agree. It is a gamble, a lottery really. And yes, of course, a reconciliation is preferable to a divorce."

I was now happily congratulating myself on having tipped the scales in favor of reconciliation and thought to be done with the fellow at last. When suddenly he picked up the little bicycle again and had edged quite near this time so he was speaking directly in my face.

"Reconciliation? Well, yes, I reckon you're right. But then I think of *him*, blast him, of that doctor, that's to say, with the pimply red face! Because that walleyed daddy of his has been going around noising it all over town anyway about His Washup's precious daughter getting a divorce. I mean, how lowdown can you get, even for a tailor? If, at least, the old fool hadn't noised it about! Because now that the whole town knows anyway, what have I got to lose? I mean, what's the saying? If the pot's broken it won't get more broken. Because as long as it was kept secret, there wasn't anything to it, really. Put a brave face on and brazen it out—that was the ticket. But the whole town is talking about divorce now, so digging my heels in seems awfully crude, even to me. So there isn't any choice left but divorce, I reckon. Eh? What about you, sir? Don't you reckon?"

"Yes, well, I am inclined to agree," I said, "as everybody is talking openly of divorce anyway, it does seem a bit crude. So I really don't see that you have any choice but divorce."

"So, what you are telling me," he said, edging his chair nearer still, so he was almost on top of me now, "so what you are telling me is I must divorce her forthwith? Now, think carefully, sir. I mean, say you was the rabbi, and I was to come to you with my wife asking for a divorce, so you ask me, 'Tell me, young man, why do you want to divorce this woman?' So what answer you reckon I might give? Now, just for the sake of argument, say I was to tell you it was because she looks at the doctor and the doctor looks at her. Well? I mean, where's the sense in that? Because, now, I ask you! What am I supposed to do, run and blindfold the woman? Only think how that would make me look! I mean you judge for yourself, sir. Because here I have just gone and divorced a woman what's called a 'real looker,' sir, a one-and-only offspring, sir, another hundred years she gets it all, that's to say, I get it all. . . . Eh? What you reckon people will say then? Mad, eh? Wouldn't you reckon? Stark raving with bells on, eh?"

"Oh, I am inclined to agree—with bells on, absolutely!"

Here my young visitor edged himself so near as to leave no distance at all between our faces, to say nothing of the inextricable confusion resulting to our feet in the consequence, and having also by now quite demolished my little bicycle, he drew my inkstand toward him instead. And uttering a sigh, he resumed his argument.

"Oh, sure, it's easy for you to say somebody else was stark raving with bells on. Only I'd like to know what *you* would do if the shoe was on the other foot. Because what if you had a father-in-law who was rude and ignorant and a mother-in-law with a Turkey shawl who won't leave off nagging and a wife who notwithstanding she was as healthy as a carthorse has took to being doctored all the time and then having the whole town pointing a finger at you and singing out, 'Ho-ho-ho, there he go, li'l miss nanny-goat's handsome billy-bo'!' Well, I reckon you'd be out of bed before half the night was done and be lighting out to where the hills are sugar candy and hens lay hard-boiled eggs!"

"Well, yes, I am inclined to agree. I suppose I should be lighting out to where the hills are sugar candy and hens lay hard-boiled eggs."

"Oh, sure, it's easy for *you* to talk," said he, "of lighting out to where the hills are sugar candy and hens lay hard-boiled eggs. Well, lighting out is all well and good. But lighting out how, sir? And lighting out to where? To blue blazes I reckon! . . . And what of her being an only daughter? . . . A one-and-only offspring, sir. . . . Another hundred years she gets it all, that's to say, I get it all. . . . Well, don't that count for nothing in this world, sir? . . . Besides! What do I have against the woman, anyway? No, you tell me, sir, what do I have against her?"

"Yes, well, I am inclined to agree. What *do* you have against the woman, anyway?"

"Man alive!" said he. "What about the doctor!? Seems you forgot all about the doctor, sir. Because as long as I see the doctor, I cannot stomach looking at the woman!"

"Well, if that's so," I said, "you really must divorce."

"Well, yes, I reckon," said he. "Only what of the practical side? Seems you forgot all about the practical side, sir. I mean, what's a young gent such as myself to do in hard times like these? Well, go ahead and tell me, sir, because I should like to know!"

"Well, in that case," I said, "I suppose divorce is out."

"Divorce out? But the doctor! Because as long as . . ."

"Why, then, divorce it is!" I said, thinking to make an end.

"Divorce? But the practical side! Man alive . . ."

"Well, then, for God's sake, don't divorce!"

"But what of the doctor?"

I don't know what came over me then. For the blood had suddenly rushed to my head and I was in a blind rage and I had taken my young visitor by the throat and was pressing him against the wall and screaming uncontrollably at him:

"Divorce her, you horrible little man! Divorce her! Divorce her! Divorce her!!!"

Our outcries had brought the entire house rushing to our side. "Goodness, what is wrong? What has happened?" "Oh, nothing! Really, it was nothing!" Though catching a glimpse of my livid features reflected in the glass, I scarcely took them for my own and was next apologizing profusely to my visitor, pressing both his hands in mine and craving of him over and over to put the unpleasantness between us out of his mind. "It happens sometimes," I said, "that a man may be put out of humor." My young visitor, still shaken and confused, allowed as how if a man loses a grip on himself, he is sometimes put out of humor. . . . And executing the same mincing reverence he had made me upon entering, he took his departure now: the same retreat of a couple of paces, the same bow from the waist, the same rubbing of palm in palm: "Your pardon if I have presumed on your time, sir, but I am most beholden to you for your advice, sir. . . . Deeply beholden, sir. . . . Well, good-bye, sir!"

"Not at all, sir, not at all. . . . And Godspeed."

Joseph

The "Gent's" Story

Oh, have your little joke. Go ahead, do a lampoon of me, make it a dashed whole book, if you wish—because you don't scare me. I want that made clear at the outset. Because I'm not the sort of a chap that scares easily. Writers don't scare me, I'll have you know. And, no, I don't go all grovely and weak-kneed in front of a fella only because he's a doctor, nor truckle to him because he's a lawyer, and if you was to tell me a chap's been studying to be an engineer, I'd be the last to drool over him on account of it. Because I've put in my time studying, too. Was a student myself once, y'know. Not that I finished. But that's only because of a scrape I got into over a girl. Fell in love with me, don't you know. Head over heels. Well, I'm a good-looking enough fella for it, always have been. Swore to do herself in, she did, if I didn't have her. Swallow poison, she said. But I wasn't any more interested in marrying the girl than, say, you might be. Well, now, it wasn't as if she was the only fish come to net, if you take my meaning. . . . But the thing had got out of hand, and one of her brothers stepped in then. Fella was a licensed chemist at a pharmacy, don't you know. Said if his sister was to swallow poison, *he'd* know what to do. Had just the thing to splash me with, he said. . . . So I had to take the gal. Worst three years I ever spent. Wanted just two things of me: keep at home and keep the old eye from roving. . . . So how d'ye like that for a bargain, eh? Well, it's not my fault God made me with a face that drives all the women and the girls wild. What's that you say? . . . Good God, no! . . . Why, no, there isn't "any more" to it! Fall in love with me, y'see. End of story. Finis. You know, wherever I go—I mean to say, I'll be getting off the train at some place? Well, they'll be all over me, like bees at the old jam jar: marriage-broker chaps, oh, just hordes of 'em, buzzing about, pestering the life out of me. And why's that? I mean, here I am your progressive, modern young chap really: good looks, good health, good name, good income, scads of the old ready, which I don't much mind parting with, nor miss any if I do, et cetera, et cetera. So it's only to be expected I'd be fair game, now, isn't it? Well, y'don't suppose I intend to let them have their way? "Leave off," I tell 'em, "Already got my fingers burnt once.". . . . But they only persist then, saying, "So where's the harm in looking a new girl over?" . . . Well, now, what chap turns down an offer like that? So here I am, looking girls over in the meantime, and the gals look me over, all of 'em at each other's throats, always clutching at me, clinging to me like limpets, hanging on for dear life, I tell you, for that's only the God's honest truth. They all want me, every one of them. But what good is it to me, all of them wanting me, if I don't want any of them? Because nobody but myself knows of the one I want. . . . So that's my trouble, y'see. It's what I've been meaning to tell you about. Ask a small favor first, though. Keep it amongst ourselves. Mum's the word, eh? You, me, the lamppost. Much the best way. Oh, not on my own account! Good God, no. I've already told you. Don't give two hoots myself about being "characterized," as you fellas call it. Not much point, though, in letting the thing get about, now is there. . . . Well, that's settled, then. So I'll get down to telling my story.

Now, I'm sure you appreciate why I shall say nothing to you about who the girl is or where she is from. I'll allow, though, she is female. Young. Beautiful. Mind you, no money. None whatsoever. Half an orphan, you see. Lost her dad. Lives with the mother, don't you know. Your young widow-lady type. Quite the looker herself, by the way. Keeps a Jewish restaurant. Kosher. Oh, about that: well, I confess, for all I'm your progressive modern chap really, good income, scads of the old ready I don't much mind parting with nor miss if I do, et cetera, I make it a point to eat kosher. Oh, it's nothing to do with being observant. Good God, no! Don't entertain the least scruple anent your grunting livestock myself. Sensible regard for the old turn is all it is, really. That's one reason. Besides, you'll agree Jewish dishes are far and away the tastiest. . . . Anyway, keeps a restaurant. The widow, that is. Does all the cooking on the premises herself, don't you know. Daughter serves. Though what cooking, what service! I tell you it's a song! It sparkles, it gleams! Sheer paradise, eating there. But the pleasure's not in the eating so much as in feasting your eyes on the mother and daughter both. Toss-up, don't you know, which one is the more beautiful. Eyeful, if ever there was one, that woman. Seeing her standing at the stove, cooking, bustling about, don't you know, never a hair out of place, always as fresh as the morning dew. Face as fair as the newly fallen snow; hands and arms, gold and silver; eyes, burning coals, passionate, fiery. . . . Oh, you can take my word for it, a man might easily fall in love with that woman still. . . . So you can only imagine what that little girl of hers must look like. . . . Well, now, I don't know how well-versed you are in the subject yourself. That's to say, in the subject of girls. Though as for the daughter, now there's a treat! Perfect little face, don't you know: peaches and cream complexion; soft dimply cheeks like two cream puffs; eyes like black cherries; silken hair; teeth like orient pearls; neck, throat, alabaster; sweetest little hands, with fingers, knuckles, palms, wrists all made for kissing; rosebud mouth, with that sort of a Cupid's bow upper lip, has that delicious little lift to it, don't you know, like a child's—oh, surely, you must know the sort of thing I mean! The girl's a picture. Perfect picture, I tell you. Chiseled is what I call it. Everything prinked out and polished smooth—exactly like one of those dainty porcelain figures that gets set out on the mantelpiece as if to say, "There, bust a gut feasting the old peepers on that awhile, sonny!" . . . And to boot, she has got her own kind of a tinkly laugh that sets her dimples a-playing Bo-peep in her cheeks, which alone is worth the price of a meal. Because when she is set to laughing, everything laughs along with her: you, the table, the chairs, the walls—why, life itself laughs along. That's the sort of laugh she has got. Well, you try an eyeful of that for a spell yourself sometime and see if you can learn to hate it!

But why should I go on boring you with this when the simple truth of the matter is that, nearly from the first afternoon I began taking my meals there, I just knew I was done for. Goose cooked, so to speak. Spitted, basted, and roasted, don't you know. Smitten. Head over heels! Though, concerning myself and gals? Well, I suppose you know all about that by now, anyway, without any of my prompting. I mean, I'm not exactly your sort that goes about putting girls on a pedestal, now, am I? And as for that silly business about "love"—or "romance," if you prefer—well, never took any stock in it myself, I'm afraid. Bagatelle's all it is, really. Just so: it's there, so why not have a crack at it, is what I say. I mean to say, all's fair in love and war, and all that. But for a chap to blow his brains out over such a thing—pish! Now, that's plain foolish. Sort of thing a schoolboy will go and do, don't you know, not a grown man.

Well, now, seeing as how I was smitten, I took the old mum aside. Mind you, not to, as you say, "ask for her hand." Oh, nothing like that. Good God, no! Y'know, I'm not your precipitous sort of a chap, to snap a thing up first instant it's offered. . . . Nothing wrong, though, is there, with taking an idle turn now and then round Ye Olde Shoppe, as it were. Give the merchandise the once-over, don't you know. . . . Anyway, had a word with the mum, looking to get the lie of the land, so to speak, test the waters, and so forth, "So how do matters stand anent your daughter, madam?" said I. "Well, now, that would depend on what you meant by how matters stood, wouldn't it, sir," said she. "What I meant, madam," said I, "was practically speaking. Future, and all that, don't you know." . . . "Oh, well," said she, "not much to worry about on that head, I shouldn't think. It's quite settled, you know.". . . Well, I confess, hearing that gave me quite a turn. So I said: "What do you mean, it's quite settled?". . . "Why, sir," said she, looking past me then, "you can judge for yourself about how matters stand, as you say. For here's our little worrywart now." . . . And no sooner were the words out than *she* appeared, the daughter herself, that is, in person, just lighting up the whole place, don't you know, like the sun in the morning.

"Mummy, have you seen Joseph?" she said. And when she said the name, Joseph, she pronounced it with that odd sort of a tuneful glide. Like a song. The way a gal might call to her "intended," don't you know. . . . At least, so it seemed to me; no, that's to say, I'm quite sure it was so. And not only this one time I'm telling of, but always, whenever she said the name, it came out with that same tuneful little glide: "Jo-seph." Know what I mean? Not plain: "Joseph!" More like: "Jo-seph."

Well, I mean, it seemed all you ever heard that girl say was "Jo-seph," over and over again, "Jo-seph." I mean, here we'd all be sitting down to table, and the first thing out of her mouth was "Where's Jo-seph?" . . . "Joseph won't be in today" . . . "Joseph said" . . . "Joseph wrote" . . . "Joseph came." . . . "Joseph went" . . . "Joseph sent" . . . Joseph-Joseph, Joseph-Joseph! Well, I must say, I was grown pretty impatient by now to get a look at this "Joseph" fella for myself, finally take the chap's measure, don't you know.

So not unnaturally I came to detest this "Joseph" chap. Oh, absolutely hated the fella sight unseen, don't you know. Though, what had I to do with him, anyway? God knows! Some perfectly horrid little twit, no doubt, boon companion, probably, to that set of snots that always hung about the place, one of the "bu-oys," as she used to call 'em, with that tinkly laugh of hers. "The bu-oys"! This title quite suited them, y'know. Oh, to an absolute T. I mean, that's all they were, really. Bunch of schoolbu-oys! Queer little chaps, though, most of 'em. The sort that likes letting their hair grow and favors those vulgar long black peasant blouses.[1] You know, with the high collar which buttons at the side and the shirttails hanging out and that silly cord knotted round the middle? Just the sort of getup I hate. . . . Oh. Meaning no offense! Though I see where you, too, seem to like wearing your hair long and have got the same kind of black blouse on. Well, if you think that's stylish, you are dead wrong, sir. Dinner jacket and white waistcoat's the thing. Infinitely nicer, I'll have you know. Take my word for it. Wouldn't trade them for all the blessings in the world. . . . Now, speaking for myself, whenever I catch sight of chaps wearing long black blouses like that with their shirttails flapping loosely about their bottoms (asking your pardon), the first picture comes into my mind is a worn-out trouser seat. . . . Think I didn't tell them so to their faces? I most certainly did! Because I'm the sort of a chap that prefers being aboveboard, don't you know. Oh, absolutely. None of your bootlickers, I! Why, you'll never catch *me* sucking up to a fella. Not ever. And if, say, you had something bad to say about me? Well, you'd be free to spit it out, say it right to my face. One thing I won't abide, though. That's being called "bourgeois." Because anybody calls me bourgeois risks getting a pretty stiff biff in the old mazzard. . . . I mean, in what way am I bourgeois? Why, I am any man's equal in that department. I am up on everything, and I keep abreast of everything. Why, I'll have you know, I read all the latest magazines and take in all your modern, progressive-type newspapers, like everybody else—so how am I bourgeois then? Is it because I happen to have on a neat white waistcoat and dinner jacket, while you go about in that black blouse with your shirttail hanging out? Oh, not yourself! Good God, no. I didn't mean you, but only that unsavory lot of "bu-oys" I've been telling you about and their ilk, and that "Jo-seph" chap and his. . . . Anyway, held converse enough with the lot of 'em, whilst at the board together, so to speak, by way of table talk, as it were, and of a kind which gave me pretty well to understand they were about as taken with me as I was with them. You know: "Heart to heart e'er listeth," that old song? Well, never you mind. Because as far as the business of baring

1. The narrator is describing the so-called Gorky shirt worn by leftists to show their solidarity with the peasants; Sholem Aleichem also wore this garb, as Y. D. Berkovitsh attests in his biographical reminiscences. See "Memories of Sholem Aleichem," below, "With the Family of Writers," section 1. In *Ha-rish'onim ki-vnei-adam*, chapter 15, Berkovitsh notes that Sholem Aleichem wrote this story immediately after visiting his daughter in Vilna—where the Jewish Socialist Party (the Bund) was especially active in 1905.

one's soul went—well, I didn't much see myself as being under any obligation in the way of such intimacies. Anyway, not vis-à-vis that lot. Though, apropos, I will confess to doing a bit of cozying up, used some of the old largess to buy my way into their good graces, as it were, try and get myself in with them, so to speak. Oh, not on their account! Good God, no. More on account of that "Joseph" chap, and not so much on his account either, as on account of her; I mean to say, on the gal's account. Well, it did eat away at me considerably, y'know, her mooning over him all of the time the way she did. Anyway, made myself a promise: if it was the last thing I did, whatever the cost, whatever the reckoning, come what may and damn the consequences— I must, no, shall! make the acquaintance of this "Joseph" personage. And don't think I didn't manage it, what's more. Because, now, I'm the sort of a chap, when he sets his mind to a thing, will allow nothing to stand in his way. Though, mind you, money's no object with me, either! Well, now, I mean, after all, here I am your young man of commerce, prosperous chap really, good income, scads of the old ready I don't much mind parting with nor miss any if I do, et cetera.

Though, now, pretty obviously, the business of buying my way in with that lot wasn't as easy as you may think. Had to proceed in easy stages at first, don't you know, one step at a time. So I set things rolling by sticking the occasional oar in from the sidelines, as it were, though always mindful of giving out with the mournful sigh or cluck of sympathy now and again, anent parlous times—oh, you know the sort of thing: days of trouble, public weal, and so forth—and letting it be known that in *such matters*, when push came to shove, money was no object, certainly not where I was concerned, no, sir, because, well, after all, I mean to say, it was only right for a chap to toss out a bit of the old ready if it's in a worthy cause. Well, I expect you know what I meant just now by "tossing out" a bit of the ready. See, now, there's your sort of a chap that will "toss" his money out whilst another only *takes* his out. Well, I mean, you'll agree there is a difference there. Y'see, "tossing out" the old ready is when a chap will dig down for a bit of Ye Olde Coine of the Realm, giving it a careless toss with an air as if to say, "Here y'are, my good fellow, *pas de quoi*, I'm sure—and dash the cost!" See, now, that's how I like going about things. Oh, but don't get me wrong, now! Not always. Good God, no. No, what I mean is, only when it's wanted. And when what's wanted is, say, for you to be forking out a twenty-fiver or half a century or, say, a cool hundred, well, you absolutely cannot allow the old hand to tremble. No, sir. Not a tremor.

Well, I mean, suppose you are dining out with a party of chaps, say, it was for lunch, or supper maybe, and the reckoning's been brought round, and you pick up the tab. Well, now, what you must do is flash a quick look at what's called your "bottom line," the while talking airily of this and that, don't you know, and then when they bring round your change next, well, you must never stop to count it, like a market woman selling onions out of a basket, but must sweep it up without looking and toss it into your pocket straight away. End of story. Finis. Y'see, life's a school which you must get through, learn to make your way in, so to speak. I mean to say, one has got to *know* how to live. And if there is one thing I pride myself on, it's that I know how to live. Because it's all a question of knowing when to do a thing and when not to do it and how much. I mean to say, you won't ever catch *me* overbidding my hand, and I defy anybody to read my cards from my face, so to speak, make fish or fowl of me, as it were. I mean, you ought to have seen me amongst that lot of "bu-oys" then. Why, you'd never in a million years have guessed I wasn't one of the "bu-oys" myself. Oh, absolutely looked the part! Not that I ever let my hair grow long or took to wearing peasant blouses or anything like that. Good God, no! Had on the same trusty old dinner jacket and white waistcoat then as now. Only difference was, I let on like I was interested in everything they were interested in, and talked about the same things they talked about: "Proletariat" . . . "Bebel" . . . "Marx" . . . "Reacting," and so on . . . anyway words of that sort, which I bunged into the conversation every time they got to talking. Funny thing though. The more I tried cozying up to them, the more they seemed put off by it. I mean to say, any time I'd try on some of that patter, you know: "Proletariat" . . . "Bebel" . . . "Marx" . . . "Reacting," and so on, anyway words of that sort, I noticed how they'd suddenly go very quiet then and be exchanging funny looks and pick away at their teeth the while. . . . Oh, and another thing! I noticed, too, how when it came to money, they would all take from me gladly enough. Like on Mondays and Thursdays, when they'd be putting one of their concerts on, don't you know? Well, without fail, I was always the first brand snatched from the pyre, as it were. "Now, surely," they'd say, "the Gent wishes himself to be put down for a front-row seat tonight. Usual three rubles, sir?"

"The Gent"—that was the only name they ever knew me by. So, naturally, "the Gent" had to fork out three rubles every Monday and Thursday for a ticket. Well, I mean, it wasn't as if I had any choice, now, was it? Which, I suppose, is why every time the "Gent" walked in on the "bu-oys" in the middle of one of their powwows, a great hush would fall over the proceedings then. Mum's the word, don't you know. Could have heard a pin drop! . . . Well, pretty obviously this got the "Gent" fairly pipped, oh, just seething, if you know what I mean, mad as all get out, in fact. Problem was, though, what to do about it. But, as I said, I'm the sort of a chap, when he's got hold of a notion, never counts the cost. Sky's the absolute limit then. So I pulled all the stops out this time, plugged away for so long and hard at buttering 'em up, don't you know, until I managed finally to work myself in amongst them, or at least sufficiently anyhow, for them to consent to letting me attend one of their "discussions," as they called it—at which time, they said, this "Joseph" chap himself would be holding forth before one and all then. . . . Now, you have no idea how happy that made me. I mean, to be allowed to see the fella at last, and actually to hear him speak!

Though about when and where this discussion was supposed to take place—you'd never have got a peep out of them, even if you asked. And I can't say I much cared to ask, either. Because I only reckoned they'd come round to telling me in the fullness of time anyway, sooner or later, so why bother? I mean, these chaps set very great store by secrecy. Throve on it, you might say. Had their own special word for it, too: "conspirashun." That's what they called it. Made a point of memorizing the word myself. Here, see? Even wrote it down in my notebook. Because, see now, I'm the sort of a chap, when he hears a fine word, will jot it down straight away, make a note of it, don't you know. Well, maybe you can't really tell if it will come in useful or not, only neither will you lose by it either is what I say.

Anyway, upshot came one fine summer's day, Saturday it was, when two of the "bu-oys" breezed round without warning, beetled in by the front door, in black blouses, as per usual, and tipped me the nod: "Come!" they said. "Where to?" I asked. "What's it matter to you?" they answered. "Just follow along, and we'll see you get there." . . . Well, that was that. Had to tag along with them, you see. . . . So we all pushed off then, trudging along together to way past the edge of town and, fetching up at the woods beyond, we plunged in amongst the trees and then trudged along some more together, and every so often we'd come across one or another of the "bu-oys," seated under a tree alone and staring off into space, making out he wasn't paying us any mind, you see, though the instant we got abreast of him, he'd shoot us a side-mouthed whisper, "Go right!" or "Go left!". . . . Now, I'd look pretty foolish, saying I was scared then. I mean, after all, what harm could come to a fella at the hands of only a couple of Jewish chaps, anyhow? Safe as houses, really, when you come to think about it. Thing is, though, it did put me off. Wanted dignity, don't you know. Well, I mean to say, here I am your young man of business, chap of substance, really: good name, good income, scads of the old ready I don't much mind parting with nor miss if I do, et cetera, letting myself be led about by a pair of snotty school kids, mere "bu-oys"! If you get my drift.

Well, cut a story short, we walked and we walked and we walked some more, and then we walked some more after that. And, just as I was beginning to wonder if our little woodland jaunt should ever end, we struck a very considerable hill. Which it was only after we clambered up to the top of and had cleared the rise and then begun our descent that I beheld such a great crowd of heads as fairly blackened all of the ground below: oh, just a sight of "bu-oys," don't you know, young chaps in black blouses, squatting down on the bare earth, and gals, too, who had got themselves up in the feminine variety of the garment and then a whole bunch of just ordinary young people mixed in with them. I mean, you wouldn't believe the turnout! Must have been all of three thousand there, easy. Maybe more. And quiet? Not a whisper! Even the flies had quit their buzzing. And we crept in amongst the crowd of heads then and sat down on the ground, and I took to searching the faces, thinking I might spot this "Joseph" chap in the meantime. And then I saw. . . . Well, I mean, you'll never guess! Chap who I dare say I was acquainted with well enough by now. One of that lot of "bu-oys" I'd been eating at the widow's with all along. Damndest thing, y'know!

I remember thinking, This it? . . . Nah, can't be! . . . This all of him? This, the "Joseph" fella? . . . And here all along I'd thought he had to be God knows what. Horns maybe! . . . Though, if you must know, it was a sight that almost gave me pleasure—no, I mean *real* pleasure, at the way things had turned out. . . . Y'see, I began stacking myself up against him. Mind! Not that I have such a high regard of my own person as to think there wasn't anybody handsomer than myself. Good God, no! Well, I mean to say, I'm not so blind as all that! I know very well that you are apt to find chaps handsomer than myself around. Only compared to *him*. . . . Well, I suppose you know what I'm driving at. . . . I mean, if you like, I can describe for you exactly what he looked like when I first caught sight of him. Stood leaning against a tree, I recall. Slight, pale little fella on the whole, mainly: gaunt, wasted, narrow chested, with hollow white cheeks that were a mite flushed, you know, like high-colored about the bone, and a growth of tiny fair-haired stubble about the chops; impressive high forehead, though, broad, absolutely white; oh, and gray eyes, like a cat's, except they were het-up, intense, don't you know; and a mouth—my God, how it talked! But dammit, I'm hanged if I know where the little fella got his strength from to talk so loud and so fast and for so long and with such a heat and such fire and such passion! I mean, this wasn't any of your ordinary talk. Inhuman, that's what it was. Devil's work. Had to be, or some dashed infernal machine someone had wound up to talk like that somehow or they'd put up a device overhead, which the words gushed out of and it shot flames into the air, or maybe it was really the tree that was doing the talking. . . . And the whole while I kept imagining how any minute this runty little bagabones with the hollow flushed cheeks and gray eyes might work up such a terrific head of stream with his talking as suddenly to lift up off the ground and then phut! go hurtling off somewhere into the blue, words and all. . . . No. You may say what you will! For I tell you I have been privileged in my lifetime to hear some of the best lawyers in the country plead before the bench and never have I heard anything to beat it, or even come near, nor I ever shall, I suppose.

I can't say how long he talked. Never even looked at my watch. I only looked at him and at the crowd of heads seated on the ground, gulping down every word the same as it was meat and drink to the hungry and thirsty. . . . But nobody who hadn't seen *her* on that day can truly say he ever saw something fine and splendid in all his life. I picked her out at length from amid all that crowd of heads, sitting on the ground with her feet tucked underneath her and her hands folded, palms down, on her breast: her face shone, her cheeks flamed, and her upper lip parted from the lower with a little lift, like a child's, and her black cherry eyes were smiling only at him—smiled only at *him* y'see. . . . No, I won't deny it. I became jealous of him then. Oh, not just because of how he talked. Good God, no! Y'see it wasn't his gift of the gab so much, nor even the rattling reception afterwards with all the cheering and hand clapping he got when he was through. No, it wasn't for any of these things that I was so jealous as for her way of looking at him then. I mean, *how* she looked at him. Oh, I'd have given anything for such a look from her! Because that look spoke words, you know. For it seemed to me I heard her voice in it, speaking with that same tuneful glide it always had, when she said, "Joseph!" Though, as I said earlier, I'm not your sort that goes about putting girls on a pedestal. What I mean is, well, after all, I have known my fair share of gals, y'know, seeing as how I'm not half bad-looking, as I think I can safely say, as being also your progressive, modern chap, really: good income, scads of the old ready which I don't much mind parting with nor miss any if I do, et cetera. . . . But even my wife had never looked at me in such a way as *that*, not in our salad days even, when she still loved me, worshiped the ground I walked on, so to say. . . . I had a mind then to get up and walk straight over to her, plump myself down beside her, which I in fact did, or sat down close enough, anyhow, to be bobbing and twitching about in plain view of her the whole while, like a fly buzzing at her ear or a mosquito maybe—only the lady wasn't buying! No such luck. Because twitch and bob as I might, her eyes never once strayed from *his* eyes, hanging on to them, sucking at them like a pair of leeches, and his eyes, too, only hung on hers. And it seemed to me that both of them, that's to say, *he and she both,* saw nobody but each other then, *needed* nobody but each other. Oh, it was agony! I can't begin to tell you what a rage I was put into. Though I hardly knew who it was I was raging at so. Was it at "her" or at "him" or at them both? Or was it myself I was raging at. . . . And at night, when I came home, my head hurt awfully, and I went to bed, promising myself I should never cross the widow's threshold again. I'd as soon see all of them in perdition as go back! Because who needed these people, anyway? I mean, am I right, or am I right? . . . But when I got up the next morning it was all I could do to wait for the hour, no, the very minute, when two o'clock rolled around again, so it might be lunchtime once more. And don't think I didn't go back either nor run into the same crowd of "bu-oys" there at the board together, same as always, and *him* amongst them. . . . I don't know about you, but me when I see a celebrated "artiste," say, or a government minister or just some famous person or other, well, even if we all may know he's human, like everybody else, that he eats and drinks, as it were, like everybody eats and drinks—only no sooner I am told the same chap is an artiste, say, or government minister or just some famous person or other, than I immediately think he is *not* like everybody else, that there is something special about him which you cannot really put your finger on, if you follow me. . . . Well, that was how it was with me when I saw *him* again, that's to say, after that tub-thumping oration; seemed pretty much the same old fella on the whole, just another of the "bu-oys" same as before, yet not *quite* the same. Something about him. Like maybe an air or special mark of favor stamped on his face. Anyway, something. Though, as to what that something was exactly, hanged if I could tell you what it was even now! Still, I'd give anything to have it. Oh, not that I need it! Good God, no. Dashed if I need it! I mean, why would I want such a thing for, anyhow? No, the reason I wanted it at all then was only on account of *her*, because she couldn't keep away from *him* for a minute, you see, and even when she came over to talk to me for a bit, it was always only *him* she was thinking about anyway, never about me. Well, see now, I'm an expert about such matters, I'll have you know. I mean, God knows, I've paid dues enough for it by now. . . . Anyway, I was in hell all over again. Because earlier, you see, that's to say before I actually knew who Joseph was, I'd painted him up in my mind as being this great big handsome strapping chap, *manly*, don't you know; yes, that's the word I want, definitely manly. Couldn't stick the fella then, y'see. Envied and hated him at the same time, I mean to say. Only now that I'd found out just *who* this fine figure of a man so-called really was, that he was only another "bu-oy," no different from the rest of the "bu-oys," if you fellow me—well, it absolutely gave me the pip. No, I mean *really* upset me. . . . Though I can scarcely say who I was upset with most. I mean was it with *her*, for idolizing him so (because you'd have had to have been half blind not to see how she absolutely idolized him!), or was it with *him*, for God having so bounteously bestowed on him such a great thumping power of the gift of the gab, or was it really myself I was so upset with, for not having the same gift of the gab as him? . . . Not that I have a great need of the commodity myself, mind! Good God, no. I mean, what would *I* be wanting it for anyhow? Well, I mean to say, it's not as if I was altogether helpless in that department. Far from it! Me, when I want to hold forth—well, you just see if I can't do it. Why, I even spoke before a pretty fair-size audience once, and that was at a meeting of the Merchants' Club, I'll have you know. And just about everybody that was there said I hadn't spoken badly at all then, not badly a-tall! . . . Though about me being so upset. Well, now, I can't really describe it for you in so many words. You have got to experience it—no, you have got to *feel* it, for you'd have had to be in my shoes then, have gone into that establishment every day, have watched *her* every day, have seen her go about every day in that trim little white apron that shimmered when she walked, have seen her bright pretty face, seen how it glowed, how it sang, have heard her sweet voice that perked up a body like a healing cordial, heard her tinkly laugh that went all through and through you and then just settled in amongst your vitals, and to have seen *him*, then, and have known that the whole performance first to last had been only for *his* sake all along, all for his sake and for no one else! No, he'd have to be got rid of somehow, got out of the way. But how to do it, now y'see *that* was the question. Well, of course, I wasn't about to poison him or shoot him. I mean after all I'm no murderer, and it's not exactly the sort of thing a Jewish chap goes about doing anyway. . . . Challenge the fella to a duel? Faugh! Storybook stuff. It's what they do in novels. Don't believe a word of it myself. I mean, it's all only done "for effect," now, isn't it? Makes the story more interesting, don't you know. . . . Anyway, that's my opinion. . . . But I finally did come up with an idea. Pretty fair one, too, I thought. Now, what if I took him aside, had a word with him in private. Like, what's the adage? "Make a thief keeper of the key." . . . Sharp, eh? I mean, what could be safer? Anyhow, you may be sure I didn't waste any bother thinking it over—because frankly I don't much hold with thinking too long about things, anyway—and first opportunity after dinner once, I said to him:

"Y'know, I've a proposition I've been meaning to put to you. Matter of mutual interest, so if you'll oblige me?"

But him? Fella never moved a muscle. Oh, not him! Just dumb-quizzed me with that set of deadpan gray eyes as if to say: I'm game, son, so what's the pitch?

"No," I said, "No, no, not in here. Keep it amongst ourselves. You, me, the lamppost, eh? Much the best way."

"Come!" he said, and led me out into the street and turned around facing me, waiting as if to say: Well? Come on, out with it, son.

"Not out here," I said. "Oh, I say, when are you usually in?"

"I can be at your place," he began; but then pulled up sharp and said: "Though if you'd rather. . . . All right, my place, then, say——" and he pulled out his watch, "say, morning, nine thirty, half past ten, tomorrow? . . . Here, take my address."

And so saying, he clasped my hand, gripping it, and he looked me straight in the eye as if to say, "conspirashun," eh?

"Oh, absolutely! Conspirashun it is." I said, "You may count on it!" And with that we parted, each to his own repose, so to speak.

Though you can well imagine I hardly got a wink of sleep. Put me in an awful fret, y'know, thinking what I should say to him. Where would I even begin? I mean, what if he was to say:

"Now, see here, Sir Gent, or Mr. Whatsyerface, where do you come off butting into business that's not your own? And what sort of a suitor are you anyway, Sir Gent Mr. Whatsyerface, to be courting a girl whom one of us 'buoys' has been pleased to regard as his intended since away back when?"

I mean, what can you say to a thing like that? Or suppose he laid violent hands on me and heaved me down the stairs. What would I do then? Mind you, not that I was scared. Good God, no! I mean why would I be scared of him, anyway? All I meant was to put a proposition to him. Take it or leave it: Y'want? So take! — Y'don't? So don't! End of story. Finis. No. Hardly a cause for mayhem, though, is it!

And that's how I spent the night in tortured musings anent this and that, and nine thirty prompt the next morning found me clumping upstairs to a poky, dashed-to-all-dammit garret somewhere on a top-floor landing where he lived — I mean, there must have been two or three hundred steps to the thing, easy — and, presenting myself at his door, I saw I was in luck and he was in. Him plus a bonus of two "bu-oys" besides, who were exchanging funny looks, as if to say, Now, what business d'ye suppose the "Gent" might have here? But my little bird tipped them the wink, which the "bu-oys" were quick enough on the uptake to accept, and they took up their caps and made themselves scarce.

So the pair of us being alone, just him, me, and the lamppost, as it were, I commenced pouring it on, full tide from the pulpit, so to speak, giving him an earful: Well, y'know, blah blah, this, that, anyway in a nutshell, I'm a chap on his own, single fella, don't you know, though, notwithstanding, I'm only your commercial sort, simple man of business really, good name, good income, scads of the old ready I don't mind parting with nor miss if I do, et cetera, still and all I keep abreast, right on top of things, your *progressive* type, if that's the word I want, modern chap really, know everything, read all the latest newspapers and magazines — and I went and unreeled the whole spiel of funny words then: "Proletariat" . . . "Bebel" . . . "Marx" . . . "Reacting" . . . "Conspirashun," and so on, anyway, words of that sort. Well, he heard me out. Though I must say he was dashed civil and polite in answering. Modest, you know. None of your high-flown talk, came straight to the point, saying,

"Yes, well, how can I be of use to you?"

"Oh, a small matter," I said, "I want your advice."

"Advice? . . . From me? . . . You?"

And so saying he dumb-quizzed me with his deadpan gray eyes as if to say, Where does a li'l bit of a chap as myself come to be giving advice to such a swell gent as yourself? . . . Y'see, he was beginning to feel a mite, what's the word I want? Yes, ill at ease. Distinctly ill at ease. Come to that, so was I feeling ill at ease. Only what was I to do? Die already cast, so to speak. I mean, I'd already plunged in, so I had to follow the thing through to the end. So I commenced unburdening, laying my griefs at his feet, confessed all that was in my heart from the minute I laid eyes on her, even to this day, my life has been an absolute agony, haven't known a moment's rest, y'see, that's to say, *she* won't give me any rest! . . . "I mean, I should never have believed," I said to him, "not in a million years, that over a mere gal, I mean to say, even if she was the Grand Duchess herself, that I should be so, so—now, what's that word I want?—yes, should be 'Reacting' so, because, well, dash it all, notwithstanding I'm your modern sort, that's to say progressive, still and all I'm a man of business really, commercial chap pretty much, good income, scads of the old ready I don't much mind parting with nor miss any if I do, et cetera."

Well, he heard me out. Though dashed civil and polite in answering, I must say. Modest, y'know. None of your high-flown talk, came straight to the point, saying,

"Yes, well, if you want my advice, I think you might start by talking with the girl yourself." . . .

"Yes, but what about you?" I said.

"Oh, I don't want—" he began, but then pulled up sharp and said, "Well, I can't, you see, I haven't the time to concern myself with such things."

"Oh, I say, you don't think—" I said. "No, but that's not what I meant at all! I'm not asking you to have a word with her on my behalf. I mean, how could I? I only wanted to know what *you* have to say about it."

"Yes, well, what *can* I say?" he said. "Should your feelings toward her be reciprocated, why, then, I imagine. . ."

And so saying he came straight to the point and pulled out his watch—none of your high-flown talk, mind, only civil like and polite, as if to say, Well, I did so enjoy our little chat. Though as regards that business with the watch, I dare say I'm familiar enough with it. Should be, y'know. Apt to use the same dodge myself when I want to get shut of a fella. Trouble is, some chaps never take the hint. Slow to catch on. Well, as it happens, I'm not, and, getting to my feet, I beseeched him to keep this little matter amongst ourselves, under the old hat, mum's the word, eh, that's to say "conspirashun," and took my departure. Well, what can I say but glad's a dirty dog next to what I was feeling then. Joyful? Pooh, not even close, I was in seventh—no, by God, in seventieth heaven! I tell you, I felt like hugging and kissing everybody I met along the way. Everything and everybody seemed to me all at once to have the most extraordinary charm I never noticed before. To say nothing of Joseph! Because I came to love him like a brother that day, no, really, as dearly as my own brother. Why, if only I hadn't been so shy, I'd have turned round and gone back and kissed him, and if I wasn't afraid of offending him, I should have brought a present along, a gold watch with a smart *breloque* and a chain.

But my good spirits got the better of me in the end, and I went to the club. I like looking in at the club in what's called the shank of the afternoon, mainly. Not that I like playing cards myself. Good God, no. I never play cards myself. Though I like watching others play, and once in a great while, that's to say very-very occasionally, I take a sporting interest in a chap's hand and will put down what you call your "kibitzer's stakes" on him, in which case it's one or the other: either you win big, or you lose big. Well, this time I won handsomely. Oh, absolutely on velvet. I mean, you talk about the cards coming a fella's way! Well, I gathered up my winnings and gave Ye Olde "Bummer's Mob" a hail—which is the name chaps at the club go by who have been relieved of their pocket money—and stood champagne dinner all around, had the good stuff brought up, too, that's to say, Rederer's Champagne Wine, and when I came home it was well on to midmorning, and there was a telegram sitting on my desk calling me away urgently on business. Well, you know how it is with us "gents-at-trade" chaps. The minute we get the summons, it's over. End of story. Finis. Drop everything and dash the rest, as we like to say. Off like a shot, y'know.

Well, I left thinking I'd be gone for two days, but, of course, I was away for three weeks, and first thing I got back I made straight for the restaurant to eat and found the place in a turmoil. Of the "bu-oys" there wasn't a sign, and such as were still about looked considerably short of their usual chipper selves, if you know what I mean: distraught mainly, uncommonly so, all of a dither, don't you know. Made short work of their meal, too, eating on their feet, as you might say, and then moped off separately with their heads down, like dogs after a rain, one going this way, the other that way.

But the thing that really set me to wondering, though, was where Joseph was. Why wasn't he around? And looking the "bu-oys" over then, I observed they certainly were acting mightily standoffish for a change, all of a huddle shushing each other the while: ssst-ssst! ssst-ssst! . . . Well, this wasn't just your ordinary conspirashun anymore—it was what you'd call "conspirashun to beat all conspirashun"! . . . And herself, well, she, too, appeared strangely quiet and pensive, quite "conspirashunal" on her own account, I thought. . . .

The flame was gone from her cheek and the smile from her black cherry eyes. And her Bo-peep "kiss-me-sweet" dimples were gone, and her tinkly laugh which when she laughed everything laughed with her: you, the table, the chairs, the walls, life itself laughed along!

Though I suppose you may have already guessed, I wasn't missing this Joseph chap all that much, anyway. . . . Still, I was at my wits' end to know where had he got himself to. And was it for a short time, or was he now well and truly gone? And had he written, or had there been no letters from him at all? Well, you try inquiring about such things of the "bu-oys" — see if they'll favor you with a civil answer. Because they'll only gawp and be picking away at their teeth, as if to say, "Listen, son, you'll grow old pretty quick if you go on wanting to know everything."

But then arriving at the restaurant in the early morning once, I found the "bu-oys" all forgathered there already, sitting around the table, and one of them was reading from the paper and the rest listening raptly to him as he read. Well, I reckoned it was news of Joseph. Knew it right off, y'see. That's to say, I knew it on account of her. Standing apart from the rest, y'know, black cherry eyes and trim white apron, with her hands folded palms down on her breast: her face shone and her cheeks flamed and her upper lip parted from the lower, with a little lift, like a child's — the same as in the woods. . . . Only difference was that her pretty black cherry eyes had gazed upon Joseph then, whereas now they groped for him somewhere far off, but always for him, always for Joseph! . . . Well, cut a long story short, I couldn't wait for the paper to be put down, and I tore it open, and I knew then: MY JOSEPH WAS IN THE SOUP, NECK OR NOTHING NOW!!! . . . Though I'm bound to say I always knew he'd come to a bad end, known it all along, y'see, if not today, then tomorrow — anyway, someday soon he'd be landing himself in the soup, just had to, y'see, inevitable. . . . Though, of course, you couldn't really tell how it would turn out yet, I mean to say, know the exact outcome, but it was pretty much a foregone conclusion, wasn't it, that he wouldn't be let off with just a pat on the head, as you say, never mind being allowed to lick honey or breathe the fair fragrances of Araby for it.

I couldn't even begin to describe to you how I felt then; well, I won't say I was greatly upset because, after all, he'd stood in my way, been an awful thorn in my side, hadn't he. . . . But if I said I was overjoyed, that wouldn't be the whole truth either, now would it? I mean, it's not exactly what you'd have wished on your worst enemy, now is it? No, believe me when I say that I really wished him well with all my heart, wished for his sake that God wrought a miracle somehow, and they wouldn't. . . . Well, you couldn't very well expect that he'd be let off scot-free, could you, because that couldn't be allowed, now could it? Only—well, maybe they'd let him off easy, oh, I don't know, give him a light sentence just for form's sake, maybe? . . . I mean—anyway, I expect you must know what I mean, now don't you?

Well, for the next few days I went about in a fog, not knowing what to do with myself. And when I learned that the business was finally over, thank goodness, and the sentence would be announced on the following day, well, I give you my word, swear solemnly, on my life—which rest assured I hold dear—that I did not, no, could not fall asleep but lay tossing restlessly in my bed for half the night, till finally I got up and tried looking in at the club, not so much for the cards though, good God, no, as thinking maybe it might help me forget, even if for a minute, that . . . because, y'see, I had had a premonition, a feeling, no, I knew, almost for certain, *that it was all up with him now.*

End of story, finis. I went along to the restaurant at the usual hour, and as I approached, two "bu-oys" came tearing out of the door looking greatly discombobulated, I must say. Quite nearly knocked me down! Coming inside, I met two strangers seated at the table, eating. She didn't appear to be serving, for her mum had taken her place. Nor was mum looking any the better for it either, because I'd have laid odds she'd been crying. Well, I'm never one to stand on ceremony, so I called her aside:

"Just wondering, madam, where your daughter might be keeping?"

"In her room," said she, giving a nod over at a hole in the wall with a door hung on it.

We'd been playing an amusing little game me and the mum all along, y'see. Oh, nothing was actually *said* amongst ourselves about the real business in hand, not outright anyhow, I mean, not in so many words. But I took it as read that she wanted the match: y'know, modern chap, good name, good income, scads of the old ready I don't much mind missing, et cetera, so why shouldn't, I mean, why wouldn't she? Well, I should think she would! I mean, I'd already dropped several hints to her, *broad* hints, mind you, that I had conceived quite an interest in her daughter, quite a considerable interest, in fact. Well, I mean, what surer proof was there than I couldn't bear for her to be serving at meals. . . . So what answer you think she made me?

"Can't bear her serving? Well, perhaps serving yourself may suit you better!"

Her very words, the mother's, that is, whipping a naked elbow across her face to wipe it as if to say, "And you can like it or lump it!"

Yes, so where was I? — Hole in the wall with the door. If you were to ask me about letting myself into that small bit of a room she had, how I up and walked in suddenly, and the first thing I said to her, directly when I came in — well, I couldn't say, because I'm hanged anyway if I can recall any of it. No, what I meant to say is I only recall seeing her still wearing the trim white apron she always walked about in, sitting by the window, with her hands folded on her breast, palms down, her face gone pale and her cheeks white without a drop of color in them, and her upper lip parted from the lower, with a little lift to it like a child's, and her black cherry eyes without even a tear but misted over as if groping for something far-far off somewhere, with an air of dumb mourning all about her sweet white brow, wrinkling it a mite with a thoughtful, broody sort of a ripple you'd otherwise never have noticed in it. Oh, I give you my word, sir, swear it solemnly on my life, which rest assured I hold dear, that in that instant she appeared to me so beautiful, so, so — what's the word I want? — so divine, so absolutely divine, I was fit fairly to fling myself down on the ground before her and smother her feet in kisses! . . . Though, catching sight of me, she took no sudden alarm, as I thought she might, nor rose from her place taken aback nor even asked to know what I wanted. So unbidden I took up a stool and sat down facing her and I commenced talking away, talking without pause. The words seemed to come of themselves, came in torrents then, and I just talked, and talked, and talked. Hanged if I even know what I said, only I suppose the gist of it was mainly this. I wanted to console her, buck her up, let her know that it didn't make any sense, her "reacting" so. . . . In plain language, she mustn't take it to heart because, in a word, she was still too young, too fresh, too beautiful for that just yet. . . . I urged that no one could say for certain what the future had in store for her. . . . Well, now, take me, for instance, because here I am your young man of business, modern chap really, good name, good income, scads of the old ready I don't much mind missing, et cetera. . . . I mean, what better proof did she want than that I should be prepared instantly, at her mere word, if she but declared herself willing to forget all that had heretofore transpired, as if none of it ever was, none of your Joseph, none of your "bu-oys," none of your "conspirashun" had ever even existed, all of them gone, end of story, finis.

You know, I haven't a clue as to where I had got such a power of the gab from then. But you think she gave me an answer for my troubles? Oh, forfend! Perish the thought! No, all she did was to only just sit and stare, sit and stare, sit and stare. Though it really beats the daylights out of me what all that sitting and staring signified anyway. Was it: "You really mean it? Oh, it's too grand to be true!" . . . Or, "I shall want the time to think it over, you know" . . . or "Go away!" Or maybe really it was: "Jo-seph" . . . know what I mean? Not plain: "Joseph!" More like: "Jo-seph."

I mean, you simply cannot imagine what a complete ass I felt then. Why, I was too humiliated to show my face for days afterwards! . . . Never mind feeling simply too wretched for words, almost as if I had had a personal hand in any of that ghastly business myself. . . . I mean, try as I might to get the fella out of my mind, absolutely to forget him, that's to say the Joseph chap, it was simply no go—just couldn't do it! . . . Now, it isn't as if I took any stock in dreams myself, because I don't, and certainly dead people have never scared me any, and I most emphatically do not believe in witchcraft, but I swear to you, by all that is holy, not a night has gone by since, that he hasn't appeared to me in a dream, that's to say, Joseph hasn't, and woken me up, pointing with his hand at that, preserve me, that mark like a blue ring, going round and round his throat. . . . You don't *really* think there might be anything to dreams? Because I know for a fact—Well, it did happen to an uncle of mine once that. . . . Oh, let it go! I don't take any stock in dreams, anyway! . . . It's only that I wasn't quite myself, off my feed, don't you know, just couldn't sleep. . . . You wouldn't be thinking I was scared, maybe? Good God, no. But, I mean, after all, chap I knew personally. Broke bread with together, shared the same table with for so long. Well, I mean to say! Anyway, I thought better of it, let the chips fall where they may, so to speak, and directly I'd worked myself up to it, I made straight for the restaurant where I knew I should find them.

Though, coming up to the restaurant—What restaurant? Gone! Premises vacated! Absolutely no sign of the place! "Oh, excuse me (sir, madam), but where is the restaurant?" "Packed off a couple of days ago!" "How do you mean, packed off? Packed off where to?" "Packed off's packed off! Where to's another thing!" . . . Well, so I went round to the front gate and rang: Ding-a-ding! Gate was opened; went in, looked up the landlord: "Where's the restaurant? Dash it all, man, but where have they removed to?" Oh, lots of luck! Nobody seemed to know; couldn't say where they had gone. But that only fired up the old ambition, and once the old ambition gets fired up, it's heads up, for I'm the devil! So I went dashing about all over the place, looking here, there, everywhere, intent on leaving no stone unturned. . . . And the "bu-oys"? Well, wouldn't you know, but they'd gone and made themselves scarce; out of spite, as I've no doubt, now I needed them. Because I couldn't find hide nor hair of them anywhere. Not a trace! So, wanting to leave no avenue unexplored, I next went down to the police station, *pour faire des recherches*, that's to say, make official inquiries. Well, coming into the station, I got what you'd call your standard-form salutation: "State your business!" So I says, "Well, y'know, blah blah, this, that, so where's the restaurant?" So they says, "Which restaurant?" So I says, "Well, y'know, restaurant at blah blah, corner blah." So they says, "State your business anent said restaurant!" . . . Well, I mean to say! Would you believe it? I mean, about wanting me to tell them what *my* business there was? . . . Well, I clammed up, I mean who wouldn't have done? But they wouldn't let up, and kept putting the same question to me over and over again. . . . So, to cut a long story short, I'd landed myself in the most awful kind of a mess, and that's the truth. I mean, you simply have no idea what a runabout I got from them on account of it with the devil bring-ing up the rear! . . . Though, on the other hand, thinking back? I mean, what had I to be scared of anyway, seeing as how I am your commercial chap really, good name, good income, scads of the old ready I don't much mind missing, et cetera? . . . Because I'm not the sort to get himself mixed up in such busi-ness in the first place. I mean, after all, *si l'on ne mange pas de*. . . . Well, par-don my French, but there's no smoke without fire. I mean, you cannot eat garlic and expect your breath to smell like roses. Thing is, though, I hate it! No, I mean, *absolutely hate it*. End of story, finis! . . . Well, I was fed up to the back teeth with the lot of them and heartily wished them all to the devil: dash the restaurant! dash the gal! dash Joseph! . . .

I should welcome nothing more than to be over her finally. Make an end of it, basta! But, you see, the damnable thing is, she simply won't be gone from my thoughts. I keep picturing her in that trim white apron that shim-mered whilst she walked and her cherry black eyes like cordials and her Cupid's bow lip with the little lift to it like a child's and her "kiss-me-sweet" dimples a-playing Bo-peep and her tinkly laugh going right through a body and settling in amongst his vitals. . . . And often, at night, when I'm asleep, I'll suddenly hear her voice calling: "Jo-seph! Jo-seph!" . . . And I'll awaken in a cold sweat and with a start. For no sooner I'm reminded of her, than I'll be thinking of *him*.

See? I never wait for a chap to pull out his watch. Because I know well enough that all good things must come to an end. . . . And you do forgive me for taking up so much of your time? Here, give me your hand, then. There's a good chap! All to remain amongst ourselves, agreed? Like, what d'ye call it: "conspirashun," eh? . . .

Adieu!

A Business with a Greenhorn

How Mr. Tummler, a Business Broker, "Loined" a Greenhorn
Who Got Merry Wid a Goil for Business.
Retold Here in His Own Words

You was saying how America was a lend of business? Never mine! Det's how it's suppose to be. But a fella getting merry wid a goil for business? Det, you'll poddon me, is mean end doity. Now, I ain't preaching no morality here, but I am telling you it's a fect; when nine-end-ninety procent of grinnhorns in dis country is getting merry for business, it is making me med! End if I am meeting op wid such a kind of grinnhorn, belive me he don't get off dry. You live it to me! Wanna hear a good one? Listen!

One day I am sitting rond in mine office mailing de post when a grinnhorn come in. Yong fella, just a boychick. Him wid his wife — end what a wife! — a doll, pitchers end crimm. So, coming in he says, "Hiye! You Mr. Tummler Business Broker?" "Siddon! Yeh, so what's de good void?" So he put his cods on de table end stotted telling me so-end-so, abot how he was a new boy just ten yiss in de country, by trade a knee-pents maker, abot how he fall in loff wid a goil which she was a woiking goil which got a tousend dollar in kesh, so den he got merry wid de goil, so now he was looking for a business so dey can make a living widdout boddering woiking in a shop because he got de rheumatism bad like you don't wanna know, end so on. Minnwhile, I am giving de liddle woman de once-over, end I says to him, "So what business you got in mine, mister?" "Stationery!" he says, because det's de kind of business he got in mine. Den he come out wid how wid a stationery store *she* can help out in de store. I minn, how you like det for a smotty-pents grinnhorn wid a noive? Because it ain't enough he got his hends on soch a poifec peach to make whoopee wid plus make hay wid her tousend dollar in kesh, but he wants she should woik so he can sid rond wid his pels all day playing pinochle, end so on — because, mister, I know my pipple! Tinks I: You want

130

stationery? I give you stationery! Busted bladder widdout a pot is all de stationery you gonna get outta me, bub! Because I gonna fix it so you wish you was dead, mec. Because you gonna get a laundry, jeck. Wid me, you gonna be a laundrymen. End why a laundry? Because it so heppen I got a laundry on my hends to sell den. So I says to my grinnhorn: "What ye wanna bodder anyway wid a stationery store for," I says, "pudding in a eighteen-hour day, looking out in case some schoolboy run in end swipe a penny-candy off de counter, end so on? You live it to me — because I can let you have a nice business, a laundry op in de Bvonx, det way you gonna woik reggler hours, end live like a king!" So den I take out a pencil end figger it out for him — so much de rent, so much de shoit-ironer, de femmily-ironer, de delivery boy, de laundry bill, end so on, which live you in de bleck wid over toity bucks a vick, clear — so what you want more? "How much it gonna cost?" So I says: "A tousend, we got us a bargain, only live it to me — for you, I'll do it for eight honderd. All you gotta do," I says, "is hend over de jeck, pick up de key, end you gonna be alright, mec. You do it blind. Minnwhile," I says, "so long, pel, end come beck in tree more days, on account I ain't got no more time now — so bye-bye!"

Me? I get myself over to my laundrymen right away end tell him *mazl tov*: because God just finish sending a pigeon my way, a grinnhorn, so seeing how he got a chence now of getting rid of de laundry at a good price, provided he was a mentsh he'd know what to do abot it, end so on. . . . So de gonnif take de hint okay, end he says: "You just make sure you bring de pigeon over, mister, end everything gonna be alright!" . . . Minnwhile, tree days later — my grinnhorn show op, pud down a deposit, den hubby end wife go to woik, figgering to give de laundry de usual vonn-vick trial, end you betcha my laundrymen make soiten de vonn-vick trial is alright, wid a bonus even, which is making it "end-how" alright wid room to spare — so den de business is settled. De grinnhorn is paying op de couple bucks what's owing, de laundrymen is hending over de books end keys, end yours truly is collecting his fee from *both* parties — because Mister Tummler Business Broker knows his business — end, how you saying over in Rossia: *finita la commedia!* Oh, yeh? Says you, maybe. By me is de comedy only stotting. Because after everything was sewed op neat all arond, den it really stotted getting to me abot de grinnhorn; because why did det momzer desoive getting soch a plum dropped in his lep anyway for, a pretty wife, a tousend in kesh, plus a ready-made business hended to him on a silver platter widdout no sweat?

No, I gonna fix it so he gotta sell out at half price end give de laundry beck to de foist laundrymen. Except you asking how? So det's de rizzon why I am Mister Tummler Business Broker because dere's notting I cannot do if I wanna. So I went across de stritt opposite from de laundry end rent a nice room on de corner dere from de agent, which after slipping him ten bucks advence on de rent, I put op a sign in de vinder:

Laundry opening here soon!!!

Well you betcha a day don't pess end my grinnhorn come rond again, looking like he just lost all his mobbles: Gevalt! He's a dead men! "Yeh, so what's de beef, pel?" So he stotted telling me de bad news abot how some momzer just now rented a store across de stritt from him end was opening op a laundry! "So what d'ye want from me, Grinnhorn?" So he says he wants me to find a buyer for him for de laundry, which he'll make it woit my while if I do end re- member me in his prayers for de rest of his life, end so on. So I calm him down, saying it ain't so izzy now finding a buyer. Only live it me, I am trying mine best. Minnwhile, so long, pel, see you in tree more days, on account I am op to here in woik right now—so bye-bye!

Me? I sent for my old laundrymen right away end tell him so-end-so: he got de chence now of buying beck his laundry for only a song, at half price, end so on. So he says, "So how you gonna do it, mec?" So I says, "So what's it to you, jeck?" So he says, "Alright." So I says, "I'm gonna get a commission out of it, yeh?" So he says, "Alright." So I says, "It's gonna cost you a honderd, yeh?" So he says, "Alright." End so on. Minnwhile, tree days later, my grinnhorn show op wid de liddle woman, which I notice she was looking con- siderable paler but odderwise still beautiful like a rose. "So you got any news?" "News?" I says. "Well it took some doing, but I finally found you a buyer. Except you gonna have to take a loss." "Yeh, so how much?" "Don't esk how much you loosing, better esk how much you winning. Because anything you get is gonna be like hitting de jeckpot. Tink you can play games wid American competition? Because you do, end dey gonna drive you into soch expenses you gonna end op taking a moonlight powder wid only de shoit on your beck!" . . . Well whatcha tink, but by de time I finish, I put soch a scare into hubby end wife dey was gled to take beck half de money dey put in, plus dey paid me my commission, because I ain't obliged to give away my soivices for free, end so on, end det's det—no more laundry! . . . But hang onto your hat, mister, dere's more to come yet. Because if you been kipping count, you remember I popped de agent a tenner advence on de store, which I henged op a sign abot a laundry? So I esks mysef, why should I trow ten smeckers out for widdout getting my money's woit outta it foist? Whatsa madder, Mister Tummler Business Broker, soddenly don't know de value of a dollar? So det's vonn rizzon. Besides which I was still plenty boined op yet abot de grinnhorn, end it was eating me op: because de momzer still got a couple of honderd simoleons steshed away in his pocket, not to mention de sweet little dish he got for himself—soch a poifec peach! So why should he have it so good, anyhow? Because here you got Mister Tummler Biggest Business Broker on de East Side, which he is stuck wid a old lady det's got a face on her which you'll podden me will stop a clock, end all she do is neg, neg, neg—while God is giving de grinnhorn soch a pretty baby doll, you know, a reggler knockout— well, I gonna see him choke on it foist. So I don't sid rond just twiddling my tumbs, but I write him on a postel cod he should come see me by appointment on soch end soch a time because I got a business proposition for him. So de fella don't wait to be esked twice end showed op on de dot, as per appointment, plus he brung *her* along, det's to say, de liddle woman. So I am pudding ot de red carpet, telling dem plizz to be sitted, make youselfs at home, end so on, end den hending dem a line, saying so-end-so: "You simple got no idea abot American bloffers! You wouldn't belive what kinda trick det gonnif de old laundrymen played on yez—it make ye hair coil!" . . . "Yeh, how's det?" "How's det?" I says, "Because it was him all along what rent de store across de stritt den henged op a sign abot a laundry to scare yez into selling out so's he'd get his old laundry beck for half de price." Hearing soch a story, de hubby end wife look each other over, end dey was positive steaming, especial de liddle woman. Her eyes was boining like hot coals. "So it only be fair," I says, "if you was to get even wid de gonnif in soch a way he got something to remember yez by!" "Yeh, only how we suppose to get even wid him?" "Live it to me," I says, "because I'm gonna settle det smott aleck's hash for good," I says, "so he gonna wish his mudder never had him—end youse two," I says, "you gonna come op smelling like roses; because," I says, "yez gonna get a business outta it better den before!" By now my pair of pigeons was looking at me like somebody is saying, "From your mouth into God's ears, long may you prosper, end so on!" So I laid de gig out for dem: Why buy somebody else's business if you gonna pay through de nose for it anyhow? But say I was to go down to de same landlord end rent de same store off of him which de old laundrymen wanted to rent, end for abot three, maybe four honderd dollars I fixed op a laundry right opposite his laundry, end den I stotted giving him competition, no matter what he was charging, I am charging less, well, I betcha I get him outta dere in three vicks' time—or my name ain't Mister Tummler! Well, whatcha tink, but by de time I finish, hubby end wife was simple delirious; de grinnhorn looked fit to kiss me on both my cheeks, end his pretty wife was blushing so she looked even prettier den usual. So de same day I rented de store for dem, end I got a laundry fitted out in no time, de whole kit end caboodle, wid a sign, tables, de woiks, end my hubby end wife rolled op dere sleeves end got down to it. So pretty soon my couple end de old laundrymen was having a bang-up time undercutting each other. If he was asking twenty-four cents a dozen "flat," dey went right down to eighteen cents a dozen plus a free "spread"; if he knocked down shoits to only eight cents per, dey dropped to a penny end a half a shoit-collar, so netcherly he had to come down to a penny a collar, end so on. So de clincher is—dey plugged away for so long at cutting end slashing prices till de grinnhorn was shook loose of his last dollar, cleaned out widdout a red cent to even pay rent wid. So he closed down de laundry end left wid his pockets toined out because like it says in Provoibs Chapter Whosit Verse Whatsit: *easy come, easy go.* Right now he's sidding rond on his keister taking it easy in Ludlow Street Jail—det's my doing because I fixed de liddle woman op wid a lawyer, which he is putting de squeeze on him, on de grinnhorn det is, in his wife's name for three things: (1) her money, which it's her tousend dollar dowry; (2) a divorce; end (3) until such time as maybe she finally get a divorce out of him, he gotta support her according to de laws of de country—so det'll loin him, goddam grinnhorn!

Translated by Ted Gorelick

I. L. Peretz

By permission of the YIVO Institute for Jewish Research.

The Shtrayml

I'm a hatmaker, but what really matters is that on rare occasions I make a magnificent fur hat, a shtrayml. The truth is that I earn most from peasants' coats and porters' furs. And sometimes Leyb Milner drops in with his sable fur coat.

Seldom, very seldom, does a shtrayml turn up, for who wears a shtrayml? A rabbi! And the shtrayml outlives him.

It's also true that when I chance upon a shtrayml, I make it free of charge, or at least I throw in my labor. I admit all of this, and yet the main thing is that I'm a shtrayml-maker, because I like making a shtrayml!

When a shtrayml comes my way, it's a delight—that's when I feel who I am and what I can do.

What else—you tell me—should I enjoy doing?

I used to enjoy making peasants' coats. Why not?

I said to myself, "The peasant gives us bread. I can't protect him from the sun while he works so hard and bitterly during the summer. When it's winter and he's resting, I'll shelter him from the cold!"

I sang a fine song while I worked.

I was a young man and had a voice like a bell. I used to sew and sing:

> Stick the needle in,
> Leather tough as tin.
> To keep the peasant warm,
> I'll make his coat to form.
> I'm thirsty Mirele, my dear,
> So bring me borsht and beer!

And so on, for a few more verses. . . . Of course, the whole song was made just for the refrain—so that these words would come out: "I'm thirsty Mirele, my dear, so bring me borsht and beer!"

Because, you should know, the dignified Miriam-Dvora of today was not yet a leading lady in the synagogue. She didn't call me "Berel Sausage," like today, but "Berele," and I'd call her "Mirele, my dear." There was a great romance between us, may we be forgiven for our sins, and no sooner had she heard the refrain about being thirsty, than she would bring me a dram of schnapps! Schnapps has a strong effect on the blood pressure, and while speaking I would catch her by the dress and plant a burning kiss on her cherry-red cheeks. Doubly refreshed, I would go back to the peasant coat!

Today, those cherries are no more!

She calls me "Berel Sausage," and I call her "Miriam-Dvora."

Since then I've also learned that land is scarce and there are many peasants . . . some say too many. The "surplus" peasants go hungry; one can't even live from six acres of land; so the peasant no longer rests in the winter.

That's when he delivers goods. Some rest he has in the winter! Entire days and nights he delivers wheat to Leybl's mill.

What do you think? You think I get peace of mind from knowing that my coats, my handicrafts, stay soaked all winter, crawling along behind two dying horses that carry Leybl Milner's grain five miles for six kopecks per sack?

Pshh! And what satisfaction do I get from a porter's fur? All winter it carries sacks of flour to Leybl Milner's mill and all summer it lies in the tavern, pawned for ten kopecks. At the end of the summer, when it is brought to me for repairs, I get drunk from the smell of bad whisky!

When Leybl Milner's sable fur coat, in all its glory, falls into my hands, do you think it gives me any pleasure? It is indeed an expensive coat, an honor, and people in the shtetl respect it; but nothing good comes of it for me.

I've gotten into a filthy habit: whatever I see, I like to think, *where* does it come from? *Why* is it this way? Can't it be *otherwise*? And when I get my hands on Leybl Milner's fur coat, I start to ponder: Master of the Universe! Why have you created so many different kinds of furs? Why does one person have a sable fur coat, a second a porter's fur, a third a peasant's coat, and yet another has nothing at all?[1]

And as soon as I start to think, I sink into my thoughts, my needle stops moving, and the dignified lady Miriam, long may she live, throws something at my head, whatever comes to hand.

Like everyone else, she wants "Berel Sausage" to think less and work more. . . .

---

1. The phrase "and yet another has nothing at all" was not present in the original edition of this story, but was added later.

But what should I do if I *must* think? And if I know that Leybl Milner doesn't have his fur coat repaired until he tears a coin from the pocket of the peasant coat and steals another from the porter?

From *that* I should get satisfaction?

Oh, I almost forgot!

A week before Penitential Prayers I was offered a strange new job. . . . What women are capable of doing! Freydl, a prayer leader at the women's synagogue, came in with frightfully large gloves on her hands. When I took a closer look and saw a pair of peasants' boots, I thought I would laugh so hard I'd burst!

"Good morning," she says to me in her forced, sweet voice. "Good morning, dear Berele!"

She's my wife's friend and, like everyone else in the shtetl, usually calls me "Berel Sausage." But today it's "dear Berele." And so sweetly that you could use her words to make preserves. So I understand that she needs something from me.

I figure that she "plucked" the boots from some peasant's wagon (it's no worse than taking change from an alms box) and wants to hide the merchandise with me. So I say to her severely:

"What do you want?"

"So angry," she answers even more sweetly, honey running down the sides of her old mouth. "You ask what I want and don't even say hello!"

"All right, hello, let's get it over with."

"Why are you in such a hurry, Berele?" she says and smiles even more sweetly. "I've just come to ask if you have a few pieces of fur."

"And what if I do?"

"I'd make a deal with you," she says.

"Well, go ahead! Talk!"

"If you wanted to be nice, Berele, you'd pad these boots with pieces of fur. I'd have something to wear to Penitential Prayers, and you'd get yourself a cheap mitzvah!"

You understand the bargain, she wants to trade me a "cheap mitzvah"!

"You already know," I say to her, "that Berel Sausage doesn't trade in mitzvahs."

"So what? Will you take money from a poor old woman?"

"Well, forget the money. I'll do it for a trifle: I'll pad the boots if you tell me the sins of your youth."

She doesn't want to and I send her to a bookbinder!

I don't pad boots! Anyway, as things are I'm sick of life. You laugh? And yet, when I don't have a shtrayml, it's all the same and everything seems tiresome to me. Why? What do I work for? Just to keep this bit of flesh going! How? With bread and potatoes, bread without potatoes, and often with only potatoes and no bread. Is it worth it?

Believe me, if a person works for fifty years and eats potatoes every day for fifty years, he *must* become sick of life! Some day he'll end up doing something terrible either to himself or to Leybl Milner. If I go on calmly eating my potatoes and working, I have only the shtrayml to thank!

When I hold a shtrayml in my hands, the blood in my veins pumps faster. I remember why I'm alive!

I think that I am a born shtrayml-maker!

Making a shtrayml, I feel as though I'm holding a bird in my hands, and when I open them, the bird will fly up and away, as far as the eye can see. I will stand and revel in it: that's *my* bird—I made it, and I tossed it up into the heights!

In town, thank God, I have no influence and I'm never called to meetings. I'm no busybody who goes without being asked, and I almost never walk the streets. I have no place in the synagogue, in the House of Study, or in a prayer minyan! I have no business anywhere. . . . At home, Mistress Miriam sits in the rider's saddle. Before I can open my mouth to say a word, she rains curses on me. She already knows what I want to say, what "Berel Sausage" thinks, and her blood boils!

So what am I? Nothing! But when I let loose a shtrayml into the community, people bend over backward!

I sit silently at home, and in the seat of honor my shtrayml blesses a wedding, a circumcision, a special celebration. The shtrayml lords it over everyone when there are elections or when a matter comes before the rabbinical court! My heart swells when I remember the greatness of my shtrayml. . . .

Across the street lives a lace maker. . . . I assure you I don't envy him.

Just let the epaulette on one of the uniforms he makes try to pronounce one ox kosher and another treyf. Let's see what happens! But when my shtrayml states that four oxen are not kosher, one after the other—the butcher is cleaned out, the apprentices grind their teeth, the whole shtetl goes without meat for a week, a company of Cossacks gets cheap beef, and that's the end of it. No one says a word.

Now, that's power!

You think I don't remember? A year ago there was an epidemic among sheep.

People said that the sheep were acting strangely, going in circles until they became dizzy and fell down dead! I wasn't there; spinning around in circles is serious, but of course Jacob the butcher soon had cheap lamb's meat.

The veterinarian came and said: Not fit to eat! People listened to him about as much as to a cat in heat!

The veterinarian brought half a dozen officials in all sorts of uniforms with epaulettes. People stole the meat out from under their noses, and a few days later the whole town had cheap, kosher meat for lunch!

But no one steals from my shtrayml. There's no need for uniforms with epaulettes, and the shtrayml doesn't need to make a move. Until my shtrayml tells them to eat, not a mouth in the shtetl opens.

Do you think that the power lies in what is *under* the shtrayml? God forbid!

Don't you know what is under there? I, thank God, do know.

The creature used to be a tutor in an even smaller town. My father, may he rest in peace—before he saw that nothing could be done with me—sent me to study with him. God help us, what a shlimmazl he was. The things you see in this world! He was a one-of-a-kind teacher.

The respectable people of the town saw that he knew nothing in any shape or form, and they soon cut his salary in half. They paid the remaining half in loose change and torn bills. The rabbi's wife saw that nothing good would come of him, and every day she used to tear at his beard!

And you shouldn't blame her. First, they had no livelihood; second, a Jewish woman likes to give a good pull; third, he already had the kind of beard that cried out to be pulled. Apparently it also called to us, the pupils, so loudly that we couldn't restrain ourselves either—so we took turns crawling under the table, grabbing the rabbi's beard, and tearing out a whisker!

Well, you tell me! Can any power lie in such a creature? What do you think, that he's changed over the years? Not a chance! He hasn't changed a bit. His little eyes are still dim, running with pus—the frightened eyes of a beggar!

It's true that, because of their poverty, his first wife died. What's the difference? So his *second* wife pulls his beard instead. When it begs and pleads to be pulled, who can resist? When I see it, even I get a strong hankering to give it a yank!

But what happened? Nothing other than I ended up making him a shtrayml. . . . Let me state openly that it wasn't my idea. It would never have occurred to me.

The community ordered the shtrayml and I made it. But when I, poor "Berel Sausage," had scarcely finished making the shtrayml they ordered, and the rabbi put it on — the community found out that it was coming and only a mile outside town, and there was celebrating in the streets! Everyone from great to small ran out of their houses, and sick people stood up from their beds! They unharnessed their horses from their wagons, and everyone wanted to go hitch up and help pull my shtrayml. God knows what sort of disputes might have broken out — it could have come to blows and slanders. But a smart fellow came up with an idea: hold an auction! Then Leybl Milner gave dozens of gold coins, and he led the procession!

Well, doesn't my shtrayml have power?

Apart from "Berel Sausage," my pious wife also calls me lusty, brazen, obscene, jack-of-all-trades, and whatever else springs into her mouth.

It's true that a man is no pig! I get pleasure from straight talk, and sometimes I like to stick it to Leybl Milner, right in front of his eyes or behind his back.

And why should I deny it? The servant girls who pump water from the well across the square are no saints saying the Priestly Blessing, God forbid, and I like to take a good look at them. . . .

But believe me, *that* is not what keeps me going.

What keeps me going is one thing: I know that once in a blue moon I send a Golden Calf out into the community, and everyone bows down to my handiwork!

I know that when my pious wife hands the keys over to me, that's because my shtrayml told her to. She listens to me like I'm the cat mewing, but she has to obey the shtrayml!

On Saturday eve or before a holiday, when she comes home from the market without meat and rains curses on the butcher, I know that he's not to blame. It's my *shtrayml* that won't let her make kugel today!

I know that when she takes a perfectly good pot and throws it out on the street, it's really my shtrayml that threw it out! When she follows the pre-scribed ritual, breaks off a piece from the leavened dough and throws it into the fire—rolling her eyes and raising her hands up to the uncomprehending ceiling—I know that it was really my shtrayml that threw the piece of dough into the fire.

And at the same time I know that my pious wife is not alone in the com-munity, and ours is not God's only community. There are many pious women like her in the community, God has many communities like ours, and I know that my shtrayml rules over millions and millions of pious women!

Millions of keys get handed over, millions of women don't make kugel, millions of pots burst when they hit the cobblestones, and I could sustain an army of paupers with the bread our women throw into the fire.

And who does all this? All of it comes from my handiwork, my shtrayml!

There's the lace maker again! From my window I can see him sitting there, and his face is shining as if it were covered with grease.

Why is his face shining, and why are his runny eyes twinkling? He's just woven a pair of golden epaulettes!

First, we know the difference between gold and dirt. Second, I know that two epaulettes have ten times more soldiers serving under them than Leybl's sable fur coat has peasants' coats or porters' furs!

But let the grandest golden epaulette try to give an order: "Slaughter ten oxen and cook only half of one"; "You can go hungry, but be sure to have all sorts of dishes and eat spleen off the left side of your plate";[2] "Throw a piece of every bite you eat into the fire or water!" Or: "Every groom must first show me his bride, and every bride her groom!" "With me, everything is possible, even under duress, while without me, not a taste!"

The grandest commander's epaulette wouldn't dream of it, wouldn't dare try. To do this, it would have to strew the entire country with new recruits: at every bed, it would have to station two Cossacks, each keeping an eye on the other and both guarding the bed!

Yet, in spite of this, how much stealing and smuggling would occur. How much deception! Master of the Universe, how does one manage that?

2. "Eat spleen off the left side of your plate": Peretz is poking fun at ultra-orthodox notions of kashrut. Perhaps, because of the prohibition against mixing meat and milk, a cow's spleen would fall into a special, problematic category.

My shtrayml does all this, nice and quiet, without whips or Cossacks!

I sit quietly at home and know that without the permission of my shtrayml, no Moshe will touch any Hannah—not even look at her, God forbid!

On the other hand, if my shtrayml pairs off a Moshe or a Hannah with some rotten dregs of society, it's for life. You can't get free except by leaving this world! If you don't want to wait that long, you have to come and beg, plead before that very same shtrayml: Save me! Shtrayml, release me from these chains! Let me out of prison!

At the end of the street there's a tavern.

Since my pious wife became a leading lady of the women's synagogue and never pours me schnapps any more, I sometimes stop by there to revive my spirits. Especially on a fast day. . . . In any case, I am not obligated to fast; after all, my own shtrayml is in charge.

I've known the tavern-keeper for a long time. . . . Like me, he doesn't live off mitzvahs and good deeds—but that's not what I'm getting at now.

He had two daughters! Two full-blooded sisters. What am I saying? They're twins, I tell you, as I'm a Jew.

Was it possible to tell them apart? Such a charming pair, thank God!

Their cheeks were red as apples on the flags people carry during Simkhes Toyre. Fragrant as the cloves in a spice box. Tall as lulavs, and such eyes—God should guard and protect them! When one of the girls looked up, it seemed as if a diamond was sparkling! And they were decent kids, living in the tavern and yet far from it. You couldn't have raised them to be better or more honest inside the Holy Ark itself!

Born in the tavern, they were princesses! Not a single drunk spoke a bad word in front of them. Not a watchman, not a tax collector. When the most important men came in, they didn't dare to pinch one of their cheeks, leer, or even think lewd thoughts! I was on the verge of saying that *the sisters* held more power than my shtrayml. But that would have been a crass mistake.

The shtrayml was stronger, as later became obvious, a thousand times stronger than they were!

Twins! They went everywhere together. If one felt a pain, the other felt the same. But how quickly they parted ways.

They did the same thing, with hardly any difference, and yet. . . . Suddenly a change came over them: sometimes they were happier, sometimes sadder, and more lost in thought than usual. I can't describe what happened to them. The right words are on the tip of my tongue, but I can't spit them out. . . . People don't learn how to talk about such things. . . . Something in them became deeper, firmer, and at the same time sadder and sweeter. . . .

But we knew who was responsible. People pointed fingers at two Moshes who made the Hannahs even prettier, better, more charming, somehow loftier!

Well, I'm waxing poetic; that's no way for a hatmaker to talk! What's with me? I'm getting teary-eyed. My modest wife will say I'm a lusty one.

I'll keep the story short. The two sisters did the same thing, by God, exactly the same—not for nothing are they twins! Both became attached to Moshes, and soon after both needed to add fabric to their dresses.

Don't be embarrassed, that's the way of the world. God wants it to be like this, so what's the disgrace?

But how differently it happened with each of them! One sister carried her baby openly—before God in the synagogue, before people in the street, and before the watchman and the tax collector in the tavern. Far from the drunks, in a quiet and well-heated room, this sister lay down in a bed with white sheets. People draped the windows, covered the street with straw; a midwife arrived; they called a doctor. . . . And then there was a celebration, what a celebration!

A new, little Moshe started to grow—raised up for Torah, the wedding canopy, and good deeds. When she saw how good it was, she bore little Moshes every year and is a respected housewife to this very day. . . .

But the other sister carried her baby secretly, gave birth in a cellar, and a black cat took the child away. . . . For years her little Moshe has lain outside the cemetery fence and she will have no more Moshes. God only knows where she is now—she ran away!

Some people say that she is a servant somewhere out in the wide world, that she eats off strangers' plates. Others say that she is no longer alive. . . . Came to a bad end!

The only difference is that the first couple was united in the synagogue courtyard, on an old pile of refuse, under a filthy woolen fabric with silver lettering—*with* the shtrayml—while the second couple came together somewhere in a warbling woods, on untrodden grass with fresh flowers, under God's blue sky, strewn with stars—*without* the shtrayml.

Not fragrant flowers, not warbling woods, not God's sky, not His stars, not even God Himself can help![3] Power doesn't lie in *them*, but in the shtrayml! Not in uniforms or epaulettes, not even in Hannahs who are a thousand times prettier, but only in a shtrayml, in the shtrayml that I, "Berel Sausage," make.

And only that keeps me alive in this foolish life, eating potatoes.

Translated by Ken Frieden

3. The phrase "not even God Himself," included in the 1894 edition of this story, was effaced in some later editions.

Kabbalists

In bad times, even the value of Torah—the best merchandise—falls.[1]

Nothing was left of the yeshiva in Lashtchev but the head of the yeshiva, Rabbi Yekl, and a single student.

The head of the yeshiva is an old, thin man with a long, disheveled beard, and the light in his aging eyes has gone out. Lemekh, his most beloved student, is a young man—also thin, tall, pale, with black, curly forelocks and burning, black, downcast eyes, feverish lips, and a quivering, pointy Adam's apple. Wearing rags, both of them are without shirts and their chests are exposed. The head of the yeshiva can barely drag his pair of peasant boots across the floor, while the student's coarse shoes are slipping off his bare feet.

That's all that remained of the famous yeshiva!

As the impoverished town gradually stopped sending food and supporting the students with "eating days," the poor boys scattered. But Rabbi Yekl wants to die here, and his student will place the shards of clay over his eyes.

They often suffer from hunger. From having little to eat comes insomnia, and from long nights without sleep or food comes a desire for kabbalah!

In any case, if one has to stay awake all night and go hungry all day, why not put this to some use? So be it: they would fast, mortify their flesh, and open all the gates of the universe—with its mysteries, spirits, and angels!

They have been studying kabbalah for some time.

Now they are sitting at the long, solitary table. For most people in town it is after lunch, but for them it is before breakfast. They have become accustomed to that. The head of the yeshiva speaks, staring into space with glazed eyes, and the student sits listening, propping up his head with both of his hands.

---

1. This opening sentence alludes to the Hebrew saying, "Torah is the best merchandise" (*tova Torah mi-kol s'hora*; in Yiddish, *Toyre iz di beste skhoyre*). Another pertinent saying from *Ethics of the Fathers*, quoted by Sholem Aleichem's Tevye in "Hodel," runs: "If there's no flour, there's no Torah; if there's no Torah, there's no flour" (*im ein kemah ein Torah im ein Torah ein kemah*). See Pirkei Avot 3:21.

"In this matter there are many different levels," the head of the yeshiva is saying. "One person knows just a small part, another knows half, and yet another knows the whole melody. The Rebbe, of blessed memory, knew a complete melody together with its harmony!"

He admits sadly, "I have scarcely had the privilege to know a tiny bit, so little. . . ." He measures out a short length on a thin finger and continues:

"There is a melody that needs words—that's a low level. . . . On a higher plane is a melody that is sung, completely without words, a pure melody! But this melody still needs a voice, and it passes through lips. You understand that lips are part of the material world. And even the voice, although it is a refined materiality, remains materiality. Let us say that voice stands on the border between spirituality and materiality!

"Anyhow, the melody that is heard by having been sung, shaped by lips, is not yet pure, not yet entirely pure. . . . Not yet true spirituality!

"The true melody sings itself without a voice. It sings within, in the heart, in the bowels.

"This is the secret of King David's words: 'All of my bones shall speak.'[2] That's where the melody must be—it must sing, in the marrow of our bones, the highest praise for God, blessed be He! This is no melody of mortal flesh, and it is no invented melody! This is part of the melody with which God created the world, and part of the soul he breathed into it. . . .

"That is how the heavenly retinue sings. That is how the Rebbe, of blessed memory, sang!"

The lesson was interrupted by a disheveled youth with a cord tied around his waist—a porter. He entered the House of Study and placed on the table, next to the head of the yeshiva, a bowl of grits with a piece of bread. In a coarse voice he said:

"Reb Tevel sends food to the head of the yeshiva!" He turned and, as he was leaving, added, "I'll come back later for the bowl."

Sundered from divine harmony by the coarse voice of the porter, the head of the yeshiva rose heavily and, dragging his large boots, went to wash his hands at the sink.

While walking he continued to speak, though with less enthusiasm, and from where he sat the attentive student followed him with his burning, dreamy eyes.

2. Psalm 35:10.

Rabbi Yekl said in a sad voice, "I have not been privileged to attain even a low level, through any gate. You see," he added with a smile, "I do know what is needed, I know the mortifications of the flesh and the mystical combinations—and perhaps even today I will pass them on to you!"

The student's eyes bulge out of their sockets; his mouth falls open, to catch every word; but the rebbe breaks off, washes and dries his hands, and mumbles a blessing. He goes back to the table and, with trembling lips, he says the blessing over the bread.

With thin, shaky hands he lifts the bowl. The steam covers his bony face with a warm vapor; then he puts it down, takes the spoon in his right hand, and warms his left hand on the side of the bowl. At the same time his tongue presses the piece of salted bread, which he is still chewing after the blessing, up against his toothless gums.

Having warmed his face with his hands, he furrows his brow, rounds his thin, pale blue lips, and starts to blow.

All the while, the student never took his eyes off him. But at the moment when the rebbe's trembling mouth came in contact with the first spoon of grits, something stabbed at his heart; he suddenly covered his face with both hands and drew back completely into himself.

A few minutes later, another youth entered with a second bowl of grits with bread, saying:

"Reb Yosef sends lunch to the student!"

Yet the student did not remove his hands from his face.

The head of the yeshiva put down his spoon and went over to the student. For a while he looked at him with pride and love, and then wrapped his hand in his caftan and touched his shoulder.

"They have brought you food," he roused him in a friendly voice. Sadly and slowly the student removed his hands from his face. He was even paler, and his downcast eyes burned even more wildly.

"I know, Rebbe," he answered, "but I will not eat today."

"Your fourth day of fasting?" the rebbe asked, astonished. "And without me?" he added haughtily.

"It is another kind of fast," answered the student. "This is a penitential fast."

"What are you talking about? You—a penitential fast?"

"Yes, Rebbe, a penitential fast! A moment ago, when you started to eat, I felt that I was about to transgress the commandment, 'Thou shalt not covet.'"

. . .

Very late that same night, the student woke up the rebbe. They were sleeping opposite one another on benches in the House of Study.

"Rebbe, Rebbe!" he called in a weak voice.

"What is it?" said the head of the yeshiva as he awoke, frightened.

"I was just now at a high spiritual level. . . ."

"What happened?" asked the head of the yeshiva, still half-asleep.

"There was singing *inside* me!"

The head of the yeshiva sat up quickly and said, "Tell me more! Tell me more!"

"I myself don't know, Rebbe," said the student in an even weaker voice. "I couldn't sleep, so I immersed myself in your words. . . . I wanted to know the melody . . . and from the pain I felt at not knowing the melody, I began to cry. . . . Everything in me cried—all of my limbs wept before the Master of the Universe! At the same time—it was a wonderful thing—I pronounced the mystical combinations you gave me . . . but not with my mouth; they came from somewhere inside me, by themselves! Suddenly a brightness came over me . . . I kept my eyes shut and everything was bright, very bright, overpoweringly bright."

"That's it!" said the head of the yeshiva, leaning forward.

"Then, from the brightness, I began to feel so good, so light. . . . It seemed to me that I was light as a feather, that my body had become weightless, that I could fly."

"That's it! That's it!"

"After that I became joyful, lively, full of laughter. . . . My face didn't budge, my lips didn't move, but I laughed—and I laughed so well, so heartily, with such pleasure!"

"That's it! That's it! That's it! From ecstasy!"

"Next something inside me started to hum, like the beginning of a melody."

The head of the yeshiva jumped down from his bench and stood beside the student, saying, "Well, what next?"

"Then I heard it begin to sing inside me!"

"What did you feel? What? What? Tell me!"

"I felt that all of my senses were blocked and closed, and something was singing inside me . . . just the way it should—but without words, just so . . ."

"How? How?"

"No, I can't . . . a moment ago I knew. . . . After that the singing became . . . became . . ."

"What did it become? What did it become?"

"A kind of playing . . . as if I had a violin inside me, or Jonah the klezmer musician was sitting inside me and playing Sabbath songs, like at the Rebbe's table! But the playing was even better, more refined, with even more spirituality. And everything was without a voice, without any sound—with pure spirituality!"

"You are blessed! You are fortunate! You are blessed!"

"Then everything vanished!" said the student sadly. "My senses have opened again, and now I am tired, exhausted, so exhausted that I . . ."

"Rebbe!" he suddenly cried out, grasping at his heart. "Rebbe, say the final confession with me! They have come to take me! There, in the heavenly retinue above, one singer was missing. An angel with white wings! . . . Rebbe! Rebbe! Hear, O Israel. Hear, O Is . . ."

The entire town, as one, wished for such a death, but it wasn't enough for the head of the yeshiva.

"Just a few more fasts," he groaned, "and then he would have died with the kiss of God on his lips."

Translated by Ken Frieden

Teachings of the Hasidim

It is known unto all — the whole world knows that our master and teacher, the Rebbe of Nemirov, served God in ecstasy.

Happy is the eye that was privileged to see the joy,[1] the fire and fervor, the sheer ecstasy that emanated from him — as from the sun — and covered the entire world in a golden, fiery glow. What a delight that was to behold!

A person could forget the long Jewish exile, the calamities, the greatest torments; one could even forget oneself when the souls of all his disciples merged into one flame together with his soul, may his memory be blessed. How joyful we were! How full of life and burning with a joy that streamed forth as from a spring!

There are righteous men who are granted ecstasy on the Sabbath and on holidays; the Rebbe of Vonvolitz, of blessed memory, boasted that his soul held a spark of the ecstasy that comes after the Day of Atonement fast. Others are granted ecstasy at a festive meal, at a circumcision, or when a scribe finishes writing a Torah scroll. . . . But our Rebbe, of blessed memory, possessed divine ecstasy every day — until his final minute on the day he passed away. May his merits protect us!

Now, as for his singing and dancing! His Sabbath songs and his dances were infused with God's holy spirit.

Once, as he spoke to us, we saw that his eyes shone with the very splendor of the Divine Presence.

"I reveal unto you," he once exclaimed, "that the entire world is nothing more than a song and a dance before God, blessed be He. All of us are choirboys singing His praise! Every Jew is a choirboy, every letter of the Holy Torah is a note, and every soul in every body is also a note. For every soul is a letter of the Holy Torah, and all of the souls together are the entire Holy Torah — both are one song before the King of Kings, blessed be He."

---

1. "Happy is the eye" (Yiddish *voyl iz dem oyg*, based on the Hebrew *ashrei 'ayin*) is a formulaic phrase that is often found in hagiographic books about hasidic rebbes — such as in Nathan Sternharz's *Shivhei Moharan* about Nahman of Bratslav.

He added that just as there are all kinds of musical notes, there are all kinds of musical instruments, and every kind of melody is joined with the instrument that can play it, and every instrument has its melody. For the instrument is the body and the melody is the soul of the instrument.

Every person is a musical instrument, and a person's life is a melody—either a happy or a sad melody. When one finishes the melody, the soul departs from the body, and the melody—the soul, that is—reunites with the great singing before the Throne of Glory. . . . "Woe unto the person," he said, "who lives without his melody. That is a life without a soul, a grinding and a groaning—that is no life at all. . . .

Every community is a separate melody, and standing before the community, the Rebbe conducts the communal melody. . . . Every person in the community knows his part of the melody, and each must sing out as necessary at the right time. If not, he ruins the melody; only the conductor must know the entire melody and make corrections, when necessary, and ask the choir to repeat it, when necessary. . . . If he hears a false note that has entered the melody, he must drive it out like a dybbuk, God save us, so that it does not spoil the melody!

"Happy are you," he said, "if you are destined to sing a joyful melody. . . ."

The Rebbe, of blessed memory, spoke a lot about this matter.

"Talmudic scholars, who can only study on the surface," he said, "are like strangers who enjoy looking at the king's palace from outside, but who cannot go in. They do not even dare to knock on the gate, for fear that no one will open it for them. . . . They can only see the walls, the windows, the chimneys, and the flags flying high above the roof of the king's palace. Sometimes they see the smoke that rises from the chimneys, and sometimes they hear voices of the workers and servants who move around in the front chambers of the king's palace. . . . But people who immerse themselves in the essence of the Torah, and who unite with the soul of the Torah, enter deep inside the palace; they see the entire glory of the king and hear how courtesans extol the king, sing the king's praise, and unite with the singing for the king. . . .

"Those who walk around outside the palace," he said, "are like craftsmen who work on musical instruments. They can repair an instrument, but they themselves can't play it. Some of them have fine, skilled hands for making musical instruments, but their ears are stopped up, and when someone plays the instrument they made, they don't hear it; others have clogged hearts and neither understand nor feel what they hear. A great craftsman who does bring the instrument to his lips can only test it or repeat what someone else has played—coldly, without soul. Even the very great ones cannot play a melody of their own."

"But I, thank God" he said, "although I am no scholar—that is, no craftsman, and cannot make or repair musical instruments—I *can* play all of the instruments."

"Scholars are the instruments," he said, "and we are the melody. They are the outer garments and we are the people! They are bodies and we are souls."

Happy are the ears that heard this!

And happy are the eyes that were privileged to see the ecstasy at the court of our master and teacher, the Rebbe; but all of that was like a drop in the ocean compared to the ecstasy at his daughter's wedding.

Whoever did not see Feygele's wedding has not seen anything!

On that occasion the Divine Presence descended and rested on everyone, and a bright, holy spirit encompassed everyone. . . . From great to small, everyone was exalted and crowned. People saw this clearly, even the cooks, the waiters, and even the coachmen who brought the in-laws to town. . . . Even the peasants, the Rebbe said, he would raise up to the level of the righteous people among the nations of the world.

The eldest among us, Reb Zatz, told me—and he never said such things lightly—that this was the first true ecstasy since the six days of God's creation.

Imagine the pandemonium in the higher spheres when the Rebbe went out to dance before the bride!

Oh, how I wished one could bring all of the heretics, the scoffers, and everyone who grumbles and pretends to be wise, to see the delight, the greatness, the ecstasy. They say they are content with the here and now; let them see how the World to Come can permeate our world—how the entire world, in ecstasy, entered our house and shone like the sun. Only then would they see how little their here and now is worth, and they would kiss the Rebbe's feet!

For the Rebbe's dance, even his everyday dance as glided across a room, was one sixtieth of Paradise. At his daughter's wedding it was no doubt a third or even fully one half!

At the time the klezmer musicians were playing a *freylekhs*. As at other weddings, people were spread throughout the room. Some danced a few steps off to the side, in pairs, in threes, or made a small circle; others sang or drank, a bit like in a wedding in the olden days.

Suddenly the Rebbe, of blessed memory, stood up, went to the middle of the room, and stopped. He gave the musicians a sign with one finger and they stopped playing.

The Rebbe stood in the middle of the room, his face blazed with holy spirit, his eyes lit up the room like stars, his satin caftan mirrored and flashed, his shtrayml teemed with hundreds of silver arrows—all this caught hold of your eyes and captured your heart.

The room fell silent as all eyes were drawn to the Rebbe and cleaved to his form. People held their breath and could hear the motion of the grandfather clock several rooms away, and in this sweet stillness the Rebbe began his quiet melody.

In the middle he broke off his song and began to let out special, separate voices, and the people soon understood what these separate voices were! He was sending good tidings out into the world, announcing and proclaiming that Feygele's wedding would take place under a good star and in a lucky hour. . . . It seemed to me that I clearly saw white doves, like snowflakes, flying out of the Rebbe's mouth. Later he would have to concede that these voices were emissaries he was sending out to the entire world—to all of the animals, to all of the trees and grasses, to deserts, forests, seas and streams, to heaven and earth, to Gehenom, to Paradise, to the Patriarchs, to the heavenly court. He was inviting them all to the wedding.

When the people felt that the heat in the room had suddenly become many times more intense—and when the Rebbe, blessed be he, saw that they had arrived—he went back to his sweet melody and began to sing it with words, with sacred phrases! Then he began to dance, and all eyes looked down and cleaved to his holy feet. . . .

Happy indeed is the eye that saw this!

It is known to all that immediately after the passing away of the Rebbe—and after there occurred what should not have occurred with his son-in-law, with Feygele's husband—I was left like a sheep without a shepherd. I traveled through all of the lands of the Jewish diaspora and searched . . . and nowhere did I find what I wanted, what my heart longed for. I looked at many things, and what I saw made my hair stand on end, but nowhere did I see ecstasy.

Sadness, melancholy, broken hearts . . . and when I did meet up with a little joy, it was merely the joy of a holiday or special occasion, so long as a bottle was near at hand! After the rebbe, no one attained the wholeness of a melody. . . . Everyone just grumbled, and no one even thought of dancing!

No one sang—the voices were wooden; no one danced—the feet refused to budge; the hands were clumsy and the body was lazy—cold, frozen. When people did sing or dance, once a year on Simkhes Toyre, it was chaos: the words went one way, the melody went another way, and the feet did their own thing separately. There was no connection among them—three strangers came together and each paced the floor alone. . . .

Together with the Rebbe's passing away, ecstasy also died. Only he knew the soul of dance, melody, and song; only he knew which bodily movements belong together with one or another melody; only he knew which music we needed for these or other words.

But let us return to the matter at hand.

The Rebbe was standing in the middle of the wedding celebration, singing and dancing, while we stood around him in circle after circle. We saw the sounds and heard the dance, and everyone around began to sing and dance—even the musicians, caught up in the enthusiasm, dropped their instruments and began to sing and dance. I was privileged to dance with the Rebbe, our master and teacher, face-to-face. Amidst all this I saw that the groom was silent, that the groom alone neither sang nor danced.

"Rebbe," I cried out in a voice not my own, "even the musicians are singing and dancing, but he isn't."

The Rebbe danced closer to me and said: "Don't worry, have faith in Feygele's good fortune, she should live and be well."

Later, before the banquet, he whispered to me: "You will hear him teach Torah in harmony with my dancing."

And so it came to pass. . . .

I don't remember the Torah itself, which the groom discussed in his speech; you know that I am no prodigy in revealed wisdom. I did not grasp everything, in particular because he spoke Yiddish with a thick Lithuanian accent—and so fast, that we became dizzy from the fiery gears that were turning before our eyes.

The Talmudic topic he discussed was profound, a very deep matter. . . . Around him, a few dozen learned men stood staring with open mouths.

The rabbi's assistant from Kovel, with his staunch intellect, never listened to anyone; he would jump up, point his bony finger at a person, and yell, "Ignoramus!" Even he sat quietly, with a sweet smile on his face, listening and nodding his head.

Everyone heard the groom, but only I knew the secret—that he was speaking what the Rebbe had danced. They all heard the outward words he spoke, and I alone knew the inner meaning of his speech. . . . And when I shut my eyes, I could see the Rebbe dancing!

The same thing happened as when the Rebbe danced. . . .

It was quiet, so quiet that one could hear the motion of the Rebbe's grandfather clock several rooms away. . . . In the middle was the groom, and the people stood around him in circle after circle, with their faces blazing and their eyes burning, holding their breath.

Upon the groom rested the glory of the Torah, and light streamed out as from the sun, kindling the souls—all around stood flaming souls!

His lips danced like the Rebbe's feet. All eyes hung on his words as they had followed the Rebbe's feet, and everyone around filled with pleasure and devotion.

At that moment, he too was a master and teacher . . . the soul of the community.

They were drawn to him like iron filings to a magnet. As if by magic he carried them along with him, far out into the street, far from the city, over valleys and mountains, beyond seas and deserts.

His eyes gleamed like the Rebbe's, and the groom's hands worked like our Rebbe's pure feet. . . .

As I sat staring dreamily into space, suddenly someone touched me on the shoulder. I looked around—it was the Rebbe, who said:

"You see! That's how I danced. But one melody is missing, blocked at the door: he is a student of the Vilna Gaon![2] Ach!"

This "Ach!" pierced my heart like a knife.

Suddenly he said, "Haim, go give whisky to the peasant coachmen."

I have not yet begun to understand what that meant.[3]

Translated by Ken Frieden

2. "Vilna Gaon": Elijah ben Solomon Zalman (1720–1797) was a renowned Talmud scholar and opponent of the hasidim.

3. Peretz signed the original, Hebrew version of this story (1894) with the pseudonym, "The Orphan from Nemirov."

The Rebbe's Pipe

You don't have to be an old timer to remember how, a while back, Sarah-Rivka lacked not only children but bread, God help us! Pure and simple — bread.

Her husband Haim-Barukh was *always* a great hasid. From the very beginning, ever since his father-in-law (may he rest in peace — an honest man) brought him back from a town outside Lublin.

It was soon obvious that he was a holy vessel, a blessing from God. He was a person who, if he did not bring the Messiah, could at least tap wine from the wall.

That's the sort of reputation he had!

In his deep, downcast eyes, a kind of hidden gleam constantly trembled, as if someone were walking around with a lantern in a darkened room.

His face was pale, but somehow it blossomed like a rose, so fine was his skin. At his temples you could always see something beating, pounding. He was so thin that he wrapped his simple caftan belt around himself at least ten times.

Obviously, such a person was not content just studying the Talmud. He went deeper and deeper: to *The Zohar, The Tree of Life* . . . you name it!

He used to sit for hours with the Rebbe, long may he live, without speaking a word — they exchanged glances, winks. Well, would you talk to such a man about taking a job?

Why, then, did people in the House of Study call him, "Haim-Baruch, Sarah-Rivka's husband," or just "Sarah-Rivka's husband"? Why did they hang all his wisdom on the pot of peas with yeast that Sarah-Rivka sold at the market? It was incomprehensible.

It caused her, Sarah-Rivka herself, terrible anguish. She felt it really was an honor that he was known by her name, but she also knew that this would diminish her joy in the *other* world!

Very often, two or three times a week, she would come into the House of Study with her pot of peas.

158

"Haim-Baruch," the yeshiva boys would cry, "your provider is here!"

It seems that Haim-Baruch had heard her coming up the stairs and had hidden himself long before in *The Zohar*. The greasy, jaunty tip of his yarmelke quivered above the prayer stand. But she didn't even look at that, or look at all in his direction, because she didn't want to see how the Divine Presence hovered over his studies. Her eyes shouldn't feed on delights of this world, she thought, but there, in the World to Come! Still, her heart filled with warmth and satisfaction.[1]

She left the House of Study feeling taller, greater, and with a brighter, freer look. It was impossible to tell that she was already almost thirty—without a wrinkle on her brow, with a charming, blushing face, she looked as though she had just stepped out from under the wedding canopy!

And precisely this, when she remembered herself, caused her anguish. She brooded, sick at heart, that nothing would be left for the other world. She would rise up like a plucked goose, without merits to her name. For what was she *doing?* She wandered around in the street with her pot of peas, from one Thursday to the next, carrying yeast to a few houses! What good was she to him?

So long as her father, may he rest in peace, was still alive and the wheels were turning, there was a place to live, something to eat, and plenty to drink. Today? She wished it upon all the enemies of the Jews!

The dowry had somehow been lost, and the little house was sold.

Breakfast was fish-grits—potatoes and water. At night they had soup and a stale bagel. That was his portion in this world!

In the past seven years she had never even made him a caftan. From one Passover to the next—a single hat, a pair of boots, nothing more! From Sabbath to Sabbath, she gave him one shirt to wear—it looked more like a spider's web than a shirt. She held her glasses up to his shirts and darned them until nothing was left.

"Master of the Universe," she thought, "in the world to come, if they place one letter of the Torah he has learned on one scale, and all of my soup and fish-grits on the other, together with my bad eyes, which will tip the balance?"

---

1. At this point in the story, the 1895 version contains the following passage that was later omitted: "Sometimes she felt almost intoxicated, as if she had downed a flask of whisky at a bris. The yeshiva boys knew this and . . . treated her accordingly, took a larger portion and stole a few of her peas. It was no use!"

She knew that what is linked in *this* world remains connected in the *other* world. Man and wife are not so quickly separated there! Would he, such a gem as he was, allow it? At meals, didn't she see how he also wanted her to take a taste? Of course he wouldn't speak of such foolish matters, but he gestured with his eyes. If she pretended not to notice, he muttered under his breath, like in the middle of the Silent Prayer. No, he wouldn't allow it! He wouldn't sit beside the Throne of Glory among saints and patriarchs while she wandered around somewhere among sinners in desolate woods, in the realm of chaos!

But what good would it do? First, it would be disgraceful for her to lift up her eyes among the matriarchs—the shame would burn her up! Second, she had no children, while the years came and went. They'd been married seven years, and after three more accursed years he would divorce her! Could she object?

Another woman would be his footstool in Paradise, God knows, and she would rot in hell with some lowly tailor. . . . Did she deserve anything better?

More than once a tailor or cobbler appeared to her in a dream, and she woke up moaning. He would wake up terrified and ask her, in the dark, "What's the matter?" But she would answer, "Nothing!" She would cry and pray to God that a blessing would come to her from the peas and yeast.

He really was a precious gem! Foolish woman, he thought, what she was going through! He reckoned that something had to be done about it. She should indulge herself, take a bite of food now and then. He looked and looked for a solution in sacred books. But it often happens that the one thing you're looking for is what you don't find. Instead, you come across such things inadvertently, unawares!

Occasionally, it seemed to him that when he was onto something, he became confused—the devil take it!—and he had to start over from the beginning.

He thought about it and decided to have a talk with the Rebbe, long may he live!

But it wasn't easy.

The first time, the Rebbe was distracted and didn't hear him; the second time, he nodded his head—it was neither here nor there; the third time, he answered:

"Hmm. Certainly the right thing to do would be . . ." But someone came in and interrupted the conversation.

Another time he made a special trip to the Rebbe and asked him: "Well?"

"Well, well!" answered the Rebbe, and nothing more.

Once Haim-Baruch was sitting with the Rebbe, before the Sabbath arrived, and gave a sigh.

"That's no way to be," the Rebbe said angrily. "A hasid of mine doesn't sigh. What's the meaning of this?"

"The yeast!" answered Haim-Baruch.

"All over the world Jews have finished baking challah," the Rebbe replied. "One doesn't talk about yeast on Friday afternoon!"

Saturday evening Haim-Baruch spoke his mind openly:

"Rebbe," he said, "perhaps you could enter into the matter?"

Again the Rebbe became angry and said, "And you—are you ill? Are the gates of heaven, God forbid, closed to your prayers?"

Haim-Baruch heard clearly the "God forbid," and so a stone fell from his heart. Nevertheless, a few months passed and nothing happened.

He came to the Rebbe again on Rosh Hashanah. After the holiday was over, suddenly the Rebbe slapped him on the back in front of the whole community and asked:

"Haim-Baruch, what do you lack?"

He became embarrassed and answered, "Nothing at all!"

"Untrue!" the Rebbe said. "You need something."

"What?" asked Haim-Baruch, trembling, and on the tip of his tongue was *the blessing over the yeast and peas.*

But the Rebbe didn't let him say a thing and counted out a few words like pearls:

"You—Haim-Baruch—need—a long-shank tobacco pipe!"

The congregants were astounded.

"You smoke from a measly little pipe, like a coachman!"

Haim-Baruch took the small pipe out of his mouth and just managed to stammer:

"I'll tell Sarah-Rivka."

"Tell her, tell her," the Rebbe said. "She should buy you a big, long-shank pipe. Take my holiday pipe with you, for size; that's how it should look." And he handed over his pipe to him. And that's all!

Even before he came home to the shtetl, everyone knew that Haim-Baruch was bringing the Rebbe's long-shank, holiday pipe with him.

"When? Why?" people asked in all of the streets and houses. All of the

Jewish townspeople trembled in awe. "What's it for?" Then they answered their own question: "For children, no doubt!"

People realized that Haim-Baruch was suffering from what besets all scholars who burn the midnight oil. Evidently the smoke from the Rebbe's holiday pipe would have an effect on this. And something else: Sarah-Rivka suffered from bad eyes. She'd been wearing glasses for twenty-two years; the Rebbe no doubt had this in mind. This was no small matter, Haim-Baruch's wife!

Simply put: what could such a pipe, a holiday pipe no less, *not* do?

And even before Haim-Baruch stepped down from the wagon, a hundred people had already asked that he lend them the pipe—for a month, a week, a day, an hour, a minute, or a second. They were ready to shower him with gold!

He answered all of them:

"What do I know? Ask Sarah-Rivka." He had spoken prophetically.

Sarah-Rivka had a good business. A draw from the Rebbe's pipe cost a ruble. A ruble, not a kopeck less!

And the pipe worked!

People paid, and Sarah-Rivka already has her own little house, a nice little shop with a lot of yeast and many other goods.

She herself is fuller, healthier, taller! She made her husband new clothes and put aside her glasses.

A few weeks ago men came to get the pipe for the feudal lord! They put down three silver rubles, what else?

"And children?" you want to know.

Of course! Already three or four. And Haim-Baruch has become a new man!

In the House of Study there's an ongoing debate. Some people say that Sarah-Rivka doesn't want to give back the Rebbe's pipe and will never return it! Others say that she gave it back long ago, and the one she lends is a copy. . . .

Haim-Baruch keeps quiet.

What difference does it make? So long as it helps![2]

Translated by Ken Frieden

2. Peretz signed the original Yiddish version of this story with the pseudonym, "The Orphan from Nemirov."

If Not Higher!

A Hasidic Story

Every morning during the week of Penitential Prayers, the Rebbe of Nemirov would vanish—disappear without a trace!

He was nowhere to be seen: not in the synagogue, not in either of the study houses, not in a prayer minyan, and certainly not at home. The front door stood open, and anyone could come or go at will. No one would steal from the Rebbe, though not a living thing stirred at home.

Where could the Rebbe be?

Where *should* he be? Up in heaven, of course! Does a rebbe have so little business to take care of up there before the Days of Awe? God save us from the Evil Eye, Jews need sustenance, peace, health, and good matches for their children. Jews want to be good and pious, but many are the sins and Satan—with his thousand eyes—sees from one end of the world to the other, submits complaints, and denounces people. . . . Who should help us, if not the Rebbe?

That's what his disciples thought.[1]

But once a Litvak came to visit, and he laughed! You know the Litvaks—they look down on books about everyday moral teachings, and they stuff themselves with Talmud and commentaries. So the Litvak points to a clear passage in the Gemarah, he pokes out your eyes with it. He shows that even Moses, in his lifetime, was unable to ascend to heaven—he remained ten hands' breadths below! Well, go argue with a Litvak!

"Then where does the Rebbe go?" the people asked.

"How should I know?" answers the Litvak and shrugs his shoulders, but at that moment he decides to find out. What won't a Litvak do?

That very day, soon after evening prayers, the Litvak steals into the Rebbe's room, crawls under his bed, and lies there. He would wait all night to

---

1. This line, not in the original (1900) publication of the story, was added later.

see where the Rebbe goes and what he does during the week of Penitential Prayers.

Another person might have dozed off and slept away the hours, but a Litvak knows what to do: he studies a complete tractate of the Talmud from memory! I don't recall whether it was *Hulin* or *Nedarim*.

At dawn the Litvak hears people being called to Penitential Prayers. The Rebbe has been awake for some time. For almost an hour, the Litvak has heard him groaning.

Anyone who has heard the Rebbe of Nemirov groan knows how much anguish, how much sorrow for the people of Israel is contained in each groan. Hearing him groan would break your heart! But a Litvak's heart is made of stone, so he listens and stays where he is! So does the Rebbe. The Rebbe, long may he live, lies *on* the bed, and the Litvak lies *under* the bed.

Then the Litvak hears the beds in the house start to creak. . . . He hears people in the house climb out of bed, murmur a few words, pour water over their hands, and open their doors. . . . Next the people leave the house and once again it becomes still and dark. A single ray of light from the moon shines through the shutters.

The Litvak later admitted that, when he was all alone with the Rebbe, he became terrified. His skin was crawling with goose bumps from fear. The roots of his forelocks pricked his temples like needles.

It was no small matter, being alone with the Rebbe one morning during Penitential Prayers! Who knows what can happen and who might appear?[2]

But a Litvak is stubborn, so he quivers like a fish in water and stays where he is.

Finally the Rebbe, long may he live, gets up.

First he does what a Jew must do. . . . Then he goes to the clothes closet and takes out a bundle. Peasants' clothes appear: canvas pants, oversized boots, a coat, a large fur hat, and a long, wide leather belt with brass rivets.

The Rebbe puts it all on. The end of a rough peasant cord peers out from the pocket of the coat.

The Rebbe goes out and the Litvak follows! As he passes through the kitchen, the Rebbe bends down and takes an axe from under a bed, sticks it into his belt, and leaves the house. The Litvak trembles but doesn't give up.

A quiet dread of the Days of Awe hangs over the dark streets. Often a cry es-

---

2. This sentence, present in the original printing of the story, was later omitted.

capes from some minyan saying the Penitential Prayers, or a sick person moans behind a window. The Rebbe keeps to the sides of the road, in the shadow of the houses. He slips from one house to the next and the Litvak follows.

The Litvak hears the pounding of his own heart merge with the sound of the Rebbe's heavy steps; but he keeps walking and leaves town together with the Rebbe.

Outside the town there is a small forest.

The Rebbe, long may he live, enters the woods. He walks thirty or forty steps and stops beneath a small tree. The Litvak watches, amazed, as the Rebbe takes the axe out of his belt and starts to chop down the tree.

He watches the Rebbe hack and hack, and he hears the tree groan and crack. The tree falls. Then the Rebbe chops it into logs and splits the logs into thin pieces of wood. He makes a bundle of wood, ties it with the cord from his pocket, hefts the bundle onto his shoulders, sticks the axe back in his belt, leaves the forest, and returns to the town.

On a back street he stops at a poor, broken-down hut and knocks on the window.

"Who is it?" someone asks, frightened, from inside. The Litvak recognizes the voice of a woman, a sick old woman.

"*Ya*. It's me!" answers the Rebbe in the language of the local peasants.

"*Kto ya?* Who?" comes a voice from the hut.

"Vassil," the Rebbe answers again in Russian.

"What Vassil? And what do you want, Vassil?"

"I have wood to sell!" says the Rebbe.[3] "Very cheap wood, a bundle of wood for almost nothing." And without waiting for an answer, he goes into the hut.

The Litvak also sneaks in and, in the gray light of dawn, he sees an impoverished room, in shambles, with squalid furnishings. In bed lies a sick Jewish woman wrapped in rags, and she says in a bitter voice:

"Buy? How should I buy wood? Does a poor widow like me have money?"

"I'll lend it to you," answers the disguised Rebbe. "Just three kopecks!"

"And how will I ever pay you?" moans the old woman, half in tears.

---

3. Here the translation follows the 1900 text, which works better in English. The later version replaces "the Rebbe" and "the disguised Rebbe"—here and several lines later—with "the disguised Vassil."

"Foolish person," the Rebbe moralizes. "Look, you're a poor, sick woman and I trust you with this little bit of firewood. I have faith that you will be able to repay me, while you have such a great, strong God and don't trust in Him. You don't even have faith that He will give you three kopecks for the bundle of wood!"

"And who will kindle the fire for me?" the widow grumbles. "You think I have the strength to stand up? My son is off working."

"I'll even make the fire for you," the Rebbe says.

Placing the wood in the stove and sighing, the Rebbe began to say the first part of the Penitential Prayers.

When he lit the fire and the wood gave off a cheerful glow, the Rebbe's voice became livelier as he continued the prayers.

The Rebbe finished his prayers after the fire caught and he had shut the oven.

The Litvak who saw all this became a disciple of the Nemirov Rebbe.

Later, whenever a hasid told a story about how the Rebbe rises every morning during the period of the Penitential Prayers and ascends to heaven, the Litvak no longer laughed. He would only add quietly:

"If not higher!"

Translated by Ken Frieden

Between Two Mountains

You've no doubt heard of the Rabbi of Brisk and the Rebbe of Biale, but not everyone knows that Noah, the pious Rebbe of Biale, was once a brilliant student of the Rabbi of Brisk.[1] He studied with him for a few good years, then disappeared and "went into exile" for a couple years before he was revealed as a hasidic leader in Biale.

He left for this reason: at the yeshiva in Brisk they studied Torah, but the Rebbe felt that it was dry Torah. They would study, for example, the laws concerning women's matters, kashrut, or money. Well and good! When Reuven and Shimon come for a legal decision, or a servant comes with a question, or a woman asks about ritual purity, at that moment Talmudic study takes on new force, comes to life, and rules the world. But without them, the Rebbe felt that the Talmud alone—the body of the Torah, revealed Torah, and what lies on the surface—is sterile. That, he felt, is not the *living Torah*. Torah should live!

In Brisk it was forbidden to study books of kabbalah. The Rabbi of Brisk was an opponent of the hasidim and, by nature, "vengeful and vigilant as a snake." If someone touched *The Zohar* or another kabbalistic work, he would curse and place the person under a ban! When someone was once caught reading kabbalah, the rabbi sent some local peasants to shave off his beard. What do you think happened? The man went mad, fell into a deep depression. And what's even more surprising, not a single person could help him. Don't play around with the Rabbi of Brisk! So how does someone leave the rabbi's yeshiva?

He hesitated for a long time. But once a vision came to him in a dream. He dreamed that the Rabbi of Brisk visited him and said, "Come, Noah, I will lead you into the lower realm of Paradise." He took him by the hand and led him. They entered a grand palace. In the palace there were no doors or win-

---

1. This story assumes some familiarity with the protracted conflict between the hasidim and their opponents, the *mitnagdim*—in this instance, between the hasidic Rebbe of Biale and the scholarly Rabbi of Brisk.

dows except for the door through which they had entered. Yet it was bright in the palace because, it seemed to the Rebbe, the walls were made of crystal and cast a bright glow.

They walked and walked, and there was no end in sight.

"Hold on to my coat," said the Rabbi of Brisk. "Here there are endless chambers, beyond number, and if you become separated from me, you will be lost forever. . . ."

That's what the Rebbe did, and as they walked farther and farther, along the way he saw no benches, no household objects—nothing!

"Nobody sits down here," the Rabbi of Brisk explained to him. "Here people walk forever!" And he followed him. Each room was grander and brighter than the last, and the walls shone in one color after another—in one place there were a few colors, and in another place there were all the colors of the rainbow. Not a single person did they meet along the way.

The Rebbe became tired of walking. Sweat poured down his body, a cold sweat. All of his limbs went numb and his eyes began to ache from the constant glow.

A deep longing came over him, a longing for Jews, friends, the people of Israel. It was no small matter—there was not a person in sight!

"Don't wish for anyone else," said the Rabbi of Brisk. "This palace is just for me and for you. One day you will become the Rabbi of Brisk!"

But the Rebbe became even more frightened and grasped at the wall in order not to stumble. The wall burned him—not the way fire scalds, the way ice burns.

"Rabbi," he cried out, "the walls are ice, not crystal! Nothing but ice!"

The Rabbi of Brisk was silent. And the Rebbe continued:

"Rabbi, take me away from here! I don't want to be alone with you. I want to be among the people of Israel!"

No sooner had he said this, than the Rabbi of Brisk disappeared and he remained all alone in the palace.

He had no idea which way led in or out; the walls cast upon him a cold fear; and he longed even more intensely for another person, for a glimpse of another person, if only a cobbler or tailor. He began to sob bitterly.

"Master of the Universe," he begged, "take me away from here! Better to be with the people of Israel in hell than all alone here!"

At that very moment, there appeared a simple Jewish man with a red coachman's belt around his waist and a long whip in his hand. The man silently took him by the sleeve, led him out of the palace, and then disappeared. That was the dream that came to the Rebbe.

When he got up the next morning at dawn, he understood that it was no ordinary dream. He dressed quickly and wanted to run into the House of Study to ask the students who slept there to interpret the dream. Passing through the marketplace, however, he saw a large, old-fashioned wagon. Beside it stood a coachman wearing a red belt around his waist, holding a long whip — just like the man in his dream who led him out of the palace.

He understood that it was a sign, so he went up and asked:

"Which way do you happen to be going?"

"Not *your* way!" answered the coachman rudely.

"Still," he begged, "maybe I could travel with you."

The coachman thought it over a bit and answered:

"A boy like you can't travel on foot? Find your *own* way!"

"Where should I go?"

"Wherever your eyes take you," said the coachman as he turned away. "What do I care?"

The Rebbe understood and went into exile!

As I mentioned earlier, he was revealed as a hasidic leader a few years later in Biale. (I will not retell the story as it has been passed down to us, although it's a gripping tale that would make your hair stand on end.) About a year after he was revealed, Reb Yehiel — a respected man in Biale — brought me into his home as a tutor.

At first I didn't even want to accept the position. Reb Yehiel, you should know, was a wealthy man of the old school, stuffed to the gills with money. He would give his daughters a dowry of a thousand gold coins, and he arranged matches with the greatest rabbinical families. His last daughter-in-law was, in fact, the Rabbi of Brisk's daughter!

You must have gathered by now that, if the Rabbi of Brisk and all of his in-laws were opponents of the hasidim, so was Reb Yehiel. But I happen to be a disciple of the Rebbe of Biale — well, how could I get involved with such a household?

I was, nevertheless, drawn to Biale. Living in the same city as the Rebbe is no small matter. I racked my brains over it and decided to go!

It turned out that Reb Yehiel himself was an honest, righteous Jew. I can even attest that, against his will, his heart was drawn to the Rebbe. He really wasn't a scholar, and he no doubt looked at the Rabbi of Brisk the way a hen looks at a person. He didn't forbid me to be an adherent of the Bialer Rebbe, but he himself kept his distance. When I told a story about the Rebbe he pretended to yawn, but I saw that he pricked up his ears. It was only his son, the Rabbi of Brisk's son-in-law, who furrowed his brow and looked at me with a combination of anger and scorn. But he didn't argue; by nature he spoke little.

Then came the fateful day when Reb Yehiel's daughter-in-law, the Rabbi of Brisk's daughter, was about to give birth! You think that for a woman to give birth is no big deal? But there was a story behind this. It was known that the Rabbi of Brisk—because he had ordered that a hasid's beard and forelocks be shorn—was being punished by the saints of our generation. Both of his sons passed away in five or six years, may such a thing never befall you, and none of his three daughters gave birth to a son. What's more, all three of them—God save us—had difficulties in childbirth, and each time they came out of it looking more dead than alive. The heavens had decreed that there would be a difference of opinion between the hasidim and their opponents, and everyone saw and understood that the Rabbi of Brisk was being punished by the righteous men of our generation. Only he himself, with his bright eyes, couldn't see it. Perhaps he didn't want to see! He carried on his opposition to the hasidim with an iron fist, using bans, appeals to higher authorities, and even soldiers, as in former days.

I pitied Gitel—that was the name of the Rabbi of Brisk's daughter. I pitied her very much. First, because she was a Jewish soul; and second, because she was a pure Jewish soul, such a saint as could be found nowhere else on earth.

Poor brides all went to her for help before their weddings; she was such a refined creature! And she had to be punished because of her father's rage. For this reason, as soon as the midwife began to stir in the room, I worked with all my might to have them send word to the Rebbe of Biale. Just a note of entreaty without any payment—as if the Rebbe needed money!

In any case, the Rebbe of Biale did not approve of the custom people have of sending money to their rebbes.

But who was there to talk to? I tried with the Rabbi of Brisk's son-in-law, for I knew that his soul was deeply bound to hers. Wherever he was, the harmony of their home was evident in every corner, from each of their movements and gestures. But he was, after all, the son-in-law of the Rabbi of Brisk! He spit and walked away, leaving me with my mouth hanging open.

Then I went to Reb Yehiel himself, and he answered me:

"It's the daughter of the Rabbi of Brisk. I won't do that to the Rabbi of

Brisk even if her life is in danger, God forbid!" Next I tried with his wife—an honest, simple Jewish woman. She answered me in these words:

"If my husband requests it, I will send the Rebbe my own holiday kerchief and earrings—they cost a fortune! But without my husband, not a kopeck, not a pip!"

"Just a short note. . . . What harm could that do?"

"Nothing, not without my husband's knowledge," she answered, as a virtuous Jewish woman should answer. Then she turned away and I saw that she was fighting back tears—a mother's heart understands, and already she sensed the danger.

As soon as I heard the woman's first shriek, I *myself* went running to the Rebbe.

"Shmaye," he answered me, "what should I do? I will pray for her."

"Rebbe," I begged, "give me something for the woman—an amulet, a charm, or a coin. . . . Give me whatever you can."

"It would only make matters worse, God forbid," he answered. "Without faith, such things can do harm, and she doesn't believe in them."

What could I do? It was in the early days of Sukkot, she was having a difficult time giving birth, and I couldn't do anything to help, so I remained with the Rebbe. I was a member of the household, and I thought that at every moment I would implore the Rebbe to intercede, and perhaps he would have mercy.

We heard that things were not going well. On the third day the birth pangs stopped. They had already done everything they could: they left no stone unturned, prayed to the dead, burned hundreds of candles in the synagogue and in the House of Study. And as for charity—they gave away a fortune. It's beyond words. They opened all of their clothes closets; there was a mountain of coins on the table, and poor folk came in and took whatever they wanted, as much as they wanted!

It pulled at my heartstrings.

"Rebbe," I said, "it is written that charity preserves us from death."

Without any reproach in his voice, he answered:

"Perhaps the Rabbi of Brisk will come!"

At that moment Reb Yehiel came in. He didn't speak to the Rebbe, as if he hadn't seen him.

"Shmaye," he said to me and caught me by the lapel. "In back there's a wagon. Climb in and ride to the Rabbi of Brisk—tell him to come!"

Apparently he sensed what was going on, because he added: "He ought to see for himself what's happening! He should tell us what to do." And Reb Yehiel's face—what should I tell you? He looked like a corpse.

So I went! I thought to myself that if the Rebbe knew he was on the way, something good would come of it. Maybe even peace! That is, not between the Rabbi of Brisk and the Rebbe of Biale, because they themselves were not fighting, but between the two sides. Indeed, when he arrived, he himself would see! He had eyes, too.

But apparently the heavens don't allow such a thing to happen so quickly. The heavens waged war against me. As soon as I left Biale, a cloud spread across the sky, and what a cloud! It was a heavy storm cloud, black as pitch. Abruptly the wind began to blow, as if all at once spirits were flying in from all sides.

Peasants understand such things, and the coachman crossed himself, pointed his whip at the sky, and said that, God forbid, it could be a difficult journey. As he was speaking the wind blew up even stronger, tore open the cloud cover like a sheet of paper, and started to drive one bit of cloud into another like sheets of ice on the water. Above my head were two or three layers of clouds. At first I wasn't even scared: getting soaked is nothing new to me, and I'm not afraid of thunder. First, because it doesn't thunder during Sukkot, and second—because the Rebbe had blown the shofar on Yom Kippur! Everyone knows that after such a blowing of the shofar, for the next year thunder has no power over us. But then the rain suddenly struck me in the face like a whip once, twice, three times. All the blood drained out of my face and I saw clearly that the heavens were slapping me and driving me back!

The coachman, not one of us, also begged, "Let's go back."

But I knew that a life was at stake. Sitting on the coach in the storm, I heard the woman's groans and how her husband was cracking his knuckles. He was wringing his hands; I also saw before me Reb Yehiel's ashen face and his burning, sunken eyes.

"Keep going," I insisted, and on we went.

It poured and poured down from above while water spurted up from under the wheels and from beneath the horses' feet. The road was deluged, completely covered by water. On top of the water was foam. It seemed as if the coach was starting to swim, what should I tell you? What's more, we had lost our way . . . but I persisted! I returned with the Rabbi of Brisk during the holiday of Hoshana Raba.

To tell the truth, as soon as the Rabbi of Brisk climbed onto the wagon, the storm calmed! The clouds split open and the sun shone through the crack. We arrived in Biale dry, safe and sound. Even the coachman noticed it and said in his own language, "What a great and powerful rabbi!"

But the main thing is that we arrived. The women who were in the house fell upon him like locusts. They wailed and practically bowed down to the ground before him. We didn't hear the woman in childbirth, from the next room, either because of the other women's wailing or because, God forbid, she no longer had the strength to groan. Reb Yehiel didn't even see us—he stood with his forehead pressed against a windowpane, evidently because his head was burning.

Nor did the Rabbi of Brisk's son-in-law turn around to welcome us. He stood with his face to the wall, and I clearly saw his body shaking and his head knocking against the wall.

I thought I would collapse, so deeply had the anguish and fear penetrated me. All my limbs went numb, and I felt that my soul was going cold!

But did you ever meet the Rabbi of Brisk? That was a man—a pillar of steel, I tell you! He was a very tall man, towering head and shoulders above us. Like a king, he spread terror before him! As if it were today I remember his long, white beard. One point was tucked into his belt and the other point hovered over it.

His white eyebrows were so long and thick that they hid half of his face. When he raised them up—dear God!—the women fell back as if struck by lightning, such eyes he had! Glistening daggers flashed inside them. He called out like a lion, "Women, away!"

Then he asked more gently and politely:

"And where is my daughter?"

They showed him. He went in and I stood stock still, almost out of my wits: what eyes, what a look, what a voice! It is an entirely different path, another world. The Rebbe of Biale's eyes shine so kindly and gently that it enlivens your heart; when he throws you a glance, he sprinkles you with gold. And his voice, his sweet voice, his velvet-sweet voice—Master of the Universe!—pulls at your heart, caresses your heart so delightfully. No one is afraid of him, God forbid; instead, your soul dissolves in love, in the sweetness of love, and it wants to leave your body to merge with his soul. The soul tears itself from your body like a butterfly drawn to a bright flame! But with the Rabbi of Brisk—fear and trembling! A sage, like the sages of yore. And he was entering the room of a woman in childbirth!

"He will turn her," I said fearfully, "into a pile of bones!"

I ran off to the Rebbe. The Rebbe met me at the doorway with a smile and said:

"Did you see the splendor of the Torah?"

I calmed down. If he was smiling, I thought, all would go well.

It really did turn out well. On the last day of Sukkot she pulled through. On the holiday of Simkhes Toyre the Rabbi of Brisk spoke words of Torah at the table. I wanted to be somewhere else during the meal, but I was afraid to leave. Especially since I was the tenth man for a minyan. We would say the blessing "Nevarekh Eloheinu."

Well, what should I tell you? The Rabbi of Brisk's Torah? If the Torah is a sea, he was the Leviathan in the sea. In one motion he swam through ten tractates of the Talmud; in one motion he reconciled the Mishna with its commentaries. It resounded and spattered, seethed and boiled, just as people describe the real sea. He turned my head until I became dizzy. . . . But "a heart knows the bitterness of its soul." My heart still did not feel the joy of the holiday. That's when I remembered the Rebbe's dream, and I froze in place! The sun shone through the window, there was no lack of wine on the table, I saw that everyone else in the room was sweating, but I—I was cold as ice. Across town at the Rebbe's court, I knew, someone was speaking another kind of Torah. . . . There it was bright and warm. Every word was interwoven with love and steeped in spiritual intimacy. One felt that angels were flitting around the room, and people actually heard the rustling of their great, white wings. Oh, dear God—but I was unable to leave!

Suddenly the Rabbi of Brisk broke off and asked:

"What sort of rebbe do you have here?"

"Someone named Noah," was the answer.

It cut me to the quick to hear him called "someone named Noah." Oh, the lie, the hypocrisy!

"A wonder-worker?" he asked further.

"Not often—one doesn't hear much about it. . . . Women tell stories, but who listens to them?"

"He takes money just like that, without performing miracles?"

They tell him the truth, that he seldom takes money and gives a lot away.

The Rabbi of Brisk thought it over and asked:

"Does he study the Talmud?"

"They say—he's a great scholar!"

"Where does he come from, this Noah?"

No one knew, and I had to answer. That's how a conversation started between me and the Rabbi of Brisk.

"Wasn't he once, this Noah, in Brisk?" he asked.

"Was the Rebbe ever in Brisk?" I stammered. "I think so!"

"Ah, here we have one of his disciples!" he said, and he gave me a look, I thought, as if I were a spider.

He turned to the other people and said:

"Long ago I had a student named Noah. He had a good head on his shoulders, but he was drawn to the higher realms. I spoke to him about it once, and I spoke to him about it a second time. I wanted to warn him a third time, but he disappeared. Isn't he the one?"

"Who knows?"

He started to describe him and hit the mark: thin, short, with a black beard and black, curly forelocks, always lost in thought, with a quiet voice.

"It could be him," the people said. "You're not far from the truth."

I thanked God when they started to say the blessing after the meal.

But after we said the blessing something happened that I could never have dreamed of. The Rabbi of Brisk rose from his seat, called me aside, and said quietly to me:

"Take me to your Rebbe — my student. But listen, no one should know!"

Of course I did as I was told, but along the way I asked him in terror: "Rabbi of Brisk, what is your intention in going to see him?"

He answered me simply: "It occurred to me, while we said the blessing, that until now I have passed judgment on something without having seen it for myself. I want to see, I want to see for myself." Later he added: "Perhaps God will help me and I will be able to save my student."

"You should know, *sheygets*," he went on light-heartedly, "that if your Rebbe is the Noah who studied with me, someday he can be one of the greatest scholars among our people and become the Rabbi of Brisk!"

Then I knew for sure that he was the same person, and my heart skipped a beat.

The two mountains came together. . . . [2] It is a miracle from heaven that I was not crushed on the spot.

2. Peretz's narrator alludes to a folk saying in Aramaic: *tura be-tura lo pagʻa, enosh be-enosh pagʻa* (a mountain does not meet another mountain, but one person meets another person). This is especially evident in the Hebrew version of this story.

The Rebbe of Biale, of blessed memory, used to send his hasidim walking around the city during Simkhes Toyre. He himself would sit on the porch, watching and deriving satisfaction from them.

It was not the Biale of today. Then it was just a small shtetl. The houses were very small and built close to the ground, except for the synagogue and the Rebbe's House of Study. The Rebbe's balcony was on the second floor and from there you could see everything like the back of your hand—the low mountains to the east and the river to the west. So the Rebbe would sit on his porch and watch. When he saw a group of hasidim walking along in silence, he threw down to them from above the commencement of a hasidic melody. They would pick up the tune and sing as they continued on their way. Group after group walked by and went through the city singing, with true joy, with true joy in the Torah. The Rebbe did not move from his porch.

This time, however, the Rebbe apparently heard other steps, and he stood to welcome the Rabbi of Brisk.

"Sholem aleykhem, Rabbi," he said humbly, in his sweet voice.

"Aleykhem sholem, Noah," the Rabbi of Brisk answered.

"Please sit down, Rabbi!"

The Rabbi of Brisk sat and the Rebbe of Biale stood before him.

"Tell me, Noah," said the rabbi, raising his brows, "why did you run away from my yeshiva? What did you lack?"

"I lacked air," answered the Rebbe calmly. "I couldn't catch my breath. . ."

"What does that mean? What are you saying, Noah?"

"Not me," the Rebbe explained in his quiet voice. "My soul was suffocating."

"Why, Noah?"

"Your Torah is all judgment, Rabbi, without mercy! There isn't a spark of kindness in your Torah. For this reason, it is joyless and can't breathe freely. . . . It's all bronze and steel, ironclad rules and copper-plated laws. All of your exalted Torah is for scholars, for exceptional people!"

The Rabbi of Brisk was silent and the Rebbe continued:

"Tell me, Rabbi, what can you offer the people of Israel? What do you have for woodchoppers, butchers, coachmen, and other simple Jews? In particular, what do you have for a sinful person? What can you offer people who are not scholars?"

The Rabbi of Brisk remained silent, as if he did not understand what was being said. The Rebbe of Biale went on standing before him and speaking in his sweet voice:

"Forgive me, Rabbi, but I must tell you the truth. Your Torah is hard, hard and dry, because it is only the body and not the soul of the Torah!"

"The soul of the Torah?" asked the Rabbi of Brisk, rubbing his high forehead.

"Of course! As I said, Rabbi, your Torah is only for extraordinary people, not for all Jews. But the Torah must be for all the people of Israel. The Divine Presence must rest on all of us. Because the Torah is the soul of the people of Israel."

"And what is your Torah, Noah?"

"Do you want to see it, Rabbi?"

"See Torah?" said the Rabbi of Brisk, astonished.

"Come, Rabbi, I will show you my Torah. . . . I will show you its glow and the joy that shines from it on all the people of Israel."

The Rabbi of Brisk didn't move.

"I ask you, Rabbi, come with me. It's not far."

He led him out to the porch, and I followed them silently. But the Rebbe sensed my presence and said:

"You may come along, Shmaya. Today you will see . . . and the Rabbi of Brisk will also see. You will see the joy of the Torah. You will see a true celebration of Simkhes Toyre."

Then I saw the same thing as on every other Simkhes Toyre, but I saw it differently—as if a curtain had been lifted from my eyes.

A great, wide sky—infinite and blue, such a bright blue that the sky was a delight to behold. White, silvery clouds swam across the sky, and if you looked at them closely, you could see how they trembled with joy, how they danced along with Simkhes Toyre! Farther off, the city was surrounded by a broad, dark green belt. But the green was alive, so lively, as if a life force were flowing through the grass; now and again, it seemed, this force burst out into existence, a smell, a new life. We felt clearly how the flames leaped and danced among the blades of grass, as if they were hugging and kissing.

Group after group of hasidim walked among the flames in the meadows. Their satin caftans and belts gleamed like mirrors—both those that were torn and those that were whole. The flames that moved among the blades of grass caught onto the mirroring holiday clothes, and it seemed as if they were dancing around every hasid with love and burning passion. And all of the groups of hasidim looked up toward the Rebbe's porch with wondrous, thirsty eyes. I saw clearly that these thirsty eyes drew light from the Rebbe's face on the porch, and the more light they took in, the louder they sang—with greater exhilaration and holiness.

Each group sang its melody, but all of the melodies and voices mixed together in the air; and one harmonious melody floated up to the Rebbe's porch, as if they were all singing one song. Everything sang—the heavens, the planets, and the earth below sang. Everything was singing!

Master of the Universe! I thought I would dissolve into the sweetness. . . .

But it was not meant to be.

"It's time for the afternoon prayers," the Rabbi of Brisk said suddenly and sharply, and everything vanished.

Silence—and the curtain fell back over my eyes. Above was a simple sky; below was a simple pasture with simple hasidim in torn caftans. There were broken bits of old melodies. The flames were extinguished. I looked at the Rebbe and saw that his face had also gone dark.

They didn't resolve their differences; the Rabbi of Brisk returned home and remained an opponent of the hasidim, as before.

But it did have some effect! He no longer persecuted us.

Translated by Ken Frieden

Biographical Essays

A Celebration of Yiddish Literature

Solomon Moiseevich Abramovitsh
and His Twenty-Five Years of Literary Activity

Lev Binshtok

On the occasion of the twenty-fifth anniversary of Solomon M. Abramovitsh's literary activity, I would like to share with readers of the journal *Voskhod* [Sunrise] a few fragmentary items about the life of the person we are honoring, and to offer a brief survey of his works. The reader might find something here that is interesting and instructive. A rather voluminous book could be written about the life and upbringing of our writer, but in the space of a magazine article we can only mention a few prominent aspects of his life.

I have known Solomon Moiseevich since my early youth. On a number of occasions he and I privately exchanged very detailed stories about our entire past. Those stories serve as a reliable source for my description of him now. I hope that my honored friend will not fault me for impropriety, since his unblemished name could easily stand up to any public scrutiny on its own merits.

Chance constantly intervened in Abramovitsh's life and carried him along, until he embarked upon a smoother path that, incidentally, is still not exactly strewn with roses. His life is a microcosm of the tragic history of our entire hapless tribe, which still senses it stands on rather shaky ground and continually moves with the wind—like a shipwrecked traveler on an ice floe at sea in the arctic—without plan, purpose, or sight of firm ground anywhere. From time to time the traveler comes upon an enormous sheet of ice on

Yehuda-Leyb (Lev) Binshtok (1836–1894) completed his studies at the Rabbinical Institute in Zhitomir in 1858. He was a friend of S. Y. Abramovitsh and collaborated with him on several literary projects. *Source: Leksikon fun der nayer yidisher literatur*, vol. 1 (New York: Alveltlekhn yidishn kultur-kongres, 1956), 297–98.

which he might take a respite from the relentless storms and hurricanes around him. But then, once again, storm clouds gather, the winds become stronger and turn into a hurricane. The ice breaks up under the feet of a frightened people, and in just another minute it might crack apart. . . . The skies clear, the ocean waves recede, and another huge block of ice comes to the rescue; but alas, this too is not solid ground, but only floating ice over a yawning cold abyss!

The basic everyday upbringing of Jewish children doesn't represent anything of particular interest. Every Jew educated in the good old way remembers well all the unattractive circumstances of his heder, where he spent joyless days of his childhood and youth. Every Jewish man remembers well his eternally menacing teacher [melamed] who never smiled and who was never satisfied with anything. What boy in an old-time heder did not curse in his heart the terrible teacher's ruler and the eternal useless poring over tomes whose meaning was harder to crack than a coconut?

Solomon Abramovitsh was born in 1835 [or 1836] in Kopyl [Kapulye] in Belorussia, near Minsk, and he began his education exactly as did all of his contemporaries. Still, the heder he attended was above the ordinary, and we shall dwell somewhat on this heder where the future writer obtained his first childhood impressions. Abramovitsh's father was considered one of Kopyl's best Talmudists. He was respected and honored at the House of Study not only for his Jewish scholarship, but because he was also considered the prime authority in the village. People came to him for advice—both for explanations of difficult passages in the Talmud and in regard to difficult everyday problems. As a prosperous man, the elder Abramovitsh wanted his son, who from early childhood demonstrated exceptional talent, to be in a better position than his contemporaries in the study of the holy Torah (which, of course, meant not only the holy scriptures, but the Talmud and the entire vast rabbinical literature). In other words, he wanted his son to study more than children ordinarily do and didn't want his child to waste valuable time. There was at the time a teacher in Kopyl named Yose Rubens who was well known as a remarkable Hebraist and Talmudist, and as an absolute original. Indeed, how could he not have that reputation given the fact that here was a Talmud scholar who was extraordinarily skillful in carpentry, who worked expertly with wood and stone and who, in addition, had an eye for painting? The wooden carvings on the synagogue ark in Kopyl are his. Most of the engravings on the tombstones in the Kopyl cemetery are his work. His hands crafted engravings on steel and copper and he personally designed embroidery patterns for the entire fair sex of Kopyl. He decorated the walls of the great synagogue with various sacred emblems and intricate designs. Moreover, whenever someone suffered from an unfamiliar disease, he alone was able to prescribe an assortment of incantations and remedies made from almonds and beans. On a number of occasions, Solomon told me that this self-taught artist was a noble soul and possessed an excellent gift for teaching. In spite of his many vocational talents he was extremely poor, and Bible teaching was his principal means of support in life.

This exceptional teacher was assigned the task of training our gifted lad. Although the teacher conscientiously carried out this obligation and did not try to distract the youngster's attention with extraneous activities, they nevertheless aroused the inquisitive boy's curiosity and drew him toward something else, as yet unknown, to the dreamlike faraway place that must lie beyond the limits of the Talmud and its interpretation. The boy's ready imagination was further influenced by two other unique personalities who were close friends of the teacher and whom he had occasion to observe quite frequently. One of these exceptional people was a member of the local scholarly Jewish aristocracy who broke off all his ties with it and, against all tradition, gave up his study of the Talmud for carpentry, which afforded him a comfortable living. In some way or other, he also learned to play the violin, which became a constant companion during his leisure hours. He delighted all of the children of Kopyl with his unpretentious music. This artist-carpenter was quite childlike when among children. He strolled and played with them and only in the presence of children did he find true pleasure and happiness. Solomon became attached to this eccentric person with his whole innocent young heart and avidly listened to his cheerful songs as well as his fantastic tales of hoary antiquity. The other unique person was this man's exact opposite—a realist and a freethinker. His activities and very appearance violated all the norms of Kopyl. He was a barber-surgeon (*feldsher*) by profession. He always dressed like a German, was clean-shaven, and he generally lived more freely than the others in that he ignored certain time-honored customs and rituals. Although Kopyl residents considered him to be something of a renegade, no one dared speak out against him since he was the only medical person to whom they could turn in need. Besides, in spite of all his freethinking, he had solid Talmudic knowledge and wrote a Torah scroll on parchment in beautiful quadratic handwriting, which he presented to the Kopyl synagogue as a gift. This learned barber-surgeon frequently agreed with the teacher Yose Rubens about scholarly matters in the Talmud, and as he drew the full attention of the quick-learning youngster, he perhaps implanted the first seeds of analytical thinking into his young and open mind.

Until he was eleven years old, Solomon was constantly under the teacher's supervision. During that period he thoroughly studied all of the holy scriptures, together with the Aramaic translation, and acquired a considerable knowledge of the Talmud. Word about the exceptional scholarship and talent of the youngster spread far beyond the confines of the village, and all who came to know him predicted that he would hold a rabbinical position in some large Jewish community. When Solomon turned eleven, his father took upon himself the task of furthering his son's education for his future calling. It goes without saying that this consisted exclusively of studying the Talmud in depth, along with its innumerable commentaries and the entire rabbinical literature. His studies under his father's supervision did not have any fixed time or systematic structure. Sometimes our young man would go three or four days in a row without anything to do. But at other times his father would awaken his beloved son at four in the morning and work with him without any break until the boy was exhausted. At times both teacher and pupil would become engrossed in the most intricate casuistic questions of Jewish law or other matters, and at other times the teacher would entertain the fatigued mind of his pupil with marvelous tales about Jewish life and Talmudic legends.

Solomon made such amazing progress in his studies of the holy scriptures and Talmud that by the age of fourteen he was considered a man of sharp intellect, a *kharef* [Yiddish, from Hebrew *harif*], and boldly took to the battlefield where he often performed with surprising marksmanship and astonished warriors who were battle-hardened in casuistics. In addition to the Talmud, he knew the entire Bible perfectly and wrote in the language of the ancient prophets just as easily as some grey-haired scholars write in their own native language.

Firmly ensconced in the world of antiquity as represented by the Bible and Talmud, and without having any real knowledge of European literature, Solomon instinctively reached out for a literary career. While other boys played children's games, he was already writing a sort of drama-tirade in Hebrew as well as a number of poems in praise of his natural environment. This dramatic work, which we shall describe below, did not of course have any real literary merit, but it does prove that Solomon began very early to develop the literary talents that would later become a powerful force.

The young Talmud specialist's early days may have been extremely monotonous, but they were not unhappy, since he was able to satisfy all the modest demands that could be expected of a fourteen-year-old Kopyl resident who had never seen anything but his father's house, the House of Study, and the fields and woods surrounding his village. But when he was still too young to have sufficiently developed his physical and moral strength, he lost his one and only guide, mentor, and protector. His father died at the age of forty-one. Almost immediately he came face to face with the sort of extreme deprivation that can only befall a fatherless Jew. His mother was a good-natured woman but extremely weak and naïve. Left with quite a few children, she was unable to take over her husband's activities after he died. The small inheritance he left her quickly disappeared. Her circumstances deteriorated with each passing month. In order to alleviate the plight of the grief-stricken widow, her next of kin decided to send her eldest son to the Slutsk yeshiva so that, in the first place, the boy would not roam idly about; and in the second place, so that he would not be a burden to his mother. For everyone knew that boys at a yeshiva had the full right to starve at public expense and could go barefoot and naked at the expense of Jewish philanthropy. The episodes of his life at the yeshiva are extremely absorbing. But eventually Solomon himself will probably acquaint the reader with that aspect of Jewish life. His masterful pen will doubtless produce something much more complete and artful than could come from my second-hand description.

As soon as Solomon entered the yeshiva, Abramovitsh's widow, at the insistence of those very same relatives, married again and moved with her children to a small village nearby where her second husband leased a flour-grinding mill. The only relatives remaining in Kopyl were Solomon's older married sister and an aunt on his mother's side. The latter's fate was closely bound to that of Solomon himself. Her husband was a tradesman. While Solomon was in Slutsk, his uncle's business ran into trouble and collapsed. Although he could not have been accused of fraud and his liabilities were less than those of Strinzberger or of the Kronstadt Bank, the suspension of payments amounting to 1,000 or 1,500 rubles at that uncivilized period of time was sufficient to alarm everyone in Kopyl. This unfortunate uncle had to leave his native village surreptitiously and flee to a place where people had not heard about his disgrace.

After two years at the yeshiva, Solomon returned to Kopyl and was immediately invited by his stepfather to work at his mill. The village in which Solomon was now obliged to live was exceptionally picturesque. It was situated along a small but clean river, surrounded by an immense forest. The mill was located beside the river, and from it narrow paths led into the heart of the forest. Our young scholar frequently took strolls along these picturesque places so full of poetry, and here his poetic talent first emerged. At the age of seventeen he wrote his first triumphant odes to nature, emulating the Book of Psalms in language, form, and manner of expression. These poems were never published and had a rather naïve, childish character, but even so they give notice of a talent that might, in the right circumstances, rise very high. Village life offered much that was attractive to Solomon's poetic nature, but his environs did not match his spiritual enthusiasm. The dry, petty accounting with millers and his uncle's clients made village life repulsive, and the House of Study in Kopyl and the discussions with scholars there seemed much more attractive than the well-fed but humdrum life at his stepfather's home. Therefore he returned to Kopyl and once again took up studies of Hebrew and rabbinical literature at the House of Study.

At that time a certain local resident named Avreml Khromoy [Abraham the Lame] returned to Kopyl after a long absence. This traveler to distant and unfamiliar lands attracted the attention of all the Kopyl residents from the first day of his return to his homeland. Everyone wanted to know where he had been, what strange things he had seen, and how Jews were getting along there. The eloquent Avreml described the lush villages of Volynia in the most colorful tones.[1] According to Avreml, there were no poor Jews in Volynia. Each farmer had his own cows and goats, and each hut was a horn of plenty. They had white bread there not only for the "Ha-motzi" blessing on the Sabbath, as in Lithuania, but all year, and even on weekdays poor people had white bread. Moreover, the poor lived no worse than prosperous Lithuanian farmers. In Volynia, he himself met some poor people from Lithuania whose satchels were filled with white bread and select pieces of the best *koda*.

"And do you 'shlimmazls' know what *koda* is?" he added with his unique laughter. "That is fat taken from sheep tails," he continued, "not like ours. Those sheep drag tails that weigh a half pound and more. Now that's a coun-

1. In Lithuania, particularly in small villages, "Volynia" [also Volin, Volyn] was understood to mean the entire southwestern and Novorossisk region and Bessarabia [Binshtok's note].

try for you," he always finished his story with a sigh. "There's a country where one can really live!"

The stories Avreml told to the Kopyl residents made their mouths water, and many decided to emigrate to Volynia because of poor local harvest years. But as we shall see, a movement for mass emigration was not at all what Avreml had in mind. After looking around the village a bit, he began frequent conversations with Solomon's aunt and persuaded her that there was no reason for her not to look for her missing husband who, he had heard in passing, was somewhere in the city of O. And, incidentally, she should take her young nephew along with her. He could get an excellent position there in Volynia since the Volynia Jews still did not understand the proper prayer procedures and were delighted when they found a Lithuanian who could serve as a teacher or ne'eman (accountant, manager). After all, it was not good for a young man to fool around and eternally pore over the Talmud. It was high time to think about a goal in life! . . . Although Solomon Moiseevich had a vague sense that the lame demon Avreml had some ulterior motive for talking this claptrap, his desire for something new and particularly something unfamiliar and untried overcame all the fears that Avreml inspired. He was eager to break out of the stifling atmosphere in which he spent his childhood and youth, and he thirsted to know things about which he had only a highly contradictory understanding. Consequently, Solomon tried to persuade his aunt that she should set off to look for her husband in prosperous Volynia where animals lived better than the people in Lithuania.

In the opinion of all the knowledgeable Kopyl residents, Avreml, as a worldly and experienced person, was the best guide to unfamiliar lands. Moreover, he owned a carriage on four squeaky, wooden wheels and a half-blind old nag with a faded mane and tail. Avreml arranged to take Solomon's aunt to the city of O. without any advance payment, since her husband would be obliged to pay for her passage. Her nephew's fare would be paid in the place where he found a position.

Preparations did not take long. Once the emigrants had celebrated Passover, they immediately took to the road. After saying farewell to his relatives, our young Solomon pushed off behind Avreml the Lame's wagon like the old Kholmogorsk peasant behind the Archangel convoy. . . . His sister wept bitterly upon his departure, gave him an entire cottage loaf of black bread and a few copper coins, and released him from her embrace with warm blessings. And so with these modest supplies, but without any luggage and without any references or addresses of friends, Solomon emigrated to the land of milk and honey—full of hope that a few drops would find their way into his mouth.

From the very first day of this journey, our emigrant realized into whose clutches he had fallen. The wagon had room for only his aunt and her little child, so Avreml himself and Solomon had to follow along on foot. One could have coped with this rather unconventional and not quite comfortable means of travel had the road been straight and dry. But it was spring, and in a number of places they ran into a veritable quagmire. The hapless carriage, in spite of its relatively light load, often got stuck in the sticky clay soil and the poor nag simply did not have the strength to drag it out of the mud every time. When this happened, the coachman himself had to help the horse and goaded his traveling companion not to stand around with folded arms.

"Don't think," screamed Avreml in such cases, "that I took you out on the road to be your servant. No, brother, you've got to help; if not, as I wear a beard and *payes*, I'll drop you in the first woods and swamps we reach. I have no intention of being your nanny!" After a few of these vigorous admonitions, Solomon understood that the lesser of evils was to obey his guide until something happened to free him from his grasp. Subsequently, whenever the carriage got stuck, Solomon put his emaciated shoulders to the task without any prompting.

The final destination of the trip, as we know, was the city of O., located in one of the remote regions of the Russian empire, but Avreml was in no hurry to get there. He wanted to prolong the trip as much as possible in order to visit the largest possible number of cities and villages inhabited by his coreligionists. At every town or reasonably sized village, Avreml arranged a rest stop and then sought out the local rabbis to whom he explained in the most eloquent and touching terms that he was traveling with an unfortunate, abandoned wife [*aguna*] to find her husband.[2] The rabbis handed him letters of reference to the charitable sons of Israel and the latter provided him with copper five-kopeck pieces to save a Jewish daughter from the shackles of being an *aguna*. After taking up a collection in one town, Avreml set off for another where he played out the same farce again. Of course, he wisely kept quiet

2. An *aguna* is a woman whose husband is missing. Such a woman was not allowed to marry again until such time as the missing husband was located or proven to be dead [Binshtok's note].

about the money he collected and assured his traveling companion that he was collecting extremely important written rabbinical documents.

There was no reason to doubt Avreml the Lame's knowledge of geography and topography. But instead of keeping to the straight and therefore shortest route, he followed a zigzag pattern that would have stumped the most experienced jokester. He visited places and settlements that could easily have been avoided or bypassed without harm to their main objective. He had little concern about his passengers' stomachs, nor did he trouble himself over sleeping quarters and overnight lodgings. Upon his arrival at any Jewish settlement, he immediately directed his young traveling companion to the House of Study where he could fully immerse himself in the subtleties of the Talmud. He put up the aunt with her child in the wagon with a makeshift canvas cover, while he himself spent days at a time going from one house to another constantly lamenting about the luckless *aguna*. At night he curled up on a bench in one of the prayer houses that, even today, serve as a permanent refuge for unfortunate Jews.

The memorable trip in the company of Avreml the Lame subsequently provided our gifted folk writer with considerable material for his stories about Jewish life. These stories, replete with humor and mild sarcasm, keenly observed and absolutely true to life, often depict places and scenes taken directly from his experience—since he had the opportunity to scrutinize closely his people's life with all of its joys and sorrows, without any embellishment or disguise.

Avreml trekked with his passengers for about one and a half months, until he arrived at the Jewish city of L. [Lutsk] in the Volynia province. He was supposed to stop there for a few days, since they arrived on the eve of the Shavuot holiday, which lasted two days. After stopping at some dilapidated house that was not quite a small tavern or inn, at the edge of town, as usual he sent Solomon off to the House of Study with the great hope that the boy would get the attention due him, and then someone would take him off his hands for a tidy sum. The perspicacious Avreml was not disappointed by his hopes. On the second day of the holiday when he came to the House of Study for services, he heard almost the entire congregation speaking about the young Lithuanian scholar, and each of the notables in the congregation wanted to have this dear guest at his own holiday table. The young people simply clung to him. He was surrounded by whole crowds who listened to his explanations of biblical texts and of the Talmud. To this day, Jews characteristically hold scholarship (Talmudic scholarship, of course) in the highest esteem. Even now it is not rare for a wealthy merchant to arrange for his quite beautiful and intelligent daughter to marry a poor, awkward-looking Talmud scholar who has no idea about secular matters and propriety. The fact that such a Talmud scholar might not be to the liking of the daughter is of no concern, because affectionate and caring parents do not have the modern habit of consulting the desires of their beloved child.

Avreml the Lame was well acquainted with the nature of his coreligionists and concluded almost infallibly that a city like L. [Lutsk] would surely have willing takers for his merchandise. He, in the capacity of matchmaker, protector, and guardian, would not give up that merchandise cheaply. Avreml's reckoning proved to be correct. As soon as he entered the House of Study, he was inundated by questions about the origins, age, occupation, and residence of the young scholar. After satisfying the curiosity of all his questioners, and laying everything out in the best light, he immediately entered into negotiations. These negotiations continued inside the walls of the House of Study. Several times a day Avreml ran over to the House of Study for a brief period and, with particular benevolence, informed Solomon that, as he had expected, God would help him and, very soon, would set him up better than he could have hoped—if, of course, he gave Avreml his complete trust and confidence. Turning a deaf ear to this, Solomon still racked his brain as to what sort of happiness this affectionate guardian and guide might bring him. Meanwhile, he was having a pretty good time among the young people of L. In those days the young people of L. wanted to start a philanthropic society to help the poor. Taking advantage of his presence, the young people turned to him for help in drawing up the by-laws for this society. He willingly took on the task. The by-laws, written in an archaic Hebrew style and beautiful script, delighted everyone. Thus the first independent work by our future Jewish writer was perhaps undertaken in the city of L.

Three or four days after the holiday, Avreml came crashing into the House of Study like a bombshell to announce that he, Solomon, had been promised in marriage to a beautiful daughter of a certain wealthy local man, and that everyone was awaiting his arrival. Avreml spared no embellishment in describing the wealth of his future father-in-law and the beauty of his bride-to-be. "You simply will be swimming in luxury," he concluded, as he took him by the sleeve and almost pushed him forcibly into the home of his designated fiancée. Solomon's distrust of Avreml the Lame, and the feeling that he had left his homeland for purposes other than marriage, gave him the firm resolve to resist Avreml's proposal. After hearing him out, he categorically declared that he didn't have the slightest intention of getting married and that from now on he would like Avreml to stop making any plans to marry him off. Realizing that a tasty morsel was slipping out of his hands, Avreml threatened to throw Solomon to the mercy of fate, saying that he would not take care of him forever, and so on. But when Avreml became convinced that threats were of no use either, he once again begrudgingly harnessed his horse to resume his travels among settlements in the Jewish Pale, in order to exploit them in the interest of the *aguna*. They rambled along for some time around the southwestern district. Along the way Avreml made two or three unsuccessful attempts to market his merchandise, and finally, in the first part of August, arrived at the city of K. [Kamenets] in Podolia province. The city was extraordinarily picturesque, situated on a high ridge and surrounded by so-called farms. Late at night Avreml and his passengers entered one of the surrounding areas on the outskirts and settled into some abandoned, dilapidated tavern without windows or doors. The exhausted passengers, who had become accustomed to unquestioning obedience, did nothing to protest the move into this uninhabitable hotel, and settled down in various corners of the building. Avreml got up at dawn and went to town to go about his business. Suddenly there was lightning and a thunderclap as it began to rain cats and dogs. The whole tavern seemed to be groaning; one more gust of wind and it would bury our travelers under its ruins. This would leave poor Avreml with neither an *aguna* for exploiting the generosity of the Jews nor a young man who might eventually be married off at a personal profit. If only Avreml had turned at this moment to the starved, soaked, and chilled Solomon, his eloquent proposal might have had some success. But fate decided otherwise. Avreml suffered a complete fiasco in the city of K.—he failed to obtain an open letter from the local rabbis for the collection of contributions for the *aguna*. In a highly irritated state, he returned late at night and announced to his travelers that as soon as it cleared up the next day they would leave the inhospitable city K. and go on to the city Kh.

"But that will be the last place I'm taking you," he said to Solomon. "If you want to get legally married there, that's fine, but if you don't, be hanged and do what you want. Of course, I won't give you back your passports until you pay for your passage, and you know what might happen without them. I hope, however, that you will finally come to your senses, understand what is good for you, and realize that I wish you no malice and that it's high time for you to settle down. Don't forget that you are, praise God, no longer a little boy. One year passes after another and before you know it you'll be an old bachelor and then no one will want to look at you."

You can imagine what kind of night Solomon spent with Avreml in the cozy tavern. He thought for a long time about his hopeless misery. Suddenly he remembered that a couple of years before a fellow yeshiva student left Kopyl and, according to rumor, became a choirboy under a famous cantor at a large synagogue in the city of K. [Kamenets]. Solomon seized upon this idea like a drowning person grasping for any object in order to be saved. As soon as day broke he set out in the mud and rain to find his former friend. After wandering at length along many streets and alleys he finally reached the famous cantor's apartment. With his heart beating rapidly, his trembling hand opened the door of the longed-for dwelling. He was met by an elderly, nicely dressed woman who informed him that his former friend was in fact a member of the choir but was now somewhere in the provinces with the cantor and would not return until the High Holidays. His last hope was lost! Despondent, dejected, and hungry, Solomon went back to Avreml at the tavern. There he was reproached by Avreml for disappearing, the devil knows where. Avreml then announced that they would immediately leave the cursed city K.

A heavy and cold downpour accompanied Avreml's departure from the tavern. It seemed as if all nature was shedding bitter tears over the two hapless victims of such cruel greed who had willingly delivered themselves into the executioner's hands. Solomon was sick at heart, with no hope left for any kind of happier future. That future appeared wrapped in the same unsightly mist that shrouded the entire city of K. [Kamenets], which Solomon had just seen for the first time, and which he might never see again. While plodding through the mire and mud along some disagreeable winding mountain path leading to city of Kh., where he was heading without any particular purpose, Solomon thought about what awaited him there and what he could expect. The rain did not let up and the poor horse exerted all its strength to pull the wagon with its miserable woman and freezing child. Avreml was in an extremely bad mood and kept silent the whole way, as if to let Solomon know that his patience was exhausted and his anger was boundless. After traveling a long distance along the winding path, they finally reached a crossroad. The road to Kh. was to the right. K. had long since disappeared over the horizon, and it seemed to Solomon that he had lost all hope of ever getting out of the miserable situation into which he had fallen, for which he had only himself to blame. While standing on an icy ledge, it seemed that just then he would fall into a bottomless pit from which there was no return. He felt that this bottomless abyss was in fact the city of Kh.—where he had neither relatives, friends, nor acquaintances, where he would doubtless find not a single sympathetic living soul, and where a spiteful Avreml would leave him to the mercy of fate without a penny in his pocket. It was a terrible moment indeed. Solomon was immeasurably desperate, his iron will broken. His energy was gone and he cursed the very hour he left Kopyl. But just at the moment when it seemed that he was standing on the edge of an abyss, a crisis occurred that had a decisive influence on his entire future. It may sound strange, but the reason for this decisive turning point in the life of Solomon Moiseevich was a horseshoe. "Go find the shoe the horse lost back there," Avreml ordered, after bringing the nag to a halt, in a tone that was half command and half request.

Solomon set off as fast as he could to carry out Avreml's order so that he might regain his patron's favor by rendering this service. He started a very thorough search over the rather extensive distance they had covered and zealously dug around the soil in a couple of places, but to his great disappointment he could not find the horseshoe. Empty-handed and dejected, on his way back he suddenly saw coming toward him a team of four horses harnessed to a Krakow wagon, which was typical of that region. He gazed with envy and curiosity at the lucky passengers inside the carriage. As he stopped for a minute, he heard someone call his name. Solomon Moiseevich could not believe his ears. Is it possible, he thought, that there could be someone in the steppes of Podolia who actually knew him—a person cast out of his hometown and wandering aimlessly at the mercy of fate like a wind-swept autumn leaf drifting among ditches and swamps? The wagon stopped and out jumped a young person who, without saying a word of greeting, embraced the desperate Solomon. Following a brief explanation, the young man who appeared on the scene so suddenly demanded vigorously that Solomon return with him to K. [Kamenets]. This young man was none other than the choirboy of the famous cantor, whom Solomon had been seeking. The cantor and the entire choir were now on their way back to the city of K. At the request of his favorite choir member, the cantor paid Avreml what was owed in exchange for Solomon's passport. Solomon then got into the wagon and went off with the cantor and the others to K., which only a few hours before he thought he had left forever.

Solomon's arrival in K. marked the beginning of a new period in his life, a period of the kind of intellectual growth and independent endeavor that he had always wanted. The one-sided, narrowly educated Talmud scholar gradually turned into a European-style thinker and writer. But we won't rush ahead. The cantor who took him along to K. turned out to be a warm-hearted person. From the very first moment of his arrival in K., the cantor took pains to see that Solomon was not left wanting, and took him to the House of Study that possessed the town's best public library. The congregation of this House of Study was comprised of almost the entire local aristocracy. Here, too, youngsters from the best families made their own studies of the Talmud. Solomon Moiseevich soon became recognized for his solid Talmudic and exegetical knowledge, and everyone vied with each other to make his acquaintance. Visitors to the House of Study admired him for his modesty and exemplary diligence. Young people incessantly turned to him for explanations of difficult passages or for source references. The longer he stayed at the House of Study, the more trusted and respected he became. Consequently, several wealthy residents commissioned him to supervise the Talmud studies of their adult sons and generously rewarded him for his services. Now that he was financially secure, Solomon could fully satisfy his thirst for knowledge. But how was he to gain that knowledge? Where would he find the initial guide who might show him the proper way? Where would he meet with the necessary guidance, and how might it be found at the House of Study? These were questions over which he racked his brain, but which he could in no way resolve. Yet once again chance set him onto the truest of paths. One venerable old man at the House of Study was permanently engaged in Talmud learning. He was respected by the entire congregation for his sincere piety and God-fearing nature. This honorable old man took a particular liking to our young Lithuanian, who quite frequently engaged him in scholarly discussions. On closer acquaintance he discovered that in addition to knowing the Talmud, the young man had a perfect command of Hebrew. Once in the course of an intimate discussion, to the amazement and delight of Solomon Moiseevich, the old man advised him to introduce himself to our venerable poet Avraham-Ber Gottlober, who at the time was teaching at the local State Jewish School.

"Drop over to visit him sometime in the evening, when no one will see you," the old man told him, "and introduce yourself. As a clean-shaven scoundrel (*sholtik*), he is not respected or trusted by our community, and we generally keep our young people away from him. But you, as a person who would know how to answer a freethinker *(apikores)*, have nothing to fear. You could get to know him safely, and because he is a great expert on Hebrew grammar *(m'dakdek)*, he could be useful to you. Remember the words of Rabbi Meir: 'Partake of the delicious fruit but throw away the useless peel.' I will tell the synagogue attendant *(shames)*, who will show you where this scoundrel *(sholtik)* lives." Solomon Moiseevich was long since familiar with Gottlober's name, and you can imagine how anxious he was to make his acquaintance. He hoped that this modern-style scholar would point the way to the genuine road of scholarship and teach him how to reach it; with his assistance, he would doubtless attain his desired goal at last.

On the second evening after that conversation, Solomon and the attendant set off for Gottlober's apartment, carrying his only literary composition, an untitled little drama written during his childhood. He hoped to elicit the great poet's opinion and get some advice and direction for the future. Gottlober, as Solomon himself told me, could not keep from laughing as he read this childish fantasy. He praised him, however, for his noble effort and predicted a brilliant literary career for him. From the very first, Gottlober could see that there was exceptional talent in this young Lithuanian. Without waiting for Solomon to ask, he offered his services and the use of his quite impressive library. The warm reception that Solomon always found at Gottlober's apartment—and the opinions, conversations, and judgments, the likes of which he had never heard before—drew him to this house, where he soon came to feel quite at home. Before he came to know the Gottlober household, he could not write any European language. There, under the guidance of Gottlober's eldest daughter, Solomon started to study the Russian and German alphabets and the first principles of arithmetic. What is more, a whole new realm of Jewish literature opened up to him. He greedily consumed whole volumes of the new Jewish [Hebrew] literature. With unusual zeal, he started to study German and Russian and was introduced to the sciences. In spite of the fact that Solomon had almost no teachers (the kind of instruction given by Gottlober from time to time could not be called genuine teaching) to direct and organize his studies, he nevertheless proceeded along a proper path in his study of scientific subjects. Just the fact of knowing a European-educated family was sufficient to enable him to break out of the archaic scholastic world, which had entirely engulfed him, into the expansive and rich fields of European science. While continuing to learn theological subjects at the House of Study, he devoted a considerable amount of time at home to studying science and languages.

Many of the wealthy congregation members at the House of Study where Solomon was always learning started to look upon him as a desirable marriage match, given his scholarship and modesty. Matchmakers (*shadkhonim*) from all over began to besiege the young Lithuanian with rather lucrative proposals. In spite of his strong will and energy, Solomon could not resist the temptation of a luxurious and worry-free life that could be completely devoted to scholarship. So he became engaged to the daughter of a wealthy local man who enjoyed the respect of the entire community for his honesty and learning. This marriage did not, however, turn out to be a happy one. The household he entered was exceptionally congenial too, as his father-in-law was a scholarly person who owned an enormous library—with books in all fields of learning, which were made freely available to him. His wife's parents were exceptionally kind to him and all the family members were intelligent people who were on very friendly terms with him. Still, his wife turned out to be so immature that she could not satisfy even such an extremely undemanding young man. He frankly related this to his father-in-law, whom he loved as his own father and who recognized that his daughter was not a good match for Solomon Moiseevich. He consequently agreed to a divorce, and the first nuptial bonds were broken. In the meantime, while living at his father-in-law's house, Solomon had managed to prepare for and pass the examination for a teacher's position, which he immediately took up at the local State Jewish School. Having achieved an independent and secure position for himself, Solomon began to work vigorously on his self-education. Just as he had earlier been completely devoted to the study of the holy scriptures and Talmud, he now became engaged with equal zeal in the study of languages and secular sciences. He was remarkably successful because of his diligence and love of labor. Without allowing himself any luxury or excesses in life, he nevertheless never skimped on spending money for useful books.

The first newspaper in Hebrew, called *Ha-magid*, started publication at this time. The newspaper was and still is being published in the Prussian city of Lyck. Well-known Jewish writers contributed to this newspaper, and Solomon also wanted to try out his writing skills. He wrote an essay for this newspaper on the subject of education. Still unsure about his talents, he left the essay on his desk among some other papers. One of Solomon's friends, an educated and forthright person who was visiting him one day, happened to see it. After reading the article, he found that, because of its sober viewpoint, logical exposition, and overall elegant style, it should be published. Upon the vigorous insistence of this friend the article was sent to *Ha-magid*. The editor of course willingly accepted it and immediately offered its author a permanent staff position on the paper. The article was enormously successful among the Jewish reading public, and it caught the attention of the well-known scholar L. I. Mandelshtam, who at the time was an official in the Ministry of Public Education. During a tour of the southwestern district in the company of Minister Norov, Mandelshtam became acquainted with Solomon and was extremely surprised to find that the author of the aforementioned article was so young.

"I was convinced," Mandelshtam told the author, "that such a serious article must have been written by a scholar in his 50s." When Mandelshtam came to know the author better he advised him to go to the then famous Padua rabbinical school in Italy, and he promised to find a way to get him a state stipend. Solomon of course agreed to Mandelshtam's proposal but because of various unfavorable circumstances the plan never materialized, and Solomon remained in Russia. We cannot now judge how useful that trip abroad would have been for him. But we can say with confidence that Russian Jewry would have been deprived of a national writer who, together with his long-suffering people, went through the bitter school of endurance, failure, disappointment, and all kinds of calamities. A writer who, while studying the entire spiritual life of his people in this school of real life, was able to convey with inimitable skill the minutest nuances of his people's soul, and who could feel the faintest beat of the people's pulse.

For a number of reasons, Solomon consequently moved from K. [Kamenets] to the Jewish Moscow, the city of B. [Berdichev], where he was naturalized. That is, he was transferred from Lithuania to the Ukrainian-Jewish community of which he is now a member. Having found a life partner to his liking here, he solidly established himself in B. and has devoted his entire life to the serving his coreligionists through literature.

The first serious work of Solomon Moiseevich Abramovitsh appeared in press in November 1859 under the title *Mishpat Shalom* [The Judgment of Solomon], and it immediately caught the attention of the Jewish reading public. This small booklet caused quite an uproar and marked a turning point in Hebrew literature. Jews who had become accustomed to hearing only praise of their own writers heard, for the first time, the bold voice of a strong, incorruptible critic. On the one hand, the booklet elicited rapture and applause, but on the other hand, dissatisfaction and teeth gnashing. Several of the established writers howled about some milksop who dared to speak against them, gray-haired bards, and dared to critique what the whole world had heretofore praised! How did he dare rise up against their works, which had been safeguarded by diverse laudatory reviews written by famous authors? Abramovitsh was not frightened by this desperate outcry and senile weakness; like an experienced surgeon, he continued to perform further operations with a firm hand. Little by little, he began to excise the weeds that had accumulated over the years in Judaic literature. Through a whole series of critical articles that appeared one after the other in Hebrew periodicals and individual brochures, he became the scourge of talentless writers and at the same time the herald of new ideas and new literary demands. One might say that he began a new epoch in Hebrew literature because, before him, there was no serious literary criticism. He gave voice to an entire army of young critics, many of whom were quite talented.

Having established himself as a literary critic, in the solace of his study he devoted himself to learning natural sciences. Although he had no instructors (not to mention natural history laboratories), over a period of three years he acquired an understanding that was sufficient for him to undertake a Hebrew translation of Professor [Harald Othmar] Lenz's work in natural history. He translated three volumes: on mammals, birds, and amphibians and reptiles. Whereas his translation of Professor Lenz's work was almost literal in the first volume, the following two volumes were not simply translations but significant independent studies that exhibited Abramovitsh's solid erudition. Wherever possible, he compared the views and knowledge of Talmud sages in the area of natural science to those of the present day—and he frequently offered remarkably astute explanations for certain passages in the Talmud. Abramovitsh made a particular contribution through his excellent Hebrew style, with its purity and deftness of language. If one recalls how limited Hebrew is in general, and particularly in regard to scientific terminology, one can easily appreciate the enormous obstacle he had to overcome in order to write these volumes on the natural sciences. This work gained the attention of the government's education officials. After each volume was published, the government bought five hundred rubles' worth of books to support their author and then distributed them to the libraries at State Jewish schools.

On the subject of Abramovitsh's literary activity we should not forget to mention his attempt to write a novel in Hebrew about Jewish life. Although the novel [*Learn to Do Good* (*Limdu heitev,* 1862)] itself has quite a few shortcomings, as an initial effort in this type of literature, it nevertheless already reflects considerable talent and a profound understanding of human nature.

Because he always felt compassion for his coreligionists and as a result of his desire to make his talents useful to them, Abramovitsh decided, to the detriment of his own fame, to write henceforth not in Hebrew—which was understood by only a limited number of select persons—but rather in the vernacular [Yiddish], presently spoken by all Jews in Russia. Thus the uneducated masses might be able to read his works and understand their own faults, which were sometimes of their own doing and sometimes caused by external circumstances. Abramovitsh undertook to write in the vernacular after studying the entire inner spirit of his people, their actual life, and the relationships both among Jews and between Jews and the surrounding world. Abramovitsh's works of this type do not flatter the crowd, to whom he has devoted all his literary activity, and they were not written to gain cheap notoriety or easy profit. He embarked upon the very thorny and thankless road of censuring all that was bad, and he attempted to guide people to a path that would lessen their suffering. He does not appear as a dull moralist, however, who reprimands all that is bad and extols the praiseworthy. No, these features emanate naturally from his vibrant stories that present to the reader a panorama of the protagonists' nature and actions. All of his characters are flesh-and-blood examples of living individuals, with all the passion and fears inherent in people with a clearly defined physiognomy and distinct character. These characters' spiritual manifestations are not subordinate to the author's will, but rather function independently. Each act constitutes an inevitable consequence of the characters' past, upbringing, and circumstances under which they have been obliged to live and act. In all of his vernacular works, Abramovitsh shows himself to be not only a subtle psychologist but often a prophet as well. As was noted earlier, he sensed the faintest beat of his people's pulse and confidently predicted the consequences of any particular national suffering or current event. Only after his predictions come to pass do people recall that Abramovitsh had long since foreseen some particular event in one of his works.

His first popular tale in the vernacular was *The Little Man* [*Dos kleyne mentshele,* 1864–65]. This biographical work describes a person from the lowest stratum of society who rises to the highest levels of society and wealth through insolence and intrigue. All of the town's residents, who suffer the oppression of this hardfisted merchant [*kulak*, literally "fist"], hate him with all their hearts, but they obediently submit to his will. Such is the power of gold. This story also presents honest, likeable persons whom the author borrowed from real life. Who would not recognize our venerable poet Avraham-Ber Gottlober in the character of Gutmann? Walk into his cozy apartment and you sense some relief from all the ugliness exhibited by the story's protagonist. But at the same time your heart will ache when you realize that, in his honest and tidy life of poverty, Gutmann must endure all kinds of privations.

The author's second story, *Fishke the Lame* [*Fishke der krumer*, 1869], acquaints us with the life of Jewish beggars.[3] This unique world, into which no Jewish writer had yet delved, is described in its entirety. The author learned about this world in B. [Berdichev], where beggars from far and wide congregated. He personally visited their haunts, talked to many beggars and cripples, became interested in their way of life, and quite frequently arbitrated their petty disputes. The type of people described by the author in his story can be found throughout the Jewish Pale of Settlement, and every reader wonders how the author could have come to know about the life of beggars in places where he had never been.

Solomon Moiseevich Abramovitsh believed that the greatest evil in Jewish social life was the tax collection box. In each city or village in the Pale of Settlement, the collection box keeper was always surrounded by a flock of parasites who lived off the kopecks collected from the unfortunate working class. Well-aimed barbs at the collection box keepers, as well as at the rich tax farmers and their stooges, appear throughout his masterful stories taken from folk life. But in addition to small skirmishes, so to speak, Abramovitsh engaged the collection box keepers in a full battle in one particular work, entitled *The Tax; or, the Gang of City Benefactors* [*Di takse; oder di bande shtot bal-toyves*, 1869]. Nowhere but in the city of B. [Berdichev] can there have been such widespread abuse on the part of tax collectors and their followers. After having investigated the entire process of tax collection and all the secret springs that moved the mechanism, Abramovitsh publicly exposed the collectors' activity in the form of a drama. The tax collection bosses almost always committed their vile, base acts under the pretense of piety and concern

3. Lev Binshtok was apparently unfamiliar with Abramovitsh's early version of *The Wishing-Ring* (*Dos vintshfingerl*, 1865).

for religious purity. The author of *The Tax* skillfully unmasks these persons, however, and shows them to the public for what they really were.

After the appearance of the *The Tax*, the fine fellows of B. [Berdichev] were so irritated that the author had to move to a more secluded place. But the popular masses extolled him and began to see him as their benefactor. From the first day of its appearance, common people adopted *The Tax* as their own, and each well-aimed sentence, witticism, or pun became a popular saying. These sayings became such an integral part of vernacular speech that to this day people who know nothing of literature will quote entire sentences from *The Tax*. The success of this drama was as great as the success of [Griboedov's drama] *Woe from Wit* in Moscow when it publicly appeared in manuscript form. In spite of the fact that Abramovitsh's drama was written in the simple vernacular Jewish language, it came to the attention of the district administration officials, who subsequently took steps to reduce the abuses practiced by the tax collectors.

All of Abramovitsh's works in the vernacular are so colloquial that they are quite difficult to translate into any European language. Translations lose the very pointedness of the satire and cleverness of the puns. The folk sayings and proverbs he cites are particularly difficult to translate accurately. If the humor of these works is to come across at all tolerably in translation, the translator must have a fine poetic sense in addition to a perfect command of the language into which the story is translated. For this reason, the translation of *The Tax* that recently appeared in print has been extremely unsuccessful.

As was mentioned earlier, Abramovitsh left B. [Berdichev] following the appearance of *The Tax*. He then moved with his family to Zh. [Zhitomir] where, at the Rabbinical Institute, he diligently began to study for the examination to become a rabbi. Although he was already well known in the ministry as a fine pedagogue and writer, without a teaching certificate he found it difficult to obtain an official position for which, unfortunately, he was in dire need. Jewish literature alone has never provided material security for its devotees, particularly for those who have selflessly dedicated the best years of their lives to it.

Upon passing the examination, Abramovitsh wrote his immortal work *The Nag; or, Notes of a Madman* [*Di klyatshe*, 1873].[4] The idea for this alle-

4. Binshtok does not cite the full subtitle, which reads: *Oder tsar baley-khayim . . . a mayse vos hot zikh farvolgert tsvishn di ksavim fun Isrolik dem meshugenem*; that is, "Or, Cruelty to Animals . . . A Story That Turned Up Among the Writings of Isrolik the Madman."

gorical story came to him as a result of a visit to B.[Berdichev] after an absence of several years. During his visit he happened to see a gaunt nag covered with sores, half-alive, hauling sand and clay to a huge construction site belonging to some local money-grubber or city boss. In his story, he depicts a certain Isrolik who suffers from hallucinations, and a metamorphosed nag; that is, a person who has been transformed by evil spirits into a nag that talks and exhibits human sensibilities.[5] During his hallucinations, Isrolik takes notes on his conversations with the nag or writes his own observations about the hapless nag's fate. This fantastic novel touches upon the entire "Jewish problem" to its fullest extent; or, to put it better, the novel analyzes all the Jewish problems that have only recently appeared in the Russian press. Through his keen insight, Abramovitsh predicted much of what his coreligionists would endure, even though those predictions seemed improbable at the time when they were written. All of the accusations that are only now being leveled against Jews, and all of the calamities recently endured by Jews, are most vividly outlined in this novel.[6] If we consider that *The Nag* was written in 1873, at a time when Lady Fortune seemed to be smiling upon the Jews, his predictions of things to come seem all the more astonishing. In order to give readers who have not read *The Nag* some idea about this story, we shall cite two excerpts.

The second chapter, entitled "Isrolik and the Nag," tells a story about the abuse inflicted upon a poor, overworked nag . . . [7]

Is it possible that the reader does not recognize in this excerpt the screaming and howling of notorious hack writers who have recently been frothing at the mouth in their angry assaults upon Jews? Surely the reader will hear in these lines the entire logic of that well-known group of present-day writers who have been discussing the Jewish question in various ways.

5. According to Chone Shmeruk, citing Y. Frankl, Abramovitsh's mentor A. B. Gottlober reworked a story about the transmigration of souls—including a horse—in 1871. This literary precursor may have been as influential as any of Abramovitsh's experiences. See "Problems in Research on Mendele's Yiddish Texts" (Hebrew), in *Proceedings of the Fourth World Congress in Jewish Studies* (1969), 2:26, n.

6. Writing in 1884, Binshtok is referring to the backlash following the period of reform (1855–81) that ended with the assassination of Alexander II and a series of pogroms.

7. Binshtok's plot summaries, intended for Russian readers who could not read the original Yiddish, are omitted. For an English translation of this novel, see Joachim Neugroschel's rendering in *The Great Works of Jewish Fantasy and Occult* (Woodstock, N.Y.: Overlook Press, 1987), 545–663.

In the ninth chapter, entitled "The Prevention of Cruelty to Animals," the author presents a conversation between Isrolik and the nag, who advises him to drop all his work on her behalf because no good will come from his feeble protective efforts. Furthermore, all his enthusiasm is no more than an adolescent outburst that will ultimately fade as the years pass. Isrolik nevertheless proves that the nag's criticism of his compassion and enthusiasm is misplaced, and that he is no dreamer. Rather, his feet are firmly on the ground. To reinforce these assertions, he reads the nag the following lines from a letter written to the Society for the Prevention of Cruelty to Animals . . . .

In response to the caustic and derisive comments of the nag and her questions about the society committee's answer to such a lofty letter, Isrolik takes another piece of paper from his side pocket and reads the following . . . .

Vividly depicting the terrible plight of Jews and predicting an even worse future for them, Abramovitsh does not in this novel pat his coreligionists on the back. Instead, with characteristic, biting satire, he castigates them for their many shortcomings, thereby showing them the way to correct those faults.

As we know, all Jews pray in Hebrew, which is quite incomprehensible to the Jewish public at large. The public prays in a completely sincere manner, of course, but it does not understand the lofty significance of the prayers that, for the most part, consist of psalms and noble poetic hymns. There have been many translations of the prayers into the vernacular, at various times. These translations have not only failed to clarify the meaning of the prayers, however, but completely obscured and distorted them. Abramovitsh took note of this fact and tried to render prayer books into the vernacular, in verse. Thus far he has translated the Sabbath songs (zmirot) and Perek shira [1875], already published, and all of the Psalms of David, which are still in manuscript form. This labor can only be appreciated by those who know Hebrew well, understand the structure of Hebrew prayers, and appreciate the difficulty of translating them. Abramovitsh has overcome all these difficulties. Without deviating from the text, he renders the prayers in easy and euphonic verse that is comprehensible to the general public. Despite all of Abramovitsh's efforts and work, this aspect of his literary activity has not yet been adequately appreciated by the Jewish public. The reason for this is quite simple: the public has not yet been sufficiently educated to understand sublime poetry. This lack of sympathy on the part of the Jewish public was the principal reason that Abramovitsh ceased to translate Hebrew prayers.

Another noteworthy work of that period is his poem in verse entitled *Yudl*

[Little Jew, 1875]. Abramovitsh employs this poem, in the form of a story based on everyday life, to depict the entire history of the Jewish people from biblical times to their intellectual development during the period of Moses Mendelssohn. The poem contains passages that are profound in meaning and expressed most artfully. Although the first edition of this book sold out very quickly, it is doubtful whether it has been understood by the public at large. In any event, the poem is a valuable contribution to literature, and it would be good to see it translated into one of the European languages.

Among other things undertaken by Abramovitsh was a popular translation of Jules Verne's *Five Weeks in a Balloon* [*Der luft-balon*, date uncertain]. I will not elaborate on the merits of that translation, nor of another booklet entitled *The Fish That Swallowed the Prophet Jonah* [*Der fish vos hot eyngeshlungen Yonah der novi*, 1870], because I participated in that work.

Since 1873, Abramovitsh has been publishing popular calendars in large editions. The sales have been quite profitable for the publishers, but they have brought very little material wealth to the author himself.

We shall cite one more humorous story entitled *The Brief Travels of Benjamin the Third* [*Kitser masoes Binyumin ha-shlishi*, 1878].[8] Benjamin the Third is a Jew from a small settlement, cut off by its very nature from all means of communication. From the time he was born until his adulthood, Benjamin has never gone beyond the limits of the village, never known any but his native language, and never taken an interest in the outside world. He is always content with his lot which, incidentally, does not exactly pamper him. Once, at the library of the local House of Study, he happens to come upon a description of countries and peoples recorded by an ancient Jewish traveler. From that time on he fancies becoming a traveler. This idea becomes so strongly implanted in his mind that he eventually becomes obsessed. He starts raving about deserts, oceans, and fantastic beasts, to the point that his village declares him to be insane. This madman nevertheless finds a worthy traveling companion in the person of Senderl, nicknamed "old woman" (because his wife runs their meager business whereas Senderl does the housework—lights the oven, cooks supper, washes the dishes and linen, and darns stockings). They set off together for unknown parts. After many

8. See Hillel Halkin's translation of this novella in *Tales of Mendele the Book Peddler: Fishke the Lame and Benjamin the Third*, ed. Dan Miron and Ken Frieden, trans. Ted Gorelick and Hillel Halkin (New York: Schocken, 1996).

strange and comical adventures, the two heroes arrive at the city of Gnilopyat (Berdichev), which they assume to be Istanbul. They believe the Gnilopyat River is the Bosporus. After they proceed to Kiev, they are sent back—almost forcibly deported—to their home town, before they get to see the mythical Sambation River, on whose shore live the "red Jews," or the mountains of eternal darkness. This story is written with such humor that the reader cannot help but laugh heartily from the very first page to the last. The scenes and characters in the story change like a kaleidoscope and are masterfully depicted. The story leaves nothing to be desired.

In 1877, Abramovitsh—who could never complain of excessive pampering in the course of his life—encountered setbacks that put an end to his interest in continuing a literary career. We believe it would be inappropriate and superfluous to dwell upon these circumstances here. Let us merely say that, because of depressing circumstances, this overflowing wellspring suddenly dried up and ceased to function altogether. On a number of occasions Abramovitsh complained to me about his morally depressing situation. He once told me that "to stop thinking is to stop living, but it seems I can no longer think. My brain feels leaden and my heart has turned to stone."[9] Abramovitsh never grumbled about his fate, but only someone with iron nerves and a tough and honest character could withstand the blows it dealt him so generously and for so long. These were attributes Abramovitsh possessed, and because of his moral strength he did not succumb to these fateful assaults. He courageously withstood an onslaught from all sides that could have crushed a giant.

The storm that raged long and hard over the head of our national writer has gradually subsided. The rain clouds that covered the horizon have scattered, and the small block of ice—to which he barely managed to cling on the boundless sea of life—has safely come to shore. Now, when we gather to congratulate him on the twenty-fifth anniversary of his literary activity, Abramovitsh finds himself in a tranquil and peaceful harbor where he once again can devote his activity to the benefit of his fellow Jews. Indeed, as one might have expected, Solomon Moiseevich has not shortchanged his public. Following his long silence, on the occasion of the twenty-fifth anniversary of

9. Compare Abramovitsh's letters to Lev Binshtok, dated 16 January 1880, 22 December 1881, and 21 October 1882, in *The Mendele Book (Dos Mendele-bukh)*, ed. Nachman Mayzel (New York: YKUF, 1959), 107–14.

his fruitful activity, he has written a marvelous drama taken from Jewish life entitled *The Conscription* [*Der priziv*, 1884]. It is now being published in St. Petersburg by his friends and admirers. We will not say anything about this drama, although we have read the manuscript, because we would like the public to judge it without any preconceived notions.

On our part, in heartily greeting our dear friend who is being honored for his twenty-five years of service to literature, we wish him with all our hearts many, many long years of activity in the noble profession he has chosen, for the benefit of his coreligionists who, for a long time to come, will need such honest, selfless, and talented sowers of good deeds as Solomon Moiseevich Abramovitsh.

Zhitomir
4 October 1884

Translated from Russian by Jack Blanshei;
revised by Ken Frieden and Rachel May

Memories of Sholem Aleichem

Y. D. Berkovitsh

Family and Milieu

It is an old, generally accepted rule that one needs to look nearby for the secret of every extraordinary person's talent: in his origins and in his childhood milieu—with parents, relatives, and sometimes also with teachers and friends.[1] If one tries to apply this rule to discover the secret of the extraordinary phenomenon of *Sholem Aleichem,* from the start this will be a bit difficult. For Sholem Aleichem, the great popular writer and master of Yiddish humor, seems to stand apart from his surroundings. Among his family and earliest childhood friends, he appears as a unique phenomenon, like a solitary, foreign plant. Neither his father nor his mother—and even less his brothers, relatives, and friends—exhibited anything externally that could have prepared and groomed the future Sholem Aleichem. His father, Nokhem Rabinovitsh, was a small-town intellectual, "religious, with a mastery of Hebrew," "a hasidic follower of the Tolner Rebbe, and a lover of [Avraham] Mapu," a quiet, reticent man with a gentle, pliant character, a gloomy

Y. D. Berkovitsh (1885–1967) was an important Hebrew writer. In 1905 he moved to Vilna, where he met Sholem Aleichem and his daughter, whom he married. Berkovitsh translated many of Sholem Aleichem's Yiddish stories into Hebrew, including the stories of Tevye the Dairyman.

1. These recollections of Sholem Aleichem are excerpted from Berkovitsh's introductory chapters—preceding each group of letters—in *The Sholem Aleichem Book (Dos Sholem-Aleichem bukh).* The passages included here are from "Family and Milieu" ("Mishpokhe un svive," p. 17), "In His Own Republic" ("In zayn eygener republik," pp. 47–53), "With the Family of Writers" ("Mit der mishpokhe fun shriftshteler," pp. 155–60, 165–67, 168–72, 187–89), and "With Friends and Everyday Folks" ("Mit fraynt un yidn fun a gants yor," pp. 285–89, 291). The length of the original chapters makes it impossible to include the full text. Berkovitsh's other memoirs of Sholem Aleichem and I. L. Peretz are contained in *Ha-rish'onim ki-vnei-adam* (Hebrew). The title of this section has been added by the editor.

person "always with a worried look on his face"—*at first glance the opposite of Sholem Aleichem.*[2] His mother, Chaya-Esther, was "a virtuous woman," preoccupied with minding the shop, and a practical housewife who was the mother of many children. She "was neither as soft nor as indulgent as other mothers," and "we often received slaps, jabs, and blows from her," because in her view "children should not like to laugh and amuse themselves," which "must have meant that children shouldn't laugh"—she, too, was not especially similar to Sholem Aleichem, who throughout his life was for children (and particularly for his own children) *an inexhaustible source of tenderness, joy, and playfulness.* His maternal grandfather, Moshe-Yossi Zeldin, who for a short time had some influence on his grandson, was a strange creature: a small-town moneylender "dressed in rags and worn-out shoes," "with an oddly coarse face," a fanatical hasid of the Chabad sect, a half-deranged mystic, a kind of Jewish, hasidic "holy fool" *(yurodivi)*, from whom Sholem Aleichem's bright, joyful character, it would seem, was unable to acquire anything. Sholem Aleichem's brothers were almost all ordinary householders; while literate, they were far removed from intellectual accomplishments, all practical men with purely material ambitions. . . .

In His Own Republic

1

"My republic"—this is what Sholem Aleichem would often call his home. With that he wanted to designate both the liberal, "republican" regime that ruled in his household, allowing each individual member to move around freely, in accordance with his inborn qualities and inclinations, and the pleasure that he himself—the free "president" of the free "republic"—enjoyed in his own environment.

He would say it in a humorous tone, but beneath this tone one could feel a deep, sincere pride, for he was extremely satisfied with his "republic."

For in that republic of his own, Sholem Aleichem derived such great and complete satisfaction as nowhere else. In contrast to most artistic personalities, whose everyday home and family life oppresses their spirits and clips

---

2. The quotations that appear in these remarks are all taken from Sholem Aleichem's autobiography *From the Fair* [*Funem yarid*, 1915–16; Berkovitsh's note].

their wings, precisely in his family circle—apart from the material burden it placed upon him—Sholem Aleichem felt inwardly freer and more able to soar than anywhere else. In order to relax mentally and strengthen himself creatively, he wouldn't run away from his home, as others do. It was just the opposite: he would always escape with pleasure from the external world to his own corner. Joyfully, because he would never come home empty-handed and always brought something along. Home was the comfortable, warm nest to which he returned loaded up with the seeds of his creations. He carried back from around the world his observations, reflections, and experiences. There he sowed them on home soil, warmed them in his own atmosphere, and there they grew—bringing forth good, natural, homemade products. For this reason, in Sholem Aleichem's works one doesn't experience the after-taste of refined, but smoky and decadent, café philosophizing.

In his autobiography, Sholem Aleichem paints a picture of his early years, which he calls "an idyll." The idyll consists of this: he and three of his older childhood friends, among which he included his father, would "with the greatest excitement and impatience" await the Sabbath, when they shared with each other the best things they had gathered together in their minds during the week. "When one of us four had something good to say, to show, or to tell, he would save it for *shabbes*." Had Sholem Aleichem reached the chapters about his later family life, in his autobiography, he would certainly have had to depict a second "idyll" of this kind—but on a much larger canvas and with richer colors: how he wandered around all day long in the streets of Kiev ("Yehupetz"), and later in the many "Kasrilevkes" of Russia, Galicia, England, and America, saving the best of what he saw, heard, and thought while underway. He would have told how he guarded and warmed it in his heart until the Sabbath, like a precious gift, until he came home and unburdened himself before his first, though it was his own, closest, and most beloved audience—his own republic. Everyone from great to small would surround him with shining, warm, and expectant faces, excitedly pricking up their ears to "hearken," to feel joy and heartache together with him. Most of all and most often, everyone would laugh with him, "cackle with laughter." And a day, a week, or a month later, all of that would be filtered, digested, and artistically transformed into bright, sweeping, creative images for the wider, external audience—for the reader.

For Sholem Aleichem, the home was not an eternal object of convenience or inconvenience, but part—and the most important part—of his entire essence. It wasn't just a means, but both a means and an end, a cause and an effect of his expansiveness of spirit, the secret and the unfolding of his life and creativity. Because of this, one would have to give a new twist to the stereotypical saying that "if you want to know a poet, visit the poet in his country": if you wish to know Sholem Aleichem, visit him *at home*. Sholem Aleichem's home was the clearest looking glass, in which he revealed himself completely and without the least blemish; his home was a strong, bright projector that shone on him and lit him up from all sides, with all of the candor and mystery of his human, artistic spirit. While he did not show himself otherwise at home than one saw him in his creative work, he did show more of himself, more fully, freely, and intimately. And because his life and work mingled in a rare harmony, the domestic Sholem Aleichem was as interesting as the literary one—if not even more interesting!

2

He was not *Sholem Aleichem* in literature and *Rabinovitsh* at home. He completely detached himself from the Rabinovitsh as soon as he truly felt his artistic mission. Everywhere he was Sholem Aleichem from head to foot. But at home he was, if one may say this, even more Sholem Aleichemesque than he appeared to the outside world. Sholem Aleichem—the gentle romantic, the sentimental, lyrical singer of *Jewish* romance (his emphasis) in *Stempeniu, Yosele Solovey, Wandering Stars,* and *The Song of Songs*—was at home the gentlest husband to his wife, the noblest and eternally loyal knight, whose refined love and exalted faithfulness constantly blossomed, fresh and young, and did not wilt with the passing years. An echo of this, full of spiritual devotion and the sadness of parting, rings out from his last will until today, as the final chord of a wonderful, romantic life symphony. Sholem Aleichem, our only writer for Yiddish-speaking children, was the melancholy and joyful singer of our impoverished and our gifted, naïve yet wise, comically moving "Topls" and "Motls." At home he was the most passionate father to his children, the happy, playful friend of their childhood, the constant companion on their long path to adulthood. And every day, in his own republic, Sholem Aleichem the humorist came out with such a wealth of humoristic ideas, such treasures of play and laugher! He was a fountain of pleasure for his people, and those who were close to him were the first to draw from that blessed source. He sensed instinctively, and later also understood consciously, that he had been given the calling of spreading joy to everyone—and who had a greater right to this than those who were closest to him?

Whoever reads through the thousands upon thousands of letters, which Sholem Aleichem wrote to his family in the different periods of his wanderings away from home, will be amazed: where did it all come from? Even for a person with great mastery of the pen, what an abundance of honest, unforced productivity on top of such extraordinary literary creativity that never stopped for a single day! How did such an intensive creator, who devoted himself completely to his fictional worlds, have so much room, such fresh energy, and such lively attentiveness for the daily interests of his family members— those of everyone collectively and of each individual separately? Perhaps the answer lies, once again, in the fact that Sholem Aleichem's private life and creativity merged into a single entity. Writing a letter to his own children was for him a kind of continuation of his literary work, and it gave him the same artistic satisfaction as writing his works for the faraway public. One might even say that for him there was no near or far. He saw before him just one person—the reader, the beneficiary, the recipient, whom he always longed to give pleasure, because his entire nature consisted of fatherliness, paternal generosity, distributing gifts left and right to whoever wanted to receive them. In his own home, where he was certain that everything he gave would be received with sincere love, his fatherliness reached its highest, most beautiful artistic expression.

3

He was an adept, artful father. At home he developed paternity into a cult. He attentively watched over every single one of his children; like a good psychologist, he studied them and knew their qualities, their tendencies, and their longings—and he constantly surprised them with his elegant goodness, which always reached its goal. He was richly inventive in his ideas and activities for the home, always bringing them to large and small in deftly thought-up, comic, and artistic preparations. In the most difficult hours of material need, of physical illness, and in the midst of fervent creative work, he had the memory, patience, and kind intention to delight one of his children in some other city, in a distant land, with something. It might be a fantasy, a chimera, or a flash of hope. And in good times, there was no limit to his kindness. In addition to his paternal generosity and protectiveness, he also possessed a mother's gentleness, a friend's warmth, and a lover's poetry. Because he could not show all of this in close contact, as a result of inborn tact, he would allow it a free outpouring in his letters.

His fatherly love was not blind. With paternal pride he sustained and encouraged the virtues of his children—by praising them at home. But he didn't ignore their faults, either. Against the fault or foolish behavior of a child he applied the same weapon as he used against the vices of Kasrilevke: humor. But that would be done with such fatherly wisdom, in such a refined, artistic manner, that it could cause no offense. Everything would burst and be resolved in a resounding, cleansing laughter.

And the children responded to him with such love! It's rare to find such a household—where children are so charmed, inspired, and enamored of their father, as in the family of Sholem Aleichem. He was the children's bright angel, the joy of their childhood, their holiday spirit. Not because they basked in the external rays of his literary fame. Perhaps that came later, when the children grew up, went abroad, and realized what a name their father had in the world. During their early childhood, raised in Kiev—in a circle of Russified Jewish plutocrats and career intellectuals, their father's fame as a Yiddish writer was seldom apparent to them. Internally, before his own family, Sholem Aleichem was the great magician, the source of joy, the family genius.

He was the head of the family, its crown and its pride. He was never a despot, however, but instead the patriarch—in the noble, spiritual sense. He never forced his opinions and tastes on the children; he offered them unnoticed, in a fine, agreeably arranged form. He had the greatest love for ancestral heritage, for the Jewish spiritual inheritance that comes down from former generations to future generations, and of itself this spirit was planted in his family life. From his own childhood he brought exquisite echoes of Jewish ethnic character, and these motifs were felt strongly in his home environment. He was free of religious dogmas, but he was bound with all his heart to the piety of Judaic traditions. He not only sang the majesty of Jewish holidays in his works; he himself also celebrated them in his own home, in the family circle, with all of their old-fashioned glory. The eve of Passover in Sholem Aleichem's home was no less tumultuous than he describes it in his Passover stories for Jewish children. The Passover Seders he led were a model of sincere, exalted holiday spirit. He led them naturally and simply, with the honest holiday joy of a child of his people—not for artificial, "nationalistic," or "educational" reasons. Because of this, his Seders affected the children naturally and joyfully.

Life in the Christian city of Kiev, and the Russifying tendencies in the surrounding region, did not make it possible to give his children a true Jewish education. The Russian high schools and universities took care of the matter of education by themselves. In similar houses of other Yiddish writers, the father's work was always entirely foreign to the children; the writing went on silently, behind closed doors, for remote, unfamiliar purposes. Such a relationship to *their* father's lifework was unthinkable. It would have been wildly absurd for Sholem Aleichem if his children had been among those to whom his creative spring was blocked. Hence he always kept his children, especially the grown-up ones, in constant contact with his creations and literary interests. He never sought solitude or an isolated study for his work; he always worked with an open door, often right in the middle of the children's commotion (which he didn't even notice while writing). As a result, the children felt emotionally connected to their father's literary activity, and his fictional characters were naturally brought into the family. "Tevye the Dairyman" was counted as a beloved, close relative, a small-town cousin; "Menakhem-Mendel" was a well-known neighbor, a frequent guest; and "Motl, the Cantor's Son" was a kind, dear, delightful sibling. When Sholem Aleichem finished a work that he was satisfied with, he would festively read it aloud to his entire household. Special preparations were made as for a family holiday. The children knew early on that, in the evening, their father would read his new piece, and Sholem Aleichem would feverishly prepare for the reading as if for a public premier. He surrounded himself with all of his writing tools, read and erased and wrote on the fresh manuscript, deftly adding new pages, reconsidering, biting his nails, erasing some more and writing some more. The family was already seated around the table in great expectation. The curious ones looked through the open door at their father's writing desk. And Sholem Aleichem was still immersed in his work. He was tinkering with something in his corner, with pen and ink, with scissors and tape, with bottles of gum arabic, and his face was mysteriously concentrated. He looked like an engineer who was testing everything and tightening the screws of his invention for the last time before he went to demonstrate it to the waiting public.

"Papa, are you ready?" an impatient child would ask from the table, to encourage his father and let him know that the curiosity was immense.

"Ready!" would be heard from the next room in Sholem Aleichem's youthful, cheerful voice, and soon he would appear before his own audience moving nimbly, with flashing, beaming eyeglasses, and with a freshly taped, bulging manuscript in his hand.

If the piece was one of his beloved works, such as a story of Tevye the Dairyman, Sholem Aleichem would wear holiday clothes to the first informal reading.

4

Most of all he would devote himself to the smaller children—to those whose brightly colored fantasy had not yet come in contact with gray reality. For them he had something that is higher than art and talent: an eternally young, childish soul. He gave them the largest space in his heart, considered their childish concerns important, and guarded their childhood feelings from outside, brutal contact. He played with them as an equal, devised interesting pastimes for them, and gave them fond, comical names. That was the best relaxation for him after his work. He was endlessly attentive to them, sincere, pliant, full of compassionate benevolence in the face of their helplessness. He knew how to speak with them in their own language, to occupy their fantasy, to interest them in all sorts of childish activities, to enchant them with outlandish gifts and with unexpected comic witticisms, infecting them with his joy and with his resounding laughter. All this was done in great seriousness, without affectation, but with great tact and deep psychological understanding of the child's spirit. That is how he was in his early years, as a young father, and he remained this way until his final years, when he had become a grandfather to his grandchildren—except that he related to them not as a grandfather but as a father. Among his many family letters one finds a bundle of short notes that were written from Carlsbad in a finely shaped script, on small, illustrated sheets, to his eldest child. He wrote exactly the same kind of letters from New York to his granddaughter Bella [Bel Kaufman, author of *Up the Down Staircase*] during the very last months before his death.

5

He was so closely intertwined with his family that life seemed almost meaningless to him without it, and his inner peace was disrupted. He liked to travel around and see new cities and new countries, to look on with curiosity at new people, and to marvel at new, strange ways of life. Everything that was new and different to his eye brought him pleasure and delight. But all of this had meaning only when he was surrounded by his family, his own republic, with whom he could share all of these novelties, properly chewing and digesting them in his unique humoristic manner. For this reason it was easy for him to pack up the whole family suddenly and travel together from country to country, whereas it was very difficult for him to tear himself away from the family even for a short time, in order to travel alone to some place in the world. When he sometimes had to part from the family, or when one of the children had to travel somewhere, he felt distraught: the entire mechanism of life was upset and paralyzed. He wrote letters daily, thought of everyone, and had something to say that would please each person. His family letters form a special chapter that clearly illuminates the harmonious blending of man and artist in his being. Sholem Aleichem wrote his family letters intimately, sincerely, revealing everything; he did this as masterfully, in comic style and form, as in one of his works or in his lifework, which should be read by his own most intimate readers. He shared everything with them: his longing, his tears, his joys — everything had to be recorded in a fitting expression, in a fine script, and in refined language. And when, on occasion, there was nothing to write, he would think up a witticism or a quaint idea that would amuse the republic he had left behind. He wrote letters from America and, from afar, he heard with a paternal ear how the "small fry" would laugh together on reading them somewhere in Switzerland. He had his own wireless apparatus that connected soul with soul. And he expected the same from every single member of the family who was away from home: being attentive to him, writing frequently about everything, and keeping up the close family bond.

If it had been up to him, Sholem Aleichem would never have let the children leave him. In the later years when he lived abroad constantly and the older children had to go their separate ways, it became the custom that every year, during the summer months, everyone would return home and spend time together with the children and grandchildren. Those days with the children, after long months of separation, were the brightest in Sholem Aleichem's solitary life abroad, and at the train station he would greet everyone who arrived with a joyful, festive reception. For someone to arrive unexpectedly without sending a telegram first, just showing up at home with suitcases, he considered a personal insult. Human life is an important matter, and one shouldn't make out-of-the-ordinary events seem commonplace.

For him life was not a corridor that one may walk through or waste. To him everything in life was important—particularly his unique moments, which must be specially marked, adorned in holiday fashion and lit up tastefully, stylishly, generously.

6

Sholem Aleichem underwent the most difficult trial in his family life during his very last days. This was the sudden death of his eldest son, Misha, and he was unable to withstand this ordeal. It completely shattered his life. He tried hard to be strong, and he attempted to write about it and get the misfortune off his chest—as he always did in difficult times. On the very evening that he received the oppressive news, he shut himself up for several hours in his study, went to his writing stand like a mourner to the pulpit, stood hunched over, and arranged the deepest pain of his soul into pearly letters, elegiac, polished letters. His glasses clouded over, his wrinkled face was covered with tears, and the bent-over paternal shoulders, which were accustomed to the heaviest burdens, could hardly bear it.

That night he wrote one of his most crystal-clear works: his will. But even in writing that he was not able to get the misfortune off his chest. His fatherly spirit was enveloped in deathly despair. He forced himself to cheer himself on, to go on living, because he had not yet *finished* everything. Yet his child's life, which had been cut short so prematurely, before he had even *begun*, hovered before his eyes. "Instead of the son saying Kaddish for his father, the father must do this for his son," he complained quietly in a letter to one of his elder daughters. He could not withstand such an injustice, and bent over, without resistance, he silently went away after his son.

This is how Sholem Aleichem—the rare artist of life, the master of his own family life—lived and died.

With the Family of Writers

1

For many years, Sholem Aleichem's being was a riddle to the literary family— especially to most of the writers who had established themselves in the War- saw literary center. Even after his creativity had flowed out like a broad stream over the young, growing Yiddish press in Russia, and his name was the dearest and best-known to Yiddish readers, he remained for most of the literary circle a kind of terra incognita. What people said about him was more legend than description. Some man was sitting in Kiev, the city of Jewish millionaires—and they said that he himself was once among them—living in a realm of grand deals and high prestige, which was so distant and foreign to what a Yiddish writer could grasp. At the same time, week after week, he was enchanting people with his indefatigable pen, increasingly radiant with the charm of a great, bright artist, such as had not yet been seen among Jews— and more and more captivating the hearts of the general Jewish readership. Who was he? A writer like all other writers? Or some sort of bizarre manifestation, a popular phenomenon? And where did he stand in relation to fellow writers? Was he one of them or a stranger? If he was one of them, why did he stay so far from the community of writers? If he was a stranger, what explained the heartfelt, intimate closeness that resounded so warmly from each line he wrote?

At the end of 1904 and beginning of 1905, when Sholem Aleichem gradually began to make appearances in the Yiddish world and was supposed to visit Warsaw for the first time, this made a stir among the writers there. The younger members of the literary family—who were more sincere and had not yet been touched by professional biases and competitive feelings, and who truly reveled in Sholem Aleichem's blessed creativity—awaited his arrival as one looks forward to a holiday. But among the elder, and precisely among the "elite" of the literary circle, there were some who showed cold dissatisfaction. Peretz's table, around which older and younger writers celebrated literary Thursdays at that time—chattering about literary-philosophical topics— once characterized him in roughly this manner: "Sholem Aleichem, a Jew from Kiev, is talented, but no more than that; neither literature nor writers can ever be certain about him." And with that they wanted to return to the interrupted literary-philosophical chatter (on the agenda was, it seems to me, Otto Weininger's *Sex and Character*). But Sholem Aleichem was a more attractive topic. People started telling Sholem Aleichem's stories and ideas, they recalled the period of his *Jewish Popular Library* [*Di yudishe folksbibliotek*, 1888–89], they retold the contents of the humorous letters that he gladly wrote to a few of his friends in Warsaw—and even the dissatisfied "elite" forgot their tense, cool relationship to the "Jew from Kiev" and laughed heartily.

Sholem Aleichem made a short appearance in Warsaw, and later in Vilna, where at that time a literary group was starting to form. The impression on those writers who didn't know him formerly was a pleasant surprise. He behaved so simply, humanely, so unpretentiously and without conceit—indeed, just like a simple "Jew from Kiev"; but something far, far *higher* emanated from him. He charmed the eye and awakened deep curiosity precisely because of the contradictions in his personality: through-and-through an artist, yet at the same time so simple, with a strong, deeply-rooted simplicity that rejected all refined "profundity." He was entirely wise and sharply ironic, yet at the same time so naïve and so friendly and trusting, especially to those who were younger and weaker than he. He was thoroughly a Jew, yet he didn't overdo it, didn't make any pious show, didn't try to be an apologist for the people. He wore long, "poetic" hair and even a black "Gorky shirt," took on all sorts of "emblems" of the writer's guild—yet, at the same time, he was inwardly far from any sort of writerly coquettishness or professional detachment, without a trace of poetic idleness or armchair psychology, without any pretense of being God's anointed. He wore his writer's crown of soft, fine, curly hair so lightly, the way a worker wears his hat to work. He stuck all sorts of pens and pencils into his pockets, as a worker does with his tools. In that he did not show off his chosenness, but his devotion to the lifework with which he was eternally engaged and united.

For those who came to know him better, all of these contradictions flowed together into a beautiful, beloved, curious harmony.

2

It was no accident of circumstances that Sholem Aleichem passed the best years of his life in Kiev, far from a literary milieu. Kiev was the metropolis of Ukrainian Jewry, the "ingathering of exiles" for all sorts of Kasrilevke-like towns in Volynia. It was the closest observation arena, where he could orient himself familiarly and intimately. Apart from this, Kiev conformed—more than all the other cities in the Jewish Pale of Settlement in Russia—to his lively, vivacious temperament and to his active, eternally searching and expectant mind. It was as if the city of broad Jewish scope and bold Jewish enterprising spirit, of rich possibilities and attainments, of great rising and falling fortunes, was created to be Sholem Aleichem's place of residence. There he both lived fully and was able to give full expression to his active, creative artist's spirit. Like a dry sponge in the energetic, fast-moving city, he immersed himself in the juicy way of life of his kinsmen from Volynia. At night, by the light of his desk, he returned the abundant overflow to the people in a re-created, purified form. For him living and creating were one and the same, and he didn't need two separate rooms. He needed no editorial offices or literary cafés to stimulate his creativity. It is difficult to imagine how Sholem Aleichem could have spent his life in a city like Warsaw or Vilna— sitting at some editorial desk like a mere literary clerk, a professional recorder of everyday life, instead of living it himself. In exactly the same way, it is hard to imagine Sholem Aleichem sitting around in a literary café, discussing literature or national Jewish problems theoretically, day after day, with a circle of writers. For him that would have been deadly boring. And who knows whether it might also have dried out his creative source? Licking his fingers was not his nature. The artistic instinct revealed to him that his source was below, in the depths, in the essence of the folk—not in any isolated heights, above the people. His subject was the living people themselves—not their abstraction, which chosen individuals lecture about and quibble over while walking ahead of the people and failing to notice that they are walking alone. For this reason, he gladly and trustingly moved among the vivacious simple folk, while he related uneasily and cautiously to people who separated themselves from the people into a higher caste. The latter, instead of sharing life with common people, abstracted it, and, *living apart*, they transformed it into a literary ersatz.

"The Jew from Kiev" was too simple and natural to push aside everyday life and be satisfied with an ersatz. He felt freer and more at home among the Kiev "peasants," and in the outskirts of Kiev, than he would have felt in Warsaw at the literary Thursdays.

3

All this may shed some light on the relations between Sholem Aleichem and I. L. Peretz. It is well known that for a long time the two great Yiddish writers not only kept their distance from each other, but to a certain extent behaved in a hostile manner. People say, on a superficial level, that this resulted from foolish matters: Peretz was angry because Sholem Aleichem revised his ballad "Monish" before publishing it in *The Jewish Popular Library*, and because Sholem Aleichem mocked his poetry in *Kol mevasser*; and Sholem Aleichem was angry because Peretz stole his yearbook and gave his own almost the same name, *The Jewish Library*. People then add that, in their later years, when the anger wore off, the two writers reconciled and became good friends.

But that is superficial. In fact, the antagonism between them was much deeper and more substantial: Peretz perceived Sholem Aleichem's great popularity with the people almost as an insult to his own greatness, and for most of his life Sholem Aleichem remained indifferent to Peretz's work *because he didn't enjoy it.*

During my first meeting with Sholem Aleichem, I happened to hear him tell the critic Bal-Makhshoves [Isidor Eliashev, 1873–1924] his heartfelt opinions about Yiddish literature in general, and about Peretz in particular. It will not be superfluous to sketch the broad outlines of that conversation.

That was in Vilna, early 1905. At the time, Sholem Aleichem was a guest in the building where I lived, on the corner of Sadover and Chopin Streets, a floor below mine. (The building belonged to a community leader named Daniel Utziekhovski, who had brought Sholem Aleichem for a reading to benefit the Jewish hospital, and who had invited him to stay with him as his guest.) One evening Bal-Makhshoves visited me and asked that I go with him to Sholem Aleichem, whom I had met just a few days earlier. We met Sholem Aleichem in a small, very tidy room, lying at rest and reading a book on the white bedspread. It was striking to see that, together with the black "work blouse" (albeit of fine material), he also wore freshly polished dress shoes.

The conversation began with Sholem Aleichem asking me whether I had written my story "Moshkele Pig"—which was published in the competition run by *Ha-tzofei* after his story "Moshkele Thief" had been published. Upon receiving from me the answer that I sent my story to the competition three months before "Moshkele Thief" appeared in the *Folkstsaytung*, he remarked:

"Although the two pieces have nothing in common, it is not good that their titles sound so similar; the average reader, who doesn't go deeply into the contents, could confuse the works." Then Bal-Makhshoves asked Sholem Aleichem, in jest, didn't he want to create around himself a "school" of young Yiddish belletrists, who would follow in his path? To this Sholem Aleichem answered:

"No! I'm no 'good Jew,' don't believe in holding court, and I don't want disciples [*khasidim*] to pick up the crumbs. I'll leave that job to Peretz."

That's how the conversation turned to Peretz. Against his nature (which I came to know later), to let others speak and himself preferring to listen closely, this time Sholem Aleichem spoke out vehemently. At present it is, of course, impossible to convey precisely what he said. I am trying to call to memory the content of his words, which was roughly this:

"Peretz holds court because he is, basically, more a hasidic rebbe than a writer. And he's not one of our simple, 'good Jews' from Volynia, like the "Shpoler Zeyde" or Rabbi Levi Itskhok of Berdichev, who were common people and understood the folk. He is of the Polish type—a kind of Ger Rebbe. He arrogantly places himself above the people, acts like a Polish lord, considers the masses to be beneath him, and doesn't speak with the people in their own language. Instead he speaks "Torah" before the people—full of obscure intentions, with allusions and omissions. He surrounds himself with young people—'hasidim,' among them a lot of nobodies, freaks who parrot his every syllable. They go into foolish rapture at his every wink, every time he lifts an eyebrow, saying 'Ai, ai, what a miracle of miracles!' It is dangerous for Peretz to become a guide for young Yiddish belletrists, because there is some doubt as to whether Peretz is himself a belletrist. People like Tolstoy or Chekhov—who have no pretenses and don't frighten the public with their deep wisdom, which one must be specially blessed to understand—may be guides. They are so genuine and sincere that *everyone* understands them. From just such people we should learn how to write! Peretz's holding court [literally "tables," *tishn*] and Peretz's teaching [*toyre*] will breed among us only literary freaks."

During this conversation Sholem Aleichem also touched on Peretz's *Yiddish*, which according to his opinion was more a local dialect of some Polish provinces than a Yiddish *language*.

"It seems to me that they could have learned to write Yiddish from Abramovitsh," Sholem Aleichem said. "Although he was born a Litvak, he blended the Lithuanian and Volynian dialects so masterfully that, out of them, a language emerged—and what a language! But no, our literary freaks have even learned how to *write Yiddish* from Peretz. And in language, that Peretz acts wildly defiant. When everyone in the world writes *emitser* ["someone"], for example, he stubbornly writes "*emits*" instead. Well, well. Now all of the disciples write *emits*—even Litvaks! Even Moyshe Taytsh [1883–1935]—now the language his mother spoke with him at home, somewhere in Smorgon or in Eshishuk, is beneath him, and he also writes *emits*! It has become a kind of passport to modernism: if you write *emits*, you are one of us, an *emitsist* [a somebody, a user of the word *emits*]."

At that moment the servant knocked on the door and brought tea.

"There!" Sholem Aleichem said, standing up and flashing his glasses at us. "*Emits* is already knocking on the door."

The whole time Bal-Makhshoves smiled more than he spoke, and he scarcely stood up for Peretz. Apparently it was interesting for him to hear Sholem Aleichem out. He himself received his share. Sholem Aleichem reproached him for not watching his language and for writing Yiddish too much like German [*daytshmerish*].

"When you used to sign your articles *Ger-tsedek* ['Righteous Gentile'], you could write Yiddish like a non-Jew, but after all, now you're called *Bal-Makhshoves* ['Master of Thought' or 'Thinker']!"

After we left, Bal-Makhshoves turned to me and said,

"It takes one to know one. In just the same way, Peretz jumps out of his skin to denounce Sholem Aleichem. And you know—it's only natural. Writers shouldn't get sweet with one another. Dostoevsky and Turgenev quarreled even more."

4

In their final years, the relations between Sholem Aleichem and Peretz became much gentler. From Sholem Aleichem's side this was apparent after the publication of Peretz's *Folktales* [*Folkstimlekhe geshikhtn*], through which Sholem Aleichem began to perceive Peretz in an entirely new light. Writers in Warsaw say that in that period Peretz used to show his close friends an enthusiastic letter from Sholem Aleichem that included a sentence like this: "When I read the *Folkstimlekhe geshikhtn*, I went to the mirror and gave myself two slaps—because until now I did not know how to appreciate your great worth." If this letter was saved, then when it is published we will know whether Sholem Aleichem expressed his enthusiasm about Peretz in precisely these words or in another form. In Sholem Aleichem's archive not a single copy of his letters to Peretz has been found. One thing I do know is that Sholem Aleichem would often speak of the *Folkstimlekhe geshikhtn* as Peretz's best work. I recall that once, in Nervi [Italy], Sholem Aleichem was walking on the beach with a well-known representative of the Russian Social-Democratic party, who was a completely assimilated Jew. Wanting to show him the high level that Yiddish literature had attained, Sholem Aleichem recommended Peretz (whose name the other man had never heard before). Then Sholem Aleichem masterfully retold "Three Gifts" from the *Folkstimlekhe geshikhtn*, in Russian, and he was very happy when his listener admired it as a literary gem.

Regarding Peretz's "revised" relationship to Sholem Aleichem in the later years I can relay this episode. Once when I was traveling through Warsaw, I met Peretz at [Yankev] Dinezon's apartment. They conversed at length about various things, and I was surprised that Perez did not inquire at all about Sholem Aleichem. Peretz said to me suddenly (*plutsem*; he would have used the word *raptem*, "abruptly"), completely unexpectedly:

"Are you writing a letter to Sholem Aleichem today? Write to him from me that he is a great artist!" I looked at him bewildered and asked:

"Why now, in the midst of everything?"

"I recently read over the novel *Stempeniu*."

"Until now you hadn't read *Stempeniu*?"

"Just imagine—no!"

I felt uncomfortable sending Sholem Aleichem such a strange greeting from Peretz in a letter. Knowing how Sholem Aleichem liked to hear all the details of a matter, I was afraid that it would only throw him off balance. When we met after some time and I told the story to Sholem Aleichem during a walk, he laughed loudly and said:

"Why did he remember to tell me this so late?"

After walking for a few minutes, wearing a pensive smile, he burst out:

"The bastard read *Stempeniu* back in the days of *The Jewish Popular Library*, more than twenty years ago. I have good evidence of it!"...

7

But Sholem Aleichem's true literary home was in Odessa, in the calm, warm family nest of the selected Odessa writers who—with a distinct intention of spiritual purity—separated themselves from the loud, mixed-up, professional crowd in Warsaw. In the cozy atmosphere of this nest, Sholem Aleichem warmed and hatched his literary self out of his youthful shell. That's where he grew his artistic feathers and spread his wings, and later he directed his mental gaze back to Odessa, when he was already gliding on his light wings over his own far-reaching territory. Odessa was his literary point of departure, and often also the point to which he returned. Sitting in Kiev, and later in foreign spas, Odessa always glimmered from afar with a special, dear, cozy glow—a reflection of young, bright mornings from his first creative ascent. "Odessa, Odessa, I am dying for you!" he once wrote in a letter to the Odessa family, in his humoristic manner, expressing his longing for that city.

The Odessa family consisted of: Mendele Moykher-Sforim [S. Y. Abramovitsh], Y. H. Ravnitzky [1859–1944], Ben-Ami [pseudonym of Mordecai Rabinowicz, 1854–1932], Simon Dubnov [1860–1941], M. L. Lilienblum [1843–1910], and later also E. L. Lewinski [1858–1910] and H. N. Bialik [1873–1934]. (Ahad Ha'am [Asher Ginzberg, 1856–1927], because he was a strict proponent of Hebrew, stood objectively outside the circle of Sholem Aleichem's connections in Odessa, while on the other hand I. J. Linetsky [1839–1935] stood outside this circle for subjective reasons.) All of these writers together, both as a tight-knit group and almost each one individually, were close to Sholem Aleichem their entire lives—and a few of them were the people who, in the early years, encouraged him to attain his great literary stature.

First of all, Mendele Moykher-Sforim [S. Y. Abramovitsh]. Sholem Aleichem already began to feel drawn to Mendele, as the source, when he took his first steps into Yiddish literature. Among the few Yiddish writers whose thin pamphlets he found in the bookcase of his father-in-law Loyev (Itzik Meir Dik, Shlomo Ettinger, Linetsky, Shatskes), Mendele immediately shone before his eyes with the genuine sparkle of a polished gem. And already in the third year of his literary experiments in the *Folksblat* [1885], feeling that something important was growing in him, he wrote a letter to Mendele and introduced himself as "an ardent admirer of his talent, who works the soil that was tilled by him," and expressed a strong intention of becoming his student. It seems that Mendele, who by his nature was not so affable with unknown "scribblers," and at the time especially viewed the *Folksblat* and its writers [*shrayber*]—he called them rubbers [*rayber*]—with scorn, gave his young, "ardent admirer" not the least attention. A few years later, in 1888, when Sholem Aleichem was planning to publish *The Jewish Popular Library* and wrote to him again inviting him to work together on his anthology, Mendele still ignored him. Only after the third letter, which Sholem Aleichem sent together with a recommendation from the Kiev scholar and Yiddish censorship official Herman Markovitsh Barats, did Mendele respond with this answer:

" 'Sholem Aleichem'—*aleykhem sholem* [peace unto you]!

"I have received both of your letters, from 3 and 18 March. If only you knew how extremely busy I am at my school and in personal and community matters; if you knew how our Yiddish scribblers of gazettes and newspapers sicken me with their requests to Write, Write! They promise golden mountains and don't keep their word; if you knew how filthily and frequently I have been deceived, in my lifetime, and been burned; and if you knew, apart from all these things, how weak and broken I am, and how much health it costs me to write anything, for when I write about my unfortunate people, I spill my own blood; I seem to laugh, but that is a bitter laughter with green worms, and every time I take up the pen I make a hole in my heart; writing with fire, I gradually burn myself out like a candle—if you knew all of that, you wouldn't be surprised and wouldn't take it amiss that I ignored and didn't reply to your first letter. . . ."

Sholem Aleichem's first letters to Mendele from this period have not yet been found, but Mendele's letters to Sholem Aleichem have been preserved in their entirety. From them one can see in part how the earliest rapprochement between them occurred, and how it quickly grew into a deep friendship. Soon after Mendele's first letter, Sholem Aleichem had already—though still unknown to Mendele—dubbed him "the grandfather of Yiddish literature" and offered himself to him as a literary grandson (at the time Mendele was, according to his true age, fifty-eight [or fifty-two] years old, while Sholem Aleichem was twenty-nine). It appears that Mendele was pleased with the name "grandfather" because in the second letter to Sholem Aleichem he already addresses him with the words, "Sholem Aleichem, grandson!" And in the third letter, "Greetings, passionate, profligate grandson!" A little later the tone seems closer and more intimate: "My dear, passionate, profligate grandson!" and "My grandson, deeply imbedded in my heart!" And that's how a warm correspondence began between the "grandfather" and "grandson," who did not yet know each other in person. In this correspondence, the reserved, staid, slow-writing Mendele could scarcely catch his breath from the moving, diligent, quickly acting and quickly writing Sholem Aleichem, who poured over him like a river in the spring. "You're drowning me with letters!" protested the worn-out "grandfather" to the tireless "grandson". . . .

The main topic of the earliest letters was Mendele's *The Wishing-Ring* (*Dos vintshfingerl*), which he began to write for *The Jewish Popular Library*.[3]

3. See S. Y. Abramovitsh, *The Wishing-Ring*, trans. Michael Wex (Syracuse: Syracuse Univ. Press, 2003).

Incidentally, it should be remarked here that the editorial work on *The Jewish Popular Library*—which Sholem Aleichem treated with the same complete diligence and full seriousness with which he always treated literature—gave him a good schooling. It played a major role in improving and solidifying his literary tact, so that afterward he was strengthened and refined for his own work as well. One can see this clearly when one compares his early works such as *Sender Blank* [1888], *Child's Play* [1886], and others (mainly in their *first* editions) with *Stempeniu* [1888], *Yosele Solovey* [1889], and the other things that were printed in *The Jewish Popular Library*.

8

Sholem Aleichem met Mendele personally at the end of 1888, when he was on a short visit, and at that time the friendship between the grandfather and grandson was sealed. Mendele enchanted Sholem Aleichem with the very interesting personality of a wise, bright mind and a true, original, Yiddish master; and Sholem Aleichem impressed Mendele with his freshness, the purity of his ebullient humor and with his youthful, sincere fervor to work, to accomplish, and to turn the world upside down. It became apparent to them that the names "grandfather" and "grandson" were not just flowery language but suited them very well. In the subsequent letters, Mendele becomes even more familiar with Sholem Aleichem. He already calls him "my flame-fiery, sugar-sweet grandson!" And Ravnitsky, Sholem Aleichem's loyal friend and correspondent, writes this report to him after his departure from Odessa: "I must tell you that you made a very favorable impression on your grandfather and also on Ben-Ami. Yesterday I was with the grandfather for a while and saw this very clearly. But you should take even more pride in finding favor in Ben-Ami's eyes. The merits of your ancestors must have interceded, because very rarely, only once in a jubilee, does Ben-Ami like someone so much."

At this time [1888] the first volume of *The Jewish Popular Library* appeared. It made a great impression everywhere, and it marked the beginning of a new period in the budding Yiddish literature. A short time earlier, the first volume of M. Spektor's *Home Companion* [*Der hoyz-fraynd*, 1888] had also been printed, and criticism that was able to compare the two editions placed *The Jewish Popular Library* on top. But in Odessa there was a small group of writers, with Linetsky as their leader, who for certain ulterior motives took the side of the *Home Companion*. They couldn't bear to see Mendele's "patriarchy" in Yiddish literature, and they carried over their hostility toward the "grandfather" to the "grandson." Among Mendele's friends in Odessa, this group received the name "the other side" [*di sitra-akhra*, traditionally a term used to denote Satan and the forces of evil]. At that time Spektor traveled to Odessa in search of subscribers for his *Home Companion,* and "the other side" exploited his visit in order to raise their own prestige. In Spektor's honor they made a feast at which they praised the *Home Companion* and tore into *The Jewish Popular Library.* They attacked not only *The Jewish Popular Library* but also the "grandfather" and his "grandson." They told exaggerated stories about Sholem Aleichem, such as that he regaled Mendele and his entire circle with ten ruble cigars—but that he left Mendele's servants small tips. Sholem Aleichem's Odessa correspondents relayed all of these petty stories to him. And although Sholem Aleichem pretended not to hear and knew that Mendele was above such "small fry," it seems that he wanted to give Mendele some satisfaction against his detractors. And at the first opportunity, after the second volume of *The Jewish Popular Library* was published, Sholem Aleichem went to Odessa with his wife in summer 1890; he honored Mendele with a banquet at the most opulent hotel in the city, the "Sievernaya gastinitsa," to which he invited all of the close friends and admirers of the grandfather. People in Odessa didn't only talk about that banquet then; for years to come, they told stories about it. All of the "lords" of the literary colony came together, celebrated, talked about the importance of the emerging popular literature, heard the grandfather's strict teachings and incisive parables. Young intellectuals who were not privileged to be inside hung around all night by the windows of the hotel, wanting to catch a word, an expression, a gesture from the "grandees." The celebration continued until dawn, when Moshe Leib Lilienblum—who served on the city burial society—looked out the window, stood up from his place and said in his stammering speech: "*Oy, vey,* it's already daytime! It's time to go bury Jews!"

That was Sholem Aleichem's last affluent gesture in the intimate circle of his Odessa friends. Because soon after, the crisis in his affairs took place, and he lost his entire fortune. Afterward he remained abroad for a time, away from his creditors, and when he returned it was not to Kiev but to Odessa, where he settled with his family for a few years. He had to give up publishing further volumes of *The Jewish Popular Library* (he put out *Kol mevasser,* which was supposed to serve as a forerunner to the third volume of *The Jewish Popular Library,* but that was the end of it). But there, through the true affection of his Odessa friends, he was convinced that his exalted place in Yiddish literature was secure; if he was no longer the wealthy Kiev publisher, he remained *Sholem Aleichem*—and that was immeasurably more important!

During those years that Sholem Aleichem spent in Odessa (from spring 1891 to fall 1893), he matured inwardly and finally found his own path. At precisely that time there was a period of stagnation in Yiddish literature; no periodicals appeared, and for financial reasons Sholem Aleichem happened to write in Russian (a series of feuillitons and lyrical sketches in the *Odesski listok*), and out of passionate ambition also in Hebrew. But in that stillness there grew in him the consciousness of his own independent power. Mendele's proximity certainly also had an effect. Under Mendele's personal influence he freed himself from Mendele's literary influence. Sholem Aleichem himself gave us an inkling of this in the splendid memoir of this time, in the chapter called "Auto-da-fé." He recalls how Mendele, without showing any mercy, told him to burn one of his works, which was written "under the grandfather's influence"—"a sort of copy of *The Nag*, and Mendele said it was *Feh!*" That was apparently the last work in which the grandson was still under the wing of the grandfather, because during this period the first series of Menachem-Mendel's letters appeared ("London," in *Kol mevasser*)—Sholem Aleichem's own open and wide-ranging path.

The Odessa period remained in Sholem Aleichem's memory as a time of comfort and spiritual enjoyment. Most of all he retained the aftertaste of the frequent, long conversations with the grandfather. Sholem Aleichem's eldest daughter recalls that in those years Mendele often visited their home, and as a child she was quite afraid of him. It always seemed to her that "the grandfather wanted to hit Papa." This impression came from Mendele's resounding lion's voice and from his aggressive, hot-tempered way of speaking.

The love between the grandfather and grandson, which was deeply rooted in those days, remained with them all of their lives. It was a moving affection, as between a real grandfather and grandson, and the same kindred relations were established between the two families. The literary success of one only delighted the other. There was no trace of "writers' envy." It is a fact that Sholem Aleichem would feel shocked whenever someone said that he had surpassed the grandfather. No one could compete with the grandfather because he was a grandfather—*the first*. To Mendele, in turn, Sholem Aleichem's honor was precious; he followed his steps in literature like a true, loyal grandfather. I recall how dissatisfied he was in 1913, when Sholem Aleichem gave Menachem-Mendel a new role in the newspaper *Haynt* [*Today*]—as a journalist. "Oy, listen to me," he said during a conversation. "I'm afraid that he will ruin his Menachem-Mendel, God forbid. Menachem-Mendel is a finished character, and one shouldn't tamper with him! What more does he want to do with him? Add a nose? Why does Menachem-Mendel need two noses? One is enough! Oy," he continued, rubbing his high, furrowed brow, "it is urgent that someone write him a short letter about this!"

I remember how he then spoke about Sholem Aleichem for a long time, with genuine grandfatherly warmth. In those days my Hebrew translation of Sholem Aleichem's "Dreidel" was printed, and Mendele started to talk about it as if he had been reading it for the first time.

"People don't know where their greatest strength lies," he said. "He pulls out of his sleeve such little things, true pearls, and never looks at them again. He thinks it's just some foolishness, a dreidel. I doubt he even knows what sort of dreidel that is!"

In the Odessa literary world, it was well known that Mendele had a habit of contrasting his own writing with that of Sholem Aleichem's:

"When I ponder writing something," he said, "who am I like? Like a Jewish woman who has conceived and is carrying a child. Oy, the pain of carrying, one should only be spared that! First, as occurs with a woman in such circumstances, nausea besets me—you should be spared from the likes. It seems that, from the mere thought that I must sit down and write, I become ill. . . . Afterward there begins a series of reflections, deliberations, hearkening to what is going on inside. Then comes pampering oneself, watching out for false turns, from a too-sudden movement; one shouldn't even be tempted! So one must sit locked up in a room, as if nursing an injury, especially in the final months. Then come the awful thoughts that one will miscarry or give birth to a freak, woe is me! Well, and when the birth pangs finally arrive, the real pain of childbearing, it's beyond what can be told—the heavens open up! You think you can play around with a woman in childbirth? —But with Sholem Aleichem the story takes place in a completely different way. A hen moves about the room clucking a little song to herself, *pikt-pikt*, a peck here, a peck there, and before you look around she has already sat down in a corner and—aha! *mazl tov*, she's laid an egg!"

In this incisive characterization, there was truth only in regard to the outward appearance and prolific nature of Sholem Aleichem's creativity. Inwardly he would agonize over his important works, like every other true creator. More than once, while writing, he would bite his nails until they bled. The distinction between Mendele's and Sholem Aleichem's creativity would have to be drawn in another way: while Mendele was like the kind of woman who *seldom* bears children, and so has difficulty giving birth, Sholem Aleichem was like women who have many children and are not afraid of the pain of childbirth. Moreover, very often the miracle would occur—with which Jewish women in Egypt were once blessed: he gave birth to six babies at once.

9

After *The Jewish Popular Library*, the grandfather and grandson had no further literary business together, and their correspondence was purely friendly—or, better, familial. No extended period of time passed without Sholem Aleichem sending a good, short letter to Mendele, to show him his attentiveness and loyalty. It was a joy for him to give pleasure to the grandfather. When Mendele's seventy-fifth birthday was celebrated in 1910, in honor of the event Sholem Aleichem wrote two articles: "How Beautiful Is That Tree" and "Auto-da-fé" (published in *Moment* and in *The Siren* [*Hatzefira*]). If he'd had the opportunity to print more in other newspapers, he would not have tired of writing more, because he could tell story after story about the grandfather.

After the pogroms of October 1905, when Sholem Aleichem had ended his journey across Galicia and America, he met up again with Mendele in Geneva. At that time Ben-Ami—one of the most respected members of the Odessa family—had also settled there. And as Sholem Aleichem used to say, it was "a renewal of our days as in times of yore," an echo of the good years in Odessa. It became especially festive when Bialik visited for a short period. At the time, Sholem Aleichem's material situation was not at all a happy one, but that didn't spoil one bit his exalted mood, which this occurrence evoked: four writers who were bound together with tender, strong family connections came together in a single gathering! This encounter was described in part by Sholem Aleichem in his essays "Four We Sat" ["Fir zeynen mir gezesn"] and "My Acquaintance with H. N. Bialik." The foursome went walking in the mountains, carried on literary conversations, competed with each other in playing pranks. Once, over a bottle of Carmel wine, when they were all tipsy,

Sholem Aleichem masterfully, like a true actor, played the role of Reb Alter in his comedy "*Mazl tov*," in which the phrase is repeated, "A Jew is never intoxicated". . . .

16

Sholem Aleichem related to the writers of the younger generation—to those who emerged in the early twentieth century, together with the Yiddish press in Russia—with fatherly attention. Unlike Peretz, he didn't have gatherings [*tishn*]; that would have run contrary to his entire nature. But privately and in a simple, brotherly manner, through letters, he would often encourage a beginner in whom he sensed a true spark. Thus he was the first to nurture Abraham Reisen [1876–1953] when he started writing. He carried on a correspondence with him, praised his first experiments, made detailed comments about them and immediately showed friendly interest. After receiving the first packet of poems, which Reisen sent him in 1893, Sholem Aleichem asked: "Who are you? What are you? How old are you? Write, I'm curious to know." He was one of the first to see that Z. Shneur [1887–1959] was an important future writer, even before public criticism had noticed him. Sholem Aleichem had been quite interested in him at their first meetings in 1905 in Warsaw and Vilna, once expressed his enthusiasm in a letter, and later he followed his quick maturation with true joy. In this he showed a sensitive, astute eye and clear analytical judgment regarding his (primarily realistic) works, both in matters of style and in details of psychological conception.

Surprising as this may seem, it is a fact that Sholem Aleichem always demanded more from young writers, of the so-called realistic type, than he did from himself. From them he demanded the Chekhovian—the concentration and economy of expression—whereas at the same time his own way was the unrestrained path of broad, flowing, circuitous, and detailed explanations. Perhaps this was because he did not wish to see a continuation or imitation of himself in the new Yiddish belletristic, but instead a further development. During my first acquaintance with him in Vilna he took a few of my earliest Hebrew stories to look them over. (He suggested that I rework them in Yiddish for the publishing house "Books for All," with which he was then connected.) In a couple days he sent me the comments he had made while traveling, and then I saw his severity with regard to every superfluous sentence, and how fine was his ability to distinguish between which phrases were alive and which were dead. Later I became even more convinced of this.

The accepted view, that Sholem Aleichem felt close and at home only with "outmoded" classical literature, is incorrect, as is the view that modern, refined human thought was completely beyond his grasp. With great interest he read the new European belles lettres, and Knut Hamsun [1859–1952] was one of his favorite authors. He read *Victoria* breathlessly and considered it to be the best work of recent years. He only washed his hands of the "mitzvah" of being modern. At a time when the Russian-Jewish intelligentsia went around carrying the heaviness of Leonid Andreyev's works, as if this were a holy burden, Sholem Aleichem considered him to be a literary bomb-thrower. He used to say that it was a desecration that Andreyev [1871–1919], with his hue and cry, drowned out the fine echo Anton Chekhov [1860–1904] had left behind in Russian literature. Most unpleasant was the "mitzvah" of modernism in our own literary corner. Sholem Aleichem was repulsed by the efforts of a few young writers to turn things upside down. In this he did not see "decadence," which can be imagined in an overflowing literature, but mere ornamentation, a "modern" transformation of flowery, Enlightenment writing—beneath which was hidden, together with talent gone awry, fraudulent graphomania. A person with limited powers is unable to make such a leap: from the House of Study, over the heads of the people, to distant pathways. In that he saw a danger for the entire existence of Yiddish literature. He believed that Yiddish literature was above all a popular literature, which could only grow with the growth of the popular reader. If authors wanted to write "to spite" the people, they would ultimately remain alone, without readers—the readers would, without any other choice, return to [the trashy fiction of] Shomer [pseudonym of N. M. Shaykevitsh, 1849–1905].

Sholem Aleichem would express such thoughts when he came upon a work from the new, "contrary" Yiddish belletristic, after critics had praised it to the skies. I once met him in New York reading a novella by an American Yiddish writer. He read over the first few chapters and then leafed through the rest without enthusiasm. "Why does he need to bother me," he said with the expression of someone who is bored to tears. "There isn't a true word there! Who are the people he wants to describe? Jews? Norwegians? If it's Jews, I also know them a bit, and I can swear that *such* Jews don't exist anywhere, not even in America. So then is it Norwegians? If so, why do I need him? Knut Hamsun has already described them better."

He referred to this kind of Yiddish author, who wrote in the style of Ham-sun, as "the writers of the Berdichev fjords."

He blamed the critics for their weakness: "now we need a young David Frishman [1861–1922] to write a new *Tohu v'bohu* about the new flowery writers [*balei-melitse*]." He believed strongly in the power of criticism and in its great significance both for the reader and for the writer. His own relation-ship to his critics was remarkable: he clung to them like a child—first to Bal-Makhshoves and later to Shmuel Niger [pen name of Samuel Charney, 1883–1956]. He was thankful to Bal-Makhshoves, because he was his first "interpreter." But he believed Niger more. He met Niger when he was still very young, a "dear youth" [*avarekh yakar*], as he called him then. Sholem Aleichem admired his maturity, his goal-orientedness, and his ability to ori-ent himself in the confusion of an author's work. He saw in him the thorough literary researcher and sanctifier of the Yiddish word, and for this he liked him very much. Once he said to me: "With Niger I'm sure that he has defi-nitely read me. All of the others are busy chewing over either Tevye the Dairy-man or Menachem-Mendel—have they really read anything more than that?"

He did not understand how a writer could not be curious to read what his friends write. "I read everyone!" he would say, and in truth he was one of the most diligent readers of Yiddish literature. He would receive almost all of the newspapers and journals from countries where Yiddish was written, and in his free time he would look over everything and deftly pick up what was of interest to him. With curiosity he considered the character of authors according to their style, their wisdom, and their foolishness that appeared between the lines. He very often cut out unusual articles and sketches from newspapers, placed them in special envelopes, and marked them with short headings to indicate the "tidbits" he had found in them. In reading he was very sensitive to the writer's linguistic tendencies and stylistic peculiarities. Once he brought me a story by a Yiddish writer in which the word "hasty" was repeated a couple dozen times in the first chapter. From then on he called that scribbler "the hasty one."

In general, he read thirstily. But he was especially attentive to his closest domain—to humor. He read all of the humorists and satirists of world litera-ture, from Cervantes, Swift, Dickens, Gogol, and Shchedrin to Mark Twain, Jerome K. Jerome, and Chekhov. He felt closely related to Gogol. Among his "personal papers" he kept in a special envelope, as a sort of charm, Gogol's words (from *Dead Souls*, part one, chapter 7), which he had written on a sheet of paper in the original Russian and added his own, free Yiddish translation:

"And long after, apparently, I with this wonderful power was destined to walk hand in hand with my peculiar characters, and to observe the great tumultuous life through open laughter and concealed, hidden tears."

He reveled in Chekhov. In his final years he suffered from insomnia, and often in the middle of the night his wife or one of his children would read to him from Chekhov's writings, which he could listen to for the tenth time with the same pleasure.

He was very fastidious about humor. He couldn't stand the young Russian humorists of Averchenko's cut. "They are natural fools," he would say, "who have signed a lifetime contract to make wisecracks." He couldn't understand how such canned humor could amuse an audience that had already tasted Gogol and Chekhov. He had the same relationship to a certain category of new humorists in the Yiddish press, and particularly to those with sticky fingers, in whom he saw his imitators and popularizers. He also couldn't stand them because they designated their sketches as "humoresques": "Well, now no excuses will help; if it specifically says 'humoresque,' then one must laugh!" Another time he represented the humoresque writer as one who says harshly to the reader: "Laugh, bastard! If not, I'll smack you over the head with a humoresque!"

But he read the New York humoristic journals with great interest—first the *Kibbitser* and later the *Wag* [*Kundes*], in which he found a couple young writers with a true humoristic spirit. He especially enjoyed Moshe Nadir [1885–1943]. During the final period in New York he followed his things with true joy, and many times while sitting at home with guests, he would read them aloud in his masterful way. There was something deeply moving about their first and last encounter at the "Yiddish Bazaar" in New York, shortly before Sholem Aleichem's death, when they embraced warmly in front of a large Yiddish audience. It was both a coming together and a saying good-bye between the one who was departing and the other who was arriving.

In New York, in the cold, workaday, shop-machine brouhaha of the Yiddish press, he felt foreign and lonely. For this reason, the friendship of his few friends—such as Yehoash [Solomon Bloomgarten, 1870–1927], David Pinsky [1872–1959], Peretz Hirshbein [1880–1948], and also Sholem Asch [1880–1957] and Abraham Reisen [1876–1953], who visited when he was sick—was doubly precious to him. A pleasant surprise came to him from some of the contemporary group "The Young" [*di yunge*], like Joseph Opatashu [1886–1954], Mani Leyb [Brahinski, 1883–1953], and others, in whom he saw a completely different "America"—far removed from the bleak routine of journalism. To him Opatashu was a revelation, and Opatashu's story "From the New York Ghetto" lifted him up out of his sickbed to write the young novelist an inspired letter.

Yehoash was a great comfort to him in the last winter. Sholem Aleichem had become acquainted with him in that period and Yehoash became the closest and most coveted of his New York literary friends. With his wisdom and keen perception, with his spirited, enthusiastic conversations, and with his entire poetic-philosophic loftiness, this newly acquired friend brought many bright hours into Sholem Aleichem's last, darkening days.

In the final Friday evening, when it became known in the city that his hours were numbered, the New York literary family bestirred itself, and the house filled with the disquieted faces of friends who watched over him the entire night of his death-throes—both inside and outside, at his windows. He died with his people, surrounded by both of his families: the real family of his household and the broader family of writers, to which he clung with true brotherly love his entire life.

With Friends and Everyday Folks

1

Sholem Aleichem's relations with the external world—his dealings with close friends, acquaintances, and simply "everyday folks," who had no intimate or direct connection to his private and literary life—deserve a much broader inquiry than can be given here, in the narrow confines of this book.

Sholem Aleichem was almost the only Jewish writer who came in close contact with all levels of his people, in particular with individuals from these levels. Earlier his worldly, commercial situation and later his extraordinary literary popularity—and most of all his great simplicity, his affable, open, curious, and trustworthy character—brought him into lively intercourse with all of the typical representatives of the Jewish collectivity. The multifaceted and colorful group of Jews that moves through his works was no external group, which he observed and studied from afar, from his literary window. It was his own world, in which he himself felt at home and moved around freely, without special artistic intentions though with artistic results. He had close acquaintance with and personal connections to everyone: the rich sugar factory owners in Yehupets and the poor "gold-spinners" of Kasrilevke, Rabbi Yozifl and Berke the bathhouse attendant, Tevye the Dairyman and his nouveau riche son-in-law Podhotsur, Stempeniu the violin virtuoso and Mekhtshi the drummer, Dr. Levius-Levitan the "art patron" and Beni Gorgl the prompter, the Bundist Joseph and his competitor, the commercial traveler. All of them held deep human interest, satisfied his curious eye and his inborn desire to know about everything, to be impressed by everything. A living proof of this is the broad correspondence he carried on diligently, his entire life, with a world of people—both the letters he wrote to them and those written to him. His archive is a rich museum of human documents, on which all sorts of Jews from an entire generation stamped its physiognomy: their accomplishments and tendencies, their styles and manners of expression. There you find all sorts of letters from all types of people in the Jewish world: artists, writers, scribblers, actors, rabbis, enlighteners, party leaders, students, money-changers, bankers, merchants, workers, scholars, and small-town thinkers, gentle youths, bourgeois brides, workers, loners, advice-seekers, advice-givers, empty heads, and heavy hearts. Before your eyes pass a flowery letter from a "good Jew," the son of sainted rabbis, and even a sheaf written in pencil from an embittered prisoner who has been buried alive. Then you glimpse a naïve correspondence from a familiar Kiev tradesman, a Yankl the carpenter, who has left for America, and Sholem Aleichem is interested in his new life and writes to him in a brotherly tone, using English: "Dear Jack, How do you do?"

Was Sholem Aleichem more drawn to the "highest" or to the "lowest" levels of society? He himself lived among the privileged circles, out of habit and because of circumstances sticking with their way of life; externally he was almost the same as them. But inwardly he was wholeheartedly rooted with "simple Jews," "the real people," from whose source he drank and to whom he opened his own source. He didn't divide people up according to classes, but according to their qualities. To him "the simple folk" was synonymous with "honest folk," the untainted segment of the people who hold within themselves the honest simplicity of generations. In contrast, he pushed away one class of people, the "aristocrats"—a withered branch of the people. Not the true, spiritual aristocracy, for whom he had the greatest respect, but those whom the people themselves half scornfully call "aristocrats"—the estranged money-men, the nouveaux riches, wealthy on the outside and beggars on the inside, who take everything from the people and give back nothing. He spent his best years in close contact with them, knew them through and through, and understood their bleak spiritual poverty. Driven by bitter, concealed need, he hung around their offices and observed them through the clear lens of open mockery: poor millionaires! The small-minded Yehupets magnates certainly didn't have the ability to grasp that this "Jargon"-writing humorist who hung around their stock exchange was the only true millionaire of them all, the immortally wealthy person. Nor could they imagine that when just a sad remnant of their millions would remain and their names would evoke only dull boredom for coming generations, an entire people would enjoy his riches and his name would be blessed for generations.

Did Sholem Aleichem himself understand this in those days? Perhaps. But need is a sore temptation. "Scrounging for a ruble" on the Kiev stock exchange, at times he would feel dejected either because of his fate as a Yiddish writer or because of his limited audience, "the simple, honest folk," which was so poor and helpless. He cried out a bitter complaint to his friend M. Spektor: "Woe is me that I must go scrounging for a ruble! To hell with the stock exchange! To hell with money! To hell with Jews, if a Jewish writer can't live from writing alone and must scrounge for rubles!" In such moments of low spirits he would try to cheer himself up with all sorts of dreams, among which his favorite was "Patrons."

"Patrons" were for him a kind of idée fixe. In this he did not just see the mere material aspect, but something more: true recognition of his lifework and attention to it by the powerful and secure leaders of the people. If "the simple, honest folk" recognized him and thanked him with what they could, love, why shouldn't the fortunate individuals among the people show him recognition in their own way? Deep in his heart he believed that somewhere among the Jews was one of his hidden admirers, a man with a generous soul, who would get fired up with admiration and compensate him for all of the bitter need which he withstood in the course of his life while giving joy and laughter to his people. It might come in his final days, but it should only come. He cherished this dream, not as a personal wish, but almost as a national ideal—in this he wanted to see the exaltation of Yiddish literature, which was so miserable and cast off, and also the exaltation of the Jew, who is so stingy and not mindful of higher, noble needs.

Yet he didn't expect the "Yiddish Patron" to come from his familiar Kiev millionaires. He knew them at too close quarters to expect anything from them. In any event, he hardly ever showed them his literary side. He knew well their alienated, obtuse relationship to everything Jewish, and he did not want to debase the things that were sacred to him. Already during the early years that he spent among them, he kept his inner, artistic life separate from them. He wrote to Ravnitsky: "Because of circumstances, it has been my lot to move among a circle that sympathizes least of all with my wish to write. That circle is our exalted aristocracy, the merchant class, men of capital, who value my finances far more than my literary talent of which almost no one has any concept. My literary pseudonym is terra incognita to them, and we meet as equals on commercial soil, like berries on the same field, with one and the same narrow conception of life and its substance." Even the personal relations were almost secondary. The great popularity that *Rabinovitsh* generated under the name "Sholem Aleichem" certainly wasn't unknown to the wealthy men of Kiev. But in accordance with their own notions, they perceived it as nothing more than the extraneous pastime of an intellectual merchant who enjoyed writing "Jargon feuilltons" and so made a name for himself in "Podol" and "Demievke" (the Jewish districts of Kiev). In 1908, when the Kiev Jewish intelligentsia was preparing to celebrate Sholem Aleichem's twenty-fifth jubilee and asked the wealthy men to take part in this benefit for the ailing honoree, they were surprised: "What's this supposed to mean? Rabinovitsh was always a wealthy property holder — why does he need others' help?" It turns out that the gift that was sent to him came more from "Podol" and "Demievke" than from millionaires. The legend that Sholem Aleichem was paid to entertain the Kiev millionaires with his stories, which some writers have noted as a biographical fact, is no more than a legend. Sholem Aleichem never used his creativity as a livelihood among the wealthy men of Kiev. For a certain period he gave free readings at Zionist meetings, together with the folk author M. M. Varshavski [1848–1907], but again that was in "Podol" and "Demievke" (as he himself related in his second introduction to Varshavski's poems). Only once, in 1894, did he try to interest Max Brodsky (the intellectual in the Brodsky family, who showed special regard for Sholem Aleichem as a personality) in supporting further publication of *The Jewish Popular Library*. But because the negotiations were not direct, instead through the mediation of Eliezer Shulman [1837–1904] who carefully guarded Brodsky's millions, nothing came of this. Another time, in a moment of pressing need, Sholem Aleichem accepted an assignment from a Kiev rabbi, his friend Shlomo Luria, to write the story of the Brodskys and their philanthropic activity, to be printed in a special booklet and distributed in the Jewish cities and towns of the Ukraine. Sholem Aleichem completed the job, but instead of describing the Brodskys and their good deeds, it turned out to be a panegyric to Shlomo Luria, whom he presented as the initiator of Brodsky's philanthropic achievements among the Jews. Luria doubted whether such a description would please Brodsky, but Sholem Aleichem answered that he couldn't write about the matter in any other way. It is not known what became of this—whether the brochure was ever printed, and whether it appeared under Sholem Aleichem's name, or anonymously.

In his works, it is remarkable that Sholem Aleichem as if intentionally avoided touching directly on the circle of the Kiev Jewish plutocracy. He was surely the only one who could have artistically represented their true anatomy, but he didn't do it. Perhaps this was because he sensed that he would have had to use entirely "the path of judgment," and his way was "the path of mercy." Or perhaps he refrained from this because of his inner tact, not wanting to disturb people who stood outside Jewish life and looked down at "Jargon"; they would have seen his treatment of them as nothing more than a rabble-rousing attack on their "aristocratic" loftiness.[4] Only once did he touch on the very head of the Kiev magnates, Lev Brodsky, in the story "Kasrilevke's Burned-Out People," when the Kasrilevke delegation, with old Rabbi Yozifl leading them, is arrested by the Yehupets police at the threshold of his palace. Of course, he did not explicitly mention his name, and in general treated him very gently; but the title with which he designates him among his fellow millionaires rings sharply sarcastic: "the lion among *animals*.". . .

2

In his dealings with the outside world, Sholem Aleichem was not guarded. He didn't screen his acquaintances and rejected no one. He didn't put on airs, didn't make people feel his superiority, didn't look down on them. This wasn't in his nature. He was too busy listening and watching to get involved in such

---

4. Meir Viner quotes and disputes this passage in his important essay "The Social Roots of Sholem Aleichem's Humor," which was first published in 1931. See "Di sotsiale vortslen fun Sholem-Aleichems humor," in *Tsu der geshikhte fun der yidisher literatur in 19-tn yorhundert* (New York: Yiddisher kultur farband, 1945–46), vol. 2, 235–80.

nonsense. He received everyone with serious simplicity, looked at each person as a world unto himself from which one can learn and experience something new. He read life as an exciting book, and each fresh person was for him a new chapter. On his walks he would gladly meet people, easily start up conversations, curiously question each person, listen with great interest—and come home revived, enriched, laden with goods: a world of novelties! . . .

In America, Sholem Aleichem met a new world with new people and many novelties—which, under other, better circumstances might have evoked in him fresh powers to live and could also have broadened his horizons. His situation here was so difficult, however, and people he had dealings with were so unfriendly, so common and vulgar, that he fled from them with a cold shudder in his heart. But the last year and a half of his life—which Sholem Aleichem, as it happened, ended in New York—is a chapter unto itself. Even now it is hard to speak about that in an objective tone.

Translated by Ken Frieden

Around Peretz

Observations and Reflections

R. Peretz-Laks

Most of the memoirs about Peretz that I have come across since he died characterize Peretz the writer, the community activist, and the cultural leader. Almost no one has said anything about his life at home, his habits, his dealings with friends and strangers. This is certainly not because Peretz's private life was uninteresting, but because those who wrote about him simply did not have the opportunity to see him in his intimate, everyday life.

Peretz was a relative of mine, and I happened to live in his house for a few years. I was able to watch him in his everyday life. In those days I was quite young and paid little attention to many things that would have interested me later. I took in everything I saw and heard immediately and unreflectively, for myself, and so Peretz was never ill at ease in my presence and he behaved quite freely.

I want to tell about Peretz and about his way of life at home—his eating, sleeping, laughing, talking, loving and hating, his different moods and relations to people. He stands in my memory as if he were still alive, getting up very early and sitting at his desk. After his early morning work, before going to his office job at the Jewish Community Center, he stands by the mirror dressed in a black velvet suit and white socks, looking in the mirror at his belly. He was always very happy when someone told him that his belly had gotten smaller.

I see how he stands at the mirror and smiles—clearly he is satisfied with

Rose Peretz-Laks, born in 1894, studied dentistry in Warsaw. After her marriage to Aleksander Laks in 1923, she moved to Vilna. There she was murdered by the Nazis, presumably in 1941. *Source: Leksikon fun der nayer yidisher literature*, vol. 6 (New York: Alveltlekhn yidishn kultur-kongres, 1968), 284–85.

himself. Peretz would get up very early. He used to say, "God likes humanity best in the morning."

Often he would perform various household tasks: helping the maid press or wash, or carrying someone a cup of coffee in bed. Once I washed his Panama hat. He took it out of my hands, certain that he could wash it better. Peretz knew that you shouldn't wring the water out of a Panama hat—so he took it to his room, still wet, dripping water all over the polished floors. He was always certain that he could do things better than anyone else. This delusion didn't bother anyone; on the contrary, it made everyone laugh. If someone sewed on a button for him, right away he would try to tear it off. When it came off easily, this gave him great pleasure. In general he liked to enjoy himself—I especially remember his laughter and his gleaming eyes as he began to tell a joke.

In about 1909, Peretz and his wife Helene traveled to Kuzmir, and along the way they spent the night in my hometown Pulav. At the time I still didn't know Peretz. When I found out that Peretz was in the Bristol Hotel, I went to meet him. It was already late at night. Already half-undressed, Peretz opened the door for me. In the narrow hotel room, his wife stood making up the bed. I spoke to Peretz in Russian and explained that I was a relative. Peretz answered in Yiddish, looked at me with a sweet smile, and stroked my head. They soon dressed and we went downstairs to drink tea.

During that meeting I was very nervous and was constantly moving around on my chair. Peretz asked:

"Are you always such a crazy girl?"

He invited me to Kuzmir, where at the time Sholem Asch and his wife were also staying. I said:

"Father won't let me. Around you people don't keep kosher!"

"So you won't eat," Peretz answered.

My father, one of Peretz's cousins—similar to Peretz in his love of life and passionate nature—was religious, a hasid, and a powerful opponent of Peretz the heretic. Once, when my older sister brought home one of Peretz's books, my father tore it out of her hands and threw it into the fire.

In the morning I arrived in Kuzmir with a group of school friends. It was an unusually hot day. In an open field, lit up by the sun, Peretz was giving a speech. A large audience stood around him, with every person's face dripping sweat. Peretz spoke loudly and his eyes were moist with inspiration. Later the entire crowd, with Peretz in the middle, went home and sang "Our Rebbe." Peretz cheerfully joined in.

On the way back from Kuzmir, Peretz again stopped in Pulav. A group of his admirers suggested that he read something from his work. The reading took place in the home of a hatmaker, a simple and foolish man. The room was small and packed with people. The host went around as if he were at a wedding; his face was sweaty, he wore an open vest and white sleeves, and he radiated pleasure. It was apparent that Peretz didn't feel entirely at home in those surroundings. While he read or spoke, he had a habit of sucking on a piece of candy, so that his throat wouldn't dry out. So he asked the hatmaker for candies and a young man brought him caramels. During the reading, the listeners ate them all up.

From Pulav, Peretz and his wife traveled next to Zamoshtsh, where he had not been for many years. People said that his aged mother, who could scarcely walk supported by two crutches, was so delighted with her son that she immediately felt healthy and threw away her crutches.

A year later, when I came to Warsaw, Peretz still lived on Tsegliane Street, a quiet, half-Gentile street with red buildings that looked like barracks. No streetcars rode on that street, but one often heard the whistle of factories near Peretz's apartment.

Peretz's apartment was very small and modest—a tiny bedroom, Peretz's study, and his son Lucian's room. They usually ate in the kitchen. Only on special occasions, when there were guests, did they eat in Lucian's room. Peretz's study was always sunny and bright. The walls were covered with pictures, sculptures, and very many plants. There were large flowerpots on the floor, flowers on the windowsill and on his desk. Often in early spring, when I wanted to please Peretz, I would buy him mimosas from a street vendor and put them on his desk. That made him very happy.

Perhaps it would be better for me to convey my impressions of Peretz in the order I experienced them. But I find it difficult to orient myself in time, and besides I have a bad memory. Once I complained to Peretz of my bad memory. He was sitting at his desk writing. Half-moon glasses were on his nose. He raised his eyes above the lenses and said with a serious expression, "A bad memory is a sign of intelligence." I didn't know whether he was making fun of me or really meant it.

I first came to visit Peretz in Warsaw on a hot day in the middle of the summer. His wife was not at home. He served me coffee. I had just started drinking it when he suggested that I take a walk with him. "Where to?" I asked. "I'll take you to a tall, thin woman, with long teeth like Og, King of Bashan."

During the first period I recall, Yankev Dinezon [1856–1919] would not often come to see Peretz, but always on *shabbes*. He was constantly occupied with cutting the flowers and rolling Peretz cigarettes, which Mrs. Peretz would trim with a scissors. Meanwhile, Peretz would busy himself with his favorite work: moving paintings from one place to another. His grandson Yanek always helped and made practical suggestions. Peretz gladly listened, but under the hammer new holes kept appearing in the walls. Mrs. Peretz would get angry about this, and Peretz was afraid of her. Once I asked him why he was afraid of her. He answered, "I'm not afraid of people who are stronger than I am, but only of people who are weaker!"

Dinezon was the closest person to Peretz in the house. Nothing was done without him; nothing was bought without his expert help. Peretz kept nothing from Dinezon and never went without his advice. Even in his most intimate affairs, he didn't act guarded around him. Oddly enough, although Dinezon was quite different from Peretz—in his way of life, his character, his views—he never criticized him, neither with a word nor with a look. That was a rare, ideal friendship. Peretz trusted Dinezon greatly and held his words in high esteem. But sometimes he was quick to laugh at him.

Dinezon had a habit of telling the same story over and over. Once, when guests were at Peretz's house, Dinezon told them something. Suddenly Peretz ran into the kitchen, where he found his wife, and laughed, "Save me, Dinezon is telling about the same thing for the sixth time!" On another occasion Dinezon was at Peretz's house and was speaking to him from the next room. Peretz, sitting beside me on the couch, leaned over to me and said: "The old man, he's already dried up."

I was amazed that Peretz allowed himself to speak this way about his close friend. At the time I didn't understand that it is possible to have such great respect, almost fear, and yet at the same time, disregard. I say "almost fear," because I remember an occasion when I noticed that Peretz was afraid of Dinezon, as of a higher truth.

It was during the period when Peretz was supposed to start working with the newspaper *Haynt* [Today]. He was ashamed of this, and at first he tried to keep it secret. Once he announced to the household that he was having guests. That evening N. Finkelshteyn, Shmuel Yatskan [1874–1936], and "the Crocodile," as Peretz called him, came to visit. He was a tall, large, and lame man in a long coat; Peretz liked him, and the man spoke familiarly with Peretz. Whenever he arrived he would ask in a loud voice: "Is Reb Leybush at home?" He was an intermediary between Peretz and the editors of *Haynt*. They had apparently come to conclude negotiations concerning Peretz's work for the newspaper. Peretz himself opened the door and tried to usher them into his study, so that the people in the apartment wouldn't notice. He also announced that no one should enter the room. Mrs. Peretz was curious to know who the guests were, so she sent me in with a platter of tea. Peretz was very lively, and the guests were sitting by his desk and talking heatedly about something. I quickly left the room, and Peretz's wife couldn't find out anything from me. Late at night they all went into the city, and Peretz didn't return until dawn. Afterward I became aware that they had been in the "Aquarium," drinking to celebrate having sealed their agreement. Peretz was extremely agitated. He went to bed but couldn't fall asleep. He got up very early and asked his wife to take the streetcar and get Dinezon. She went right away, but Peretz was impatient and sent me to Dinezon as well, so that he would come sooner. Before long Peretz himself came to Dinezon's apartment, in order to tell him what he had done. That's when I understood how important a word from Dinezon was to Peretz, and that he almost feared him.

I don't remember what happened after that. I recall only that Peretz worked quite unwillingly for *Haynt*, and that his articles displeased the leaders of the Jewish community. One Saturday evening Peretz lay on his sofa, as usual, listening with eyes closed to what I was telling him. Suddenly he let out a heavy sigh. When I asked the reason, he said, "One must go work at a desk, even if one doesn't want to." I commented, "If one doesn't want to, one doesn't have to." Peretz answered, "Then they won't pay." At the time I was astonished that Peretz would do something for money, against his will, and I expressed my amazement. He smiled sadly and said, "There are many things that you don't yet know."

Around that time Peretz received a letter in which the editors of *Haynt* asked him to change his writing style because it was harming the newspaper. Soon after that Peretz finally refused to work for *Haynt*. He was sitting with Dinezon in the dining room and both of them looked festive. For the celebration Peretz suggested drinking champagne.

While Peretz was writing for *Haynt*, an article by one of Peretz's relatives appeared in a Polish newspaper. Adolph Peretz, who was a rich banker in Warsaw, declared that in spite of having the same family name, he was no relative of the "scribbler" Peretz. This declaration greatly angered the young Yiddish writers who were Peretz's friends. They even wanted to slap him around for that, but Peretz held them back. The article made no impression on him.

Yankev Dinezon told me many times how Peretz published his first things, when no one wanted to print Peretz's works. Dinezon had them [the three short stories that comprised *Familiar Scenes* (*Bakante bilder*, 1890)] printed at his own expense. In general, Dinezon very much liked to tell where and how he became acquainted with Peretz. Previously Dinezon had heard a lot about Peretz and was quite interested in him. The conception he had formed of Peretz was so accurate that, when he met him for the first time at the house of a mutual friend, he recognized him immediately without knowing beforehand that it was Peretz. From that moment on there arose a most extraordinary friendship, which continued until the last day of Peretz's life.

I remember that Dinezon abruptly began to write a novel and read me the opening chapters. I don't recall their content. The novel didn't interest me much, and it was even a little boring to hear it read. I told Peretz about this. He smiled benignly and said, "Go every day and listen to what Dinezon is writing, and then tell me."

Every one of Peretz's moods would be expressed in the most extreme way, and he would influence everyone in the house.

When he came home from his job at the Jewish Community Center for lunch, we heard and felt throughout the apartment that he was already there. He would wash, sneeze, cough, and we heard it all. He usually had a good appetite, but he would always come up with some new dish, fall in love with it, and convince everyone to eat it. One time he decided that meat bloats the stomach, makes movement difficult, and puts people in a bad mood. For a long time he didn't eat meat. Going down the stairs he would point out how easily he bounded down. Then he suddenly came to like another dish—sour cream mixed with egg yokes—and tried to convince everyone what a good effect it had on the body. He did that enthusiastically and with gleaming eyes.

In Peretz's house there was a tradition: every Friday morning, challah was bought and fish was baked. But it was eaten up early in the day, because Peretz liked warm fish and fresh challah.

Peretz had a particular dislike for porridge. Mrs. Peretz told me that, when Peretz was still a boy, to economize his parents would usually cook porridge.

That's why Peretz was so fed up with it, and later he never allowed this dish to be prepared.

For a while Peretz wore a cape, but then he got tired of it and went back to wearing a coat. Wearing boots seemed pointless to him, but it's inconvenient to go around in muddy shoes. Peretz was delighted that it was possible to buy galoshes that covered just the soles of one's shoes. But soon he lost one and it didn't pay to bring home the other, so he came home without the galoshes.

Once he found out that he had flat feet, and that this disturbed him while walking. He called a cobbler and asked him to put brass plates inside his shoes. He was happy as a child with his invention. He said to me: that's a family defect. You probably have it, too, so makes brass plates for your shoes.

However complicated his demands were, the tailors, cobblers, and other craftsmen understood him instantly and fulfilled his caprices with joyful compliance. In making the order, both Peretz and the craftsman would feel triumphant, as if both had made a very good bargain.

Peretz loved cinema. I recall an evening when he went to the movies three times. In a certain playhouse there was a silent picture called "The Andalusian Woman's Vow."[1] Peretz went once with his wife, a second time with Dinezon, and the third time with S. Anski [Solomon Rappoport, 1863–1920], who had just arrived from somewhere—he went to the same movie three times. If the screen showed something comic, Peretz would shake with laughter, whereas in real life such images hardly elicited a smile.

In the foyer of a theater Peretz was always very lively; his eyes would sparkle, he would nod in every direction with a friendly expression, and he almost always lost the tickets. He seldom liked plays and almost never sat it out until the end of the performance.

The Moscow Art Theater was visiting Warsaw and it made a powerful impression, but Peretz didn't like it. In his opinion, "A scene must not be a photograph of life. Stanislavsky's theater is too realistic. Actors should perform what people see only in their dreams."

When Peretz Hirshbein [1880–1948] was forming his troupe, Peretz was passionately interested in the selection of capable boys and girls for the cast. Rehearsals were held in his apartment, and I was amazed when young female vocalists used to come and sing for him, in order to hear his expert opinions.

---

1. Peretz's interest in this obscure film may have been enhanced by his speculation—mainly based on the name "Peretz"—that his family was of Sephardic origin.

I think that Peretz possessed no particular musical talent, and he had absolutely no ear for singing.

He would sing folk songs like marches, and he used them to keep time while striding back and forth in his room. Saturday afternoons, when the young writer Haim Gildin [1884–1944] would masterfully sing his countless folk songs in Peretz's apartment, Peretz cheerfully accompanied him and would always start off an octave higher. Even that never bothered Dinezon, who was very sensitive to music and a great lover of warm, heartfelt singing.

Peretz revised his works many times. Once he reworked a story of his into a play. But I had the impression that he didn't write plays with as much ease and talent as he did fiction. Basically, he wrote them in order to keep up with other modern writers. I commented on that to him. It pained Peretz, and he said sternly to me: Because you don't understand. . . .

Peretz was then about sixty years old and his works were world famous. Yet there were moments when Peretz doubted his literary ability. I remember a day when Peretz was particularly under the sway of such depressive thoughts. He stood by the bookcase and looked into one volume after another. He read long passages out of his books, paced back and forth across the room, and looked again at a book. His face expressed pain, almost despair, and this state endured until the arrival of Dinezon, who—with an ardent look and a few sincere words—could dispel and drive away Peretz's painful thoughts.

It is a sunny *shabbes* morning, and Peretz has just finished writing his story "Korbn" ["Sacrifice"]. He sits by the table, still half-absorbed in his creative mood. In his eyes is a strained look. His nose is feverishly white, and on his brow are small drops of sweat. Dinezon enters quietly, unannounced, and Peretz says:

"Yankl, sit down!"

Then he reads his story aloud. In the silence, Peretz's voice infuses everyone with a kind of mystical feeling. From Dinezon's enthusiastic expression, it is easy to see that Peretz's new story has made a very strong impression on him.

In the evening Peretz liked to lie on the sofa and hear me tell stories from the small shtetl. He was ready to hear everything, even things that didn't seem at all interesting to me. Later on, he couldn't go to sleep without a "tale," as he called it. At every opportunity he would beg, "Tell me a tale!" And I would tell him whatever came into my head.

I once told him a girlfriend's dream. Peretz liked the dream very much and related its content to Dinezon. Dinezon said, "Write down the tale and call it 'Haim Treger.' " Peretz replied, "I'll write it down when the tale turns up again unexpectedly." Another time he said "Tell me something!" I said that I had nothing to tell.

"Aha!" he teased, "I've already drained you dry." Peretz's favorite hero of my "tales" was Uncle Notte. Dinezon once asked, "Who is Uncle Notte?" Peretz answered, "You don't know Uncle Notte? I feel as if I can touch him."

I was about to leave for a longer period. On that occasion Dinezon commented that, when I came back, I would have many interesting things to tell about. Peretz said, "A person is not always a sponge. Only in the earliest years does one soak in everything so easily."

Peretz was reading something aloud to his guests and said, "As light as a butterfly." I said, "What sort of butterfly is that?" He said, "A sixteen-year-old girl."

Peretz loved when people read books aloud to him. I brought home books indiscriminately, and he enjoyed everything. For the most part I read him Chekhov. I remember that once he laughed heartily over Chekhov's story "Dushechka" ["The Darling"]. I read it to him a few times and he always listened with the same attention.

While reading plays he never bothered to list the names of the characters. I used to be amazed at his agility in orienting himself to a play. Often he would write something and, at the same time, he would listen to me read or tell a "tale." It seemed to me that Peretz wasn't listening attentively enough. But he could retell word for word some of what I read or told him—so remarkable was his ability to do two things at the same time.

Peretz had an interesting relationship to writers, beginners who came to him for an encouraging word. A major part of the impression that the novice made was based on his appearance and mannerisms. If Peretz liked the writer, he received him well and kindly, read his works, and asked him to come again. But if the young man made an awkward movement or seemed like a pitiful person, all was lost, and Peretz tried to get rid of him as fast as possible. Because of this, apparently, there prevailed an opinion that Peretz was not kindhearted but an egoist. More than once I saw him quickly say goodbye to such a visitor, go into another room, and wait behind the door until he had disappeared.

One time a young man came to Peretz, bringing a notebook with him. Peretz asked him to leave the manuscript for him to look over. In a few days he returned the work to its author and told him that he should try to write something else, more successful, and then we would see. I knew that Peretz hadn't read the notebook and asked how he knew that it was no good. Peretz answered: "You don't need to open a barrel of tar to know that it stinks—you sense the smell even when it is closed."

I remember another episode: Once a young man came to Peretz in the evening, when everyone was sitting in the dining room. Peretz went to his study to receive the guest. The young man had long dreamed of meeting the great writer, and he had finally traveled a great distance to shake Peretz's hand. But he was so surprised when he saw Peretz before him that he was literally speechless and couldn't say a word. Peretz spoke quietly with him and tried to calm him down, but the guest went on stammering, and it was impossible to understand him. From the front room I heard Peretz tell him: "Go home and calm yourself. Come again tomorrow at eight in the morning, and we'll chat." I understood the young man. At first, before I became accustomed to Peretz, almost every minute I was overwrought and moved almost to tears.

I recall one such instance. It occurred while they were still living on Tsegliane Street, and a Christian maid named Manie was their servant. Her fiancé wanted to leave her because someone told him about her unrefined past. To convince her fiancé that it was a false accusation, she traveled to see him in Lublin. But she came back tired, hungry, and beaten down—she hadn't accomplished anything there. She came into the kitchen through the back door, lay down on her bed, and buried her face in the pillow. Peretz was sitting at the kitchen table eating something. He looked at her with infinite compassion, went over to her, gave her his food, and tried to console her. She didn't even turn over. I looked at Peretz, enchanted, and there were tears in my eyes. Peretz noticed that and said, "You're still just a foolish girl."

Another time his servant girl was not well. He carefully took her temperature, gave her spoonfuls of medicine, and called several times from his office to find out how she was. In general it was very moving to see his concern and discomfort when someone in the house was sick.

In such cases Peretz sometimes overdid it, and comic scenes would take place. Once I arrived after we hadn't seen each other for a long time. I rang the doorbell with a pounding heart. Dinezon let me in and led me by the hand into the room. I greeted everyone at once and broke into tears from excitement. Before I could sit down I needed to try on all of the gifts that Mrs.

Peretz had brought me from abroad, over the summer—warm underwear and various strings of beads. From the trip I was unnerved and red in the face, but Peretz thought I had a fever and was sick. I felt healthy and wanted to sit at the table to talk and enjoy myself, but since Peretz had decided I was sick, it was hopeless. I needed to take aspirin and go to bed with all of the underwear and beads. Yet I absolutely had to go into the city that day—to find my friend with whom I needed to prepare for exams the next day. I tried to explain that to Peretz, but no arguments helped. Finally I started a conversation about something else, to divert his attention from me, and that worked right away. Peretz became lost in thought, soon went to his study, and totally forgot about me. I got up quickly, dressed, and stood for a while at the table where Peretz was writing. He looked at me without seeing me. In the evening I told how I had fooled him, and he laughed, saying, "You're really a clever one!"

Even apart from his great talent, it seems to me that as a person Peretz could be very surprising. Most surprising was his mixture of the most diverse traits. He was resolute and proud as a lion, yet soft and gentle like a child. Easy to deceive, Peretz's trusting relationship to people sometimes found expression in especially naïve ways. A poor relative from the provinces came to him for help. Peretz handed him a slip of paper and asked him to choose from one of the sums, fifteen and twenty-five, which were written on it. With a smile, the relative pointed to the twenty-five. Sometimes it seemed to me that Peretz consciously let himself be fooled—for the beauty of the game.

Various impressions remain in my memory. Saturday evening he was lying on his sofa with his eyes closed. In his room were guests—well-known women and writers. One woman said, "Quiet, Herr Peretz is sleeping!" Right away Peretz called out, "Herr Peretz never sleeps!"

Once we were at the theater—Peretz, Mrs. Peretz, Dinezon, and I.

During the intermission, Peretz stood by the aisle chatting with a Jewish student. The student was very tall, with a narrow and doltish face. While talking Peretz smiled the whole time. His forehead was oddly bright, as if illuminated. One could see that Peretz was mocking the student. Everyone said that Peretz looked taller than the lanky student.

At the summer house in Miedzieszyn. During lunch on the veranda I sat, as usual, between Peretz and his wife. I had tied back my hair with a red string, which I had taken from a bag of sugar. Peretz couldn't stand it and, in the midst of a lively conversation with the guests, he slipped the red string off my hair. Without anyone noticing, he angrily threw it under the table. Mrs. Peretz and I could hardly contain our laughter.

Peretz himself always dressed elegantly and tastefully, often with a flower in his lapel. For a while I remember him wearing a green hunter's cap, which suited him best. At home he always wore soft, comfortable, expensive clothes. During the winter, while working, he wore a soft green or brown shirt made of English material. His high-ankle, supple shoes were padded with cloth. He had cut open those shoes on both sides, so that his foot would slide easily into them. Peretz covered his legs in a thick white fur. He gave off a faint odor although he used no perfume and couldn't stand any perfume scent. Once a girlfriend put a strong perfume on me. Covered in fragrance, I went over to the table where Peretz was sitting, expecting to receive a compliment. Peretz took a sniff and said to me, "Move back, I can't breathe!" He also hated manicures; the polish and redness of manicured nails aroused disgust in him.

Peretz once stood in the front room dressed to go out, wearing a new suit with a red flower in the lapel. His cap was tipped rakishly to the side. His face was festive, his eyes shone, and his wife and I looked at him amazed—he looked so handsome and bright. At the door he turned to us and asked, "Am I an ugly guy?"

Once he abruptly asked me, "Do you want to marry N.?" I said no. "And would you marry me?" he asked. "What do you mean?" "I mean, a guy like me."

One evening Peretz was sitting in his room reading a book. I came in. He drew me by the hand and asked, "So, girl, what's new?" I told him I was sad. "What do you mean?" he asked, astonished. I told him that for a while I had felt that my eyes had lost their luster and that, when I was speaking with people, I saw that they became bored and something uncanny stood between us. He thought a while and advised me, "Lock yourself up in your room for a month, don't let anyone in, and everything will heal itself."

Once I showed him a photograph of an acquaintance. Peretz looked at it and said, "He looks as if he's just come out from under his mother's apron, but because of that, grab him." I didn't understand why I should grab him. "Girls should get married," Peretz said. "One can only kiss until age thirty."

An acquaintance, an eighteen-year-old Russian student, gave me a gift—a philosophical work by Max Stirner [Kasper Schmidt, 1806–56]. I showed it to Peretz. He laughed: "He would have done better to give you a couple kisses. I'm familiar with Stirner, but what's he got to do with you?"

In his bookcase were the complete works of Heinrich Heine [1797–1856]. Peretz often quoted Heine's poems, which he had also translated into Yiddish. That apparently gave me reason to believe that Heine had influenced Peretz's creativity. In Peretz's son Lucian, who had a separate world of ideas and idols, it was also possible to notice Heine's influence. He had memorized many poems and entire pages of Heine's works. I understood that to be the result of Peretz having educated him. When I knew him, one of Peretz's favorite authors was the Dutchman Multatuli [Eduard D. Dekker, 1820–87]. In the few hours Peretz had time to read, I would most often see him reading Multatuli's works.

Regarding his literary work, Peretz was quite patient. He had reworked his things dozens of times and could endure long hours sitting at his desk. But in everything else he was capricious as a young girl, and he had to gratify each longing right away. Mrs. Peretz had always been a diligent housekeeper. Before she left the apartment she used to take a long time checking the household—closing cabinets, straightening chairs, giving orders to the servant girl. Thanks to Peretz she had to break her pedantic ways once and for all. Knowing that Peretz was impatient and didn't like to wait, she learned to be ready at any moment to accompany him, when he wanted to go out.

Once we all went for a walk. Peretz walked behind me and commented that a tear in my coat made it look like a wing. He told me, "Cut off another piece of the coat, and you'll look like a bird." At home I had to cut off almost half of the coat. Then I naturally wasn't able to fly and couldn't even walk in it, so I had to buy a new one.

A cousin once came to visit me from the shtetl. She was young and very pretty. But Peretz didn't like her, perhaps because of some flattering words she had spoken to him. Suddenly he called me into his study and said to me, "Take her away from here and don't let her come back!" She asked for paper to wrap up her galoshes. Peretz handed me a stack of newspapers and pushed me along. That irked me and I asked why she bothered him so much. Peretz answered, "What did she do to her teeth?" She was missing two front teeth. I could hardly bear to look at my cousin as, terribly downhearted, she wrapped up her galoshes. I went away with her and was supposed to return for lunch. But I was delayed and didn't get home until evening. Peretz stood holding a hammer, rearranging the pictures, and making new holes in the walls. Vikta, the servant girl, brought me dinner, and I sat down to eat. Without turning around, Peretz said, "Where did you drag yourself around with her?" It was so insulting. I pushed the plate away and burst into tears. Mrs. Peretz calmed me down, saying, "Why do you listen to your crazy cousin? Eat, don't listen to him." But Peretz was pleased that I was crying.

I can still see him giving a reading in the Philharmonic Hall. He looks wonderful. One cheek has turned completely white from the excitement. His face and entire figure exude life, energy, and will. His unique eyes gleam, and his mouth utters pearls. He moves forcefully, and so does the graying tuft of hair on his forehead. All eyes are directed toward him, and everyone listens intently. Peretz goes home cheerfully because, as always, he has been successful. Around him is a crowd of people—strangers, acquaintances, all of them speak lovingly and try to get closer to him. He feels this and walks along self-assured, in high spirits, wearing his broad cape.

Peretz liked such festive days. He was especially lively when he was invited to give a reading in some other country. When he rode to Vilna for a reading, as usual he lost his train ticket. He returned from Vilna with numerous gifts, which he received from different Jewish societies.

I recall a laurel wreath with large, wide ribbons, which adorned Peretz's room for a long time. I also recall an original speech, in which Peretz was called "the eagle from the mountains." Peretz told with pleasure of the special moments and impressions from his Vilna trip. Most of all I remember that the pupils from Antokolski's high school honored him with a speech. It was presented to him by one of the pupils, "a beautiful girl with black braids." When she went up to read the speech, in her excitement she began to cry and the speech fell out of her hands.

The Jewish veterans in Chenstokhov established their own library and invited Peretz to the festive opening. On his return, he had to lie in bed for a few days. When the soldiers threw him up into the air, their belt buckles so bruised his legs that for a long time he couldn't move them. It was very touching to see Peretz lying sick in bed.

The Jewish students in Pulav's horticultural institute invited him to lecture a few times. But Peretz didn't want to travel there because he had bad memories of Pulav. Then they wrote him an awkward Russian letter, addressing him as "Dear Grandfather." Peretz didn't like that. He asked me to write an answer, so as not to do them the honor of writing a letter in his own hand, and he set strict conditions. Finally he traveled there and received such an enthusiastic reception that it blotted out all other impressions of Pulav.

Peretz was going to travel to a lecture somewhere with H. D. Nomberg

[1876–1927]. Nomberg had just learned to drive a Rover and used to boast of his fast driving. I asked Peretz if I could go along. Peretz said, "I'll travel by train and you can go with Nomberg in the Rover. You can try to catch up with me."

Peretz always dreamed of visiting Palestine, among many other things. He very much wanted to depend less on material things, and not to have to work at the Jewish Community Center. But his punctuality and diligence regarding that work were admirable. He went there even when he did not feel completely healthy. Once Peretz was not well and had a high temperature. His wife stood beside him and tried, with all her power, to convince him to stay in bed for a day. Peretz agreed, but after a while he dressed and left for work with the words, "the devil take it."

Peretz once taught me how to be punctual. "When you have to be somewhere, try to get there in time to stand for a minute by the door, and then ring at the right moment."

Peretz dreamed of having a tall house on the shore of the Vistula River. Then, when he looked out the window, he could imagine that he was in the middle of the water.

He probably wanted to be rich. When the Titanic sank, the billionaire Straus was among the fatalities. Peretz said, "Why didn't he bequeath his fortune to me?"

When Peretz was at home in the evening and lying on the sofa, we used to dream. He would say, "Nu, what would you like now?" When it was rainy, gray, and muddy outside, I would dream of a warm, bright house in the village, with a samovar boiling on a white tablecloth. At the table were dear friends, and happy, good-natured voices rang out. Peretz said, "Not bad, keep going."

During the last year I lived there (a year before Peretz's death), one quiet evening I sat beside Peretz on the sofa. I said that when I had my own money, I would make him a golden diadem for his head. He answered, "By then you'll have to place the diadem on my grave!"

On Tsegliane Street, Peretz had a cramped apartment—cozy but uncomfortable. The kerosene lamp especially bothered him, besides which the apartment was cold and impossible to heat. That greatly influenced Peretz's mood. He always dreamed of moving somewhere more comfortable.

Once I traveled from Pulav to Warsaw in the autumn. By then Peretz lived on Jerusalem Street in large, attractive rooms with new furniture and lots of electric lights. His study was especially beautiful, with many flowers and new paintings, a new desk, a new and unusually fine bookcase. On a small table was a bronze bust of Rabindranath Tagore [1861–1941]. A large oil painting by P. Minkovski depicted a female fruit merchant against the background of a sunset. In the new apartment everything looked different, especially in sunlight. In a corner of the room, on a hanging table, was a pipe that lit automatically when it was touched. Peretz was busy decorating the apartment, rearranging the paintings. For the small couch in his room he had made a thick, plush cover that hung down to the floor on both sides, recalling a certain style. It stood in a corner, hidden by large leaves from the flowerpots. But Peretz liked changes, and later he put the couch in the middle of the room, beside his desk. Everything expressed an aesthetic feel and a strong wish to make things beautiful.

In the bedroom hung fire-red curtains, and soft carpets covered the floor. When the artist Eliovitsh painted a large oil portrait of Peretz, he was kind enough to lie on the soft divans and look as if he was working.

Right after I arrived, Peretz took me to see how the new, modern cabinets opened up wide, and how the electric lamps shed different light. The lighting in his study was hazy and made it appear dreamy [*fantastish*]. The new icebox in the kitchen also drew more than a little of Peretz's attention. He was as delighted as a child by the new bathroom. When anyone wanted to bathe, Peretz hurried to light the gas and set the temperature—with the expression of a child playing with a new toy.

Peretz loved fresh air and would often go out walking. Once he didn't go out all day. Late in the evening he realized this and said, shocked. "I wasn't out on the street today," and went right out.

In general, Peretz loved the outdoors and the street. Like a true bohemian, Peretz always strove to free himself from the bourgeois household. Although his home was very cozy, for a time he ate lunch with his entire family and the cook in restaurants. Peretz's favorite pastry shop was, in 1910–1911, Ostrovski's. In early spring he liked to get up at dawn and make excursions to a park outside the city. Sometimes I joined him, and in order not to ring his doorbell so early, I would meet him at Ostrovski's. Occasionally he would eat breakfast there. He crumbled up the pastries in his coffee, made a thick stew, and ate that. In the streetcar he always stood on the platform. The sun and the spring affected him more than other people. He smiled and bowed in all directions, as if everyone were his relatives or close friends.

Peretz seldom went to other people's homes. For a time he would go only to Leon Feigenboim's house. There Peretz felt at home and sometimes when he was tired, he would even go into a side room and lie down. From there, once in a while, he would throw out a word, and soon everybody went over to him, in the dark room.

Once all of us are standing by the window of a sleeping car. Peretz and his wife are traveling out of the country (I think to Bad Neuheim). Among other people who have come to see Peretz off are Dinezon and Asch, who have just arrived. In parting, Peretz and Dinezon embrace. Now Peretz, at the window, looks like a bird preparing to take flight. He makes a broad gesture with his hand and turns to go deep into the train compartment. The train leaves the station. Dinezon stands sadly and watches as Mrs. Peretz waves a handkerchief from the window.

I recall a summer in Miedzieszyn. Until noon Peretz worked at the Jewish Community Center. Every day I would come to him from school and travel together to Miedzieszyn. Peretz always like to stand on the train platform. One of his coat pockets belonged to me; that is, I was allowed to take change from there. In his pocket was a metal container with compartments for small change of different sizes. Once a gentile boy came in and offered to shine our shoes. I was wearing white shoes. But Peretz said, "Let him earn a few groschen," and the rascal shined my white shoes with black shoe wax. My fellow students, who would give lessons at the summerhouses, would travel with us. All of them were poor, and I would treat each of them to a glass of lemonade and a cookie. The money all came from "my" pocket, because Peretz told me to let people earn a few groschen.

At our summer lodgings, a crowd of people ate at the table. Everyone looked at us, and at Peretz, wanting to hear a word from him, wanting to know his opinion. But there Peretz didn't want to be the literary man and set the tone. He wanted to be among young people, to take walks across the fields, sing, and lie on the grass. Young girls liked him.

Often Alter Katsizne [1885–1941] and other young writers would travel there. Dinezon came every Shabbat. Katsizne would bring along a manuscript and read aloud. Peretz had good relations with him and was interested in all of his affairs. Among the other young writers who had Peretz's special attention at that time was I. J. Trunk [1887–1961]. I remember him in a long coat and a small cap; Peretz was always pleased to meet him. At the time I rarely met Sholem Asch with Peretz. I heard that when Asch first started to write, Peretz said of him, "Fire brings ash, but this Asch will bring fire."

Peretz was always very kind to people who needed material assistance. I recall how kindly he treated porters, craftsmen, and coachmen. He never took back change from a coachman. Once I went with him to the Saxon Garden, and I liked to ride on the carriages. Sometimes Peretz would give me money for a carriage, which cost twenty-five kopecks. But he always told me to give thirty-five.

In 1912, at the time of the general amnesty, Peretz invited a group of political prisoners to his home. Then he called for a cobbler and ordered shoes for each of them. He took almost all of his clothes out of the closet and gave them away—without thinking, with a light heart, joyfully.

My girlfriend in Warsaw needed money. I sent ten rubles from Pulav and, in a letter, asked that he have it delivered to the indicated address. Later, when I was in Warsaw, my friend told me that Peretz himself climbed up to her fourth-floor apartment with twenty-five rubles and told her that I had sent it.

He always supported poor writers. From poor artists he ordered portraits and bought paintings. P. Minkovski was poor at the time, and I remember that Peretz bought much of what the artist showed him.

He also commissioned works by Eliovitsh, Kratkon, all in the most refined, friendly way. A poor sculptor, who had made a very large bust of Peretz, suggested that he buy a bronze Greek vase that he had acquired by chance. Peretz bought it although it cost ninety rubles.

Two of my school acquaintances wanted to travel to America. On their behalf I asked Peretz for letters of recommendation. He turned me down sharply. That was his nature: when he couldn't satisfy a request, he would angrily refuse. I was insulted and became sullen. This didn't bother him, and he didn't try to justify himself. Dinezon saw me crying and asked Peretz why. Peretz told him and laughed, "What do you think of this foolish girl?" To me he said, "My acquaintances in America aren't bankers. If I send your friends to a poor writer, he'll empty the students' pockets." The kindly Dinezon said quietly to me, "You know that Peretz turns his wallet inside out when someone asks him for money."

Once I was angry at him for a few days. The deadline had passed for paying my school tuition. Peretz became uneasy and called me on the telephone, telling me I should come to pick up money from him at work. I didn't want to go, so we made a compromise and agreed to meet halfway. In the middle of the street, between Marshalkovske and Gzhibov, we met. When I saw Peretz's face with his gentle smile, I felt enchanted. Unable to restrain myself, I broke into tears. Peretz covered my eyes with his hand and said, "Nu, calm down and learn to control your moods."

Once his finger was hurting, because Peretz suffered from arthritis. He asked me to rub his finger with a salve. I rubbed with all my strength, and the next day his entire hand swelled up. Seeing that it upset me, he answered the doctor's question by concealing the true reason for his swollen hand.

Once he was a bit gloomy and lay down to sleep. I pitied him and wanted to do something good for him. Peretz said, "If you want to bring me an offering, just pull off my boots."

On the street or in a coffee house, I always noticed that everyone looked at him. I said, "Everyone's looking at you." He would answer, "They're looking at you—they see such a crazy girl."

I used to like to stroke his hair and to touch his cheek with mine. When I didn't want to do that, he would ask, "Scratch my head, and when I die they'll say that you were Peretz's little scratcher."

Often he would joke. Once I told Peretz about my girlfriend who, in one day, visited five doctors. They checked her nose, eyes, ears, stomach, and teeth. Peretz wrinkled his nose and said, "She's gone to pieces, so there's no person left to tell about."

Sometimes an actress from a visiting Yiddish theater would visit Peretz. It happened one *shabbes* while guests were visiting. She was a very joyful, exuberant girl. She jumped, laughed, and tried to sit on Peretz's lap. Peretz said to her, "Better you should sit on Dinezon's lap—he's still a bachelor."

. . .

At the summerhouse he followed this schedule: very early, when the sun started to rise, he would dress and go out onto the balcony; his desk stood on the balcony, where he would work. He would sit there for a long time. When Mrs. Peretz and I got up and went down to breakfast, I would notice how worn out and pale Peretz was from the many hours of work. That's how it was on *shabbes*. He couldn't allow himself this pleasure on weekdays, because he had to travel to Warsaw for his work at the Jewish Community Center.

Many times on hot days he would stand on the balcony in just his pants and laugh at the young girls and women who became embarrassed and ran away. When he laughed through his teeth, a dimple always formed on his chin, and his face looked roguish.

Peretz was accustomed to being respected, and everything that looked to him like a belittlement would simply crush him.

The famous actress Esther Rachel Kaminski [1870–1925] was to appear in a new, interesting play, and she invited Peretz to the premiere. He accepted the invitation and they him sent four tickets in the front row. Peretz, his wife, Dinezon, and I went to the theater. But it turned out that, by mistake, our seats had been sold.

After the play had been going on for a few minutes, the real owners of the seats came up and asked us to move. At first Peretz didn't understand what they wanted from him. Then he leaped up and went out, with all of us following him. The play was interrupted. Kaminski and other actors ran after Peretz, grabbed his hand and cape, and asked forgiveness from Mrs. Peretz and Dinezon. But Peretz looked frightful. It was the first time I saw him so angry.

Everyone kept quiet. Silently we took the streetcar and, standing up, we rode to Dinezon's. Dinezon bent over and said to me, "Don't tell anyone about this!" That was Saturday evening. Dinezon's face was dark. The blue lampshade on his desk cast a pall over the entire room. Peretz lay on the sofa and looked crushed. Dinezon occupied himself with his stove, wanted to make tea. Peretz was a rare guest in his room, especially in the evening. Dinezon was very agitated, and everything he picked up fell out of his hands. Mrs. Peretz sent me downstairs to buy bread. We couldn't get anything other than stale, black bread. Everyone in the room was quiet and sad. I had the same kind of feeling as if a calamity had taken place. After tea, which Peretz didn't drink, Dinezon accompanied us down to the streetcar at Karmelitske. When we got home, Peretz immediately went to bed without a word. He was in a pitiable state. The incident was never mentioned again.

Peretz's age pained him, and he very much wanted to be young. But he had a bad heart, a defect he'd had for a long time. Twice he had heart attacks that were almost fatal. Mrs. Peretz thought that he developed the defect when he was imprisoned for three months [for political activities, in 1899]; he had suffered terribly, most of all from the flies that bit and swarmed like locusts.

Until today I feel regret that I once caused him pain. I had heard from people that Peretz liked young women and avoided them when they got older. A relative, who was supposed to have interested him when she was young and pretty, used to come visit Peretz at home. I noticed that he couldn't stand this cousin, and the same was true of other elderly women. Once I said to him, "I'm glad that you won't still be alive when I get old." He went pale and his entire expression changed. I don't want to tell what he said in response. But it will forever remain in my memory, and I will always regret my words.

During the last period when I lived in Peretz's home, I recall that he was often silent, wore a tired expression, and moved with heavy, lugubrious movements. Once I was sitting at the table in the dining room with one of my girl-friends. Across from us sat Peretz, who was reading a newspaper while eating. It was a quiet, boring evening. I remember a series of evenings, at that time, when almost no one came to visit. Peretz would go to the cinema or go to bed early. My girlfriend wanted to hear a word from Peretz, and she wanted him to take his head out of the paper and look at her. But he didn't move and went on reading the newspaper with a bored expression, as if no one else were in the room. I said to my friend, "Eat, Estherl!" Then Peretz raised his head a bit and said, "If you call her Estherl, she'll never get a husband!" He gave a lazy smile and returned to the newspaper.

Peretz was no longer his earlier self. I would see him undress and get into bed, and my heart contracted with pity—he was old, broken, tired. He slept very poorly. The slightest movement from the next room would wake him up. Once, on a winter evening, Peretz was already in bed although it wasn't very late. Dr. Eliashev [the literary scholar Bal-Makhshoves] came up to visit, frozen and miserable, and he wanted tea. Peretz got up from bed, helped me make tea in the kitchen, and then sat talking with Eliashev for a long time. It seemed to me that they enjoyed one another's company more than usual, and something about it was sad.

Once Peretz sat at his desk writing. I stood beside him and watched his hand moving. Usually, before he would start to write, the quill would shake over the paper for a long time, as if trying to gather force. I looked at Peretz's head and saw that long hairs were sticking out of his ears. Then I saw before me in the armchair, with its soft cushion, an old shriveled up Jew with over-grown eyebrows hanging down, long hairs coming out of his nostrils, bent-over shoulders. . . . It was so unlike the image of Peretz that everyone had that I almost burst into tears. I left the room so that he wouldn't notice.

Once, on a somber day, Peretz was unwell and lay in bed. Lying down he always looked weak and helpless, like a bird without its wings, and I didn't like seeing him that way. It was dark in the bedroom because of the cloudy skies and the dark red curtains on the windows. Beside Peretz was a guest, a cousin, who came to make his acquaintance. Peretz said quietly, "If it were possible to be born again and start life anew, I would live completely differently. First of all, I wouldn't get married." The cousin had an open and kind face, and she looked directly into his eyes. I saw that he wanted to make a confession.

During the final period I would often bring Peretz an apple or a second breakfast at work. In the morning he didn't want to take anything with him — so that his pockets would not be stretched out. Besides, he had in his pockets two or three handkerchiefs, which his wife placed there every day.

A lot of poor people, orphan boys and girls, were always sitting in the front room of the Jewish Community Center. They were almost always crying. I didn't understand the reason and asked Peretz why they were crying. "They're hungry," he said. "If you feel compassion, give them something." He would add, "Give away your money and I'll chip in." He would always give, and I would run to buy herring and bread. Later, after Peretz's death, I heard that these scenes — crying children, poor people shouting under his window at the office — made such an impression on him that he became thinner every day and looked very unwell.

I didn't see him in the last year of his life, but Mrs. Peretz told me that he lost a great deal of weight, his clothes became loose on him, and he lost his joyful humor.

Peretz expected a lot from the war. But actually I can say very little about his thoughts and moods that year. One thing I knew: he hoped for the defeat of tsarist rule. He was most concerned about the collective Jewish fate. Whatever he had at home, he gave away to the poor. Mrs. Peretz was then abroad; because of the disturbances, she could not return home and remained, for a time, in Stockholm. Before her departure she had prepared various supplies — complete bags of food. Peretz gave it all away and scarcely allowed himself to eat. Mrs. Peretz said that when she returned, she saw Peretz worn out, miserable, with a hollow face. On the table lay a small loaf of black bread, and he would cut off thin, dried-out slices. Everyone who saw him during his final year surely knows that this is true.

I learned of Peretz's death from the newspaper. I understood that I would not be in time for the funeral, but I traveled there right away to look at his room and his desk. When I arrived, a number of his relatives were in the dining room—Peretz's sister, brother, and son Lucian. All of them were anguished and depressed. Peretz's wife came in from the kitchen. She looked strangely large and unable to move, with a stony face. Every few minutes the doorman brought in more telegrams expressing condolences, which were not read but placed beneath a fruit bowl. I stayed there a few days.

Mrs. Peretz told me how it all happened: very early, as usual, Peretz got up and sat down at his desk to work. I saw his last handwritten page. From the final lines I could see that his hand was trembling as he wrote them: "Quieter, quieter, he wants to ask". . . . I imagined that Peretz anticipated his approaching death, and the words looked to me like a final confession.

He did not sit for long at the desk because he felt unwell, and he went into the bedroom to tell his wife. Then he went to the kitchen to request a glass of milk from the servant girl Vikta. He told her that his shoulder hurt him "as never before." In the dining room he opened a balcony door—he was having difficulty breathing. So that his grandson Yanek would not catch cold, Peretz awakened him asked him to lie down in his own bed. Then he went back to his study and fell down heavily at the door. Mrs. Peretz heard the crash and went to the study. Peretz lay on the floor with his face down. She called in Lucian and both tried to lift him up, to give him some wine or syrup. Peretz was still breathing, but the wine spilled out. He died in a few minutes.

I didn't see any of that, and afterward when I went with Mrs. Peretz and Dinezon to the cemetery and saw the mound of earth, I couldn't believe that Peretz lay beneath it.

Half a year after Peretz's death I happened to live in Warsaw, again with Mrs. Peretz, who was still living in the same apartment. Peretz's study had not been touched, and everything was in the same place. The furniture throughout the apartment was unchanged, in the same arrangement, but it all looked so different. The walls and everything else exuded gloom. Lucian had moved into Peretz's study, and even the air in the room had changed.

It was difficult to be there. Dinezon came seldom, just on *shabbes*. He took care of the home and took care of all the business. But how gloomy he looked sitting by the table, conversing quietly with Mrs. Peretz and recalling the smallest details connected to Peretz. It was sad. Yet Dinezon's Sabbath visits were the only ray of light for us. One could see from his face that, without Peretz, he was sinking.

Once I was at Dinezon's apartment, and we were remembering Peretz. Dinezon took out a bundle of letters from Peretz to him, written at different times. They were tied with a pink string. He said that the letters were his relics. He cried and it seemed to me that, from constant crying, his eyes had become puffy. "With Peretz's departure," he said, "everything has died for me. I hope that we'll meet again soon." When I left, he embraced me and pressed me to him several times. I understood that he felt orphaned, and that he sought in me a trace of Peretz.

Peretz's Family Life

Peretz married for the first time when he was seventeen or eighteen years old. As is well known, his first wife was a daughter of Gabriel Yehuda Lichtenfeld [1811–87]—a follower of the Jewish Enlightenment, a mathematician, and also a Hebrew poet. Together with his father-in-law, Peretz published a book of poems in Hebrew, *Stories in Verse and Various Poems* [Warsaw, 1877].

Peretz had a son, Lucian, with his first wife. After fourth grade in the Zamoshtsh public school, Lucian moved to Plotsk, where he was raised by his half-assimilated relatives, the Papierno family, and later by the Altmans. In Plotsk, Lucian completed the gymnasium and distinguished himself through his unusual capabilities.

When Lucian was still a small boy, about four or five, Peretz married for the second time.[2] Peretz's friend Dinezon told me about this: At the fair in Lentshna (a tiny Polish shtetl), Peretz went into a wine shop to drink a glass of wine. There he saw the wine dealer's daughter—Helena Nehama Ringelheym. She was very thin, slender, with a fine, pale face. He liked her very much and immediately asked her hand in marriage. At first, Helena Ringelheym—who came from a wealthy family, played piano, and was well educated—was frightened by his "dark, thin lips," but Peretz conquered her heart. They were married a few days later and departed for Zamoshtsh. There, with her five-hundred-ruble dowry, Mrs. Peretz redeemed "a bundle" of promissory notes, Peretz's debts.

Later Peretz was employed as a lawyer and took very important cases. He

2. Peretz divorced his first wife, Sarah Lichtenfeld, in about 1875.

earned a great deal of money and lived well. It is worthwhile to mention a fact that shows how popular Peretz was among the legal clerks. While I was living at Peretz's house, a man who formerly presided over the Russian court in Zamoshtsh came to visit him. He was delighted to see Peretz and, as an expression of friendship, he gave him a golden pitcher bearing his initials. But Peretz didn't want gifts with Russian letters and had them effaced.

When people without special legal training were prohibited from engaging in legal matters, Peretz and his wife moved to Warsaw, where they lived in dire circumstances. Meanwhile, as is well known, Peretz took part in a statistical expedition. Its goal was to do research into Jewish occupations, in order to show the poverty of the Jews in the country. For this purpose, Peretz traveled around to the small villages in Poland, which also gave him material for his *Scenes from a Provincial Journey*.[3]

When Peretz happened to be in Levertov (near Lublin), he lived with his relatives, the Peretzes. People still tell how strangely Peretz behaved: either lying on the couch for entire days, letting no one in to see him, or going around to visit the poor Jewish shops. He ate cutlets of raw meat and sang so loudly in his room that everyone was scared of him. He did not explain why he was in Levertov, and his relatives were left with the impression that Peretz was gathering statistics for a trial regarding blood libel, and that Peretz won the case with his fiery spirit. This story was passed down in a very confused manner. Peretz's elder relatives in Levertov were proud of their kinsman and would invent legends. They would also boast that no Peretz had ever served in the military (then viewed as a mark of dishonor) and that no Peretz had abandoned the Jewish faith. At the time, Peretz lived at his relatives' expense. And although these relatives in Levertov were not happy with Peretz "the goy," they liked him very much. They recalled with pleasure having had the opportunity to be his host.

Peretz also liked his family, and although he always kept his distance, it was evident from what he said that he considered the Peretz family to be highly talented, almost chosen. He would often refer to "a true Peretz!"

Shortly after the expedition, Peretz accepted his position in the Warsaw Jewish Community Center, where at first he received thirty-six rubles

3. See "Impressions of a Journey Through the Tomaszow Region," trans. Milton Himmelfarb, in *The I. L. Peretz Reader*, ed. Ruth R. Wisse (New Haven: Yale University Press, 2002), 20–84.

monthly, and where he remained a punctual and dedicated clerk until the last day of his life. In spite of his distaste for the atmosphere, with its assimilated bourgoisie, he went to work even on days when he was not entirely well.

Peretz's son Lucian studied mathematics and medicine, but he did not graduate. He lived for a long time in London, where he became acquainted with his wife, Helenke Ayzman—a daughter of very rich Jewish aristocrats who, as was customary in those days, raised their children abroad. Helenke was quite assimilated and a passionate Polish patriot. Her parents opposed the match and let her know that, if she gave up Lucian, she would receive a dowry of 75,000 rubles, instead of the 60,000 rubles that all of their other children received. Helenke was very ambitious and, to protest her parents' proposal, she married Lucian right away. Peretz invited the couple to visit, rented an apartment for them in his building, and for a long time he supported them completely. Lucian later received a position with a wealthy, well-known, assimilated Jew. But after working twelve years for him, he was fired because of a suspicion that he had incited the workers to strike. Lucian also tried his hand at business, though without much luck. He changed his trade too often. Certain merchants from Moscow, Peretz's chance acquaintances, offered him a position in their firm. Lucian refused to take the position, knowing that it came through Peretz's influence, in spite of the fact that he was living on his father's money in his father's apartment.

When Lucian's only son was born, Yanek, his mother's parents made peace and released the 60,000 ruble dowry. Helenke and her son supported themselves on this money until the end of her life. She had separated from Lucian shortly after Yanek's birth. Most likely they loved one another very much, but both had nervous disorders, with acutely apparent psychopathic character traits, and they were forced to separate.

When I was in Warsaw, I would sometimes visit Helenke. Each time she would speak about Lucian and ask me to be kind to him. Yet Lucian told me that when he saw her in the distance, he noticed that she hid in a doorway so that she would not meet him. He often recalled and dreamed of moments in their earlier life together—with extraordinary tenderness, and with tears in his eyes. He constantly thought about her. During a conversation about her, he once said: She used to love me, but she loved the old man even more. It was clear that he was jealous of his father. His own life was not successful, and his moods were always bleak and heavy.

When Peretz was still living on Tsegliane Street and looking for an apartment, Lucian went with Mrs. Peretz to see another apartment. In one room, Lucian noticed a long hook in the wall and burst out: A comfortable place, where one could easily hang oneself! Because of that alone Peretz didn't want to rent the apartment.

Lucian was similar to Peretz in several character traits and in his appearance, his height, his build, and something else impalpable—except that his eyes were cold and gray, his short-cut hair was prickly, and he was clean-shaven. There was something English—or, rather, American—about his face and in his entire demeanor. Like his father he was very energetic, always busy, and read many serious and belletristic books. He read with a purpose and with deep penetration, as, for example, in philosophy. While working he also, like his father, wanted someone to sit in his room and do something, to create a work atmosphere, which helped him concentrate his thoughts.

His room was always cold and unwelcoming, like that of a scholar. When Lucian occupied Peretz's bright and finely decorated study, it changed immediately, becoming cold and gloomy like Lucian's character.

He had mastered six or seven languages and read European literature in the original. His behavior was very proper.

Despite his intellectualism, at many times Lucian displayed humane feelings. He helped his stepbrother complete middle school and high school, and he always supported his mother, who remained a widow after the death of her second husband; he gave her free lessons and large sums of money whenever she turned to him. But he frequently treated his father badly and even cruelly. Always frugal, in his later years he became possessed by a mania for hoarding money. He took care of himself and Yanek like an invalid, bought whole sides of pork and kept them in his room; he used to say that the pork would help coat his body with a thick layer of fat, which would later provide better nutrition and artificial warmth.

In Lucian's maniacal chasing after money, in the last year of Peretz's life he once tore insurance papers out of his father's hands—Peretz was insured for a few thousand rubles, and he wanted to lend someone a couple hundred. He did that in the office of the insurance company, in the presence of strangers. Peretz was insulted and crushed by Lucian's behavior, and through Dinezon he ordered him to move out of his apartment. In a wild rage, Lucian grabbed and damaged Peretz's things, whatever fell into his hands.

Lucian also tormented Mrs. Peretz with his stinginess, although she was a devoted mother all her life. She valued his good qualities and showed him great compassion. Lucian was well aware of his bad character and used to state, "My father's a poet and my mother's a mathematician—a positive number times a negative number makes a negative."

From 1916 to 1917, Lucian studied mathematics intensively and even produced some works in that field. Later he was a mathematics teacher in a high school, but he soon became very ill. While he was sick, his former wife Helenke stayed at his side, taking care of him with Mrs. Peretz, and she greatly lightened his unbearable pains. Helenke even agreed to remarry him and get him a position with her brother-in-law, a wealthy manufacturer in Berlin.

In his short will, Lucian indicated how his small inheritance should be divided. Among other things, he left 300 rubles to the servant girl Vikta, who had served many years in Peretz's house and showed special friendship toward him and Yanek. The mathematical works Lucian left behind have never been published. He died in 1919.

Peretz's library and other valuable objects from his study were bequeathed to his grandson Yanek.

Lucian could not speak Yiddish, and he couldn't even grasp Yiddish sounds. Yet with some of Peretz's acquaintances he was on friendly terms, would often spend time with them, and go to their homes. Most of all he had an intimate friendship with Peretz Hirshbein, with whom he communicated in English. On the title page of a book that Peretz Hirshbein gave him as a memento, these words were written in Russian: "To a loner from a loner." In turn, Lucian gave him a silver watch with blue enamel, which Peretz Hirshbein wore for many years.

Lucian was not familiar with his father's works; he was neither interested in, nor did he recognize, his father's talent. He didn't consider Yiddish a language. Lucian viewed his father as a preternatural person, didn't believe him, and thought that Peretz elicited admiration by means of tricks. That no doubt pained Peretz because he loved his son and felt special tenderness and compassion toward him.

Once Lucian was angry and didn't want to come to the lunch table, so Peretz sent me to get him. "Ask him to come in." But I returned empty-handed—under no circumstances would he come. He became irritated with me. Peretz said, "It doesn't matter—ask him more forcefully."

Lucian was always angry. When he returned home he would hastily open the door and then shut himself up in his room, as in a fortress.

One had to enter his room cautiously—he might say something gruff. If I didn't close his door right away, he would tell me, "You must be a dog or a princess, since only they don't close doors behind them."

I never noticed that Peretz attempted in any way to influence Lucian's convictions. Apparently Peretz didn't try to have an effect on him in earlier years either, because Lucian was always an anti-Semite who also showed clearly his animosity toward his father.

Lucian stammered slightly in his speech. He thought that the defect could have been overcome had more attention been paid to it when he was a child. For that he never forgave his father. But mainly Lucian disliked his father because of jealously: Peretz's greatness and fame eclipsed and overshadowed Lucian.

Lucian's hatred of Jews was connected to his deep-seated hatred of physical weakness. He used to advise the young girls he knew to marry non-Jews, so that they would have healthy children. Motivated by this hatred of weakness, he exhausted his son Yanek with various sports. Until late in the autumn he bathed with Yanek in the Vistula River, until the water began to freeze. On cool autumn nights he let him sleep by an open window with only a light blanket.

At Peretz's apartment there was a special wall cabinet for Yanek, containing various tools: saws, hammers, and nails. When Peretz had to make changes in his room, he would get all of the necessary tools from Yanek's cabinet. Later Yanek developed a passion for collecting nails. He would say that after the war, when people start to rebuild, they'll need nails, which will become very valuable.

Lucian also took pains to acquaint Yanek with Polish and European literature, mainly English. He held England to be the most cultured country, and he thought that English people were the best. It was moving to see how, on free Sundays, he would lie for hours on the sofa with Yanek and translate poems from a book by Longfellow. He would take him to art exhibits and familiarize him with the works of the greatest artists.

On the street one would always see them together. From a distance they looked like two faithful friends. They both had large cleats in the soles of their shoes, and their walking was audible from far away. And although Lucian was older and more capable, Yanek would explain to his father how various things were made. He thought he was the master, and because of that quarrels would often arise between them. Then Lucian would honor him with his favorite word — "donkey." Yanek would become insulted and go home, but the next day they were together again, and the quarrel from the prior day was forgotten. In his father's room, Yanek had the opportunity to read books of contemporary and classic literature, and to see reproductions of the best paintings and sculptures. Once Peretz wanted to buy a gift for a guest. He let Lucian take care of it, and someone expressed surprise. Peretz said: I can depend completely on Lucian — my son has excellent taste.

Like Lucian, Yanek disliked Jews and Judaism. This was a natural consequence of the education he received from his assimilated father and mother.

Yanek lived with his mother. But he spent every Saturday and Sunday at his grandfather's home. One could often see Yanek lying with Peretz on the couch. They spoke Polish, because Yanek didn't understand Yiddish. He knew a few Yiddish words, but he mangled them terribly, and he used them when he wanted to insult or make fun of someone.

Peretz improvised stories and sang Yiddish folk songs, accompanying himself with his hands; Yanek, radiant, would help him with resounding cries. Peretz would also play "horse and wagon" with his grandson, where Peretz was the horse and pulled Yanek. Or Yanek would drag Peretz off of the couch and rush to take his place. Yanek was very handsome. On his dark, fresh face, his long velvet eyelashes cast shadows around his eyes. With a solid and slender build, at eleven or twelve he was taller than his father. He was the general favorite in Peretz's house, and all of his pranks, even the most burdensome, only aroused a joyful smile from Peretz and his wife Helene.

Yet Peretz could be very strict even with his favorite when it came to teaching character. At Peretz's summerhouse, for some reason, Yanek once felt insulted. He tearfully packed his change of clothes and, with a small suitcase under his arm, he left for the train. Peretz's wife begged her husband: Call him back, have pity on him — the child will get lost. But Peretz said harshly, "Let him go." That's how Yanek learned to be independent in that respect, and later he would travel there alone every *shabbes*. Yanek was no less attached to his grandpa [*dziadzio*], and was jealous of everyone who was close to Peretz.

Peretz would often lie on the couch with Yanek and me on either side. Peretz had to hold both of us so that we wouldn't fall off. But Yanek always thought he didn't have enough room, and he would push until I fell off. Or he would take Peretz's hand from me and place it on himself.

Later, after Peretz's death, Yanek passionately cherished the memory of his grandfather. The mere phrase "the old man" [stari] worked like a balm on his sick nerves. On days when he was in a bad mood, when Yanek was most upset, his mother Helenke would whisper into Mrs. Peretz's ear, or to me: Speak about "the old man"! Immediately Yanek's expression would change and light up with a special glow.

Helenke told me that Peretz gave her one of his books. But Helenke couldn't read Yiddish. He ordered her, "Read, and you'll learn." She was also under the spell of Peretz's enchanting power, although for some reason she stopped meeting him; for many years until the last day of his life, she didn't come to Peretz's house. But she felt special devotion toward Peretz and his memory.

A few years ago she fell ill with cancer and died. Shortly before her death, Yanek converted to Christianity. Mrs. Peretz understood, from an intimate conversation with Helenke, that Yanek did this with the approval of his mother.

Translated by Ken Frieden

Glossary

Bibliography

Glossary

Yiddish words are transliterated in accordance with YIVO guidelines, except in some cases of names or words (for example, "shmooze") that have attained currency in another form. Hebrew words are transliterated based on the Sephardic pronunciation currently used in Israel, except as spoken by Tevye and other characters who use Ashkenazic pronunciation.

Amidah: Standing Prayer that is first uttered silently, also known as the Eighteen Benedictions; a central part of the daily synagogue services.

Asch, Sholem (1880–1957): Popular Yiddish author who, when he lived in Warsaw during the first decade of the twentieth century, was part of Peretz's literary circle.

Bal-Makhshoves (pseudonym of Isidor Eliashev, 1873–1924): Important Yiddish literary scholar from Lithuania. When he began his career as a Yiddish critic, he initially signed his name *Ger-tsedek* ("Righteous Gentile") to indicate his cultural distance from folk traditions.

Bathhouse attendant (translation of *shmayser*): Literally, one who beat or whipped the bathers with twigs, perhaps the cultural equivalent of a masseur.

Bebel, August (1840–1913): German socialist leader.

Bezliude: Name of a fictitious shtetl, called Bezliudev in later editions of *The Little Man*. The word (from Russian) means "without people," probably in the sense of "without *mentshn*"—lacking in good, decent people.

Biale: Town in eastern Poland, near the border to what was formerly Lithuania.

Bitter herbs (*k'zayit maror*): Literally, an olive-sized piece of a bitter herb such as lettuce used for dipping at a Passover Seder; "olive-sized" (*k'zayit*) is the minimum quantity that fulfills a halakic obligation.

Bobruisk: Small town in Belorussia, struck by a disastrous fire in 1902.

bris: Circumcision; literally "covenant," as God makes a covenant with Abraham in Genesis 17.

Brisk (Brest-Litovsk): Town in western Belorussia, near the Polish border, formerly within greater Lithuania. Opposition to the hasidim was stronger in Lithuania than in Poland and the Ukraine.

Bunimovich: 1. Jewish banking family in Vilna. 2. Vilna epithet for anyone thought to be rich.

Chenstokhov: Polish town northwest of Krakow.

Cholera groom: Following an archaic Eastern European superstition thought to appease the cholera and end an epidemic, Jews were known to arrange "cholera weddings" at the cemetery.

Chorisch (from German): Leading services *chorisch* presumably means leading them in the fashion of German choruses, in four-part harmony.

Conscriptions: Refers to practices under the Cantonist System, when young boys were forcibly inducted into a twenty-five-year army service.

Cossacks: Ethnic group from the Ukraine, widely feared as cavalrymen in the tsar's army.

Cupping: Discredited medical procedure during which incisions were made in the patient's back and glass cups were used to catch the blood. Often associated with the practice of applying leeches to remove blood.

Davening: Yiddish *daven* (possibly from Old French, *diviner*) means to pray or to lead prayers.

Dinezon, Yankev (1856–1919): Yiddish novelist and Peretz's closest friend from the time of their meeting in 1887 until Peretz's death.

Divine Presence (Yiddish *shekhine*, from Hebrew *shechinah*): God's in-dwelling spirit, thought to have gone into exile together with the Jews; sometimes considered the female aspect of God.

Dreidel (Yiddish, from the verb "to turn"): Top bearing the Hebrew letters Nun, Gimmel, Hey, and Shin—spun by children in a Hanukah game.

Dybbuk: Spirit of someone who has died that inhabits a living person.

Eighteen Benedictions (Hebrew *shmone 'esreh*, Yiddish *shminesre*): Another name for the Amidah (standing) prayer, a central part of the daily synagogue services.

Feh! (Yiddish): Exclamation expressing disgust.

Four-cornered garment (*arba' kanfes*, four corners): The four-cornered, rectangular, linen or wool cloth with fringes (*tsitsit*) that Jewish men have traditionally worn, over or under a shirt. The fringes represent God's 613 commandments.

Freylekhs: (from the Yiddish *freylekh*, happy or cheerful): Traditional, fast instrumental pieces played by Jewish musicians (*klezmorim*) at celebrations.

Fringed undergarment (Yiddish *talis kotn*, small prayer shawl): A four-cornered garment with tassels that Jewish men have traditionally worn under or over their shirts.

Gemarah (Yiddish *gemore*): The latter portion of the Babylonian and Palestinian Talmuds, compiled in the fifth century. Together with the second-century Mishna, the Gemarah forms the centerpiece of yeshiva study.

Ger Rebbe: Isaac Meir ben Israel Alter (d. 1866).

Gevalt! (Yiddish, literally meaning "violence" or "force"): Exclamation that is a rough equivalent of "Help!"

Glupsk: Fictional place name in Abramovitsh's works associated with the actual town of Berdichev in central Ukraine. From its Russian root, Glupsk names a "town of fools."

Golem (sometimes written *goylem*): An artificial man made of clay, such as the one purported to have been made by the Maharal of Prague; also, by extension, a blockhead.

Gorky, Maxim (pseudonym of Alexei Maximovich Pyeshkov, 1868–1936): Russian author of revolutionary novels and acquaintance of Sholem Aleichem.

Grinnhorn (or greenhorn): Yiddish (or American Yinglish) for a recent immigrant to the United States.

Haftarah: Reading from the Prophets that follows the reading from the Torah during Sabbath morning services.

Haggadah (Hebrew; Yiddish *hagode*): Narrative about the Exodus from Egypt, read at home during the Seder ceremony on Passover eve.

"Happy is the eye" (Hebrew, *ashrei 'ayin*): Formulaic phrase that is often found in hagiographic books about hasidic rebbes, such as in the works by Rabbi Nathan Sternharz about Rabbi Nahman of Bratslav.

Hasid: Follower of a hasidic rebbe.

Ha-tzefira (The Dawn): Hebrew periodical founded in 1862, edited by Nahum Sokolov from 1904.

Ha-tzofei: Hebrew newspaper that appeared in Warsaw from 1903–1905.

Haynt (Today): One of the most widely distributed Yiddish daily newspapers in Europe, which began publication in Warsaw in 1908.

Heder (from the Hebrew word meaning "room"): Privately run school for children aged three to thirteen, where the teacher (rebbe, to be distinguished from a hasidic leader called "the Rebbe") taught Hebrew prayers, the Bible, and the Talmud. Usually held in a room inside the house of the teacher (also called a *melamed*).

Heine, Heinrich (1797–1856): Important German-Jewish poet whose satiric work influenced Peretz early in his literary career.

Hoshana Raba: Holiday on the seventh day of harvest festival Sukkot. During Hoshana Raba, synagogue goers traditionally made seven processions around the synagogue with the lulav and etrog.

House of Study (Yiddish *bes medresh*): Often connected with a synagogue and inhabited by yeshiva students, who study Talmud.

Hulin or **Nedarim:** Two of the sixty-three tractates that comprise the Babylonian Talmud (which is more often studied than the Palestinian Talmud).

Jargon: Dismissive name for Yiddish, often used in the nineteenth and early twentieth centuries.

Kabbalah: Jewish mysticism, more commonly studied among the hasidim than among their opponents, the *mitnagdim*.

Kamenets (Kamenetz-Podolsk, also Komenetz): Town in the western Ukraine, near the border to Austria-Hungary and hence more accessible to Enlightenment inroads.

Kashrut: The dietary laws regarding kosher (literally, "fit" to eat), ritually clean food. The opposite of kosher is *treyf*.

Kasrilevke: Fictional shtetl in Sholem Aleichem's work.

Kedusha: Literally, "sanctification"; a prayer attached to the Amidah (Standing Prayer) in congregational worship, based on verses from Isaiah, Ezekiel, and Psalms.

Khumesh (from the Hebrew word meaning "five"): The Five Books of Moses.

Kibbitser, The: Illustrated journal of humor and satire, founded in New York in 1908; a kibbitser (or kibitzer) is someone who gives unwanted advice.

Kiddush cup: Silver cup that is traditionally filled with wine or grape juice for the sanctification (*kiddush*) on Shabbat or other special occasions.

Kidnappers (*khapers*): Hired thugs whose job was to capture young boys who could be substituted for military service in place of other children.

Klezmer (from the Hebrew *klei* + *zemer*, instruments of song): In Yiddish, a klezmer is a Jewish musician; by extension, the word is sometimes used to denote instrumental music played by Jewish musicians, generally in a band including instruments such as violin, clarinet, flute, trombone, hammer dulcimer, percussion.

Kol mevasser (A Voice of Tidings): Launched in 1862, the Yiddish supplement to the Hebrew newspaper *Ha-melitz*. Abramovitsh's story *The Little Man* was published serially in this newspaper starting on 24 November 1864.

Kosher meat tax: Tax levied by Jewish communities to cover the cost of rabbinical supervision in the ritual slaughter of animals.

Kto ya? (Russian): "Who is 'me'?" — in answer to "It's me" (*ya*).

Kugel pudding: Casserole usually made with noodles.

Kuzmir: Town situated west of Lublin, Poland.

Lamentations: Special prayers said on Tisha b'Av, the ninth day in the month of Av, commemorating the destruction of the Temple in Jerusalem.

Lashtchev: Small town near the border of southeastern Poland and northwestern Ukraine.

Lease-holder (or tenant farmer, *rendar*): Literally, a *rendar* either leased an estate — usually from a feudal lord — or administered an estate, which sometimes included collecting taxes from serfs who worked the land. Isaac Abraham uses the term figuratively, to designate anyone who holds sway over a rich man.

Little man (Yiddish *kleyne mentshele*): Refers to a corrupt, mean-spirited, petit bourgeois person, or (from a childish perspective) to the reflection of oneself in another person's eyes.

Litvak: Lithuanian Jew. Lithuania was the center of opposition to the hasidim, and many of the most elite yeshivas were situated in Lithuanian towns and cities. "Litvaks" were associated with a more rational and less emotive approach to Jewish practice.

Lublin: City in southeastern Poland.

Lulav: Palm branch used together with the citron *(etrog)* during Sukkot prayers.

Mapu, Avraham (1808–67): Hebrew novelist from Lithuania, remembered for *Ahavat tzion* (The Love of Zion, 1853).

Mazl tov (Yiddish, from Hebrew *mazal* = luck, fortune, or constellation + *tov* = good): Literally, "good luck" (under a good star), but used as an equivalent of "Congratulations!"

Megile, Megillah (Yiddish, Hebrew): Literally, "scroll"; may refer to any of the five short scrolls read in the synagogue on special occasions, but by itself this word usually refers to the Purim Megillah — the Book of Esther.

Melave-Malke (Yiddish; Hebrew *melavei-malkah*): Literally, "accompanying the Queen." Refers to festivities — especially involving songs — sometimes held at the conclusion of Sabbath, interpreted as accompanying the Queen, or Divine Presence *(shechinah)* on return from a sojourn on earth.

Mentsh: In some contexts, a successful person who can cope with the world; the Yiddish word *mentsh* can also mean "a good, decent person."

Mezuzes (plural of Yiddish *mezuze*, from Hebrew *mezuzah*): Ritual container affixed to the doorposts of Jewish houses, containing the "Shm'a" prayer: "Hear, O Israel . . ."

Midrash (from the Hebrew root *d-r-sh*, to seek out or inquire): Rabbinic narrative or commentary on the Hebrew Bible, as exemplified by the verse-by-verse exegesis in *Midrash rabbah*. Midrash is associated with narrative *aggadah*, in contrast to legalistic *halakhah*.

Mikve (Hebrew and Yiddish): Ritual bath, frequented by women and (mostly hasidic) men. According to Talmudic law, the *mikve* must use natural running water, such as from a stream, but in this passage Abramovitsh is clearly attacking the lack of hygiene in some ritual baths.

Minyan: Prayer group, traditionally requiring the presence of ten men.

Mishna: First part of the Talmud, compiled around 200 C.E.

Mitnagdim: Opponents of the hasidim, epitomized by the Vilna Gaon (Elijah ben Solomon Zalman, 1720–97).

Mitzvah (Yiddish plural *mitzves*, Hebrew plural *mitzvot*): Often understood as meaning "good deed," but more accurately defined as one of the 613 positive and negative commandments from God, according to Judaic sources.

Moment: Yiddish daily newspaper, which began publication in Warsaw in 1910.

Momzer (Yiddish, from Hebrew *mamzer*): Bastard.

"Nahamu" (Hebrew, meaning "console"): Sabbath "Nahamu" is the first Sabbath after Tisha b'Av, when the Haftarah reading begins "Console, oh console My people . . ." (Isaiah 40:1).

Nemirov: 1. Town in the Ukraine; associated with Nathan Sternharz, the disciple and scribe of Rabbi Nahman of Bratslav. 2. Town near the border of Poland, Galicia, and the Ukraine, northwest of Lvov (Lemberg).

"Nevarekh Eloheinu" (Hebrew): "Let us bless God," words spoken at the beginning of the grace after meals when there is a minyan of at least ten men.

Nomberg, H. D. (1876–1927): Yiddish writer and integral member of Peretz's Warsaw circle.

Nosh (Yiddish): To nibble on, snack, or eat (especially sweets).

Obmanov: Fictional town. Its name suggests—based on the similarity to a Russian word—that it is a town of deceivers or swindlers.

Oy, vey: Exclamation of woe.

Payes: Forelocks traditionally worn by hasidic men.

Penitential Prayers (*slikhes,* from the Hebrew *slihot*): Prayers asking forgiveness for sins, based on biblical verses, said during morning prayers during the week before Rosh Hashanah and on Tisha b'Av.

Prayer shawl (Yiddish *talis,* Hebrew *talit*): Four-cornered garment traditionally worn by Jewish men during morning prayers.

Priestly Blessing: Three biblical verses, originally chanted at the end of the Amidah prayer during services at the Temple in Jerusalem. In the Diaspora, men of priestly descent *(kohanim)* pronounce this blessing on festivals. Worshipers are forbidden to observe the *kohanim* during the ritual.

Pulav: Polish town northwest of Lublin.

Purim: Holiday that celebrates the rescue of the Jews from the Persian Haman.

Rabbi Avigdor Emanuel: Perhaps alluding to Avigdor ben Joseph Hayim, an avid opponent of the hasidim.

Rabbinical judges *(dayonim)*: Rabbinical arbitrators who were authorized to settle minor disputes.

Rashi script: Hebrew typeface used in the printing of some Bible and Talmud commentaries, named after Rashi—Rabbi Solomon ben Isaac (1040–1105).

Reb: Term of respect, roughly the equivalent of "Mr." There is no connection to the terms "rabbi" or "rebbe."

Rebbe: Hasidic leader, usually associated with a specific town and group of disciples. "Rebbe" (lower case) can also refer to a teacher, especially at a heder.

Rebbetzin: Wife of a rabbi.

Red Jews: Mythical lost tribe.

Scrivener (Yiddish *soyfer*): Ritual scribe who writes Torah scrolls and the parchments for tefillin and mezuzot.

Seventeenth of Tammuz: Fast day commemorating the capture of Jerusalem by Nebuchadnezzar's army in 586 B.C.E., leading to the Babylonian Exile.

Shabbat Nahamu: The name is taken from the opening words of the Haftarah reading from the Shabbat that falls after the solemn fast day on the ninth of Av.

Shabbes: Yiddish pronunciation of the Hebrew word for the Sabbath, *shabbat*.

Shadchen: Marriage broker.

Shammes: Sexton; synagogue caretaker or servant to a rabbi.

Shavuot (Hebrew; pronounced *shavues* in Yiddish): "Feast of Weeks," spring holiday that falls seven weeks after Passover. Associated with the giving of the Torah at Mount Sinai.

Sheygets (Yiddish, masculine form of the word *shiksa*, from the Hebrew root meaning "unclean" or ritually impure): Pejorative term for a non-Jewish man; sometimes used to denote an impudent Jewish man.

Shive (Yiddish; Hebrew *shiv'a*, from the Hebrew word meaning "seven"): To sit *shive* is to mourn a person's death for the prescribed period of seven days.

Shlimmazl: Literally, bad luck; by extension, a clumsy, accident-prone person who is characterized by misfortunes. Also used to describe a person who always gets the short end of the stick.

Shm'a: Prayer that begins, "Hear, O Israel, the Lord our God, the Lord is one," declaring God's unity and providence.

Shmargon: Vilna Yiddish pronunciation for Smorgon, a nearby town.

Shminesre (Yiddish): Eighteen; see **Eighteen Benedictions**.

Shmooze (from Hebrew *shmu'ot, shmu'es* = things heard): To converse intimately, picking up rumors and gossip.

Shofar: Ritual ram's horn that is blown in the synagogue during Rosh Hashanah and Yom Kippur.

Sholem aleykhem: Greeting that literally means "Peace unto you" and alludes to the song addressed to the ministering angels that introduces the Sabbath on Friday evening.

Shpoler Zeyde and Rabbi Levi Itskhok of Berdichev: Aryeh Leyb of Shpola (1725–1812), opponent of Nahman of Bratslav (1772–1810), and Levi Itskhok of Berdichev (1740–1809), popular hasidic leader known for his doctrine "love of Israel."

Shtetl (diminutive of *shtot*, city or town): Small, provincial town.

Shtrayml: Expensive fur hat made with mink tail, traditionally worn by respected hasidic men, especially rabbis.

Shul (Yiddish): Synagogue.

Silent prayer: See **Amidah**.

Simkhes Toyre (Yiddish; Hebrew *simhat torah*): Holiday after Sukkot, celebrating completion of the annual cycle of Torah readings.

Sirota, Gershon Isaac (1874–1943): Cantor of the late nineteenth and early twentieth century in Warsaw and Vilna; once a household name among Russian Jews.

Spektor, Mordechai (1858–1925): Yiddish literary writer and editor, based in Warsaw.

Spice box: Often filled with cloves, cinnamon, or other fragrant spices, and traditionally used during the Havdala ceremony at the end of Sabbath on Saturday night.

Stanislavsky, Konstantin (1863–1938): Pseudonym of Konstantin Sergeyevich Alekseyev, an important Russian director and teacher who founded the Moscow Art Theater.

Stempeniu: Sholem Aleichem's novel (1888) about a klezmer violinist, Stempeniu, based in part on the life of an actual musician.

Sukkah (Hebrew): Temporary booth or hut built during the holiday Sukkot.

Sukkot (Hebrew; pronounced *sukkes* in Yiddish): Referred to in English as the Feast of Booths or the Feast of Tabernacles, a seven-day harvest festival commemorating the ancient wanderings of the Israelites. Jews traditionally build a *sukkah*, or temporary dwelling, during this period.

Tabernacles: English word for the Jewish harvest festival of Sukkot, when Jews often eat their meals in temporary huts.

Tagore, Rabindranath (1861–1941): Prolific Indian writer who received the Nobel Prize for Literature in 1913.

Takif (Yiddish from the Hebrew *takif,* meaning "strong"): Name for a rich and powerful man in the shtetl.

Talis: Prayer shawl with knotted fringes on the four corners, traditionally worn by Jewish men during morning prayers.

Talmud-Torah: In some contexts, synonymous with heder: a one-room school for children. Elsewhere it refers to a larger school for poor Jewish pupils.

Tashlikh: Ritual during Rosh Hashanah when Jews symbolically cast off their sins, sometimes emptying their pockets and throwing bread crumbs or other remnants into a river.

Tassels (Yiddish *tsitsis*): The specially knotted fringes on a prayer shawl *(talis)* or fringed undergarment *(talis kotn).*

Tatenyu (Yiddish): Literally, "dear father."

Tax collector: A tax collector or tenant farmer *(rendar)* leased or administered land from a feudal lord and collected taxes from the peasants who farmed it. They were among the wealthiest Jews in the Pale of Settlement.

Tefillin: Small leather cases known in English as phylacteries, containing parchments inscribed with biblical verses; traditionally placed by Jewish men on the forehead and left arm during weekday morning prayers.

Tisha b'Av: The ninth day in the month of Av, commemorating the destruction of the Temple in Jerusalem.

Tree of Life, The: Kabbalistic book by Haim Vital (1543–1620), an important follower of Isaac Luria (1534–72).

Tsadek: Righteous person; term used by hasidic groups to describe their leaders.

Tsores (from Hebrew *tzarot*): Troubles.

Tsviatshits: Fictitious name of a town, taken from the Yiddish pronunciation *(tsvies)* of the Hebrew word *(tsviut)*, meaning hypocrisy.

Tuneyadevke: A fictional town in Abramovitsh's works; its name, drawn from the Russian root *tuneyadets*, suggests that it is Parasitesville. Possibly associated with the town of Zhitomir, near Berdichev, or perhaps meant to represent a typical Eastern European shtetl.

Vayomer: Hebrew word meaning "and he said," commonly used to introduce biblical dialogue.

Vey iz mir: Literally, "woe unto me."

Vilna: Yiddish name for Vilnius, the major Lithuanian city and center of Talmudic scholarship. The Jewish Socialist Party (the Bund) was founded there in 1897.

Vilna Gaon (Elijah ben Solomon Zalman, 1720–97): Renowned Talmud scholar and opponent of the hasidim.

Volynia (also Volin, Volyn): Region in western Ukraine.

Vonvolitz: Town situated to the west of Lublin, Poland.

Wedding bard (*badkhen*, from the Hebrew root *b-d-h*, to amuse; also called a *marshelik*): Entertainer at a traditional Eastern European Jewish wedding, who sang rhyming verses during the ritual of seating *(bazetsn)* and veiling *(badekn)* the bride.

Wine 'n' Candles Alter *(Alter yaknoz)*: This eponym refers to a mnemonic containing the ritual obligations for Sabbath eve; "yaknoz" is an acronym for yayin (wine), *kiddush* (blessing over the wine), *nerot* (candles), and *zmirot* (songs). Hence Alter's name links him to traditional Judaic practices and presumably to some of the artifacts he sells in addition to books.

"X-squeeze-doory" courtyard *(eksvidorske hoyf)*: Garbled expression based on Vilna Yiddish usage, referring to inherited property that consists of a block of apartments around an inner courtyard, jointly owned.

Yarmulke (Yiddish; Hebrew, *kipah*): Skullcap, a head covering traditionally worn by Jewish males, especially during prayer and meals.

Yarmolinetz (or Yarmolintza): Town located southwest of Kiev.

Yehupetz: Fictional town in Sholem Aleichem's works, based on Kiev.

Zamoshtsh (or Zamość): Peretz's birthplace, a relatively modern and cultural city in southeastern Poland, near the border to Austria-Hungary.

Zhitomir: Heavily Jewish shtetl in the Ukraine, where Abramovitsh lived roughly from 1869 to 1881.

Zohar, The: "The Book of Splendor," seminal kabbalistic work from the thirteenth century. Usually attributed to Moses de Leon but supposedly based on the work of the second-century sage Simeon ben Yohai.

Bibliography

S. Y. Abramovitsh

Dos kleyne mentshele oder a lebensbashraybung fun Yitskhok Avrom takif. Supplement to *Ha-melitz,* serialized beginning on 24 November 1864. *Kol mevasser 2,* nos. 45–51 (1864), and 3, nos. 1–4, 6 (1865).

Dos kleyne mentshele oder a lebensbashraybung fun Yitskhok Avrom takif. Odessa: Nitzshe and Tsederboym, 1865.

Fishke der krumer. Zhitomir: Shadov, 1869.

Ha-'ishon ha-katan: Dos kleyne mentshele [Bilingual Hebrew-Yiddish edition]. Trans. and ed. Shalom Luria. Haifa: Haifa University Press, 1984.

K'tavim b'ibbam: T'b'at ha-mofat/Dos vintshfingerl, Fishke ha-higer/Fishke der krumer [Bilingual Hebrew-Yiddish edition]. Trans. and ed. Shalom Luria. Haifa: Haifa University Press, 1994.

Sholem Aleichem

"A mayse mit a grinhorn." *Di varhayt,* 16 January 1916.

"An eytse." *Der fraynd bayloge* (1904), no. 20.

"Der yontoyvediker tsimes." *Der fraynd 2,* no. 207 (23 September 1904).

"Hodl." *Der fraynd 2,* nos. 193, 194, 196 (2 September, 4 September, 6 September 1904).

"Khave." *Dos yudishe folk 1,* nos. 2–3 (24 May 1906 and 31 May 1906).

Monologn. In *Ale verk fun Sholem Aleichem.* New York: Folksfond Edition, 1917–23, vol. 21.

"Yoysef." *Der veg* (22 September, 24 September, 25 September 1905); also *Dos yidishe togeblat* (5 October, 6 October, 8 October, 10 October, 11 October 1905).

I. L. Peretz

"Dem rebin's tsibuk." *Yontev bletlekh* (1895), no. 2, *Der omer.*

"Dos shtrayml." In *Literatur un lebn: a zaml-bukh far literatur un gezelshaft.* Ed. I. L. Peretz. Warsaw: Funk, 1894.

"Ha-mekubalim (sippur)" (Hebrew). *Gan perahim* 3 (1891).

Khasidish. In *Ale verk fun I. L. Peretz.* Ed. Shmuel Niger. New York: CYCO, 1947, vol. 4.

"Mekubolim." *Yontev bletlekh* (1894), no. 4, *Der tones.*

"Mishnat hasidim" (Hebrew). In *Ha-hetz: yalkut sifruti.* Ed. I. L. Peretz. Warsaw: Shvartsberg, 1894.

"Mishnes khasidim." *Der yud* 4, no. 19 (1902).

"Oyb nisht nokh hekher! A khasidishe ertseylung." *Der yud* 2, no. 1 (1900).

"Tsvishn tsvey berg: tsvishn dem Brisker rov mit'n Bialer rebin: a simkhes-toyredike mayse." *Der yud* 2, nos. 40–41.

Biographical Essays

Berkovitsh, Y. D. [Introductions to chapters.] *Dos Sholem-Aleichem bukh.* Ed. Y. D. Berkovitsh. New York: Sholem-Aleichem bukh komitet, 1926.

———. *Ha-rish'onim ki-vnei-adam: sippurei zikharonot 'al Sholem-Aleichem u-vnei-doro.* 3d. ed. Tel Aviv: Dvir, 1976.

Binshtok, Lev. "Prazdnik zhargonnoi literatury" (Russian). *Voskhod* 12 (1884).

Peretz-Laks, R. *Arum Peretzn (zikhroynes un batrakhtungen).* Warsaw: Literarishe bleter, 1935.

Printed in the USA
CPSIA information can be obtained
at www.ICGtesting.com
CBHW020022210524
8863CB00002B/61

9 780815 607601

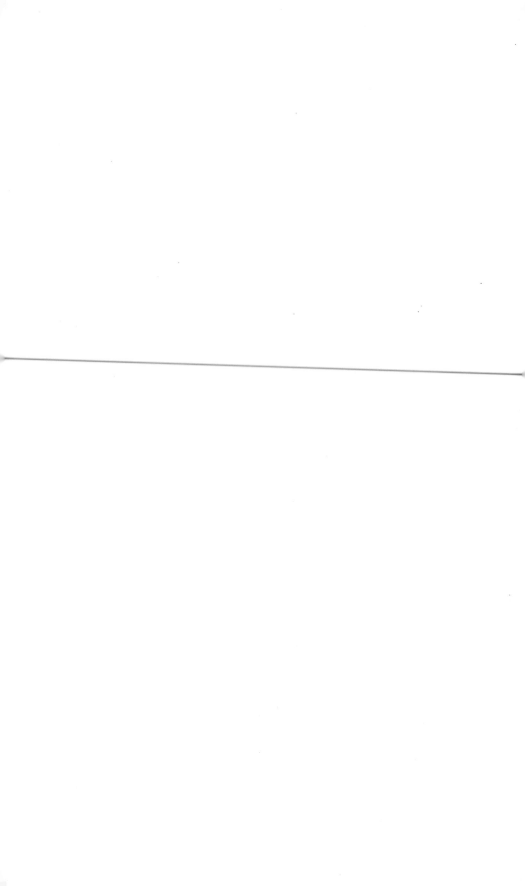